A PENNY FOR THE VIOLIN MAN

Eli Rill

A PENNY FOR THE VIOLIN MAN

Eli Rill

CIRCLE OF LIFE PUBLISHING
Canoga Park, CA

A PENNY FOR THE VIOLIN MAN
by Eli Rill

Published by: Circle of Life Publishing
8901 Eton Ave., #109
Canoga Park, CA 91304
Phone/Fax: 818-341-7713
Website: www.apennyfortheviolinman.com
E-mail: info@apennyfortheviolinman.com

Although based on actual events, this is a work of historical fiction. All names and characters, with the exception of historical and public figures, are products of the author's imagination and are not to be construed as real. Where real-life historical and public figures appear, the situations, incidents, and dialogues concerning those persons are fictional and are not intended to depict actual events. In all other respects, any resemblance to persons living or dead is entirely coincidental.

ISBN: 978-0-615-33807-1

Library of Congress Control Number: 2010922529

First Edition. Printed in the United States of America
0 9 8 7 6 5 4 3 2 1

Edited by Arthur V. Coyne

Cover and Page Design by One-On-One Book Production, West Hills, California.

To all those working for Teachers Unions and
those countless others who struggled
during the Great Depression,
a mirror image of present times.

"BE KIND, FOR EVERYONE YOU MEET
IS FIGHTING A GREAT BATTLE"

An old Hebrew proverb

Prologue

A SENIOR SHUTTLE VAN PULLED into the parking space outside the New York skyscraper, its windows blinking at the bright sun.

Unsure of itself, the van bumped the curb, crawled up toward the sidewalk and went into reverse, rolling back to the street.

Engine turned off, the sputtering motor argued for more oil, shivering for a moment before coming to rest.

The driver, an elderly man, his alert eyes and occasional wrinkles belying his many years, smiled triumphantly, speaking over his shoulder to the younger man seated behind him.

"Well, Arnie, the old man got us into port, didn't he?"

"I'll take over now, Mr. Schecter."

Norman Schecter, the most senior of the seniors at SHALOM ASSISTED LIVING, had asked Arnie to permit him to drive the last block of their outing, but his request was turned down. Schecter persevered, arguing that because the DMV had notified him that they had decided for safety's sake his license be terminated on his 100th birthday, he was now pleading for one more chance to sit behind the wheel.

Reluctantly allowing Schecter to take over, Arnie had strongly cautioned him to not go faster than five miles per hour.

Schecter, under Arnie's watchful eye, had carefully followed the instruction, the taxi in back of him impatiently blowing its horn twice, then finally pulling into the next lane.

Seeing Schecter intently hunched over the wheel, his hands grimly clutching it, the taxi cab driver, mumbling 'old fart,' gave him the finger. Now safely parked, Schecter slid a cell phone from the pocket of his jacket hanging loosely on his spare frame.

"Gotta let Miriam know," quickly, expertly dialing, "that je suis arrivé."

Miriam, pleased that her grandfather had come as planned, suggested that she would meet him downstairs and they would go, as usual, to the Carnegie Deli to celebrate her birthday with a slice of blueberry cheesecake for her and Schecter's once a year treat: a hot pastrami on rye washed down with a cream soda. Schecter objected, insisting that he finish his adventure in style, taking the elevator up on his own; then both of them coming down together.

Because Miriam had perceived that in recent years Schecter had become increasingly short-tempered when not getting his own way, she didn't argue the point.

"You remember the office number?"

"Why," testily, "you think I've got Alzheimer's?"

"Okay, Grandpa, come on up."

Getting out of the van, Schecter glanced up at the impressive building before walking steadily to the entrance.

Arnie waited in the van parked in front of One World Trade Center. His well-thumbed Racing Form on his lap, he squinted in the clear September sunshine in order to read the bettor's odds for that day… the eleventh.

1

Summer, 1937

Amboy Street, Brooklyn

TIME-RAVAGED FIVE-STORY TENEMENTS lined both sides of the street: a canyon of grimed brick.

The buildings' dirt encrusted thick glass doors were framed with black wrought-iron, the peeling paint a surrender to time.

The chipped-tile lobbies had long ago lost the battle against the countless scuff-marks and stains of stepped-on roaches.

Norman Schecter, who lived in one of the aging tenements, '179,' once described to himself the street's ambience: "When I look at it through an imaginary telescope, the squalor is magnified, oppressing the spirit; but viewed from the other end, the weather-beaten façades soften into reassuring familiarity."

Impressed by his observation, he fancifully continued the image: "This double-vision must be because of my being born just before midnight on New Year's Eve ushering in the Twentieth Century, my perceptions having been permanently affected by seeing two different centuries at the same time."

For a few minutes of the Nineteenth Century and thirty-six years into the Twentieth, Norman had lived in Brooklyn. The Brownsville section was one of the Borough's many decaying areas, its pit-marked pavements crowded with boys playing stick-ball and girls playing jump-rope and jacks. Their shouts and screeches cut through the muted sidewalk conversations of the older people driven out of their airless apartments, attempting to catch some elusive cooling summer breeze.

The enervating heat discouraged any discussion about some of them having lost their meager savings because of the many bank closings; or the ever-present threat of being evicted for non-payment of rent for their soiled-wall and cracked-ceiling rooms, a fertile feeding ground for roaches and rodents.

The dispossessed tenants, when forced out of their crumbling apartments, were kept company by their worn furniture thrown out onto the street with them.

Early that summer, Norman had tried to console Mr. and Mrs. Berg as they sat on unmatched kitchen chairs next to the rest of their possessions in front of '179.'

Norman shook his head in commiseration, his usually warm dark eyes now flashing in anger. "That bastard Kotchman!"

Kotchman was the building's owner, an aggressive collector of the hard-to-come-by monthly rents.

Berg was quick to caution Norman. "Better you don't let him hear you talk like that, Schecter."

"What? He'll make me move out of this palace, too?"

Norman watched Berg staring at his disassembled bed, its streaked walnut-stained headboard, sagging mattress and spring separated from each other, no longer providing comfort for work-tired bodies.

Constant struggle had etched extra years into the Bergs' strained faces making them appear far older than their years, parents of the two young girls playing hopscotch nearby, their sounds of laughter and fun drowning out the silent screams of the family's journey to failure.

The children's few threadbare clothes were tied to a folded dirty canvas cot, the girls' shared cramped sleeping quarters. Another piece of frayed string held together a worn gameboard and box of playing pieces. Mr. Berg had bought the BIG BUSINESS game on sale for 35 cents, several months earlier when he was flush with having earned 17 dollars for what turned out to be his last week of work since then, repairing sewer pipes for the city.

BIG BUSINESS had been put on the market the year before, its company hoping to compete with the established best-selling MONOPOLY. BIG BUSINESS had been designed on a grander scale, the denominations of its multi-colored paper money being many more times than MONOPOLY'S bills, the 'business' transactions astronomically higher. The developers of the game hoped to appeal to people's fantasy of being able to amass great wealth in the midst of the Depression poverty surrounding them.

However, the leap to this gaudy income level was too much even for the public's needy imagination to accept.

BIG BUSINESS in short time proved a failure, collapsing almost as suddenly as the stock market had done in '29, also a victim of misplaced faith in the virtue of the greedy pursuit of the big dollar.

The Bergs sat quietly, as other tenants, sensitive to the delicacy of the moment, would relate to them in various ways. Most of them just nodded in support; one of them, the next door neighbor, Schwartz, was genuinely surprised, "I wondered what the tumel was, moving furniture around all morning. I didn't know about this, Berg."

"And if you did?"

Schwartz, uncomfortable, murmured, "A good luck to you, wherever."

Yes, Norman thought, wherever you don't have to beg the landlord for the once-every-five-years painting of overpriced 24-dollars-a-month apartments, and constant requests for roach exterminators. "Please, Kotchman," Norman once sourly pleaded, "they're so big, they're even eating the bedbugs."

"So, you complaining?"

Norman had been the only one who risked offending the Bergs. "So what are the plans, Sid?"

Berg shrugged. "Some of the stuff we can store, and maybe a dollar or two from Isaac the junkman for some of the leftover pieces."

"Well," Norman gestured toward the mound of furniture, "I can help you carry."

"Don't worry about it, Schecter."

A weight of responsibility fell from Norman's shoulders even though he himself wouldn't have been able to offer the Bergs a place in Apt. 2 with his family, or could he?

"Sid, until you get another place, maybe Gloria and... what's the little one's name?"

"Debby, but —"

"Listen, they have a cot, we have a living room."

~

In the midst of Brownsville's spirit-draining climate of hardship, a badge of distinction had recently been pasted onto the brick wall of '179.' by a traveling-circus bill-poster. The colorful thick paper boldly proclaimed:

Ringling Brothers and Barnum & Bailey
Proudly Present
Frank "Bring 'Em Back Alive" Buck

Brownsville-East New York Hippodrome

Buck was displayed in vivid hues with his whip and fierce stare, holding at bay a cage of snarling lions and tigers. Buck's defiant glare was mocked by crudely crayoned eyeglasses and a Van Dyke beard, compliments of an unknown neighborhood artist.

Since the first time Norman's son, Ira, had seen the poster, he had paid silent homage whenever he passed the swashbuckling, jodhpured hero. The boy recalled the good fortune of two years back when, on his tenth birthday, his parents had taken him to see the famous lion tamer in action.

As Norman exited '179,' Ira caught his eye, gesturing toward the poster and its anonymous vandal. "What a—!"

Unable to find a word to match his anger, he just shook his head. Norman tried to help him through the moment.

"When people do things like that, Ira, it's probably because they're envious, that's all."

Ira puzzled through his question. "About what, Pop?"

"About Buck being so famous, maybe."

"That's a dumb reason to ruin the whole picture, Pop."

The poster began to assume a larger meaning for Norman, a metaphor of survival: the lions and tigers valiantly fighting for their existence, struggling against Buck's skill and bravery; and the crayon wielder ruthlessly wiping out all the combatants. Tumbling through Norman's memory were proverbs; biblical and *Reader's Digest* send-in observations; axioms for the struggle to the top by men who had from humble beginnings risen to the top of society's economic summit.

These desperate Depression years, with their oppressive weight of want, heavily burdened Norman and many other 'have nots' in their Sisyphean struggle for financial security.

Norman and other public school teachers like Frank Buck were forced to try to tame their dangerous beast: the Board of Education's budget limiting salaries to less than what would be commensurate with teachers' contribution to the educational and social issues of the day.

Norman headed a small splinter group he had helped form within the Teachers' Union, hoping to affect change by pressuring the Board to vote more funds for higher wages and benefits. It was a quixotic mission but Norman was committed to the struggle, the members distributing petitions for local residents to sign in favor of raising teachers' salaries. However, most people had little sympathy for the financial problems of teachers, viewing them as a privileged class, already paid more than workers in the labor force who were constantly in danger of losing their low-paying jobs. The union activists managed to attract only a small number of signatures, scarcely enough to impact the Board's decisions. Several members of the group felt that Norman, who had temporarily lost his teaching job, his family falling on hard times, was making it very difficult for himself to be reinstated because of his militant activities. Besides, they argued, bureaucrats would just throw the petitions into a trash can or use them for wallpaper.

"Yes," Norman acknowledged, "there's very little chance of success, but it's a beginning. The battle must be joined! City Hall take notice!"

He had adopted the battle cry after certain events several years before when he had been teaching English at the Abraham Lincoln High School in the Coney Island section of Brooklyn.

2
1934

ELISSA JACKMAN, a leader of the politically active National Student League, had organized a campus peace strike. Abraham Lincoln's principal, Gabriel Mason, assigned Norman, a trusted enforcer of the school's regulations, to deal with the situation.

"I perceive this demonstration, Norman," he intoned, "a threat to the very foundation of this school's Jeffersonian concept of majority rule."

"Well, Mr. Mason, there are a number of students here who feel that their protest is valid."

Mason answered Norman's point in his practiced way of appearing to be fair. "Of course the minority voice should be heard, but danger lies in its becoming too loud. Therefore, Norman, we must take every precaution to protect our bailiwick here."

"I'll talk to them. Elissa Jackman is in my English Lit."

"Good. She has to be made to realize that her continuing as a student in good standing at Lincoln will be based on her adhering to our rules."

When Norman did not agree as quickly as Mason would have liked, he added, "Indeed all of us, Norman, should keep in mind that students... *and teachers alike must conform to our agenda or suffer the consequences.*"

Later, when Norman spoke to Elissa, he quickly realized that the clear-eyed, pert-faced girl, although barely seventeen years old, was very politically sophisticated. Her parents were active officers in Local 5 of the Teachers' Union and apparently helped shape her liberal ideas.

"It's not just war we're against, Mr. Schecter, and the lack of Negro history in our texts, but other evils of the school system."

"And those evils are —?" Norman asked patiently.

"Well, for one thing, the school newspaper editors have been criticized because of their dissenting articles about increasing class sizes by some 20-30 percent."

"Unfortunately that might be so, Elissa, but do you also realize that teachers will be forced to work that much harder?"

"Of course, the sword of larger classes cuts both ways, Mr. Schecter."

"Teachers do not write the budget, Elissa. We also suffer from there being fewer tools available to solve curriculum problems.

"Which proves that student problems are really teachers' problems, so you should join us in our protest."

"Do you intend to go into law, Elissa?"

Thrown by the question, Elissa became edgy. "Why do you ask?"

"Well, you seem to be quite expert at maneuvering facts in order to make your case."

"It's very easy, Mr. Schecter, if you're interested in public service. Right now the League has to deal with the fact that unless we apologize for our activities, our vigilant Principal, will find a way to keep us out of college. In *my* case, he'll probably short circuit my application to Princeton."

"I think he intends to do that, Elissa."

"And what are your feelings about it, Mr. Schecter?"

"I believe that sometimes measures have to be taken to bring order to chaotic public behavior."

Elissa hesitated for a moment before plunging ahead, "I honestly have to say, Mr. Schecter, that there's been nothing in the way you conduct your classes that prepared me for that fascistic remark."

"You may be the brightest student in my class," Norman stated genuinely, "but I'm not about to debate a premise which is fallacious at its core."

"Well, I don't think-"

"You know the Principal's stand on whether or not League members should be recommended for college. The next move is yours."

Whenever she was upset, Elissa usually tugged at one of her pigtails. By the time she had reached Norman's office door, she had nervously yanked on both of them.

After she slammed the office door behind her, Norman turned to stare out the window at the tree that usually bloomed its green promise of spring but at the moment seemed to Norman to be as leafless as his behavior: moral ambiguity at best; at worst, compromising his ethics in order to protect his position at Lincoln—a permanent substitute teacher without tenure or salary increments. It was vital for Norman to remain in Mason's good graces, since the principal had the absolute power to replace him with a regular teacher. As long as Norman did not behave in any way contrary to Mason's dictates, he would be able to continue at Abraham Lincoln... as a favored lackey of his principal.

~

On the bus taking Norman to the Schecter apartment in East Flatbush, his thoughts were interrupted as he caught a look at himself in the bus driver's rear-vision mirror. His face seemed taut and haggard, but his wife, Marsa, had once privately told him that although she loved her son with 'all my big Russian-Jewish heart,' Norman was better looking, even handsome, whereas Ira was 'a wonderful, wonderful boychik, but on his looks, not so hot.'

Norman smiled at the memory of his wife's affectionate observation. Now his thoughts went to the possibility of trying to convince Mason to modify his position of withholding his college recommendation for the League members, but quickly dismissed the idea since the principal was apparently intractable on that point. He grasped at the idea of telling Jackman that he would discuss her case with Mason when a propitious moment presented itself. However, sensing that Jackman would easily see through his equivocal stance, he decided it would be more politic not to say anything at all. After all, he had the responsibility to not endanger the financial security of his family. He felt his anger growing at the thought that his young student, hell-bent on curing the ills of the world, would expect him, with the country sinking into a deeper economic depression by the day, to jeopardize his hard-to-come-by job. This evaluation satisfied him although he dimly heard the disapproving voice of his conscience, distant and far away, in a place hidden by denial and fear.

Marsa Schecter was waiting for her husband with his usual end-of-the-working-day cup of coffee, along with a slice of Muenster cheese and a few grapes placed decoratively around it.

In recent years, because of Norman's modest but steady substitute-teacher's salary, the family had been living with some small degree of ease. Staple foods were not wanting if the Schecters lived within their carefully worked out, no-frills budget; clothes also, especially if purchased at discount prices, which Marsa was adept at ferreting out. With Marsa guarding the budget, the Schecters had recently even started to save 5 or 6 dollars a month. Unfortunately, a sudden catastrophic financial reversal would soon quickly exhaust their slim savings, forcing the family to move from their small modest apartment. This pleasant section had a large Jewish population and was ethnically diverse with many Irish and Polish and a few pockets of Italians. Also, a scattering of colored people had started to move in from over-crowded Bedford-Stuyvesant, where tenants of the once-upon-a-time stately brownstones were shoe-horned into four-walled decay and helplessness; its low-income laborers, domestics, and sprinkle of professionals struggling for an economic toe-hold in a white world extremely protective of its own meager earning power.

When the Schecters were forced to move to Brownsville in 1935, it, too, was a homogeneous neighborhood, nearly everyone of its 200,000 people were Jewish, with a small handful of Italians and Colored, living in the run-down part of this run-down area where the Schecters lived in the cramped apartment 2, in '179.' The few dollars for food, rent and minimal expenses that the City Relief provided was barely enough to live on.

Marsa was about Norman's age, about his height, about his intelligence, but vividly different in the way she addressed life. Where Norman seemed almost light-hearted when facing adversity, Marsa's response was almost always an anxious one. Where Norman would quickly recover from a disappointment, his wife would remain in its grip until with Norman's help she allowed herself to be prodded to a more optimistic state.

In this way, Norman had been helpful, counseling and consoling Marsa in her constant stressful concerns about her family still in Germany.

This day, polishing the family heirloom silver samovar, she drew comfort from her memories of its position of prominence in her former home on Bleibtrue Strasse in a high-toned section of Berlin. Here in Brooklyn, the centerpiece of the apartment's decor was the tea-server, its place of honor on the coffee table in the center of the very small, tidy living room.

The samovar had been sent as a gift to Marsa from her parents in Germany, immediately after the World War I Armistice. Receiving it marked the first time she had heard from them since she had arrived in New York to visit her aunt just before the Kaiser declared war on the Allies, blocking Marsa's return home.

As a young married couple, her parents, the Slipoys, had carried the heirloom to Germany from Odessa, a major city in the Ukraine, because the Cossacks had started another brutally violent Pogrom against the Jews. Max and Esther Slipoy were not aware at the time that the fire they jumped into was much hotter than the frying pan of Russia.

Marsa religiously kept the ornate silver at a high shine, and sometimes if she stared at it, the brilliant surface would mirror a young girl, her deep brown eyes peering back into time, to when the sounds of graceful living swirled through the large airy rooms of her childhood Russian home, her brother Leo's and her dedication to playing the baby-Grand in the carpeted comfort of the wood-paneled drawing-room, caressing them all with melodies of Mozart and Beethoven.

The past was dead. She knew that, but she had never been able to put it to rest. The scar that covered her loss was often torn open, the pain shooting through her spirit.

Most of the time, she tended to the wound herself, feeling it her own responsibility, her solitary burden to bear.

After the war, Marsa's family had made plans for her to return home, and she was packed and ready to go back, when she met and fell very much in love with Norman, just discharged from the Army, still romantically uniformed with decorations.

Both were just 20 years old, and the heady excitement of their physical attraction for each other and mutual optimism for their future and the world's, after this 'war to end all wars,' bonded them. Within a year, they were married.

So Marsa unpacked and found a job as seamstress in a garment sweatshop in order to support the family while Norman went to CCNY, a college which was tuition-free to high school students who had B grades or higher, essentially drawing the enrollment from low income, working class families who could not afford Columbia or N.Y.U.

A few weeks into Norman's first semester, they were washing the dinner dishes together when Marsa, exhausted, slumped onto a chair. Norman, concerned, spoke warmly as he took her dish towel away. "I'll finish 'em."

"No, Normie, my body was tired for just a minute but I'll—"

Norman gently stopped her from getting up. "Marsa, I don't like our arrangement."

"Arrangement what?"

"You work very hard on that sewing machine at Tuckman's Tots and then you run back here, make dinner."

"You don't like my cooking?"

"It's the best, my dark-eyed angel, but I'm going to drop one of my classes; have some time to sell encyclopedias or something, so you won't have to work so many hours."

"Don't worry your head, Normie, your job is just to read those smart books so you can be a good teacher like you want."

"But—"

"And then I can retire like a princess."

Norman lovingly corrected her, "A Queen."

Concerned, Norman was able to find a part-time job for a few hours a week, making linen deliveries to restaurants. The few dollars he earned made it possible for Marsa to not have to work overtime at Tuckman's, and appreciative of her efforts to keep the family afloat, struggled to express his deep affection.

He once wrote a few lines of poetry when she went to visit her aunt in the Bronx.

"To express my love,
Don't get me started;
The heavens wept
when you departed."

Marsa translated the poem into Russian and German, framing and hanging the three different versions on the wall, now an altar decorated with photos of Ira as he grew up.

Marsa and Norman were very much in love; amused at their both sharing a modesty about their nudity, always getting into bed wearing some undergarments, which were tossed aside from under the blanket. Affectionately laughing at each other's physical exertions, they shared a sense of humor about the different body contortions they would get into while pleasuring each other, chuckling their satisfaction. Now, Norman, still trying to shake his hard day, reached for the comfort of Marsa's body, her lushness and warmth enveloping his unspoken need even as he returned the delight to her.

3

SPEAKING TO ELISSA JACKMAN the next day after class, Norman tried to stay on neutral ground. "I hope this Sunday is one that passes… *un*eventfully."

"We hope, Mr. Schecter, that our cause will prove to be an *eventful* one."

Stopping at the classroom door, Elissa hesitated for a moment before turning back to Norman.

"You're invited to our rally Sunday, Mr. Schecter."

"Thank you, Elissa, but I think it's prudent that I not be present."

Having been refused permission by Mason to use the school auditorium for the meeting, Elissa and the Student League had decided to hold the rally at the athletic field.

Anticipating this, Mason had the custodian padlock the two gates to the stadium.

Elissa and the League, on their part, were aware of the lockout, and were able to find a few step-ladders which were to be used to scale the fences, avoiding the illegality of cutting the gate-locks and being accused of vandalism and trespassing.

Instead, there were classmates greetings, salutary hails of hand-waving; welcoming smiles; hugs, youth. Visions of change; harmony of dreams; a warless tomorrow!

The *RALLY FOR PEACE NOW* flyers would protest several of the conflicts around the world: Japan's rape of Nanking; the puppet state violently carved out in Manchuria; the roiling unrest in Spain threatening to burst into a civil-war conflagration.

The minor inconvenience of scaling the gates underlined the common thread of brother/sisterhood struggle. The camaraderie was challenged by an unexpected light rain, but the students' good humor was tested for only a moment before there was an unspoken pact of good-natured response, turning the threatening weather into just another obstacle for the healthy bravura of youth to conquer.

As soon as Elissa and the others had arrived at the field gates, the custodian phoned the principal at home, who quickly called the police and Norman asking him to be the school representative to meet the police when they got there. Norman arrived at the field just as two mounted policemen were ordering the custodian to unlock the gates so they could enter.

By now, the crowd, without an umbrella among them because the *Daily News* weather forecast had promised a clear, seasonally warm day, were proudly wearing their wet clothes as a badge of discomfort shared by all for the greater good of a brighter future fought for.

The mounted police moved slowly into the crowd, dispersing it, but when several students stood their ground in front of them, not moving, one of the officers waved them out of the way with his billy club.

Norman shouted to Elissa to help the officers clear the field. "You had your meeting, Miss Jackman, but the law is in charge now."

"No, Mr. Schecter, for what we have to do, the *truth* is in charge."

One of the mounted policemen, losing his patience, threateningly waved his club.

"Let's move it, kids. Twenty-three skidoo."

Elissa, her dress soaked through, ran to one of the ladders and quickly climbed to its top, shouting down to the crowd, some of them uncertain as to whether they should continue the meeting or leave at the belligerent request of the police.

"We've still got unfinished work to do," Elissa shouted, "don't let them scare you off."

Norman called up to Elissa now 20 feet above him.

"It's not safe, Elissa, come on down."

Elissa, as if on the barricades, straddled the top step, dramatically shouting through the rain pouring down her face. "Tom Paine is watching what we do here today. Yes, 'these are the times that try men's souls, the summer soldier and the sunshine patriot'—"

Norman noticed one of her feet slide off the step that was anchoring her.

"Elissa, careful!"

Her arms spread wide, she shouted "The battle must be joined! City Hall take notice!" Then she lost her footing. As Norman rushed forward to cushion her fall, she fell past his desperate, outstretched arms, her body hitting the ground with a thud, and a sound like a twig breaking.

She lay there, unmoving.

Many years later when the 911 emergency system came into use, Norman wondered if it would have made a difference in what eventually happened to Elissa because it had taken so long to finally get her to a hospital.

A couple of days later when Norman went to visit her, he met her parents in the waiting room, who quietly told him that the doctor had put Elissa through extensive examination and tests related to her spine.

Mrs. Jackman explained calmly, "Our daughter may be paralyzed from the waist down."

Mr. Jackman, fists tightly clenched, his words coming between short, labored breaths, murmured, "We gave her a surprise birthday party just last week. She was seventeen."

Donna Jackman patted his shoulder consolingly, "She's going to be all right, Max."

"Yes," Max obediently repeated, "She's going to be all right."

Donna, glancing toward Norman, managed a half smile, "Thank you very much for helping our daughter."

In Elissa's room, Norman attempted to be reassuring. "If there's anybody who has the will to overcome this bad fortune, you—"

The morphine for her bruised body wearing off, she abruptly cut him off, "I can do without the pep talk," calling out, "Nurse, I need my medication!"

Norman stayed for a few more minutes as the morphine was taking over Elissa's pain, and speaking as he started to leave, offered a comforting, "She's going to be okay." At the door, he turned back to the Jackmans, "I have to leave, it's my wife's birthday," almost apologetically, "I'm taking her to see City Lights."

"We saw that Chaplin last week," Donna said, smiling at the memory, then stared down at her sleeping daughter, and in a mock-chastising tone, "but you were just too busy organizing the Protest."

"Trying to do too much, little girl," her father, fighting back tears, reached out to clutch his wife's hand.

Donna turned to Norman proudly, "She even came down to our local meeting, collecting information about some of *our* past rallies. It's actually a lot of work," Donna offered, not complaining. "Come down to Local 5, take a look at what we're trying to do."

At school, Mason told Norman that he had written to Elissa's parents, extending his condolences for her injury. He assured them that the school would be sure she would get the necessary class assignments. The fact that she was in the upper five percent in her grades was an encouraging factor for Mason.

"But on the other hand, Schecter, I hope she helps her recovery by not expending any more wasted energy on her extra-curriculur activities."

"But it's a vital part of her life, Mr. Mason, and from the doctors' prognosis, she may have to live it in a wheelchair."

"That would indeed be tragic, Schecter, but what must be faced is that it would be an unfortunate consequence of her involvement with a renegade group."

Norman was quiet for a long moment before speaking slowly, in italics.

"The rest of her life in a wheelchair."

Mason stared at Norman intently before finally glancing at his appointment book.

"It looks as if I have a meeting coming up. If you will excuse me, Schecter?"

It was Norman's turn to stare at Mason intently, finally turning and leaving.

4

SEVERAL DAYS LATER, arriving at Abraham Lincoln for his first period, Norman was greeted by two excited students outside his classroom.

The shorter young man, Terry, hardly five-feet tall, proudly introduced himself as Elissa's aide-de-camp, politely asking Norman if they could speak with him.

Norman, recognizing the two students from the Peace Rally, was already opening the door for them.

"Let's talk, fellars."

The other student, Jim, six feet six inches of varsity football player's muscle, followed Norman into the room. On first sight, the disparate heights of the two students invited humor, but their no-nonsense mien discouraged anything but the most serious response.

Jim explained the reason for their visit.

"Elissa told me and Terry to let you know about our plans for the League's next move."

"I haven't seen her for almost a week. Is she —" Norman's words trailed off — "still —?"

Jim managed a muted answer, "Yeah, she's still paralyzed."

Nodding solemnly, Terry brightly added, "But we know she's made of strong stuff. She's really swell."

Jim, his voice and aggressive body language as if coming out of a football team huddle, barked signals. "Elissa has diagramed the entire operation."

Terry again finished the thought. "The parent-teacher-student protest!"

Jim caught the ball. "To stop the extreme overcrowding of classes; this time featuring one of the worst—Public School 225!" And carrying the ball to the touchdown, "Too crowded!" He demonstrated the point by adjusting his large frame in the standard classroom chair, his body and legs clearly too large to be comfortably accommodated. His knees 'cracked' as he stretched his long legs, both he and Terry chuckling at the unintentional sound effect.

~

Several years later, in 1937, Norman was unexpectedly reminded of the visit of the two serious students: It had become extremely heated in Schecter's ground floor apartment in '179' Amboy. During the summer, a small electric fan set up in the living room provided little benefit in this hotter-than-usual summer. Even that small help had become unavailable. The fan had broken down some weeks before, and Marsa had refused to give it to a repairman.

"To pay a single dollar will make me feel a thousand percent hotter."

So the Schecters were forced to suffer through the near unbearable heat. Occasionally, when the thermometer went over 100 degrees, the sweltering apartment sent most of the tenants up to the tarred and pebbled roof in search of some respite, some faint cooling breeze in order to sleep. Each family would bring with them a bed sheet that would be used to mark out their roof territory. A bottle of water and a couple of house slippers or shoes used to weigh down the corners would make the area theirs until dawn. As the night darkened, the stars not yet bright enough to help the 'campers' thread their way through the narrow maze spaces between the many blankets. The flashlight that Norman, with foresight, occasionally brought with him would help keep people from trampling into each other's domain.

Because it was too hot to easily get to sleep, sometimes Duddy Cohen from apartment 14 on the second floor would play his harmonica, not too well, but he hit most of the notes of *The Music Goes Round and Round* and some of the new hits; *It's a Sin to Tell a Lie*, and *Red Sails in the Sunset,* but the crowd pleaser was the one most of them knew the words of, and which usually drew a laugh and applause; *You Can't Stop Me from Dreaming.* Duddy would play it even as some of the people were starting to get some welcome sleep. The blankets could not mask the prickly uncomfortable feeling of the pebbles underneath, and occasionally when someone complained, Norman would gently kibbutz him; asking "What the hell you complaining about? You the princess or the pea?" It was a sure laugh.

This hot afternoon, Norman had gone outside hoping for some cooler air, but the blazing sun had heated the street as well.

Disappointed, Norman decided that the street was a lesser evil, so he sat down on the top step of the shallow three-step unit that extended out a few feet from the front of the building. It was as if an architect had copied the way European royalty had placed their monarch's throne on a rise separating it from the common folk, adapting this touch of aristocracy for the enjoyment of the peasants of Brooklyn. A man's castle with a terminally rotting foundation.

It was then that a similar 'cracking' sound carried his memory back to his meeting with Terry and Jim: Ira was 'cracking' his knuckles as he watched his friend Eddie Baker playing with his Hi-Li racquet.

Eddie, a couple of years older than Ira, had started his daily exhibition of Hi-Li expertise. He had become the block champ, having spent the whole summer perfecting his skill with the racquet and the long elastic band stapled to the center of it with a small rubber ball at the end of it. Each time the ball hit the paddle and sprang back, Eddie proudly announced the count, always in diligent pursuit of a new Amboy Street record.

Ira's 'cracking' knuckles started to create an annoying problem for Eddie's concentration.

"Nynee four... cut it out Ira... nynee five... ya shmuck, nynee six."

Norman's memory circled around the after effects of the student-parent-teacher rally at P.S. 225 in 1934. Along with Jim, Terry and the Jackmans, they had all shared a cab, compliments of Local 5, to go to the Kings County Hospital. They were anxious to tell Elissa the positive results about the reporter from the *Brooklyn Eagle* who had covered the event.

They arrived at the hospital; the energy of the rally surrounding them, the day's victory, a glimpse of their vision of bettering school conditions.

Passing through the lobby on their way to the elevator, the ambience connecting to some memory echoing in each of them, of fear, of relief, awe, comfort, pain, gentleness, a mix coloring one's response to this hallowed place and the empathic magic of the men and women in uniformed white.

Elissa had had a particularly painful day. After a moment of watching her writhe in pain, it was clear that the information that Norman and the others were carrying to her should wait for another time. Gesturing to Jim and Terry, he motioned for them to follow him out of the room. The Jackmans nodded in approval, but Elissa's whispering a pained "What happened today?" stopped them.

The Jackmans gave a brief recounting of the rally as a nurse entered with a hypodermic, a doctor right behind her.

"We're going to take away the pain now. It's going to be all right, young lady."

As he left, Norman wondered if it *was* going to be all right. It would be awhile before Elissa's medical problem was finally resolved.

5
1937

PARKED IN FRONT OF '179,' a roofless truck loaded with large blocks of ice fighting the melting heat drew Norman's attention, perched on the three-step unit in front of the building. From his well-worn leather briefcase he always carried with him, he carefully removed several mimeographed flyers and a sheet of paper: Teachers List. Copying one of the names onto an envelope, he inserted one of the flyers announcing a special meeting the following week. In one smooth move, he licked the flap, sealed it and anxiously put the important dispatch into his briefcase.

The list of teachers had been collected back in '34 when he had, at the Jackman's invitation, become involved with progressive Local 5 of the Teachers' Union. His activities with the Union had expanded over the next few years and by this summer of '37 he was at the center of many of its campaigns.

The owner of the parked truck, Tony Falacarro, a lean, hard-muscled 50, ice-picked at one of the blocks with quick expert strokes, working hard and quickly in order to sell his wares to the apartment-dwellers for their ice-boxes. Tony had to rely on the harvest of the hot summer, for in the cooler months when ice would not melt away as fast, he had to live off the seasonal bounty.

Tony would often give the same cheerful, Italian-accented offer to his customers: "Five-a cent apiece is-a cheap to cool the food, thatsa right?" If his customers complained about the smallness of the piece they were buying, Tony would give them a cracked-tooth grin: "Take-a tenna cent piece. Makes-a da whole kitchen cold like-a Eskimo house!"

Often, the customer would bring a towel to wrap the piece in to carry home or Tony would put the ice into a large wooden-slatted bucket, sling it over his shoulder and follow the customer to their apartment.

Tony, noting that Norman was busily bent over his envelopes, called to Ira without interrupting the rhythmic stabbing of his ice pick, the melody of his Italian inflection wrapping itself warmly around his business inquiry, "Ask-a da Mama, five-a cent... tenna cents?"

Ira, who had been admiringly watching Eddie and his Hi-Li technique, glanced up at a ground-floor window as it was opened by Marsa.

"Hey Mom, go back in, it's too hot."

Marsa waved affectionately at him, her hand at the same time trying to escort some breeze into the window.

"Tony, five cents," commandingly, "but big."

Her voice softened as she spoke to Ira, "Answer me, if you please, why you left some mashed on the plate?"

Ira explained, complaining, "I'm starting to look like an Idaho potato, Mom."

"Well, Mister Clark Gable no more, remember to pick up the *à-la-carte* menu today."

"I'll get it on the way back, Mom, don't worry."

Eddie proudly continued his exhibition of great skill, "Hunnerd 'n seven... hi Missus Schecter... hunnerd 'n eight."

Ira watched Eddie's technique for a moment longer before going toward a worn flight of stone steps leading down to the cellar of '179.'

Marsa held her hand outside of the window, testing the temperature. Not finding it any cooler than in the apartment, shrugging in helplessness, she stepped back into the room, closing the window.

~

Unyielding darkness. Ira's shoe scuffed the cement floor of the musty cellar, cautiously probing. His hesitant voice attempted a song... a thin melody challenging the dark.

"Six o'clock in the morning I looked upon the wall—"

A hint of bravura deepened his tone.

"The bedbugs and the roaches were having a game of ball—"

A match flared; a flickering spotlight.

"The score was six to nothing—"

The melody wavered for a moment as the match dipped to light a much used wick struggling up from a stub of a candle.

"The roaches were ahead—"

Ira carefully held the fluttering orange glow in front of him, exploring the cobwebbed darkness, his song soaring,

"A bedbug hit a home run and knocked me out of bed!"

The wavering light reached toward a battered children's carriage. He grasped its grimy handle familiarly, its feel carrying with it a long-ago moment: he had wanted to push his carriage, but his mother said, no, he was too small. His father had insisted, yes, that he be permitted to.

Shrugging off the recollection, the 'intrepid explorer' edged his way into the basement's darkness, softened by the candle dot of light, distorted shadows bouncing threateningly off the white walls. A splintered broom lay on a urine-stained mattress, its bedmate a rusting tricycle... proud, jaunty travelers in a sea of discarded relics.

Ira bravely made his way to a once-upon-a-time-blue-painted door. With a key drawn from a frayed pocket of his knickers, the 'safe cracker' wrestled the ancient lock open, the candle held high, its flame blinking at a small storage bin jammed full with an old bedspring... scarred end-tables... and several stacks of newspapers reaching to the low, plaster-flaking, cracked ceiling.

Pulling out one of the bound bundles, Ira noted that one of the careful knots he had tied in the string, rested on a photo of Roosevelt on the front page of the *Daily News*...

right on his mouth. Ira pushed the offending knot away as if to ease the President's discomfort.

His eyes adjusted to the dark, he packed as many of the newspaper bundles into the carriage as he could, then, sure-footed, he carefully negotiated his way back to the basement door. Opening it, he stepped into a wall of pungent odor coming from the opened garbage cans stored at the bottom of the steps leading up to the street. He carefully maneuvered the carriage past them and up the steps to the street with more ease than he had anticipated in his solo maiden voyage to the bowels of '179.'

~

On the sidewalk outside of '179,' Eddie Baker, almost reaching his old record of one thousand, three hunnerd 'n thirty, glanced over at Ira, exiting the cellar steps, and his concentration split, missed hitting the ball with the racket, quickly pretending to have purposely stopped in order to counsel his friend.

"Ya takin' the papers to Lensky or Big Nose Nathanson?"

The 'busy business man' shrugged as Eddie continued conspiratorially.

"If ya take 'em to Big Nose, ya can wet 'em."

Ira's expression asked for more information. Eddie patiently explained.

"Ya soak 'em in water, ya shmuck, 'n they weigh more. Ya get a nickel, maybe a dime even more."

Ira considered the advice as Eddie confidently reassured him.

"I'm tellin' ya, the guy there don't know the diffrunce."

Having decided he had spent enough time away from more important matters, Eddie stepped into a shaded area and attempted to set a new Hi-Li record. Ira's eye caught the front page of the New York Daily News on top of one of the bundles. "HITLER MARCHES INTO RHINELAND."

That's a peculiar way of putting it, Ira thought, not to say "GERMAN ARMY MARCHES INTO RHINELAND," but just "HITLER." He worked it out: when someone gets really famous, they become more important than even a whole country, like "NAPOLEON DEFEATS AUSTRIA"; or, "THE GAULS WERE VANQUISHED BY CAESAR"; or, "GHENGIS KHAN CONQUERED EUROPE," Hitler, then, must be very special. Also, a real shmuckhead from everything Ira heard about him. A 'First Class Anti-Semite,' his Rabbi-Teacher, Mr. Mintz, called him, spitting fine spray each time he mentioned Hitler's name.

The Rabbi would also spit at the mention of Father Coughlin; so Ira once asked him why this father upset him so much. The Rabbi's eyes almost apoplectically popped out of their sockets.

"Why? Ask your father! He listens to the radio!"

Ira didn't understand why listening to the radio was the key to all this passion, but when he asked Norman about it, his father also became emotional.

"Almost as many people listen to that Father Coughlin lunatic on the radio as Roosevelt. He's dangerous to the whole country, not only because he's a Jew-hater, but he's against workers, unions and everything that decent people need for a better life!"

This was one of the times that Ira really felt proud of his father, even though he thought that his father was acting dramatic like an actor in a movie.

He easily figured out why Coughlin was the crazy man his father said, but for some reason that Ira couldn't completely figure out, he felt an odd kind of guilty respect for the Nazi chief, Hitler. Sure, Ira hated him for all the evil things he was doing to the Jews, but you had to hand it to him. He had made himself so powerful that everybody in Germany had to call him Führer, which as Norman had explained, meant leader. *Leader* means you're first, and Ira put great store in being first, no matter what his father would say to him about how important it was just to play the game well, so even if you didn't win, you would feel good anyway. Maybe that works sometimes, Ira reluctantly thought, but you don't get to be a leader if you can feel okay about being second.

6

1934

A *NEW YORK TIMES'* FRONT PAGE announced that President Roosevelt's pet legislation, the National Recovery Act, a watershed law, allowing workers to organize, had been declared constitutional by the Supreme Court. The top of Principal Mason's highly polished mahogany office desk framed the newspaper. Moving his paperweight bust of Abraham Lincoln off to the side, he carefully placed a manila folder between Norman and himself. Flicking an imaginary dust particle off the folder, he ceremoniously opened it.

Norman stared down at the sheet of school issue blue-lined paper. In neat precise writing facing Mason were just three words.

"I wrote this, Norman, immediately after our talk about Miss Jackman unfortunately ending up in the hospital."

With a flourish, he turned the sheet toward Norman, enabling him to read it; in block letters: SCHECTER WORRIES ME. Mason solemnly continued, "The last several months, I've hinted more than once that since Harkin was planning to retire next year, I was considering a couple of teachers on staff who have an administrative degree, to recommend one of them for my Assistant Principal. You recall these conversations, Norman?"

"Vividly."

"And their significance, Norman?"

Norman nodded, tersely responding, "That I was one of those being considered for the position."

"Your perception is valid, Norman. How do you, at this time, perceive that Assistant Principal contest?"

"Well, Mister Mason, I must admit that certain past events have muddied the water somewhat."

"Well, do you have any input that might clear it up for me so I can make the proper selection, Norman?"

"May I first ask you a question?"

Mason, interpreting the request as an indication that Norman was going to be more accepting of his proper position as a loyal team player, congenially answered, "Of course, Norman, one must always question ways in which one can learn to temper one's behavior in these difficult times."

"Sadly, that may be so, Mr. Mason."

Now Mason readied himself for whatever strong-fisted, velvet-gloved diplomacy was needed to ensure that Norman was once again lock-step with him. Norman, on his part, prepared to walk an ethical tightrope, the footing slippery with self-preservation.

"Well," Norman paused for a moment before venturing into dangerous territory, "over the years, other teachers who have been on staff here longer than myself have told me that during the war, you were a conscientious objector."

Mason, very surprised, pivoted his body around in order to stare directly at Norman. "What was that, Norman?"

"Is my information correct, Mister Mason?"

Completely thrown off balance by the unexpected question, Mason almost sputtered his response, "Who...? What...? Who told you that?"

Norman, ignoring the question, spoke with growing intensity. "I was in the war myself, Mister Mason, and when I was with my outfit in France and heard there were a number of 'conshees,' as far as I was concerned, if their beliefs were sincere, I was okay with it. Truly."

After a long moment, Norman took the silence as confirmation of Mason's past during the Great War. He continued in an easier tone, "Your war objections were sincere, I'm sure, yes?"

Speaking slowly, deliberately, Mason's answer was genuine. "Yes, Norman, they were very much so."

"Well then, Mister Mason, why did you—?"

Mason's uneasiness accelerated, abruptly interrupting Norman, his voice strident. "That will be quite enough, Norman." However, Norman politely but firmly continued. "Mister Mason, I find it difficult to reconcile your past objection to war, with your present objection to peace."

Mason nearly shouted in frustration, "Let me attempt to educate you into the world of harsh realities of professionalism." After a short impassioned lecture on the necessity of not playing fast and loose with economic imperatives, his tone became more moderate.

"My having remained as a teacher during the war, provided me an excellent advantage; learning that many officials on the Board of Education desired staff to be loyal to authority and not, under any condition, 'conscientiously' object to any rules and guidelines set down by it."

"I'm not sure I understand, Mister Mason, why that would force you to change your views which had been accepted by the U.S. government itself."

"I," Mason was becoming impatient, his tone sharpening, "did not so much change my liberal views, Norman, as much as adapt them to the prevailing political climate."

"Well, it sounds to me that you were actually denying your obligation to your personal beliefs in order to accommodate the Board."

"Your observation, Norman, is an ill-conceived one."

"Well, it's clear to me, Mister Mason, that becoming principal is a step toward higher administration status, and if you keep trimming your sails in order to catch whichever way the political wind blows, you might very well become a Superintendent of a school district, correct?"

"Your smug appraisal of my behavior is duly noted, Schecter, but yes, I believe my qualifications may eventually help me achieve that position and its rewards."

"Qualifications?" Norman asked, "or opportunism?"

"That is quite enough, Norman! I've heard all I want to about your assessment of my actions; which will, not immodestly, eventually profit the young students under my tutelage."

"Well, the effect of your compromising behavior can eventually color their own code of ethics."

"You are beyond ludicrous, Norman, preaching your self-righteous morality. Only when you, yourself, are in a pitched battle, torn between your beliefs and what is expeditious for the good of all, do you earn the right to be the arbiter of things honorable. You are in simple terms, a phoney." His anger escalating, rage encased in ice, his voice pitched in chilling threat.

"Out of my office! Out! I have work to do, work that deals with real problems!"

For the next several days, Norman, now fully realizing that his job was in jeopardy, avoided any further one-on-one interaction with Mason. However, Norman's participation with other teachers, parents and students at the Public School 225 demonstration against overcrowded classrooms, lit the fire again.

Incensed at Norman's flagrant disregard of the Board of Education's position and his own authority, Mason called him to his office.

The Brooklyn Eagles' feature story, with photographs of Norman and other demonstrators were on Mason's desk, along with the opened file folder. The yellow paper had three words added to the first ones, in block letters again: SCHECTER MUST GO!

"I am transferring you from Abraham Lincoln as soon as the ink on my letter dries, requesting the Superintendent to confirm my move."

~

Although the Unemployed Teachers Association vigilantly championed Norman's protest about being transferred, demanding an open hearing for him in front of the Board of Education, Superintendent O'Shea supported Mason's action, 'for the good of the system.'

Answerable to the pressures of politicians who had helped to appoint him to his well-paying position and who, in tandem with powerfully wealthy business leaders, dictated the dollar amounts of school budgets, O'Shea would often attempt to leaven his hard-nose rulings with some amount of compassion. Once a teacher himself, he would try to make the cutting of the sharp ax of 'fiscal necessity' as painless as possible.

The Teacher's Association's representative argued that Norman's transfer was obviously punishment for his 'protest' activities.

"That may or may not be," O'Shea quietly explained, "but the point is a moot one, since we've had emergency budget cuts, so Mr. Schecter, along with a large number of substitute teachers, will have to be temporarily laid off."

"But, Mr. O'Shea, I've had a number of excellent teacher's evaluations by Mr. Mason himself, prior to his arbitrarily transferring me."

"Which have been duly noted by myself and the other Board members, Mr. Schecter, and you are to be congratulated on your good," seeming to underline the rest of his observation, "past record."

"Then, Mr. O'Shea, is my reinstatement based on my… *future* activities?"

"Absolutely not, Mr. Schecter," O'Shea continued carefully, "although the Board would hope that your behavior would not create problems for the system."

O'Shea breathed easier now that he had handled another one of those difficult situations which were invariably kicked up to his desk.

Within two months, Norman with only a few dollars left of his savings, reluctantly moved his family out of East Flatbush and into Brownsville, only a bus ride away, but closer to soul-deadening poverty.

7

ELISSA JACKMAN STARTED HER DIARY-JOURNAL on May 1, 1935:

Kings County Hospital, May 1, International May Day.

This is a new experience! My friend Helen bought me this diary for my birthday two or three years ago, but I never felt like draining away my time from all the other things, like classes, homework, hanging around Local 5 with Mom and Pop.

Now, I can sit around in my wheelchair, and if they give me my morphine regularly for the pain, I can read, write letters to the members in the Student League, and sit and sit and sit.

I don't want to start pitying myself, but I've got nothing but time to sit, and take some therapy that the nurse claims will help. Mom and Pop bought me this Zenith radio, but I'm sick of listening to *Fibber McGee and Molly,* and that Bergen and his dummy, Charlie McCarthy, who sometimes makes more sense than the Board of Education.

I listened to *Amos 'n Andy,* but had to change the dial when they really got stereotypical more than usual. I know they're white men playing Negroes, and I guess I wouldn't mind it if once in awhile they had a program about somebody who isn't a member of their stupid lodge or a garbage collector or a drunk bartender. Like how about Amos 'n Andy going to a Negro doctor's office or even a Negro teacher (we have a lot of them who joined the union this year).

I've got to admit that sometimes I'm really angry at Mom and Pop. I know it's not their fault, but maybe they should've talked me out of the peace protest and I wouldn't be here.

If I never get out of this wheelchair, I'll be a hero, but screw it, I want to walk again.

Maybe I should be gratified that more people are out there who know about the peace movement. Some nights when the drugs get to my mind and the pain is too much... anyway — I can't even cry anymore. Schecter came for a visit last week, but I think he sees what happened to me only as a kind of trophy of his newfound liberal values. I don't trust him.

8

1937

A SIMPLE WOOD-FRAMED PHOTOGRAPH of Clarence Darrow hung on the wall in the Schecter's cramped, yellow gloss-painted kitchen. Below the frame, a cardboard plaque stated the credo of the successful defender of the thrill murderers, Leopold and Loeb: "FEAR IS THE CHILD OF IGNORANCE." Picture and quotation had hung in Norman Schecter's classroom all during the time he taught English and Civics.

Norman had admired the famed criminal lawyer ever since he came across a moving emotional speech made by Darrow in honor of John Brown. While a student at Tilden High, Norman, researching a history class project on abolition, was extremely moved by Darrow's humanity, and quoted a line from the Address in his composition, printing it in large red block letters: "AND OTHER MARTYRS TAKE UP THE WORK THROUGH OTHER NIGHTS, AND THE DUMB AND STUPID WORLD PLANTS ITS WEARY FEET UPON THE SLIPPERY SAND, SOAKED BY THEIR BLOOD, AND THE WORLD MOVES ON."

His teacher, Mr. Sirota, gave him only a B-, explaining he was concerned that Norman 'be alert and careful not to be seduced by Darrow's well-known Socialist views.'

Now, twenty years later, the event flashed through his memory as he picked up a Trade Unionism book from the shelf in the living room. Glancing over at Marsa, who was solemnly peeling a potato, he spoke gently.

"You've got that sad look on your pretty face again."

"I'm all right, believe me. Just read your book, already."

"I guarantee you, Marsa my Russian beauty, that things will look better soon; you'll see."

"You told me last week the same story, twice... Just another week."

Marsa was used to 'waiting another' week because of anxiously watching for a letter from Germany. 'Another week' had turned into months. Although the Schecters were struggling through difficult times, across the ocean, the fortunes of her family, as well as those of other Jews, were living through even more down-turns of another sort; the growing overt anti-Semitism reflected in laws excluding them from most of the professions.

Marsa's father had felt that his managerial position at the Philharmonic was secure, and anyway, eventually the Nazi influences would be washed away by the public's good sense.

However, as the 30s marched along to the frightening boot sounds of the growing militant storm troopers, her father finally came to feel that he should, after all, make new plans for his family's survival.

Her brother, Leo, had written to her how their father, Abe, had become very good friends with one of the major philanthropic supporters of the Philharmonic, Jorgen Yablonski, a Jew who, through his excellent business acumen in the trading of essential supplies like rice, tobacco, oil, had achieved a unique position. His work had become so important to the leaders of the German economy, that even though he was well known as a Jew, he and his family were protected to the extent that he had been designated by Nazi high authority to be an Honorary Aryan, an Ehrenarier. This status was held by less than a handful of Jews, guaranteeing him absolute protection.

Slipoy visited Yablonski in order to ask his assistance. As Yablonski finished getting the information of Slipoy's Philharmonic responsibilities in order to take the necessary steps for visas and passports, a German military officer hurried into the office, apologizing for his intrusion; he needed some immediate information and help regarding a very large oil shipment of which Yablonski was in charge.

Yablonski hurriedly told Slipoy that he would assess his problem and get in touch with him, and just as Slipoy got up to leave, the officer gave him the by now standard official 'Heil Hitler,' his hand raised in the accompanying salute.

Slipoy hesitated for a split second before responding with a weak 'Heil Hitler'; and as Slipoy left the office, the officer watched him through cold, disapproving eyes.

The next day, an officer arrived at the Slipoys with a visa for Leo and his mother to travel to Hungary.

Of course Slipoy was very pleased at the prompt action that Yablonski had been able to take, but he felt uneasy about the travel plans that had been set up for himself. The officer reassured him though, that Slipoy's help was needed temporarily to set up an orchestra in a recently built work camp.

Leo and Mrs. Slipoy would leave in the morning in a limousine that would drive them to the airport for their flight, to Budapest. Abe would also be driven, but to the train station for his connection to the camp outside of Munich... Dachau.

~

Marsa tried to shake off the memory of that information as Norman entered the kitchen, placed his briefcase on a small bookcase which held several teacher manuals, some books on trade unionism, and a collection of Clarence Darrow's most important cases of defending unpopular causes. As he started to pick up the Darrow book, Marsa reached down under the ice-box and carefully drew out a pan, filled almost to the top with rust-tinged water. Lifting it was an exercise in slow motion; legs straightening almost imperceptibly; arms straining to keep her balance; shoulders hunched to meet the demand so that the water would not slosh over the sides.

Norman quickly put the book down, and rushed to her assistance.

"Why do we always wait till it's so full, Marsa?"

"Sh..." She cautioned him. Perfect concentration was needed for the journey of the porcelain pan, and not until it rested on the edge of the sink would she answer.

"Could it be maybe because you forget to empty it?"

The pan was tilted, the pale orange waterfall almost filling the shallow sink before the sluggish drain slowly gurgled it down.

"No, I think there must be a simpler explanation."

The pan emptied, Norman started back with it toward the icebox.

"I think it's because..."

He appreciatively embraced his wife's ample body.

"... we like meeting at romantic, out of the way places like this."

Laughing, Marsa returned his hug; both of them enjoying the physical closeness of each other, just as there was the sound of the lobby door squeaking open. Gently pushing Norman away, she moved rapidly to the apartment door, confidently throwing it open. As usual, she had timed it perfectly; Tony was standing there, his arm arched upward over his shoulder; his strong hand holding the top of the ice-bucket riding easily on his shoulder, as he entered and moved familiarly toward the kitchen.

Opening the top door of the ice-box, Norman noticed the small smooth piece of ice remaining inside. Staring at the graceful curve of the melting ice finally connected him to the past: Several years before, he had taken one of his classes on a field trip to the Metropolitan Museum. The exhibit was of the works of the celebrated surrealist, Salvador Dali, featuring his most famous painting, THE PERSISTENCE OF MEMORY, and its limp, melting watches scattered around a landscape of futility.

Many years later, Norman would revisit that moment in front of the ice-box, not for the image of the painting itself as much as its meaning for him... memory... melting memories.

Now Tony deftly maneuvered his fresh piece of ice onto the corrugated tin shelf as Norman locked in on the image of the smaller one melting away.

Waiting long enough for Marsa to nod her head in appreciation of the size of the fiva-cent-piece, Tony slammed shut the ice-box door.

Norman gave him a nickel, reaching into his pocket for a two cents tip.

"Grazia, amici, Tony."

Tony waved it away. "No grazia, amici."

Tony left and Norman picked up a Trade Unionism book, as he spoke to Marsa, attempting casualness.

"I'm going to the store and give Bennie the Butch a few hours."

"Five customers a day, if your father is lucky. He needs Norman Schecter's company?"

Marsa finished peeling a potato and brought the knife down hard, cutting it in two, one of the halves sliding off the table. Just like life, she thought sourly; it's so easy to end up on the floor.

Norman offered the neutral ground of mentioning one of their friends. "First, I'm going to meet Alan."

Marsa pounced on the information. "Tell him I'm sorry he had to be a waiter for the summer, but," pointedly, "for some people, a job is a job."

Norman fought against being defensive, but an edge crept into his voice, "I made a few dollars tutoring that college kid last week."

Marsa could not resist a derisive chuckle, "A dollar was for the doctor bill we owed Rabkin for taking care of Ira's whooping cough and the other dollar for pants and shoes for Ira from Madame Jay."

"Madame Jay" was the romantic euphemism for junk store, Marsa bestowing the aristocratic title on all the small shops along the pushcart-crowded streets that sold second-hand clothing.

Norman stared down at the cucumber he had taken from the ice-box. He vigorously salted it, but spoke quietly.

"I have to have time to work on the Union committee."

"That's a Union? Ten meshiguna teachers fighting City Hall?"

Norman almost shouted his defiance, "But we're going to win!"

Marsa was far from convinced. "In the meantime, they found out what you were doing, so they fired you, Mr. Union Man."

The Union Man denounced the system, "That son of a bitch, Mason, picked up some easy 'under the table' money, using PHG."

"What's with this alphabet business?"

Norman patiently explained, "Principals can sell a job to an unemployed teacher by PHG: Papa Has _____," rubbing his thumb against his first two fingers, "Gelt!"

"So go!" Marsa's frustrated emotion almost choked her words, "You know how it kills me to live like this! How it used to be better for me even in Russia," angrily finishing her litany of deprivations, "before those crazy Bolsheviks grabbed everything away from us."

As Norman rolled up his shirt sleeves in order to fight the heat, an envelope from his shirt pocket accidentally fell to the kitchen floor. Marsa picked it up, reading the return address.

"So, Normie, what's with this Board of Education letter?"

"Board of Education," evasively, "is Board of Education."

"Is the letter something maybe good, Normie?"

"They're asking some of us from the Union to come in and talk."

"About a job?" hopefully, "A definite?"

"No, I think they just want to find out about our plans to use the Wagner Act."

"The wonderful new law," Marsa's voice was scratchy with frustration, "you yelled about that was going to make the teachers millionaires?"

Norman and Marsa had argued heatedly about the Supreme Court's ruling that the Wagner Act, permitting workers to bargain collectively, was constitutional.

"Maybe not millionaires, Marsa, just decent salaries."

"So where does it say, Mister legal expert, that a teacher is the same as a worker?"

Norman climbed a righteous barricade. "We are all workers," his passion mounting. "All of us in the trenches of serving society… all of us!" He stopped abruptly, feeling that he sounded like a street corner Red, haranguing the crowd, hungry for political solutions to their financial plight. He lowered his voice so as not to be mistaken for one of those wild-eyed Communists, at the same time aware that the Party was after all preaching from the same book as he was… equity and fairness for all.

Moderating his voice, he continued, "Even though the government has ruled that it's illegal for public employees to strike, we'll find some way of testing that Wagner Act. Oh yes, we'll make them take their feet off the backs of our necks, pushing our noses into the ground."

Even before Marsa started to applaud in mock appreciation, Norman had stopped again, uneasy about his high-strung rhetoric. Marsa, recognizing his self-doubt, pressed her advantage.

"So, what's to hurt if you go in and talk to them?"

"Look, Marsa, it's just a game they play."

"So, what's special with this game?"

"It's called 'bribe the teacher' by putting him on staff again if he tells the Board about Union plans."

"So play the game," Marsa easily solved Norman's problem, "and get a job."

"I just don't like them trying to make me a labor spy."

Marsa snapped back, "And I don't like no money, so my son has to eat only potatoes, a few string beans, and if he's lucky, sometimes an egg sandwich."

"Neither do I, Marsa."

Marsa continued in high-volume, "So now there's a chance to make some dollars for your son to live better, and you run away to your Union instead?"

Ira, rushing into the apartment, halted the argument from escalating further. Marsa continued her potato peeling as she watched her son fill an empty milk bottle with water from the sink-tap.

"Pardon me prying, my busy son, but is it a big fire you're putting out?"

Staring down at Ira's well-worn tennis shoes, Marsa shook her head negatively as she reached over and tapped the back of his calf. Continuing to concentrate on the slowly filling bottle, Ira routinely lifted his foot for his Mother's smitty-like inspection, the first shoe passing her grudging approval.

The milk bottle filled, Ira started away from the sink but was stopped by his mother's quick grab of his other leg. Dutifully lifting his foot, he exposed a worn-through sneaker and threadbare sock. As Marsa glanced accusingly at Norman, she steered her protesting son toward a chair.

"Sit!"

Glancing up, Ira silently asked for assistance from his father who returned the boy's desperate look, with a quizzical one. After a moment, Norman spoke 'perplexedly,' "You remind me a lot of… uh… uh…"

As Norman pretended to earnestly wrestle with his memory, Marsa rummaged through a cluttered cabinet drawer, her 'treasure chest,' triumphantly extracting a roll of black electrical tape. She started to put a piece of it on the hole in Ira's sneaker just as Norman suddenly snapped his fingers dramatically, 'remembering.'

"Of course! You look just like Ira Schecter!"

The boy shook his head in good-natured despair.

"You're absolutely peculiar, Pop!"

Finishing her shoe repair, Marsa, after a moment's deliberation, took a penny from her change purse and shoved it at Ira's hand, masking the gift with brusqueness.

"So you won't yell later, 'Mama, gimme a penny.'"

Smiling his pleasure, Ira hurriedly left with his bottle of water as Norman turned back to Marsa, attempting a conciliatory tone.

"Should I ask Alan to come over Saturday night with Janet?"

"Ask if she's got an extra pillowcase to bring."

"But don't we have?"

Marsa's sharp "No" spoke for many other things the Schecter's also needed.

Picking up the *Trade Unionism* book, Norman started to the door.

"Don't worry about my supper, Marsa."

"Alan buying you a hot pastrami, maybe?"

"They're not doing so good, either."

"But Janet doesn't have to worry about Alan and Unions."

"Look, Marsa, eventually there's going to be certain protection in Union membership." Norman felt himself sliding into a pedantic tone, but it was too late to stop. "However, in my own case, the negotiating power was still too weak. If it'd been a little stronger, the School Board would've had to keep me on staff."

Marsa's curt interruption broke his pose.

"You made so much trouble, why should they kiss you and take you back? It's like you quit with them."

Norman clenched his teeth.

"I didn't quit. They forced me out."

"To me that's a quit, and to them, it's a quit."

A piece of the cucumber had lodged in Norman's throat and as he attempted to speak, he gagged slightly. Marsa patted him hard on his back, speaking more gently.

"Don't talk."

Norman cleared his throat as he stepped back to the ice-box to return the uneaten piece of cucumber.

"You're right," he sighed, "there's no point in talking."

Norman turned away quickly toward the door, speaking as he moved away from her.

"Don't worry, I'll be back before Mr. 'Relief' gets here."

Marsa went to the sink and held her hand under the tap and watched the water wash away the blood from one of her fingers she had cut while peeling the potatoes.

As Eddie, batting his Hi-Li ball, watched approvingly, Ira poured the bottle of water over the newspapers in the carriage. Ira studied the wirephoto of the German troops marching into the Rhineland blur as it soaked in the water. Glancing up, he saw his father's gaze from the doorway of '179,' and turned back to his work self-consciously, busying himself with tying the newspapers. After a moment he again glanced over at his father. Norman shook his head disapprovingly, turned and walked away, his book and briefcase tucked under his arm, hoping that Ira, on his own, would reconsider his petty larceny.

Straightening up from the carriage, Ira squinted into the sun as he watched his father walk deliberately down the street.

When Norman reached the mailbox at the corner, he removed the sealed envelopes from his briefcase. Glancing furtively around for a moment, he quickly put them into the box, and with purposeful strides, walked toward Stein's Deli where he had arranged to meet Alan.

Marsa watched the blood-red tinged water as it trickled slowly down the always clogged drain. The bleeding would not completely stop. With her other hand, she rummaged through the 'treasure chest.' Finally, from under a rusting pair of scissors and a worn Russian-English dictionary, she drew out a battered box of band-aids. Anxiously opening it, she discovered it now held only a few thumbtacks and a piece of old, frayed red ribbon.

Using the scissors, she cut a small corner from the copy of the Daily News on the kitchen table. Wrapping the paper tightly around the cut finger, she secured it with a rubber band she had been using to hold her thick black hair in place. As she picked up the piece of ribbon, she glanced up at the kitchen cabinet door above the sink where a faded photo was thumb tacked: a 12-or-13 year old girl in a tasteful ribboned blouse and skirt, along with a younger boy; both joyfully playing a piano.

As she studied the photo, she gently fingered the red ribbon a moment, before carefully placing it back into the band-aid box and putting it into the treasure chest, touching it affectionately before covering it again with the dictionary.

She glanced again at the photo. She tapped her finger rhythmically on the counter, her left hand joining in to 'play' the piano. Humming at first, she started to sing in Russian, her lovely voice caressing the words as she sang:

OT CHA CHUNIYA
OT CHA SKUCHIA

As she 'accompanied' herself on the piano, Marsa's cut finger accidentally struck the counter, causing her to wince in pain. Her singing abruptly stopped; her present sad life started again.

9

NORMAN GLANCED INTO the showcase window of Eppy and Eppy's shoe store where a small placard advertised for a part-time salesman.

The freshly decorated store was an oasis of elegance in a desert of shabbiness; 'high style' several cuts above the attempts of the desperate Mom and Pop businesses to merchandise an assortment of goods ranging from factory 'seconds' of irregularly cut underwear; to odds and ends of cheap linoleum; remnants of dress and curtain material and old used radios.

Eppy's credo, in the expertly calligraphied sign printed boldly on the store door, QUALITY FOR QUALITY PEOPLE, had apparently appealed to the public, hungry for anything that would elevate their sense of dignity while spending any of their hard-earned dollars.

Now glancing at the salesman sign, Norman decided to inquire about the job but he wondered if he would be able to convince Eppy that he could sell shoes. After all, a vitae of teaching High School English and coaching the school chess club was hardly a recommendation for being a shoe salesman. And he certainly would not be able to mention his union activities since it might worry Eppy's, as it would most businesses at this time. The newspapers had recently reported on the sit-down strike of F.W. Woolworth employees for more pay and benefits. They had barricaded themselves into the store until some basic concessions regarding salary, working conditions and overtime had been met. The ripple effect had reached many other businesses, causing owners to be sensitive to anything that might incite the low paid, frightened docile workers to collectively strike for higher wages.

The urgency of earning a few dollars impelled Norman to seize this opportunity to help his family.

As Norman placed his hand on the doorknob, Eppy picked up the 'Salesman Wanted' sign and handed it to a man standing beside him, who then nodded in appreciation as Eppy shook his hand in congratulation.

Disappointed, Norman wheeled around, starting to cross the street to Stein's Deli, but suddenly stopped, his ears cocked to a sound drifting over from around the corner. He smiled in recognition as it joined the street noises of old sputtering model-T's, infrequent Chevy's, and for this poor neighborhood, the rare, solid sound of the haughty, up-scale Buick.

In a moment, a wagon drawn by an arthritic, old horse started its way down the street.

Clop! Clop of horses' hooves and the long groaning squeak of the protesting wagon's old wooden floor, heralded Isaac the Junkman's arrival.

"Ahlta Shick! Ahlta Klayda"! Norman then intoned the translation of Isaac's urgent announcements:

"Old shoes! Old clothes!" Isaac's "Ahlta Zahchen" was followed by Norman's "Old things!"

He knew that Isaac would not mind his joining in to alert the neighborhood to the junk man's arrival, and the promise of a few cents for old, outworn articles that might otherwise eventually find their way into the garbage can.

"Clop! Clop! ... Squeak!"

Several months before, as Isaac and his wagon were passing through Amboy Street, some pots had fallen off in front of Norman, who helpfully had handed them up to Isaac. They became friends, connected in some way by the muted sound of the pots nestled among the assortment of old clothes, torn underwear, blankets, socks, towels that time and many washings had caused to meld into almost indistinguishable, sad unnamed colors; suits, long out of fashion, some buttonless, soiled with memories of long-ago family dinners, banquets, celebration of weddings, bar-mitzvahs, funerals; jacket linings of scarlet red, sky-blue, black and white polka dots, that once proudly knew astonished, wide-eyed applause when displayed as its wearers twirled in the carefree, celebratory dance of a Hora or syncopated tango, his partner wearing what was once shimmering colors, richer in imagination than any rainbow, awing the audience at the Grand Ball.

Clop-Clop! Squeak!

The material frantically holding seam-ripped beauty together, revealing its former glory.

All a distant, unshared memory, now lost among rusted pipes, broken cameras, torn window-shades and the tin flue of a kerosene lamp which once attempted to light velvet darkness that only the yearning imagination could illuminate: the darkest dark of once-upon-a-time, free of all its toil, of the 'then' that the heart searches for in vain, never finding, searches, never finding… never.

Clop clop! Squeak!

Over the following several weeks, whenever his route took him down Amboy Street and Norman happened to be outside, they continued their growing warm relationship.

Isaac Baumgarten was an Austrian Jew and like virtually everybody in his country, spoke German, but with a softer more melodious sound, similar to the Yiddish language which Norman had assimilated from having listened to his Russian-Jewish parents and other neighborhood émigrés.

At first, Isaac was reluctant to talk about his difficult journey to get to America, but despite some language difficulties, Norman managed to piece together his remarkable odyssey before finally reaching New York a few years earlier.

Isaac had decided to leave Austria shortly after being summarily dismissed as the head of the History Department at the Graz University.

He had been charged with 'unacceptable teaching methods' but the apparent intrusion and pressure of Hitler's emissaries to clean out the 'impurities' of Jewish influence, was clearly the first step to eventually purge Austria of anybody not of the pure Aryan race.

What impressed Norman most about Isaac was his extraordinary sense of dignity. Here he was, a highly educated man, a full Professor of one of Europe's renowned Universities, forced by circumstances to earn a meager living, driving a junk wagon.

Once, when Norman explained to him about his Union activities, the conflicts and hardships it presented for himself and his family, Isaac expressed his strong feeling about Norman's life.

"Du bist mahzeldik, Norman."

Norman thought Isaac had misunderstood him.

"You think me 'lucky'?"

"Ya," Isaac insisted, "du bist lucky."

It was at this time that Isaac told Norman about some of the obstacles that he, his wife, and their young child faced in order to cross the Italian border to Trieste.

Because Norman's parents had come from the Balkan states area, he had studied the various routes across Europe and the problems facing anybody trying to escape the growing Nazi oppression.

"Boat? Shiff?" Norman inquired.

No, Isaac had not been able to get passage on a boat sailing down the Adriatic into the Mediterranean, and then on to Spain or Portugal for some means of transportation to the United States or South America.

Norman asked about the train going across Italy to France. Again, Isaac shook his head 'no.'

Norman knew that the only other way to get to Switzerland and the first step to safety, would be to challenge the dangerous Brenner Pass across the Alps.

When Norman inquired about that trip, Isaac hesitated, started to say something but then shook his head, unable to continue.

~

Isaac's story caused Norman to reassess the perception of his own difficulties. Although he realized that there were many problems created by his becoming more involved in the Union's ever-growing militancy, by weighing everything into the equation, he felt he was indeed 'mahzeldik.'

On the other hand, after he had brought Marsa to the hospital to meet Elissa, on the bus ride home she had sympathetically, sadly observed, "That poor girl has no mahzel."

Marsa liked Elissa immediately and during a few visits over the next several months, Marsa had developed strong familial feelings toward her; a sort of surrogate for her younger brother, Leo, whom she had not seen for over twenty years.

Since she had received a letter and photo from him the year before from Budapest, he and his mother both wearing the Nazi mandatory armband with the yellow star of David, there had been an ominous silence.

Norman had patiently consoled Marsa on a number of occasions when she would be overcome with anxiety about her family, particularly her father, from whom there had been absolutely no word.

Although Norman was able to keep his own spirits up, the devil's advocate in him that always lurked around the edges of his reason waiting to puncture his optimism, suggested that if he turned his ever-present 'telescope' around he would be able to see that *his* 'luck' was running out; that because of his attempts to walk a tightrope between the Union and his family obligations, he was in danger of slipping off and crushing not only himself, but his family and the Union's dreams.

The events of the recent past had dramatically demonstrated the difficulty in keeping that balance.

Norman and the group's second-in-command, Danny Watkins, had decided to organize a meeting where future steps to advance their goals were to be discussed. It would only be through collective bargaining, Norman was convinced, that the Union would eventually be able to effect growth for the teaching community in all those areas that bound them to administrative decisions however inequitable they might be.

"Look," Norman would remind Watkins, "while Roosevelt is getting legislation passed to maybe brighten the country's economy, we teachers have to do whatever we can to make sure some of the light shines through to *us*."

Watkins, the nuts and bolts man of the group's leadership, energized by Norman's usually passionate rhetoric, would work to coordinate the practical aspects of their activities.

"Okay, Norman, let's try some more petitions, but I just don't know —"

The group met weekly at the Hebrew Educational Society in Brownsville; the use of its small auditorium was donated by the H.E.S.'s Rabbi Landsman, who hoped that the good will engendered would be used to strengthen neighborhood relations, encouraging donations that could help keep its doors open for children's craft classes and adult Hebrew learning seminars.

Numbering less than thirty members, the union group was made up of many different colors of the political spectrum. Most were liberal Roosevelt Democrats; a small number of conservative Republicans still hoping for a return to the good old days of non-intrusive government, rubbing shoulders with those tinged with the ever-more-popular Socialist views, plus a few outspoken Communists.

The mingling of these disparately different political ideologies created a volatile mix. Seasoned with contrary personalities and stirred by impatience, the pot periodically boiled over, scalding the cooks with combativeness and suspicion.

Now on the table was a plan that Norman and Watkins presented to the group. It spelled out the need for the Board of Education to upgrade the salaries of teachers who were kept on as 'permanent substitutes' for several school- terms in order for the City not to have to pay them full teacher's salary and benefits.

Mark Dysart, arch-conservative and very vocal dissenter, almost shouted his objection.

"What the hell are you trying to pull off, Schecter?" his voice rising as he stood up, an imposing barrel-chested man almost a foot taller than any of the others. "I thought we were meeting just to make a few suggestions because the School Board was starting to act as if they had the right to make any goddamn rule their little autocratic minds wanted to."

Loud murmurs of agreement supported Dysart's statement. Watkins tried to use it to get the others back on track. "That's exactly why we're arguing for changes in their handling of substitute teachers. Credentialed full-timers are reasonably safe *now*, but unless the inequity regarding substitutes is corrected, the Board can exert their high-handedness and decide to, let's say, cut back on sick days or summarily take away preparation periods and make us teach an extra class."

"Or take away," Norman was now as loud as Dysart, "every step of progress that Mary Barker struggled to achieve!"

"I'm glad," quickly added Connie Washington, one of the two colored members of the group, "you mentioned her because she helped pass some of our most important legislation. She was quite a lady."

As President of the American Federation of Teachers, Barker had worked many difficult, stressful years to achieve a balanced view of the colored people's history in school textbooks and for racial tolerance.

"Well, maybe it's time now," growled Dysart, "for a *man* to take over to get the really important things accomplished."

Jerry Goldstein, one of the card-carrying Communists in the group, condescendingly offered an observation. "Maybe if we can get beyond sexual bias, and deal with what the worker really needs to fight against: capitalist exploitation."

"Goldstein," Dysart said, pushing a chair aside in order to stand in front of Goldstein and tower over him, snarled through clenched teeth, "you are a goddamn pain in the ass, so if you have anything to contribute, fine, but otherwise, keep your Marxist bullshit ideas to yourself!"

"Bourgeois malcontent!" was all that Goldstein thought was necessary to silence any reactionary counter-attack.

10

ALAN MULNICK HOPED HE WOULD be able to use today's meeting with his best friend, Norman, to turn this bad day around.

More than this day alone, he had a bad *week*, a bad *year*.

And now he was having a bad time at Stein's delicatessen.

"Are you kidding, Stein? Two cents for 'extra'?!"

Stein had just put a hot dog in the bun and Alan had told him to go 'heavy' on the sauerkraut.

"A joke I'm not making, Mulnick. Go over to Persky's, go, see. By *him*, 'extra' is *three* cents."

Alan gestured his reluctant acceptance of the sauerkraut tariff as he glanced out of the store window before hopefully addressing Stein again.

"Was Normie Schecter here before?"

Stein looked up from where he had started to print something on a paper bag as he answered.

"The gentleman was not in my store."

"You sure?" Alan asked anxiously.

"Him," Stein sneered, "I'd remember. He can't even afford a *penny* for 'extra.'"

Alan shook his finger vigorously in Stein's face, lacing *his* sneer with anger.

"*You* should only be half the man *he* is, you shmuck!"

Stein had finished printing his sign: 2 CENTS FOR EXTRA SAUERKRAUT, turning to Alan angrily, "Don't shmuck me, you shmuck! You don't like the prices in my establishment, go to Persky's."

Alan looked out the window again, this time spotting Norman across the street, waving goodbye to the Junkman. Gulping down the last bite of his frankfurter, he hurried out of the store, calling out, "Normie!"

As Norman crossed the street toward him, waving his hand in salutation, a surprised look came over Alan's face. "Hey, your fly's open!"

Norman glanced quickly down at his buttoned trouser fly to confirm the fact that his fly was indeed *not* open. As he reached the sidewalk, he earnestly greeted Alan.

"It's been a long time since —"

He interrupted himself, pointing to Alan's face.

"What happened to — ?"

Alan's hand went to his upper lip.

"That shmuck headwaiter at the fancy Catskill Country Club made me cut it off. So what can an out-of-work furrier in-the-summer say to that?"

"I thought," Norman said, disappointed, "the Furrier's Union was going to —"

Alan's angry interruption was not aimed at Norman.

"Today, a Union card and a coffin can get you into any cemetery."

"Well," Norman said, smiling, "that's a start, Alan."

Alan laughed derisively; the pros and cons of unions was a constant heated, not-always-good-natured, debate between the two.

"It'll take a little time," Norman argued, "but unions are going to get a lot stronger if we all just —"

"*If* my aunt had balls, she'd be my uncle," Alan countered. "It's a boss's market today, you know that."

"*Today*, yes, my friend, but the hands on the clock move."

"Yeah," Alan pounced, "like shit floating upstream."

"All right, wise-guy, how's Janet and the kid?"

"My good wife," Alan shook his head in despair, "continues to slice up my nuts, and Esther needs braces —" touching his upper teeth, "If I can dig up ten dollars."

Norman and Alan had been walking down Sutter Avenue, and they stopped to watch a couple of men with sticks poking at the remains of a burnt-out store.

Alan's "Aha," was a word carrying the implication of much more to come, "Lichter's Haberdashery wasn't doing too good, so… pht!"

He sang to the melody of the Israel national Anthem, the Hatikvah, using an exaggerated Yiddish accent.

"Once I hed a candy store,
Business was so bed,
I asked my wife what to do,
this is what she said."

"Stop that stereotype crap, Alan!"

Alan teasingly sang a little louder, with an even thicker Yiddish accent.

"Take a ken of gasoline,
Put it by the door,
Take a metch,
Make a scretch,
No more kendy store!"

Alan steered angry Norman into Paddy Flynn's Neighborhood Bar, where they sat at one of four scarred wooden tables.

"Look, Alan, I'd expect something like that coming from Paddy, maybe, but —"

"F'chrissake, Normie," Alan spit out, "don't get your left testicle in an uproar."

"Just because Lichter," Norman shot back, "wasn't doing too well isn't enough reason to assume that he —"

Interrupting, Alan shook his head in disbelief, "Normie my boy scout, that place has gone 'poof' four times in the past two years. The ice cream parlor, Rizzo's Hat Store, the —"

Alan had held up two fingers to Paddy, behind the bar, who now served both customers a beer.

"Anyway, Norman, champion of the underdog, don't stay up all night bleeding for the insurance company, their rates went up again last month."

Withdrawing from the argument, Norman warmly offered, "Maybe I'll be able to help you out with Esther's braces. I mean when I get back teaching."

Alan, pleased with his friend's gesture, smiled affectionately. "Thanks, shmuck," then took a long swallow from his glass.

"My Pop is gonna be sixty eight next week."

"Well, wish Sam a real—" Norman's words were genuine, "'Happy' from me."

"He just won't listen to reason, Normie."

"He won't even take the day off?"

"He could take the whole week off, and it wouldn't matter. The store didn't even make enough to pay the overhead last year."

Alan had told his father the same thing that morning when he was helping him re-arrange the furs in the modest store window of "Mulnick and Son."

"Popa, you can change the display *every* day, but the cash register still won't ring enough to pay the rent."

Sam felt that as a man who had done a great deal of reading when he was a young rabbinical student in the Shtetl in Russia, and knowing that his son was not the scholar *he* was, felt that his erudition might stop Alan from lecturing him further about business problems.

"Alan, mein zindel, Spinoza said you only worry about the mortgage in your dreams."

Alan knew that whenever his father argued by using a famous man's quote, it meant that he was worried about the practical warning that Alan had presented.

"Yeah, Popa, and I bet he wrote a big fat philosophy book on the fur district, but the handwriting's ten feet high on the old walls here. You've got to do what I'm telling you; my plan is our only chance!"

Sam suddenly gasped in pain and frantically clutched at his chest. Alan quickly went to him, his hands reaching out to support his father's sagging body.

"What's the matter, Popa?"

Sam pushed aside Alan's help.

"A little gas, that's all, but maybe I should sit down for a —"

He eased himself into a chair as he held his hand up to silence his son from saying anything further.

"And no more I wanna hear those crazy ideas from you. The covenant of law must never be broken, you hear? Never!"

As Alan spoke to Norman, recalling his father's desperate situation, he repeated what he had said earlier.

"The store didn't even make enough to pay the overhead last year, Normie!"

"Why doesn't he just sell it?"

'You're funnier than the Marx Brothers. Pop couldn't *give* it away."

"Well, Alan, maybe by next year the business will —"

"By next year, Normie, he'll have another heart attack worrying about the business."

Norman, concerned, asked, "So what do you figure on doing?"

Alan was long waiting for that question. "Normie, you've got to help me to —" the words spilled out now. "...take a match... make a scratch."

"What —" Norman taken by surprise, managed "the hell you talking about?!"

"It's the only way we have."

"You've got matzoh balls in your head, Alan."

"Look, he's always liked you a lot, so if he knew you were going to help me, maybe he'd —"

Norman, overcoming his surprise, exclaimed, "Hold it! First of all, it's your *father's* business."

"Norman, it's just four dirty walls and a few shmahta pieces of muskrat."

"Look, Alan, what happens to the store should be up to him. I mean, the man has worked there forty years. The man has fought and struggled. The man—"

"The man," Alan was becoming very emotional, "the man'll have to hock his false teeth to pay the rent next month."

"Look," Norman was trying to hold onto his resolve not to become involved in Alan's plans; "if your Pop is crazy enough to do... this thing... do it and just don't tell me about it!"

"You used to come crying to our house when your mom made fun of you pissing in bed."

"And you saved my life at Belleau Woods, so?"

"My Pop's gonna go bankrupt in three months, 'n what's Mom 'n him gonna do? Move in with us? And share a pot we haven't got to piss in."

"Alan, I'm not going to talk Sam into burning down his own store."

"Then at least you've got to help me do it… two people are needed to carry out my plan to set the fire."

"Look, what you want to do is—"

"I'm hard of hearing, Normie, so don't give me one of your famous honesty speeches."

Alan's hand tightened around the beer glass. As he increased the pressure on it, his arm started to shake. Norman, attempting conciliation, spoke quietly.

"Alan, I just don't think I could—"

The glass in Alan's hand splintered and broke, the beer sloshing out, mixing with the dust and specks of hard-boiled egg on the scarred tabletop.

Paddy had turned toward the table at the first sound of the glass cracking. Rag in hand, he came around the bar, mopping up the beer as it slopped over the table. After checking that Alan's hand wasn't bleeding, he barked, "Hey Mulnick, easy on the property."

"I'll give you the nickel for the glass, okay?"

"Just like every Kike," Paddy thought, "figuring they could come into your house, piss on the floor and get away with it by throwing you some gelt." He tossed the rag on the bar and started to empty the ash trays as Fred the Mailman came in, unslinging his shoulder pouch and hanging it over a chair. He slid into another one where he could get a better view out of the window to watch the passing women in their thin summer dresses.

Glancing around the bar, he caught Norman's eye, nodded a salutation and turned back to stare out at two tightly sweatered girls, walking and talking in youthful animation. Craning his neck to follow their jiggling walk, he lightly touched himself.

Alan spoke low as he leaned closer to Norman.

"I think he's gonna beat his meat under the table."

Fred suddenly slid his chair forward. What a piece of luck! There she was! Finky, the best built, sexiest body in Brooklyn, rushing to cross against the lights, her large breasts threatening to bump her under the chin. Since there were no cars approaching the corner, it seemed to be an uncontested race. Norman and Alan, watching her shake provocatively, exchanged knowing smiles. Leering, Alan nudged Norman, nodding toward Fred.

"I'll give him thirty seconds before he comes."

Fred figured Finky to be pushing thirty-four, thirty five, maybe, but she had a great ass in addition to the biggest chest since Mae West. He'd sure like to give her a Special Delivery right between them. Especially before her husband, "Hey Kid" Charlie, got out of Sing Sing after doing three years for armed robbery.

Watching Finky catch her breath just a few feet away, he thought it would've been more fun to have done some of the things "Hey Kid" had done, especially like shtupping Finky. His groin warmed in pleasure at the thought.

Finky, glancing around while standing at the corner, caught Fred's look, and smiling, she came toward the bar entrance.

Standing in the doorway for a moment, her eyes adjusted to the dimness. Waving to Norman, she bobbed over to Fred's table. The nearness of her sexuality exciting him all the more. He could feel himself harden under the table.

"Anything for me today, Fred?"

He shook his head sadly.

"Sorry, Finkelstein."

"Well , Fred honey, you don't write 'em. You just deliver 'em, right?"

He was pleasantly aware of Normy and Alan watching as he casually indicated a chair at his table.

"Wanna brew?"

Finky hesitated for a moment, toying with a blouse button.

"Gotta rush, but-"

She took the glass of beer that Paddy had set on the table and gulped a swallow, shoving the glass back in front of the startled but pleased Fred who pretended to protest.

"Hey, hey!"

"I owe you one, okay? Next time you got any mail for me, you deliver it personal to 12 and you get a whole bottle, okay?"

"Yeah, but what if—"

Finky anticipated his question.

"And if there's no mail, knock anyway, cheapskate." Smiling, she turned and swept out, leaving Fred exhilarated and proud of the encounter that had taken place in full view of Paddy and the other customers.

Alan whispered to Norman,"If he gets into her pants, I'll gladly take sloppy seconds."

Norman remained focused on the seriousness of their meeting.

"I realize you're worried about your father's business and money problems, Alan, but the sun isn't shining so hot for the rest of us, either."

Alan's voice softened, almost pleading.

"Normy, I'm in a hole. A deep one."

"I don't think you should count on me."

"What does that mean?"

Hesitating, Norman glanced around the bar aimlessly. Alan jumped on the opportunity.

"Just give it a little more thought, Normy. Okay?"
"You're asking me to get involved in—"

"No. I'm telling my friend that I'm in a box and the lid's coming down."

Norman's finger traced the still moist outline of the beer stain on the table that Paddy had wiped up.

"Alan, I don't see how I—"

"I said, just sleep on it. Capish?"

"Capish."

Alan sighed hopefully. "If I knew Jean Harlow, I'd take some pictures of her underwear and let you look at 'em."

11

THE LIVING ROOM OF APARTMENT 2 was Marsa's favorite. In addition to the samovar heirloom always being handy, there was enough space for her to take care of some household chores; sorting out the socks, shirts, and underwear that she had hand-scrubbed numerous times, their colors almost bleached out. She was also able to enjoy the task of pressing them neatly on the ironing board she would set up facing the window as she listened to the small Zenith radio, distracting static, notwithstanding. "Our Gal Sunday" was her favorite soap opera, the announcer introducing the daily 15 minute program with a dramatically intoned question: "Can this young woman from the little mining town of Silver Creek, Colorado, find happiness with England's richest, most handsome Lord, Lord Henry Brinthrope?"

"Our Gal Sunday" reminded Marsa of that part of her long-ago self that often dreamt of being whisked away from her Odessa home, by one of the Czar's handsome palace guards; and then later, when she was living in Berlin, hoping that her high school math teacher, Herr Schegel, might become her shining knight. However, being rushed out of Germany ahead of the outbreak of the World War, cut short that teenage fantasy, so she went on to adopt the American movie stars to rescue her. Douglas Fairbanks, with his athletic virility seemed for a short while, a likely romantic candidate for her salvation, although she felt that Charlie Chaplin's hilarious whimsy could help her spirit fly away. Then, when she first saw Rudolph Valentino's smouldering gaze in The Sheik she felt that he was surely *her* Lord Henry Brinthrope... until she met Norman.

Another reason for Marsa enjoying her time in the living room was the Violin Man.

The windows of the kitchen, living room, and the small bedroom all were part of a rear section of '179' that along with the adjoining building, '185,' formed a small, crumbling courtyard littered with cigarette butts, gum wrappers, popsicle sticks, newspapers, and a few paper bags of garbage thrown out of apartment windows, splattering their odorous contents.

About once a week, the Violin Man, a neatly dressed man in his mid-thirties, in well-worn clothes, carrying a highly polished violin in one hand and its well-cared for case in the other, walked familiarly into the courtyard. He adjusted his eyes to the sun managing to find its way past the densely-hung clotheslines, criss-crossing the buildings all the way from the roof, down almost to the courtyard floor.

The Violin Man slowly glanced around as if getting the measure of his personal concert hall. Carefully, professionally tucking the violin under his chin, he brought the bow up to the ready position, where it poised for a moment as if waiting for the signal from an unseen conductor. Then, delicately, expertly, he would play selections ranging from gentle Albinoni adagios to contemplative ones of Beethoven and Haydn, to lively Enesco Hungarian dances.

He played them all with the same caring attention, the same respect for the composer's dream.

After a minute, a coin wrapped in a piece of paper landed near the Violin Man. In a moment, another wrapped coin joined the first one.

Marsa would take a penny from her well-worn change purse, wrapping it in a piece of newspaper. She stood off to the side of the window, behind the curtain so as not to be seen by the Violin Man as she threw out her penny.

The Violin Man continued to play; a couple more paper-wrapped contributions joined the others, and he acknowledged them with a slight nod and glance up to the apartment windows. Never stopping his playing, he started to gather the coins by using his feet to push the pieces of paper into small piles. Marsa continued, hidden from his view, to enjoy her concert until the Violin Man stopped, bending down to pick up his audience's tributes of appreciation for his effort.

Finally, the Violin Man pocketed his money packages and stopped for a moment as if at center-stage, nodding courteously to his unseen audience, carefully picked up the violin case and walked through the back lane to the next hall.

During one of the Violin Man's earlier performances, Ira had come in sweaty from a punch-ball game, grabbing a glass of water and throwing himself on the sofa to gulp it down.

"Whew! I'm hot!" Ira announced.

Marsa shushed him as from behind the curtain she threw her wrapped penny into the courtyard.

Before Ira went out to play another punch-ball game against the Herzl Street team, which was 'challenging' Amboy Street, two cents a man to the winners, he asked his mother why she was hiding so the Violin Man couldn't see that she was giving him a penny.

"What? Are you writing a book? Go play punch-ball, already."

If Ira weren't needed as much as he was to help his team, he would have stopped to tell his mother about him and his father having talked to the Violin Man just a few weeks earlier.

Ira had been playing 'catch' with Norman in the back lane, and the Violin Man having finished in the 179-185 'concert hall,' started to walk past them on the way to the next courtyard.

Ira accidentally threw the ball wildly past his father and it headed toward the Violin Man who quickly dropped his violin case, catching the errant ball before it could strike his precious violin.

Ira, relieved, called out, "Thanks, Mister."

Smiling, the Violin Man tossed the ball back to Norman, who complimented him, "Great throw," as Ira politely asked, "Hey, what's your name, Mister? My mom only calls you the Violin Man."

Speaking with a thick Greek accent, the man, awkward with English, answered, "The name I have is Manos."

He started to walk away but turned back to Ira and Norman, urgently correcting himself, "No, I have the name, George."

"George Manos?" Ira asked.

"No, George Dakis!"

Norman attempted to clear up the name problem, "George Dakis Manos?"

The Violin Man belligerently repeated his name "George Dakis!"

Staring at Ira and Norman for a moment, he continued toward the next courtyard, pleased at what English he had learned since he arrived in New York just a year before. Speaking only his native language, he had quickly joined a Greek social club in Brooklyn in order to learn some conversational English.

When he joined the club, he decided not to use his real name, Manos Pulyakis, because of the reason he had been forced to leave Heraklion, his hometown on the island of Crete.

His mind would often race over the events that had led him to having to play for pennies in the courtyards of Brooklyn. Yes, the environment here was very different from the seaport town of Heraklion, where the vineyards outside the busy capital of Crete encircled its northern tip, rounding into the choppy sea.

He fondly recalled the aroma of the grapes mixed with the clean seawater smell, floating an umbrella of fragrance over the gentle but strong-willed Cretes.

His very first audition for the Royal Athenian Symphony, at the age of nineteen, had placed him at the head of the Second Strings. He advanced rapidly, being groomed to take over as First Violin, when the day came for Athan Karras to retire. On Manos' twenty-seventh birthday, Karras himself, in front of the entire orchestra, announced the present he was giving to his talented assistant, by leading the young man to the chair of chairs of the Concertmaster.

A touch of glory!

"Manos is the best bow—this is the truth—since I heard Joachim play the Brahms for the first time in Liepzig."

Well, joy! Pride!

The next morning, Manos received a telegram from his sister Christina, telling him that their father had had a stroke, killing him immediately.

That same afternoon, Manos sadly booked passage to return to Crete the next morning. Agnotis, the Maestro of the orchestra, himself tried to prevail on him to stay, but the grief-shocked man clearly saw his responsibility to his mother and two sisters. Yes, perhaps there might be a time when he could return to Athens if they still wanted him, but now he had to bury his father and in the tradition of Cretans, become his father.

12

Brownsville, 1937

NOTWITHSTANDING NORMAN'S chuckling appreciation of Alan's offer of photographic evidence of his intimacy with Jean Harlow's panties, he knew that he would eventually have to address his friend's financial S.O.S. and desperate plan to set fire to his father's fur store for the insurance money.

On Alan's part, he sensed that if Norman were pressed at this moment to make a decision about becoming involved in the arson, he would probably say 'no.' Alan grasped at a way that he thought might divert Norman's negative response: Chess!

The two friends had played literally thousands of games with each other from early High School on through their adult years, and even with their family responsibilities, had managed to find time to squeeze in a few matches from time to time.

Alan, extremely competitive, sought victory for the trophy of winning, but Norman asserted that for him, *the* greater prize was the quality of a game well played.

"Norman, you are so full of it. You want to win just as much as I do!"

"Well, listen close Alan, when it's a really good battle and we're both playing at optimum, *that's* the ultimate prize. We just have different values, that's all."

"I call your value a pile of bullshit!" Alan shot back, "You're just afraid to admit that at the bottom of it, you're as competitive as I am. F'chrissake, Normie, if winning isn't the most important thing, then why the hell does anyone keep score?"

In any event, Alan knew he had to keep Norman on the chess track in order to stop him from expressing an absolute negative about helping him set the fire.

"I've been working on the ALEKHINE OPENING, Normie, and I've got a defense against it so I can turn it around on any opponent," pointedly staring at Norman, "who uses the ALEKHINE, I can mate in nine moves."

"Impossible, Alan."

"Well, I've been analyzing his '32 Grand Master victory, and—"

"Alan, I've told you that if Bigolyobov hadn't castled—"

"I can show you on the board in a minute."

Although Norman could divine that Alan's argument about chess could merely be a way of drawing him away from any further negativity about setting the fire, he was nonetheless seduced by the challenge.

"All right, Grand Master, prove it!"

13

THE LARGE WEIGHING SCALE of NATHANSON'S SALVAGE COMPANY was anchored by its sturdy iron base located at the truck-wide entrance of the rotting-wood frame, its ceiling, a patched tarpaulin protecting the storaged articles from the winter snow and rain. In this excessively humid summer, it retained the heavy air's overpowering smell of rancid grease and rust, mixed with noxious odors oozing from the junk piles.

The wobbly structure rested shakily on the sidewalk, potholed by the wear and tear of heavy trucks and the corrosive scars of metal-wheeled dollies unloading their wares.

The large sprawling mounds of car parts, plumbing fixtures, and other remnants ripped from vacant buildings, waited to be compacted and shipped to construction companies and auto plants in foreign countries like Japan and Australia, hungry for American scrap metal.

Now, Isaac the junkman anxiously deposited some of his day's collection onto the scale and gratefully pocketed the money that Nathanson paid him. He glanced up and saw Ira who had been waiting near the entrance with his carriage of newspapers.

Ira had been included in one of his father's conversations with Isaac Baumgarten, and now the boy nodded in friendly salutation.

Isaac smiled back. "Vie gayst mein boychik?"

Although Ira had a limited Yiddish vocabulary, he had a good working understanding of much of what he heard, occasionally even attempting broken Yiddish-English.

"Ich bin selling mein newspaperin."

Isaac nodded in appreciation of Ira's Yiddish.

"Ehr," gesturing toward Nathanson, "ist ein," and it was now *his* turn to try an *English* expression "honest man." He gestured for Ira to bring his newspapers to the scale.

Isaac, seeing Ira hesitating, prompted him encouragingly.

"Go boychik, ehr," looking in Nathanson's direction, "ist ein qüte mann."

Ira, not understanding his growing reluctance to have Nathanson weigh his wet newspapers, took a step in the direction of the scale, but suddenly turned his carriage around, quickly wheeling it in the direction he had come from.

14
Crete

LESS THAN A YEAR after he had returned to his home, Manos' mother, dressed in her lifetime widow's black, was pulling a small cart of freshly picked grapes along a narrow cliffside road overlooking the sea, when the hem of her long skirt caught under a wheel. As she yanked it free, she lost her footing. Manos, following with another cart, rushed forward to assist, desperately trying, unsuccessfully, to grab her hand. Frozen, Manos watched his mother smile in terror, as she fell to the rocks below that jutted up through the violent crashing foam.

Her broken body was buried next to her husband's under their favorite arbor where they both had rested often from their hard labors. At the funeral service, being the oldest living male in a parentless family, Manos vowed the traditional Cretan oath: that he would devote his life to the younger children until they had themselves established their own households.

15
Brownsville, 1937

CHECKERED SQUARES WERE PAINTED on the top of cement tables in Lincoln Terrace Park. The people who played chess and checkers there every day seemed also to have become a permanent part of the small patch of park that served as informal boundary line between Brownsville and more upscale East Flatbush, where not only were the Relief Rolls shorter, but some people even owned their own five-room house.

The tables closest to the main expanse of lawn were occupied, as usual, by the older regulars who had long been in the habit of getting there early for the tables, shaded from the summer sun by two of the park's very few trees in all of asphalted Brownsville.

The growing list of unemployed men, looking for something to occupy their idle time, created the problem of too many for the too few tables.

In addition, the ranks of the players were swelled by some of the immigrants who had recently arrived in

America, despite the new stringent quota laws limiting East European immigration.

The Jews in those countries, their synagogues desecrated; roving gangs violently expressing their anti-Semitism; the growing exclusion of Jews from government and professional positions, were finally perceived by them as a serious threat to their welfare.

Reluctantly, they were forced to uproot their families, sell their homes and businesses at exorbitantly depressed values, and sadly flee the country of their birth, taking with them only what they could carry.

Unfortunately, only a small percentage of those who stayed behind were able to escape the horrors that eventually engulfed them; a deadly finality repeated in Hungary, Poland, Romania, Greece.

And so the Nazi universe was being formed by Germany and their satellites, some orbiting in approval, others in terror.

Brownsville's planetary system was quite different, screaming meteors of poverty and desperation slicing through their fragile galaxy.

Hopelessness and apathy sat side by side on the wooden park benches, in hopes that the May breeze warmth, or November's bracing chill, could touch a distant time of faith, and resolve, and arbeit, work!

A small shed supplied the recreational equipment needs of the grateful public.

Norman and Alan signed out for a cardboard-boxed set of battered wooden chessmen just as, unexpectedly, a table became vacant.

They set up the pieces for the game as they bantered about who would win if Alan used the Alekhine offense.

Surrounded by the Lincoln Terrace regulars, silent and solemn in their dedication to the game, Norman and Alan's light-heartedness was clearly inappropriate to many of the others. After a few reproachful stares and a hissed admonition from the 'regulars' at adjoining tables, silence was achieved, and a 'regular,' Heshie, went back to concentrate on the contest with his even more ancient opponent, Pinkus, who was well over 80, but could still 'mate' young pishers and recite obscure passages from the Talmud at the same time.

Norman and Alan, both excellent chess players, silently made the opening Alekhine moves. Alan placed his finger on a pawn, hesitated a moment before removing his finger. Finally he glanced at Norman, his expression almost pleading. Norman knew that his friend was querying about something much more than the game.

He spoke quietly, answering the question he knew Alan was anxiously asking.

"Alan, I really have to think it through."

Heshie, annoyed at the conversation distracting him from deciding whether or not to 'castle,' glanced sharply over at the two men.

Alan, staring directly at Norman, smiled at what he perceived to be his friend's growing willingness to help him with the arson plan.

While Alan's enthusiasm was centered in economic necessity, Norman reasoned that if he did become involved in Alan's plan, it would be because he would loyally be helping his best friend deal with a major problem.

Pinkus scratched his scraggy beard as he held his finger on his black knight in the square that he had placed it. As he considered finalizing the move by lifting his finger off the piece, he glanced up at Heshie in order to fathom his opinion of the knight move.

A look of puzzled surprise crept into Heshie's face. Pinkus took his finger off the piece, and started to clean his ear with his little finger, before noticing that his opponent's expression was not about his move.

"Vuss, Heshie, what... what?"

Heshie shrugged, returning to the game to deal with Pinkus' early threat, as his opponent turned to look in the direction of his puzzled gaze. Pinkus decided to put his spectacles on so that he could get a better view of the little boy who was running around on the lawn, spreading newspapers.

Ira had already put a load of the wet newspapers where the midday sun could reach them, picking them up as they dried, replacing them with other damp ones from the carriage. A short-haired mongrel, that had been worrying a squirrel through some hedges, switched its yipping attention to Ira's heels. Mock-wrestling with the dog, Ira stretched out on his back, the dog playfully jumping onto his chest.

When Norman turned toward the sounds of boy and dog, Ira was getting another batch of dried newspapers.

Norman considered going to the lawn to congratulate Ira about his change of mind to cheat Nathanson, but he was confronted by a sudden awareness; that his son was correcting a dishonest act even as he, himself, was considering one.

Recognizing his hypocrisy in the face of his often preached honesty ethic, silenced him, even as Alan became aware of Ira on the lawn.

"Hey, Normie, isn't that Ira over there?"

"Yeah," Norman spoke abruptly as he turned his back to where Ira was, "but let's finish the game."

Alan, aware of the closeness between Norman and his son, put his friend's harsh tone down to anxiety about becoming involved in his fur store fire plan.

Alan smiled in relief; Norman's face, tense with conflict.

Norman and Alan continued their Alekhine chess test, as Ira, unaware of them, continued to spread the papers and play with the dog.

16

TWO TEENAGERS IN VERY WORN CLOTHES exited BAER'S CHOCOLATE SHOPPE across the street from Nathanson's salvage company. In an adapted 'grown up' manner, they lit up Avalon cigarettes which they had each paid a penny for at Baer's. They casually leaned against the store's glass window, as Walter opened a pants pocket, furtively revealing an O'Henry bar to his friend, Turk.

Turk hadn't noticed it when Walter shoplifted the candy bar. Impressed, he nodded in approval.

"Whatta good fuckin' thief."

Walter watched Ira across the street, arguing with Nathanson over the price of the carriage. He saw Ira happily accepting a dollar, quickly shoving it into his pocket.

Walter took another deep drag on his cigarette and handed it to Turk, motioning him to follow. He crossed the street toward where Ira was playfully wrestling with the dog that had faithfully followed from the park. Walter started to speak to Ira even before he reached the sidewalk.

"That's a jerky lookin' dog, Abie."

Ira looked up, immediately aware of the danger as Walter approached him casually, kneeling down next to where he was nuzzling the dog. With studied ease, Walter took a wooden handled linoleum cutter from his back pocket, the curved blade sharpened to razor thinness, its wicked-looking point cutting through a dirt filled crack, separating sections of the sidewalk.

As Turk patted the dog's head, he glanced at Walter, sensing that he was going to do his usual strong-arm stuff.

Even though Walter always gave him a split of whatever lunch money he took from the smaller kids, Turk didn't like it when Walter would often hit the kids and even, a couple of times, when a kid would fight back, Walter had used the cutter to slice their arms, drawing blood. In fact, Turk had started to worry about Walter killing somebody someday.

"Hey, Walter, why not just take the mutt?"

Walter was after only one thing, though.

"Gimme it, Abie."

Ira scratched his head to mask his hesitation. Walter threateningly snarled his impatience.

"Ya betta shit dat money right now."

Ira started to straighten up slowly.

"What?"

"C'mon, c'mon."

There was a momentary hint of defiance in Ira's manner, but the size of the two older boys intimidated him. He reached into his pocket, withdrawing his hand and reluctantly emptying his fist into Walter's impatient palm. Walter looked down at a dime, a nickel, and a penny.

"Gimme da buck too."

"Wattaya talkin' about?"

Walter brandished the cutter.

"I'll rip ya fuckin' face!"

"I'm tellin' ya. I don't..."

The cutter was brought menacingly closer.

"Ya liddle kike!"

Ira hesitated for a moment, angry but fearful. Suddenly, he rushed at Walter, punching him in the groin, dodging around the surprised boy.

Walter slashed at him with the cutter, ripping his shirt and drawing blood. Ira raced down the street at full speed. Walter started to straighten up in pain, as Turk ran after Ira, the dog barking at the pursuer's feet. For a few moments, Ira pulled away from Turk, but the bigger boy started to close the gap, as Walter angrily joined the chase.

The few people on the sweltering sidewalks paid little more than casual attention to the running boys. Ira, anxiously glancing over his shoulder, saw Turk and Walter rapidly gaining ground. Prodded by fear, he accelerated, the dog keeping pace with him. One end of the black-taped patch that his mother had put on his shoe came loose, flapping rhythmically against the pavement each time his foot hit the ground. Turk and Walter were breathing hard, closing on the tiring boy, just as he suddenly cut into an alley-way he knew well. He slid through some rotting boards in a makeshift fence, with the dog scrambling after him.

A vacant rubble-strewn lot lay on the other side of the fence where the two boys caught their breath as they glanced around for their prey. Ira and the dog were nowhere in sight.

They approached a nearby livery stable, the heated stench of manure-clotted straw drifting heavily out toward them. Disgustedly holding his nose, Walter peered around the darkened stable, while an old nag in a filthy stall shuffled its hooves, its mangy tail swatting at the flies on its back.

A wizened old man in dirt-caked clothes, slouched asleep on a stool, leaning against an open dilapidated door, pushed back against the scummed wall. A grimy toilet bowl was barely visible in the small, darkened recess beside the man. Walter continued to peer around the stable, gesturing for Turk to look in the bathroom.

As Turk quietly approached, a rustling sound came out to meet him. Walter hurriedly pushed by him, just in time to catch a glimpse of a large rat disappearing behind a mound of litter in the corner of the foul-smelling cubicle.

Walter turned away in frustration, his foot hitting the toilet-bowl, dislodging it from its loosened bolts in the rotting floor.

Suddenly thrown off balance, one of his feet slid into the opening left by the bowl moving off its base. Frantically attempting to stop his fall, he grabbed at the toilet paper roll fixture, yanking it off the wall. As he continued to fall, his leg lodged in the hole, his foot plunging into the excrement of the indoor "outhouse." His face mirroring his revulsion, Walter hastily pulled himself out. Moving toward the stable door, he wiped his shoe along the floor.

Ira, in the corner shadows of one of the stalls, huddled under the restless horse, held back a sigh of relief as he watched his disappointed hunters return to the street.

Finally deciding it was safe to move, Ira crawled away from under the horse, turning back toward a sudden "shish" behind him. A steady stream of sound, the faint mist of steam, and the heavy smell of urine floating in front of his awed face told him how lucky he'd been in moving away before the horse had started to relieve itself.

Ira sighed a "wow!" while watching the deluge pour down on the spot he'd just left. Backing off cautiously, he slid through the rear door of the stable, the dog clutched in his arms, until both were safely outside, and in the schoolyard of LEW WALLACE JUNIOR HIGH SCHOOL.

The cornerstone of the school was chipped by the erosion of time and the bombardment of numerous teenage boys over the years since MXMV had been chiseled into it.

In many instances, entire sections had fallen completely away, the pock-marked façade looming its Gothic oppressiveness over the tiny concrete play area.

Inside, the main floor of the school had aged even more markedly, the inexpensive painting and plastering doing little more than bandaging terminal wounds. One long table held a couple of hundred loaves of unwrapped bread—stacked on another, about fifty sacks of potatoes and bundles of large, brown paper bags.

A policeman wandered around the area, nodding familiarly at the people who had lined up to get their bread and potatoes supplement to their regular Relief check. Hunched in a chair off to the side sat a dour man, supervising the operation, checking off the people's names against his records, closely watching as each person filled up one of the bags with potatoes, and picked up a single loaf of bread.

As Ira entered from the side door, the policeman motioned him to the rear of the line, filing in by the main door. Joining the others, Ira sneaked an apprehensive look outside, still alert to the danger of Walter and Turk.

The "Coast Clear'" he took out the Relief book, identifying his right to pick up the food allotment, the '*à la carte*' that his mother had reminded him about earlier in the trip.

17

RIDING ON THE ROCKAWAY Avenue-Canarsie trolley route in Brooklyn starting from the depot, the pungent water-scum odor surrounding polluted Canarsie Bay. It hangs heavy on the air for the first few street corner stops. The foulness of the beach's landfilled swamp is challenged as the weather-beaten wooden cars clang past Cohen's 'SPECIAL DELICACIES ON SALE HERE' pushcart with its tantalizing smells of pickled herring, sauerkraut, sour pickles floating in a barrel of garlic-vinegar brine. SOL'S NEIGHBORHOOD BARBERSHOP with its witch hazel and shaving cream fragrance joins the potpourri aromas. Wafting out from KASTNER'S DELICATESSEN is the *pièce de resistance*; breathe it in deeply, the never to be forgotten king of all pleasant food smells, almost a meal itself in a single strong sniff; the elegant exotic spiced HOT PASTRAMI!

The rhythmic metallic sound of the trolley wheels clattering over the iron rails seemed to Norman to be apt musical accompaniment for the exciting heartbeat of Brownsville, perhaps all of Brooklyn. Norman once fancifully referred to the sound as the pulse of America's great enterprise.

Pleased with his imagery, Norman dimly heard a faint voice from the shadows of his unspoken dreams. "You sound like a frustrated writer, so why not make the leap of faith, and become one?" If Norman was in any way conscious of the mocking self-query, he did not answer directly, except to remind himself that teaching was, after all, more than just a conduit for information; was a higher calling, an 'art.'

"Art shmart," Alan once tartly observed. Norman had shared the feeling about his love of teaching and that, not immodestly, he considered himself one of the better Public-School teachers he had known.

"Yes," Norman continued, "everything a person does extremely well, aspiring to the best in his field, creates some form of art."

"I repeat, Normie, art-shmart!"

The Rockaway-Canarsie trolley stopped at the busy corner of Sutter Avenue and several people, despite the summer heat, hurriedly boarded. Two men brushed by Norman, reading his Trade Unionism book, their sharp staccato speech causing him to glance up as baseball information was exchanged between the two sports experts.

"Wanna go to Ebbets Field Saddiday?"

"Who da bums playin'?"

"The Cards."

"They were okay when Dizzy Dean was pitchin,' but now—"

A colored woman with a small child contentedly sucking a lollipop, sat down next to Norman.

As the child settled in, the lollipop was brought down on the page Norman was reading.

Annoyed, Norman brushed it away, but when he turned to the child, the boy, smiling in innocent fun, stopped Norman's disapproving glance.

The woman started to scold her son.

"Albert, you are the worst—"

"That's all right, Missus," Norman interrupted, "it'll make the book," lightly joking, "taste better."

The woman half smiled back at Norman, as the boy brought the lollipop close to Norman's mouth.

"Oh," Norman said playfully, "you want to give me a lick, Albert?"

The curly-haired head nodded solemnly as his mother watched Norman hesitate. Norman realized that the woman was challenging his willingness to put something in his mouth that a colored kid had had in his.

Norman opened his mouth, the boy grinning in pleasure as he shoved the lollipop into it, glancing up at his mother for approval. When she smiled at him, he started to laugh.

The woman had pulled the cord above her window, signaling that it was her stop. As she stood up to leave, sliding past Norman, the boy started to cry, hitting at Norman's head, the woman quickly grabbing the boy's hands.

"Stop that, child, you gave it to the nice man."

Norman took out the lollipop and started to hand it back to the boy but as the woman stood in front of the opening exit door, she spoke directly to Norman for the first time.

"That's all right. It's a gift," pleasantly, "from Albert."

The woman exited, Albert reluctantly leaving his lollipop behind.

18
Crete

A YEAR AFTER MANOS PULYAKIS' father and mother had died, the family was still mourning, when George Dakis, a pleasant young man studying industriously to become a teacher, entered their lives.

Dakis asked Manos for permission to marry his sister Aglya who had just turned a full-bloomed eighteen. Manos was incensed that Dakis, who knew that the older sister Christina was not yet married, would declare himself before the proper time.

When Aglya struggled against her brother's will, he had her locked in the house for over a month until she promised to respect his wishes. Soon after, Manos unexpectedly came upon her and Dakis walking on the beach one afternoon.

Grabbing Aglya's arm, Manos slapped her and turned cold-eyed to Dakis. He placed his hand threateningly on his father's knife, worn always at his hip.

Silent, he stared at the boy for a long moment until George, realizing that he could do nothing at this time, turned and walked away.

The next day Constantine Dakis, George's father, the town's constable, called on Manos.

The meeting was cordial since Mr. Dakis was, like Manos, a traditional Greek patriarch and respected Manos' behavior toward his son and Aglya.

"I hope, Mr. Pulyakis, that when the proper time comes for my son to call on your daughter, that his rudeness will not be held against him."

Over a glass of ouzo, they spoke of family honor, and the need for young people to respect traditions. After another ouzo, Constantine sang a few lines from a sad Crete song, about a family that had to bury their son when he was killed fighting the Turks in the battle for Independence.

Manos, familiar with the song, picked up his violin that was always nearby, and played the melody.

Constantine had become very emotional, and when the song was over, he had another ouzo before he spoke again.

"Do you love your sister, Manos?"

Manos' simple nod spoke to the heart of his answer.

"Good, Manos, as I love my son." Manos poured another drink for both of them, and they toasted each other's families.

For the next six months, Aglya was permitted out of the house only to go to church on Sundays. The neighbors uniformly agreed that Manos was behaving correctly, honoring his parents' memory with such dedication. Until both of his sisters were married, he would remain in Heraklion.

19

BENJAMIN SCHECTER KOSHER BUTCHER STORE was a small one-man operation on DeKalb Avenue in the Williamsburg area. The noisy, colorful street was an ethnic bridge between the Jewish section and the Gentile world: P. MURPHY HARDWARE AND RADIO REPAIR, FRANK DEVITO CHILDREN'S SHOES, OTTO'S FISH MARKET, did business alongside the ever-increasing Jewish stores. Bennie Schecter had opened his new shop a few years before, on the same day as Roosevelt's inauguration. He had cut out the photograph of the oath-taking from the Daily News, recaptioning it with a crayon to read: "ROOSEVELT SWORN IN, SWEARS TO BUY MEAT ONLY AT SCHECTER'S BUTCHER STORE." The picture still hung on one of the meat hooks, next to the framed first dollar of business. Bennie would often tell his unbelieving amused customers about the President coming in on the GRAND OPENING DAY of the store to make the first purchase, two veal cutlets for him and his wife with the big teeth, Eleanor.

Now, after his trolley trip outside the store, Norman leaned against the window, watching his father wait on Mrs. Gartenberg. He idly ruminated over all the different butcher store windows through which he had watched his father, through the years.

Most of the times, Bennie would work for somebody else, but every few years he would open a small business like this one.

He would struggle along for awhile, before accepting the fact that although he was a very good butcher, he was a bad businessman. Reluctantly he would 'sell the key' to the new owner, providing him with good will by staying on the premises for a week or so, introducing him to the customers as they came in.

Then Bennie would report to HEBREW BUTCHER'S WORKERS LOCAL 232 and within a few days he would have a steady job again; until these Depression years had changed everything. No longer would there be the luxury of a worker having the opportunity to move from one job to another better-paying one. Now, the desperate times dictated that once a worker had found even a narrow niche of economic security, he should hang onto it. Chances of bettering oneself had to take a back seat to the immediate expedience of paying the rent. And so, this time Bennie was chained to his owning this store until Roosevelt would maybe make things like they used to be. Maybe not as good as it was after the World War, he thought, or before that shmagaggie President Hoover got the country into trouble.

As Bennie, closely watched by Mrs. Gartenberg, put three lamb chops on the scale, Norman remembered watching his father through the window of a different store. At the time, he was even younger than Ira. Seated on a low stool, his father was plucking a chicken, his hand moving in a staccato rhythm of clutch, jerk, clutch, jerk. He had glanced around the empty store slowly, and still plucking, walked the few steps to the meat-cutting block, touching it with his fingertips before flicking a piece of sawdust off it. Over thirty years ago, Norman recalled, but the moment was as warm and familiar as the sun that was now patting the back of his neck... and his father was... young again.

Mrs. Gartenberg shifted her weight in order to get a better view of the scale, as Bennie addressed her with the behind-the-counter charm that was one of his life's great pleasures.

"Tell me when your husband isn't home and I'll come deliver the meat personal, dollink."

"Did you trim good the fat?"

Bennie was always ready with his most elaborate Rudolph Valentino leer for that question.

"Doesn't Bennie know, the closer the bone, the sweeter the meat, dollink?"

"Just, keep your thumb off the..." she gestured toward the scale, "...Bennie, *dollink*."

Bennie looked up the heavens in playful protest.

"To Benjamin, the Great Lover, she opens a mouth like that? So when your husband isn't around, I'll knock on your door."

The women customers never took Bennie's flirtatious comments seriously; he was harmless.

He turned toward the sound of the store door opening. A look of surprise and mock despair came over his face and he raised his fist dramatically toward the heavens.

"Just a minute, don' go 'way, please! Tell me how I brought up my son so wrong?"

Standing in the store doorway, Norman licked the lollipop the child had given him. Bennie's clenched fist opened to point his errant son out to God.

"A grown man sucks a lollipop?"

The grown man smiled good-naturedly at the father.

"So, what did He..." gesturing up toward Bennie's heaven, "...say unto you?"

God was curtly waved away by Bennie.

"Him and you together don't know enough to cook even one good potato latka."

Norman laughed, enjoying his father's humor as Mrs. Gartenberg motioned impatiently toward the scale. "Mahk schnell, already."

With an always present touch of ceremony, Bennie deftly wrapped up the meat, as Norman strolled to the rear of the long, narrow store. He started to clean the top of the large wooden meat-cutting block, with a wire brush his father always kept next to a deck of cards on an apple crate behind the counter.

Closing the store door behind her, Riva waved away a large horsefly that buzzed in past her.

"An old girlfriend of yours just flew in, Benjamin the Lover."

Bennie commandeered the brush out of his son's hand, as he called over his shoulder.

"I love only my wife and you, Rifkela dollink."

He was already moving the brush with accustomed force and style, the sharp teeth scratching through the specks of meat and sawdust that never seemed able to be completely cleaned away.

Norman shuffled the deck of soiled, much-used playing cards as he watched his father admiringly. He noted the surface of the block, crisscrossed with the countless razor-thin scars of countless brushings; an infinite web of veins that connected Bennie with all the other butchers who had stroked their labors into the wood over the years.

At this moment, it occurred to Norman that the block was an altar on which the ritual exchange of money for goods took place. Here the order of things was pure, the transaction anointed with honesty, a barter of good blood.

"Knock Rummy, Pop?"

"So what else? Can I make an honest living winning by you in Casino, a penny a game?"

As he drew two battered chairs up to the block, Norman was already dealing the cards out.

"Mama okay?"

"If only Hitler had kidneys bad like her, we could make a celebration. It's a lovely," glancing at his cards, "seven cards you gave me."

"Did you take her to the doctor like I told you?"

"I took, I took."

"So?"

"So she has to go back next week so I can read the *Look* magazines in Rabkin's waiting room."

Bennie pounced on a card that Norman had discarded. "Thank you for the lovely six, mein zindele. And so why don't you bring my only grandson, the angel, with you?"

"He's busy growing up."

Another discard caused Bennie to look up with great pleasure and an extended groan of joy.

"Dumbbell, you put a six down by me already."

Tapping his forehead, he patronizingly instructed his son.

"Concentration, my college man."

"You going to make a speech or pick up the six?"

Bennie began to ask God to intervene, but decided to handle his son by himself.

"Wattsa matter... you can listen by the fireside chat with Frankie Roosevelt, but a word from your father's mouth, not?"

Norman picked up the card and handed it to his father.

"Which reminds me, Pop, did you hear what the Supreme Court ruled about the President's New Deal Plan?"

Bennie narrowed his small alert eyes.

"What should I hear?"

Studying his cards closely, Norman rearranged a couple of them, seeming to have forgotten about the Supreme Court.

"Well, you going to throw a good one down for me, Pop?"

"So, what should I hear?"

"Oh. They decided that, from now on, all Kosher Butchers are going to be forced to sell Goyisha meat."

This time, Bennie knew that he needed the Heaven's assistance.

"So, are you listening to my son make jokes like a Hitler?"

Not waiting for an answer, he turned back to his smiling son.

"Maybe you can tell me, should I expect better from a man who makes the Principal fire him?

The same rhetorical question had been asked many times in the last two years.

"Oh Papa, Papa."

"… and just like that, fight City Hall?"

Again, Bennie decided to ask God's help.

"Can *you* tell me, maybe?"

Glancing heavenward, Norman added his own plea. "Please… tell him."

Bennie dropped his light tone.

"You still think it was so right? A man with a family suddenly decides to make a union?"

"Pop, I'm trying to do something —"

"He's *trying*!"

"Well, the *Butchers* Union is a union."

"A butcher is different from a teacher."

As far as Bennie was concerned, he had won the argument.

"Because my brain didn't go to college doesn't mean I'm a number-one dummy."

Norman rose wearily.

"There's enough time for me to walk home."

"Stay already a minute…"

Bennie dug some change out of his apron pocket.

"… I'll give you for the trolley."

Waving the money away, Norman walked toward the door. "Tell Mama we'll be over tomorrow for her world-famous boiled chicken."

Finding his own idea somewhat less than a gourmet's delight, he rolled his eyes up to his father's heaven.

"Well, wattaya say… is that a loving son, or is that a loving son?"

Bennie rushed to the large wooden meat-storage-box, as Norman left the store.

A late-model Packard blared its horn, roaring down the almost traffic-less street. Annoyed at the driver's arrogant behavior, Norman, nonetheless, stared after the car enviously. It stopped at the corner for a moment before turning to glide elegantly down a side street. As he stepped off the sidewalk, his father's voice stopped him.

"Hey Mister, you lose this?"

He waved a small brown papered package at Norman. Rapidly covering the few feet, Bennie shoved it into his son's hand.

"Pop, You shouldn't—"

"Take. I can't sell the furshtoonkana piece anyway." Turning quickly back to the store, he waved Norman's thanks away with one hand, as he took a dingy handkerchief out of his pocket with the other to rub away a streak of dirt he'd just noticed on the store window.

"Pop?"

"If you don't like the way the meat tastes, complain to the Supreme Court already."

"Seriously, Pop, what if business doesn't pick up for you?"

"I'll ask my good friend Rockefeller for a little loan."

"Would you sell the store?"

"Sell-shmell. Who's gonna buy today? Anyway, it's almost a living I make."

"But what if you couldn't?" Norman asked, thinking of Alan and *his* father.

Bennie put his handkerchief back into his pocket and scratched his hard bristled moustache.

"What, are you asking questions for the census?"

"I'm just asking."

"So, I'm just answering. *My* store, *his* store — who cares? As long as I can get up in the morning and put in a day's work."

As long as Norman could remember, it had always been as simple as that. His father would cheerfully get up at six each morning without benefit of alarm clock, taking the first step in the day's pleasant ritual of work. Bennie drew more than a salary for his labors. Work was his joyous connection to people, feeding the enormous appetite of his gregariousness. Like most people, he had to work to live, but he was one of the few fortunates who also lived to work.

20
Crete

MANOS BEGAN A WILDLY PASSIONATE AFFAIR with Lula, a flowering twenty-year old, with raven hair framing an exquisite cameo beauty. Her gentle committed love made Manos feel a warmth and comfort he had never known before.

He was overjoyed when old Kasanotzakis, the retired wine merchant, asked him to arrange a marriage with the oldest sister, Christina. In spite of Christina's tearful reluctance, he hurried up the wedding date and let it be known that he would now entertain suitors for Aglya. As a gesture of forgiveness and good will, Manos permitted George Dakis to escort Aglya again, and even invited him and his father to Christina's wedding.

By the second day of the wedding celebration, Manos had happily played countless violin requests and drunk countless glasses of Ouzo and Retsina, and had not felt such joy for years. As soon as Aglya would marry the Dakis boy, Manos, his family duty fulfilled, would sell the vineyards, marry his beautiful Lula, move to Athens, and unencumbered by any other responsibility, become the best Concertmaster the Symphony ever had. Or maybe... there was still time, with hard work, he'd become a soloist. Who could tell?

Lula and several other guests were living in the coach house during the expected three or four days of eating, dancing, and drinking celebration. Manos and Lula had sneaked off to their favorite spot in the vineyards, making gleeful love on the dawn-dewed grass. On the second night, the moon lighting their way back to the vineyard, they held hands as they laughingly poked grapes into each other's mouth, only their eyes speaking.

A muffled sound, a little way off, silenced them. Wary of being discovered, Manos started to lead Lula off in another direction just as the sound was repeated, louder and more distinct. This time, Manos headed back toward the sound, signaling Lula to remain quietly, where she was. Removing his shoes quickly, he quietly crept closer to the sound.

Suddenly, he leaped into a small clearing where Aglya and George, partially undressed, were embracing, making love, unaware of his presence. George never knew that it was Manos who drew his father's knife violently across the boy's throat, his blood spurting out, covering Aglya's eyes which suddenly opened, and the sight of George's gaping wound and his mouth open in shock and pain, etched its horror into her eyes for the rest of her life.

Grabbing Aglya's arm, Manos dragged her from under George, bleeding his life into the ground.

At first, Aglya was mute with shock, but when Manos started to explain the need for his protecting her honor in the name of their parents, she screamed frighteningly, building into an uncontrollable hysteria. She ran, aimlessly at first, but as Manos tried to stop her, she ran back toward the wedding festivities where Constantine Dakis was dancing with the others.

From a distance, Manos saw Constantine's shocked, unbelieving look; then taking Aglya's hand, he pulled her with him back in the direction of the vineyards.

Manos rushed into the house, realizing that Constantine, in his position as Constable, would probably use his authority to exact revenge for his son's death.

The music and dancing had stopped. The guests, uncertain as to exactly what had happened, but sensing they were part of a terrible event, spoke in stops and starts of uncertain whispers.

In a few minutes, Constantine, holding his still bleeding son in his arms, the moonlight painting them in grotesque eerie shadows; the father's stricken look of such monumental grief; the son's eyes closed tight against their final memory.

Constantine's expression mirrored his soul, torn beyond repair. He walked dirge-like, a funeral procession of one.

Finally, still holding the body, he slumped to the ground, his arms soaked in the blood of his first born, cradling him in his arms as if rocking his baby to sleep.

He started a low keening sound, finally bursting into a terrible scream, echoing the greatest pain, the loss of a child.

21

SMILING, NORMAN SPOKE PLEASANTLY to the security guard posted in the reception area of the World Trade Center's North Tower.

"This is all my granddaughter's idea, yes?"

"No, sir."

Still good-natured, Norman tried to solve the problem. "It's a practical joke, yes?"

"No, sir."

"You jest."

"I just have to check your ID before you can go up, sir."

"I told you, I left it home... or maybe I lost it... I don't know."

"I'm sorry, sir, but—"

"You worried about a hundred-year-old man doing something to the building?"

"You say your granddaughter works here?"

"She's waiting for me."

"Well, how about calling her to come down and identify you?"

"Negative, my good friend; I made plans to pick her up." The security guard held up his cell phone.

"Why don't you give me her number and I'll call."

22
Brownsville, 1937

MARSA WAS VERY UPSET and puzzled. When Norman gave her the package that his father had given him, she weighed it in her hand for a moment, guessing it to be over a pound of hamburger meat as she put it into the icebox.

Marsa had become expert at estimating the weight of different foods; household expenses had to be carefully watched, the city's Relief check barely covering the necessities.

A few hours later, taking the package out of the icebox in order to prepare dinner, she was surprised at its weight, gauging it now as no more than a half pound.

Any further thought about the perplexing problem of the missing meat was interrupted by a dog's loud barking outside.

Glancing out the window facing on the courtyard, she could see Ira petting a dog next to an empty plate. Solved for Marsa was the mystery of the disappearing half pound of hamburger.

Opening the window she called out, "Please to come in mein zindel."

"Okay, Mom."

"And the plate, if you please."

A knock at the apartment door stopped her from saying anything more.

Opening the door, she nodded familiarly at a man in Orthodox Jewish black, curly-hair ringlets hanging down from under his black fedora hat.

"So, come in, Rabbi."

In deep solemn tones, Rabbi Mintz addressed Marsa, his voice resonating as a Moses coming down from the mountain.

"An important day is here, Mrs. Schecter."

"Believe me, I told Ira, absolutely."

Reaching down to the coffee table, Marsa picked up a 10-inch can, proudly labeled in bold blue letters, JEWISH NATIONAL FUND, a slot on its top for contributions.

"So, Mrs. Schecter, the boy got good people to fill it up?"

Marsa hesitated for a moment before holding the can up in front of the Rabbi, shaking it; the sound of the few coins in it hardly enough to make a jingling sound, sad proof of Ira's unsuccessful fund raising.

"So, Mrs. Schecter, the boy must go out again for the fund and the future of the Jewish people."

"He'll go... he'll go."

"With God's blessing, one more day I'll wait."

Touching two fingers to his lips, lightly kissing them, he then placed them on the mezuzah, the small strip of tin with Hebrew lettering symbolizing the Torah, nailed on the inside of Brownsville apartment doorways for Jews to honor.

After Rabbi Mintz left, Marsa, glancing out the window again, saw Ira trying to keep the dog from tagging after him as he started to leave the courtyard.

"Ira, leave the mutt out there!"

"I'm trying to, Mom, but he keeps following me."

Rifling through her 'treasure chest,' Marsa quickly found an old belt that, having lost its buckle, had been retired, waiting for the moment it could be called upon to be useful again.

Throwing the belt out into the courtyard, Marsa called to Ira, "Tie the mutt to the rail."

Following his mother's instruction, Ira looped the belt around the dog's neck, then tied it to the top of the metal stairway leading out to Amboy Street. The plate from the courtyard in his hand, Ira entered the Schecter's apartment, apprehensive of how his mother might act toward him. He thought it might be with irritation because of his not coming as soon as she had told him the first time or, he suddenly realized, she might be upset because he had taken some of the meat for the dog, which he had named "Orphan Annie."

Marsa stood rigidly facing the apartment door, waiting for her son, "a wonderful boy" she thought, "but a little crazy, 'meshugga,' to starve his family for a dog."

When Norman had returned after visiting his father in his store, he had gone into the bedroom to work on his latest protest plan that he was going to offer to his union activist group for their consideration at the next meeting. Coming into the living room now, he intended to practice his presentation in front of Marsa. Although he was aware that she would be far less than enthusiastic about hearing anything of his latest 'trouble-making' activities, he knew that it would benefit him to hear his ideas stated out loud. This method of 'auditioning' for Marsa had often been helpful, occasionally leading him to make significant changes.

Marsa, anticipating the possibility of Norman intervening in her upcoming scolding of Ira, held one hand up toward Norman, signaling that he stay out of what was going to happen between her and her son.

The boy took a hesitant, cautious step into the apartment, attempting a nonchalant innocence as Marsa barked her words at him in tight-lipped anger.

"Since when are we millionaires to take food from the table for a dog?"

"It was just a little piece, Mom."

"So, it's just a little piece less you'll have for your supper."

"But he was hungry, Mom."

"And your father and mother do not need nourishment too?"

"I'm really sorry, Mom. I..."

"No more discussion, thank you. The dog, you'll say goodbye to right now."

Tears started to well up in Ira's eyes.

Norman decided that if he, as usual, tried to mediate between Ira and Marsa, it might very well, as in the past, end up being counter productive.

He and Marsa had taken a neighborhood stroll with Ira, still a very young tot. As they reached a street corner the boy had suddenly climbed out of his carriage, insisting that he be permitted to push it. Norman had prevailed over Marsa's strong objection, but was too busy proudly watching Ira captain the journey across the street to realize that the oncoming traffic was a serious danger. Fortunately, Marsa alertly noticed that an approaching car was running a red light and quickly grabbed Ira, still holding the carriage handle, pulling them both back to the corner, the car barely missing them. After an angry sigh of relief, Marsa glared over at Norman, nonplused with guilt.

Now, although Marsa felt that the limited finances prohibited feeding the dog, she was moved by Ira's distress at the loss of the dog. She relented… slightly, striking a deal, holding up the Jewish National Fund can.

"The Rabbi's coming here tomorrow to collect, so if you go to fill this, the dog for one more day can stay."

"Just one day?" pleaded Ira.

"Take the can."

"I got a dollar for the newspapers and the old carriage, Mom."

"Good, it'll pay for a few meals for the mutt."

"So I can keep it… for awhile?"

Marsa suddenly started to hum the melody that she had sung to herself earlier in the day, then starting to sing.

"Otcha Chuniya… Otcha…"

Cutting herself off, she addressed Ira in a gentler tone.

"You know that Otcha Chuniya means black eyes in Russian?"

"I remember you used to call me that when I was a kid."

"Oh, and so *now* you're a big shot?"

"No, Mom, I'm not."

"My father, in the old country, once gave me a dog, Otcha Chuniya."

"That's swell, Mom."

"He was such a lunatic! He chewed up all my shoes." Deep in the past now, "My father would curse him, 'You're dumb like a goy!'" To be compared with a gentile's alleged lack of intelligence was the ultimate insult to dogs... and Jews.

"He was a real meshuga, Mom?"

"But every time he chewed up a slipper, I laughed all over."

"You'd laugh?"

"Out loud! He was like just another starving Jew!"

As Marsa chuckled at the memory, Norman touched her hand comfortingly.

"*All* your slippers?"

Laughing, Marsa shouted "Everybody's!"

All three Schecters laughed warmly as Marsa continued.

"Oi, you shoulda seen him... Black Eyes."

Hesitating for a moment, Marsa now faced a dark memory.

"One night, it was exactly ten minutes after nine, two drunken Cossacks came to the house. The one with the big red moustache... stuck his bayonet right into Otcha Chuniya's eyes."

Ira winced at the image.

"I'm sorry, Mama."

Norman reached out to embrace Marsa.

"I never knew about that."

Marsa waved away his condolences as she spoke to Ira.

"Okay, take the can and go to Pitkin Avenue and get a lot of money against those Nazi pishers."

Ira took the can and started to leave, turning back at the door.

"Mama?"

"No more conversation about the dog."

"You're really swell, Mom."

"So goodbye already."

23

Kings County Hospital
March 20, 1935

Elissa Jackman's Thoughts in My Journal

FOR THE PAST FEW WEEKS, I haven't been in the mood to think about what to 'journalize' on these pages, but there are two reasons now why I've decided to try to put some things down… finally.

First of all, it's the first anniversary of the peace rally, so I'm going to give it the old college try… which is actually ironic, since I may never get to those halls of ivy or any other college as far as that goes. As a mere High School student who may not even make it through my senior year, let me inform anyone who may read this about what's been happening, or *not* happening. Well, the big news (sarcastic) is that some smart aleck on the Brooklyn Eagle came up with a clever (?) story, so I'm pasting the whole article right here. I underlined the part where he calls our rally the "Abraham Lincoln Emancipation Day" but *no* freedom for students.

Well, you don't really have to read the whole thing because it just goes on about how nothing was really done about Public School 225's overcrowded classes.

Also, the students who didn't apologize for their involvement in the demonstrations were not accepted by the colleges they applied to. Which means that me and four other seniors will have to appeal our applications being turned down. Who knows, if I'm still alive next year, maybe I can still get into Princeton after all, or if I'm not able to even graduate, I can stick around and take a summer class in weaving or playing checkers. Ha! Ha! In fact, Schecter brought a chess set a couple of months ago and taught me the fundamentals. He's a good teacher. I got to like him a little, finally.

Mom and Pop were happy about me having something to occupy my time... Tell you the truth, time is a concept I don't like... Especially because I don't know if my clock is wound up right or for how long.

The second reason is because of what I read in the Daily News today plus the headlines from the front page of the New York Times which one of the doctors was reading while the nurse was bathing me. The Daily News had pictures of the riots in Harlem. Last year I went with some other members of Abraham Lincoln's Drama Club to visit the Apollo theater in Harlem to see some of the Negro performers there. Mr. Hilsenrath, the math teacher, was in charge of the group and he got us twenty cents, half price tickets to get in, but to be honest, I wasn't too impressed with most of the comedy acts. Maybe it was because I sometimes didn't understand some of their expressions, but I sort of did like one performer, Moms Mabley, who was really funny, and a tap-dancer with one leg, Peg Leg Bates.

Anyway, according to the Times story, some incident with a Negro customer in one of the stores on the main street, 125th, started it all off, and before long there was building burning, vandalism, looting, some police beatings, and a few Negroes were killed. Wow! According to the Daily News, half of Harlem is still burning. My mom called me this morning and said that she and Pop were not really surprised at the riots happening. She said Pop always said that living in the Harlem ghetto, where he once taught a Junior High School class, was like being on a Southern plantation before the Civil War, with the cops acting like the overseer for the white "massah."

Right now, I think that Principal Mason is also acting like a "massah." Oh yeah, we're not slaves picking cotton, but he's sure using the whip to keep us in our place.

The doctor had to put me back on some morphine every day now because the pain is very bad sometimes. So when I get a few hours free from it, I try to write some journal stuff, but I feel less and less like doing this.

My 'aide de camp' Terry and Big Jim still loyally came around every few weeks to say 'hello' and ask my advice on different programs our peace group was trying to accomplish, but they finally apologized to Mason about their peace activities, and because they both had applied to MIT, they were now accepted. They came around once more to say they were sorry, but I really couldn't be angry with them. After all, they tried, as Schecter said, but just couldn't withstand the pressure.

I like Schecter for all he tried to do, even getting fired by Mason, and maybe it's too demanding, but I have a strong feeling, that he also is too weak for full commitment. Maybe I'm being a purist about that, or maybe the morphine is starting to affect my logic. Or maybe it's because I've been spending too much time thinking about what my friend, Helen, told me about not being a virgin anymore. Harvey Plotnick in our class broke her cherry, she said. Well, I think he's not very attractive as far as I'm concerned, but I wonder the way things are for me, whether I'll ever be able to get out of my hospital bed and get into another kind of bed. (Joke)

In the meantime I guess I'm stuck playing chess with Schecter.

24
Brownsville, 1937

ON SUNDAY MORNINGS, at the corner of Stone and Pitkin Avenues, through blustery winter chill and stifling summer heat, carpenters, painters, electricians, and masons assembled to talk shop and find employment. Boss painters and contractors walked from group to group, picking their work crews. Behind them rose a boarded forlorn building, once a branch of the Bank of the United States, whose sensational bankruptcy in the 30's brought enormous losses to Brownsville's residents.

Through this working class area, Ira, carrying his Jewish National Fund can, walked down Pitkin Avenue, past well-lit showcase windows of large shops carrying expensive items, high-class restaurants, crowds of shoppers and strollers, offering a colorful contrast to the side streets lined with dismal houses in varied stages of deterioration, similar to Amboy street. This day was not any better than it had been before for Ira as far as collecting contributions. The financial problems burdening many Americans were much more glaringly evident in Brownsville. Even the highly respected Red Cross found it almost impossible to raise enough money to support its local chapter. In spite of the National Fund's parochial appeal in this predominately Jewish neighborhood, it was able to do little better.

Along with Ira were three other young solicitors, all vying for position among the stream of pedestrians. None of them were really successful, only an occasional coin, usually a penny, finding its way into their cans. After several unsuccessful minutes, Ira took out a piece of paper from his pocket, glancing at what was written on it. Making a few pencil corrections, he silently practiced mouthing the words on the paper. Finally feeling secure enough to chance a bold adventure, Ira, drawing a deep breath, sang the words he had written to an improvised melody/chant.

"Please help the Jewish National Fund, against the dirty Nazi Bund."

Ira took another breath as several pedestrians smiled in his direction, but walked by him without contributing as he continued to sing.

"We all give our dough to make that evil Hitler go."

People were surprised at Ira's dramatic request, passing him by, depositing their pennies into the cans of the other young boys. Ira, puzzled at the lack of positive response to his song, paused for a moment but resolutely continued louder than before, feeling that even if the world didn't appreciate his genuine cry of protest against the dark forces that his young spirit could only guess at, horrors that his imagination, and the world's, would eventually be forced to face, the reality of the Holocaust!

Norman spoke briefly to Marsa after Ira left the apartment, collection-can resolutely in hand. Obtaining a commitment from Marsa that she seriously consider allowing the dog to stay with the Schecters, and then postponing his work on the Union speech he was preparing, he hurried out toward Pitkin Avenue where he knew Ira would surely go to raise money.

Thinking that by observing Ira's behavior, he might be able to make suggestions which could possibly improve the solicitation, he took a position across the street from where Ira was making his unsuccessful attempts.

After listening to Ira's song which continued to receive smiling responses, but no money, the few cents contributed given only to the other youngsters who simply stood, holding their cans in front of them. As Ira sang, walking directly toward pedestrians, Norman thought, "My son has a lot of guts."

Ira was surprised to see his father crossing the street toward him.

"Pop!"

Norman was speaking even before he reached the sidewalk where Ira was.

"You make that song up?"

"You like it?"

"It's excellent."

"But how come the other kids get more money?"

Norman was also puzzled.

"Yeah, I would figure with that song, *you'd* do good business."

Ira had hoped his father would be able to explain his lack of success. So, disappointed, his anger started to well up.

"Then how do you explain why not?"

"I don't really know, Ira, but maybe I do have some idea."

"Yeah?"

"Maybe some people are like your mother."

Ira knew that his father sometimes explained things by indirection, but at this moment he was baffled, his anger mounting.

"What does Mom have to do with this, Pop?"

"I don't know for sure, but maybe it's like with her and the Violin Man."

Ira was becoming impatient with his father's circular reasoning.

"All right, Pop, what the heck you getting at?"

"Well, maybe the people here don't give money because *they also* don't want anybody to know they're giving, sort of like your mom always hiding behind the curtain when she throws a penny out the window."

Now Ira started to appreciate his father's logic.

"Yeah."

"But remember one thing, Ira, with your mother there's one important difference... *she* always gives."

Now Norman completed his case.

"I suppose that for her, she just doesn't like people to know she's giving."

Ira needed more explanation.

"Why?"

"'Y' is a crooked letter, 'Why'? Why ask <u>me</u>?"

"Why not?"

"A true rebel's logic, my son. The truth of the matter is that I've never been able to figure out 'why' myself."

"No kidding?"

"On matters of profound philosophic import, I do not jest."

"Then you don't have an answer either, Pop?"

"Well, perhaps the two of us can shed some light on this enigma."

"What's 'enigma'?" Ira asked.

Norman paused, trying to come up with a simple definition for Ira.

"It's something like a puzzle... like an idea that's in a labyrinth, or... you know what a labyrinth is?"

"Yeah. Maybe an enigma is kind of a riddle, then."

"As usual, Ira, you amaze me. Yes, a 'riddle' is something you can figure out."

"All right, Pop, I'll use my 'amazing' brain and give you an answer."

"Agreed," Norman said solemnly.

After a moment, Ira pursued the problem. "Well, Pop, first you have to give me the question."

Norman smiled approvingly.

"Spoken like a Socrates come to Brooklyn."

It was Ira's turn to smile.

"He was a Greek, and they killed him."

"Well, do you think we should stop before a similar fate is visited upon *us?*"

Ira shook his head vehemently, encouraging Norman to pursue the solving of the enigma.

"Then bravely together we confront this perplexing problem. Now suppose, I hid..."

Closing his eyes, Norman placed his hands over his ears, "and gave you something... or even just said something like... I love you, Ira. But now, when I say," taking his hands off his ears and opening his eyes he stared at Ira. "I love you Ira, there's a difference, right?"

"Obviously, Pop. The difference is, the first time, you couldn't see or hear what *I* was feeling."

"Ah-ha! We're getting closer, and what was that feeling?"

"That you're kinda crazy, Pop, and that I love you anyway."

"So, if I hide, does it mean that I'm afraid to see that you love me, or… does it mean that I'm afraid to see that you do *not* love me?"

"Well, Pop, I honestly don't feel like doing another riddle without an answer."

"Nor, my wise son, do I, so why don't you sing that song instead?"

"Again?"

"I find it as good a song as anything by Irving Berlin."

"Well, then now *I've* got a tough enigma."

"How's that?"

"Well, Pop, do I sing even if I'm feeling sad because Mom doesn't want me to keep the dog?"

"Oh, no! There's quite a different word for that. It's called 'blackmail.'"

"Oh? Never heard of the word."

"Then, little bandit, if you sing, maybe I'll talk to your mother about this dog riddle."

Ira linked his arm with Norman's, starting to sing the Fund song.

"Please help the Jewish National Fund."

Norman joined in the next line.

"Against the dirty Nazi Bund."

Ira leading them into the rest of the song, the two of them loudly singing as Ira jiggled the can toward the passing pedestrians… with a continued lack of success.

"We'll all give our dough, to make that Evil Hitler go!"

25
Crete

THE PULYAKIS' WEDDING CELEBRATION had been tragically aborted by the killing of George Dakis. After a rushed, tearful farewell to Lula, Manos hurriedly left Heraklion that very night, taking some money he had saved and carrying only his violin and case.

During the following year, in order to escape the enraged, revengeful pursuit of Constantine Dakis, Manos hid in small towns, leaving them as soon as he suspected that a police drag-net was closing in. Finally, in desperation, using the incognito of Spiro, his father's name, and Helio, his mother's maiden name, he booked passage on a small fishing boat going to Piraeus, the port of Athens, looking toward the Aegean Sea. Manos immediately contacted Ignotis, maestro of the symphony, convincing him to send Manos to Portugal, ostensibly to scout musicians to play in the Athens orchestra. However, once in Lisbon, using most of his money, Manos bribed a seaman to smuggle him onto a freighter sailing to Chile.

Disembarking at the port of Valparaiso, Manos gave the rest of his money to a customs official, allowing him to enter the capital, Santiago. Fortunately, able to find a dishwashing job which provided him with meals and enough to rent space in a hovel in the slums, La Chamba, Manos was finally able to feel safe. Limited to the few Spanish words he had learned on the ship, it took him some time before he was able to be hired for an engagement with a small three-man orchestra on a ship sailing around Cape Horn, docking in New York.

Aboard the ship, he befriended a passenger also immigrating from Europe, and although the two men spoke different languages, they were able to understand each other well enough to establish a friendship and provide support for each other as they adjusted to their new world.

Renting a room together on the lower East Side, his new friend having heard Manos practicing on his violin, suggested that he might be able to make money playing on the streets. At the same time, he himself also found a way of earning money, collecting bottles, cans, magazines and newspapers that he was able to sell to different businesses for reuse. The market value for this work was less than a dollar a day, but together with what Manos earned, they were able to afford a spartan life while they looked to the future to improve the lot they had both been forced to accept… for the moment.

Occasionally, Manos would give a private concert in his room for his friend, and was applauded with 'bravos' by his genuinely appreciative audience of one.

Manos sometimes playfully introduced himself at these 'concerts' as Maestro Pulyakis, or Spiro Helio, his father's and mother's names; or in one instance, Gamo Dys, explaining that it was Greek for copulation evil, the first letter of each word, the 'G' and 'D' standing for George Dakis. Of course his friend understood nearly nothing of Manos's explanation, jokingly murmuring to himself that "it was all Greek" to him.

Returning to their room one day, Manos found his friend glancing at Manos's passport. Incensed, Manos shouted at him, using some choice Greek words for excrement, 'scatto,' to be poured on his roommate's 'necro,' dead body. He punctuated his vitriolic condemnation, kicking a chair.

His anger escalating, he threateningly picked up the chair as the other man calmly sat down, writing on a small pad that he had recently bought and carried with him at all times, jotting down whatever English words he learned that might be useful. Now as he wrote, he hardly glanced up, even when Manos hurled the chair against the wall, and then started to pace frantically around the room.

Finishing the note, his roommate placed it on a table, packed his meager belongings in a shopping bag, and left the room.

26
Amboy Street

"**THIS TIME, MARSA,** I want it to be a girl… a beauty like her mother."

It was just a day after Ira's Pitkin Avenue fund raising, that Marsa told Norman that Doctor Rabkin had announced to her during her frightened visit to his office for the pregnancy test results, "the rabbit died, Mrs. Schecter."

"Oh, Normie, ich liebedich, but what's gonna be? What? Can you hear me?"

"I hear."

"The words maybe, but can you hear me?"

"I'm listening, Marsa, so talk."

"I'm trying," Marsa said, struggling to express her fear of the dark financial future. Her initial instinct of maternal celebration she had felt in Rabkin's office had been quickly squelched.

"C'mon, Marsa, I'm listening."

"Your heart don't hear me."

Norman hesitated before speaking.

"We'll manage."

Marsa's echoed "We'll manage" was barely loud enough to support her sarcastic tone. Trying to reassure her, Norman quickly said, "You'll see, Marsa."

"And when I see the rats come up from the coal bin under her bedroom?"

Unfortunately it was not until after the Schecters had moved into their ground floor apartment, that Norman had learned about coal being a rat's ideal hiding place. However, Norman weakly corrected her, "Mice," feeling foolish at his feeble attempt to minimize her disgust.

"Whatever," Marsa shot back, "I'm not going to put her asleep where they can take bites from her."

"I'm doing everything I can, Marsa."

"Well, you can live with them, but not anymore me and the children."

Norman brushed off the threat, "I hear."

"And you hear me say, I'll take Ira and..."

"And what?" Norman sharply responded. "Check into the Waldorf?"

"I talked already to my cousin, Sarah, and she said okay if I wanted to use two rooms upstairs."

Startled, Norman could hardly speak, glaring at Marsa, he managed an abrupt, "You what?"

"You can look at me murder all you want."

Angry now, Norman shot back, "I'll help you pack in the morning."

"Go make jokes with your son; I gotta think how to pay bills this month."

Other than the ticking clock they heard as they stared at each other, the room was silent.

27

ALAN HOPED THAT THE LARGE SIGN that he had put in the display window of Mulnick and Son, announcing a "SPECIAL SUMMER SALE" would attract some desperately needed customers.

Glancing through the window, he saw Norman walking with deliberate strides toward the store.

Quickly stepping past his father, who was mending a worn buttonhole on a muskrat jacket that he had just steamed to revive some of the luster to the fur, Alan spoke to Norman as he reached the door.

"Can I interest you in a special full-length mink for your wife, sir?"

Glancing up from his work, Sam spoke sharply to his son.

"Enough with the funny jokes already."

Turning to Norman, his tone warm, friendly.

"Not since Rosh Hashonna I see you."

"So invite me to supper, Mr. M., see what happens."

"So, come next Shabbus, mein boychick."

"Sorry, I'll be in Europe on my annual vacation."

Laughing appreciatively, Sam clapped Norman on his shoulder. "Come, I'll give you another lesson about dialectical materialism, and I'll tell Rose to make special for you her best boiled chicken."

Norman good-naturedly accepted the invitation.

"Oi vey, Marx and chicken soup, a real treat."

Exchanging a glance with Alan, he continued to address Mr. Mulnick.

"In the meantime, Mister M, can I take your son out and buy him an egg cream soda?"

"Life's to enjoy, Norman, take. But remember, next Shabbus."

"I'll come back from Europe… special."

When Norman and Alan had taken a few steps down the street, Alan spoke urgently, conspiratorially. "I'm glad you finally came. Pop hasn't been able to pay me anything in over four months, so the insurance money'll cover that, and…"

Norman interrupted.

"M' thinks, Cassius hath a lean and hungry look."

"I'll tell Caesar next time I see him, but in the meantime there's going to be four, five hundred left over from the insurance, and…"

"I've told you, Alan, don't count on me to get involved."

"Don't be a class A schmuck, you won't be able to buy out Wall Street with the money, but it'll pay the rent for a year for you to move back to a nice apartment in Flatbush."

It seemed to Norman it was as if Marsa had spoken to Alan with her litany of grievances. Now he felt like he was sitting on a barbed wire fence separating his family's need from pursuing an illegal act.

Rabbi Landesman was very apologetic to Norman about being able to give him only sixty cents for his week's work with the Drama Club at the Hebrew Educational Society. "I'm sorry, Mister Schecter, but only twelve children were able to give five cents this time."

After one of the union meetings held at the H.E.S., the Rabbi had approached Norman about starting a theater group there. Norman quickly agreed to organize one, feeling that it was a way to repay the H.E.S. for, attempting a light-hearted joke, 'harboring our disruptive bunch of agitators.' The Rabbi, humorless, literal minded, reassured him, "Oh no, Mister Schecter, I consider your group very reasonable and respectful."

At the first meeting with a group of eighteen early teenagers, Norman read them excerpts from the children's play, *The Emperor's New Clothes.* Based on their enthusiastic response, he typed a copy of the play and made mimeographed copies of it for the youngsters.

Because their families excitedly looked forward to the play being performed in H.E.S.'s small auditorium for an invited audience, it was agreed that Norman would receive five cents from each child for the weekly meetings.

With this week's sixty cents, Norman hurried over to the Benjamin Franklin Bank on Pitkin Avenue where he had joined the Christmas Club. With his weekly deposits of about fifty cents, he would have saved approximately thirty dollars, to be withdrawn at the year-end holidays.

The teller in charge of the Club adjusted her thick- lensed eyeglasses as they slid down her nose, and smiled at Norman.

"Welcome again, Mister Schecter."

"Thank you, Miss Dickens."

The small ebony plaque on the counter stated in simple white lettering, MAUREEN DICKENS. Norman politely continued, "I've meant to ask you several times, but could you possibly be related in some way —"

Interrupting, Miss Dickens was answering his question even before he was able to complete it. Smiling, she pleasantly said, "I've been asked that question many times."

"And —?"

"Well, I've read *A Tale Of Two Cities*, but I am definitely not a descendant of Charles Dickens."

"I didn't really think so," Norman said, putting his deposit slip and sixty cents in front of Maureen, smiling as he paraphrased the opening lines of *A Tale Of Two Cities*, "It is the best of times, and the worst of times."

Maureen laughed appreciatively, responding mock-solemnly with her version of the closing lines of the novel, "then it's a far, far better thing you do now, than you have ever done."

It was Norman's turn to laugh.

Fred the mailman was just about to enter the bank as Norman exited. As usual, Fred was feeling very good about going to the bank.

He felt it was his imagination and leadership ability that had prompted the Supervisor to entrust him with a special banking assignment. Nothing was added to his salary for this extra chore, however, Fred surmised that his superiors were checking him for possible promotion to an 'inside' administration job, so he willingly accepted the responsibility.

Norman held the bank door open for Fred as he spoke to him.

"One of the lucky ones who have something in the bank Fred?"

"Yeah... thousands. I'm a rich man... once a week... when I pick up the payroll," gesturing to his mail pouch slung over his shoulder, "for the station."

"Well, Fred, if I run into Dick Tracey, I'll tell him to keep an eye on you."

28

Manos, recognizing some of the words in the note left by his roommate as German, was able to have it translated by Herr Miermann, whom he found teaching German at the Townsend Harris High School in Manhattan.

After reading the note, Herr Miermann, who spoke near perfect grammatical English, turned to Manos.

"Tell me about the gentleman who wrote these words."

Manos, in New York for just a few months, had acquired only a limited working knowledge of English, and could only shrug his answer.

"Mr. Pulyakis, the man who wrote this is a very educated man."

Again, Manos could only shrug. Miermann wrote out the translation in his neat precise handwriting. After Manos had finished reading, he glanced up at Miermann, whose impassive features revealed nothing.

Back at his room, Manos read the translated note again.

> "Manos, I have been very patient to try to understand the strange manner in which you sometimes behave, but I am no longer willing to further accept your present actions.
>
> First, sir, I glanced at your passport only in curiosity because you appear to be confused about your name, so I am not sure you are indeed Manos Pulyakis or George Dakis as you have often referred to yourself. I have therefore been confused as to who you really are, and perhaps you are also.
>
> In these days it is dangerous to be that way. In my country, my wife and daughter were killed because their identity was not accepted.
>
> I hope that you will be able to fix your thinking.
>
> Respectfully,
>
> Isaac Baumgarten"

29

ON AUGUST 28, 1963, Norman was confronted by imminent life-threatening danger. Actually, it was not aimed directly at him, as much as it was at his daughter, Edith, just turned twenty-five.

Violence promised to engulf her if she participated in the upcoming march on Washington, D.C., led by Civil Rights leader, Reverend Martin Luther King, Jr. Of course, there were the usual ugly threats attacking King, and the fact that Edith, a low-profile white woman was also targeted, was the result of her prior activities. Several years earlier she had read, and been very much impressed by, James Baldwin's first novel, *Giovanni's Room*, the story of a man's conflicted choice between loving and desiring a man… or a woman… or both.

She adapted several scenes into stage play form, and as head of the Drama Club at NYU, she had them acted in front of an audience drawn from the student body.

Boldly, she invited Baldwin to the performance. Intrigued, he attended, and was genuinely impressed by Edith's creative inventiveness converting his prose into stage drama.

Sometime later, he returned the favor, inviting her to a reading of his newly finished play, *The Amen Corner*, about a woman evangelist in Harlem. Edith received Baldwin's permission to bring her father along, feeling that because of his storehouse of literary knowledge, he could possibly contribute to the discussion of the play's merit.

After the reading of the play by the actors, Norman was able to offer several helpful insights for its development.

Again, Baldwin was appreciative, and sometime later when the march on Washington was being planned, he spoke to Norman and Edith about it. When it was announced that Baldwin would be joining King at the rally, the news item also included Edith's name. Almost immediately, a threatening letter was received by Edith, living at home with the Schecters in an apartment that Norman was now able to afford in upscale Brooklyn Heights, just across the river from NYU where Edith was commuting to complete her Masters.

The Aryan Now hate group sent Edith several vitriolic letters addressed to the "White Slut" accusing her of sleeping with the Nigger Baldwin. The irony was that Baldwin's homosexuality was openly acknowledged. A letter was also sent to Marsa, advising her to keep her daughter at home, or her fate would be the same as the two Kikes from New York who had been lynched along with the Nigger boy from Mississippi. Terrified, Marsa attempted to prevail on her daughter not to go to Washington, but Edith was resolute about being part of what she felt would become an historic event.

On one hand, Norman was proud of Edith's stance, although he felt it would be inappropriate of her to risk her life, as well as endangering himself and Marsa. He strongly felt that because of the situation's volatility, he should protect his family's safety by staying home.

When Edith returned safely from D.C., she reported that there had been no acts of violence directed at her, or anybody else, as far as she knew. In spite of this, Norman still felt that he had been correct to err on the side of discretion, having no regrets about not attending the march.

30

Brownsville, 1937

WHENEVER FRED, THE MAILMAN, delivered '179's' mail, he thought about that sultry afternoon when Finky had drunk some of his beer, but shit, he hadn't seen her since then. Once, one of the neighbors, Mrs. Wax, had answered his guarded query as to whether Finky had moved from '179.'

"Finklestein?"

"Y'know, 12? There hasn't been any mail, so I thought—"

"So ask me—" Mrs. Wax prompted, "—what she's doing lately."

"So, Mrs. Wax, what's Finky doing lately?"

"I should know?"

Fred had thought it would be just his rotten luck that he wouldn't get another chance with Finky.

He nodded benignly, as he spoke to the small group of people, including Marsa and Norman, clustered around the rusting letter boxes at the rear of the building.

"One for Cohen."

He handed a letter to a grateful elderly woman before turning back to a younger one.

"Wax," Fred announced.

Evelyn Wax, a high energy, flaming red-headed woman in her attractive thirties, grabbed the envelope out of his hand, as she declared to Marsa, "An advertisement, I bet ten to one... it should only evaporate!"

'Evaporate' was Wax's dismissive word of finality she used to annihilate anything that was a threat to her fragile universe of uncertainty.

Mrs. Wax triumphantly held up an advertising flier from Davega Sports Store.

"See, Marsa! What'd I tell you? My Davie bought a pair of sneakers on sale from them two years ago and now they write us regular like we were in the family!"

Norman gingerly inquired of Marsa, "Nothing still from your mama and papa?"

Marsa shook her head as Norman comforted her, "No news is better than bad news."

Marsa turned plaintively to her good friend, Wax.

"Come in later for a glass of tea, Evelyn?"

"After I hang the wash, I'll put my head in by you."

As Marsa walked back to her apartment, Evelyn went up the stairs, almost colliding with Finky coming out of 12 at the head of the landing.

"Oopsy-Daisy, Evelyn."

Fred had just finished delivering the last letter when he heard Mrs. Wax and Finky's laughter drifting down the stairwell. He spoke curtly to the others as he locked the mailboxes.

"I told you before — nothing else."

Grunting their displeasure, the tenants started to leave as Fred took an extra moment to hitch the mail pouch up higher on his shoulder, waiting to see if Finky was going to come down the stairs. When he heard the seductive click of her high heels on the stairs, he pretended to be checking inside the pouch, shifting his body so that he could get a good view of the stairway.

Out of the corner of his eye, he saw one of her firm bare legs. He caught his breath. She was wearing a short, tight, pink, thin cotton skirt that hiked up as she stepped down, and he could clearly see some of the soft flesh of her thigh. Even though Fred was busily reshuffling some letters as she came into full sight, he was able to note that she had on a matching tight pink sweater, outlining her full breasts. What a pair of knockers, Fred thought. He felt himself push up hard inside his trousers.

Finky waived gaily at him.

"Hi, Mailman."

Glancing up, Fred awkwardly pretended surprise.

"Oh, I didn't hear you."

She smiled teasingly, the tip of her tongue showing between her teeth.

"Hey, you forgot my name."

"I sure didn't, Finky. And I didn't forget you drank up my beer."

He felt pleased with his quick reply, especially when her soft lips rounded into a tempting pout as she pretended disapproval.

"Ooh! Freddie the cheapskate."

She had reached the bottom stair, and standing just a bit higher than him, he was almost forced to look at her breasts, as a waft of her perfume reached his nostrils. He took the mail pouch off to hold casually in front of him, in order to hide his erection.

"Me? A cheapskate?"

She glanced quickly around the empty hallway and then turned back to Fred.

"Yeah, you made me promise to pay you back."

"Sure, next Christmas. You'll pay me… maybe."

"Oh all right, cheapskate—"

She wheeled around and started up the stairs, the fleshy full roundness of her body moving provocatively under the thin cotton. Fred watched, not sure of what he should do. Was he supposed to follow her upstairs to her door or—?

"Hey, cheapskate mailman, you don't expect me to bring it down to you, do you?"

Fred answered, trying hard to mask his excitement.

"Coming up, Finky."

He walked up the flight of stairs and stood at the opened door of '12,' watching Finky sway down the hallway leading to her kitchen. As she opened the icebox, she called to him.

"F'chrissake, Freddie, you want personal delivery? I'm not a mailman, so ya gonna have to get it ya self."

Fred held his breath for a moment before stepping into the hallway, the floor creaking loudly under his step. Nervous, he stopped, but the easy familiarity of her voice reassured him.

"And shut the door will ya, Freddie?"

Reaching behind him, pulling the door shut, Fred puzzled that the doorknob was wet. As he stood there, adjusting his eyes to the semi-darkness of the hallway, he realized that both his hands were sweating heavily, as the scent of Finky's perfume became stronger. Coming into the room, he felt excited by the way the pink-painted walls seemed to invite him in. As he turned toward Finky, he accidentally bumped into her as she straightened up from the icebox. He jumped back as if stung.

"Sorry, Finky."

She turned to him, a beer in each hand, smilingly offering him one as she kicked the pink icebox door shut with her foot.

"Grab it, clumsy, and sit down someplace before you run me down."

Fred playfully snatched at the bottle, welcoming its coolness, as he stepped to the small pink kitchen table and sat on the color-matching wooden chair as Finky mock-growled at him.

"All right, cheapskate, d'ya wanna glass, or d'ya like to chug-a-lug it straight from the bottle?"

Taking an opener from the top of the icebox, she expertly flipped off the bottle cap. Placing the foaming bottle on the table, she leaned over to open Fred's, placing one hand on the bottle to steady it, touching his fingers, shooting an intense feeling through his body, jolting his groin.

Finky brought her bottle up to her mouth, her lips slowly closing around it as she motioned for Fred to do the same. With a smile, he followed her instructions, and they both drank, trying to drain the bottle without stopping. Finishing his first, Fred held the empty bottle up in a victory gesture, as Finky gulped the last mouthful, playfully staggering, falling into the other pink chair, laughing.

"You cheated, Freddie."

"Baloney."

"You started to chug-a-lug first. We'll do it again and I'll prove it."

"Okay, Finky."

"Thanks."

"Well, it's your beer."

"Yeah, but what I mean is, thanks for keeping me company."

Since Finky's husband, Charlie, had been sent to prison, she had had no visitors to her apartment… for good reason. First of all, if Charlie ever found out about her sleeping with another man while he was in the 'pen,' he said he'd kill her when he got out! Once when she was visiting him in Sing Sing prison, he warned her that if he ever heard of her even going out with a man, he would have one of his buddies on the outside rough her up.

Another, almost equally as important reason was that there were no men in the neighborhood whom Finky had met who she felt were very different from Charlie as far as how they treated women. Even Normie Schecter, who seemed like one of the nicer guys, would sometimes speak sharply to his wife when they were picking up their mail, and Marsa would become upset about not receiving a letter from Germany. Finky had noticed that Norman would at first be considerate about dealing with his wife's disappointment, but when Marsa would continue acting out her distress, he would become short-fused.

"For chrissake, Marsa, you can be—"

"Enough with the Jesus talk, Normie!"

"—a pain in the ass waiting for news about the Nazis."

"You should bite your tongue, Normie, for talking like a Hitler."

Finky, for all her loneliness and needy desire, had not invited anyone into her apartment until now. She quickly became aware that not only was she sexually attracted to Fred, but she felt a real liking for the way he acted courteously to her. 'Yeah' Finky thought, not only did his body look good wearing his snug summer greys, but he had a likeable puppy-dog manner.

For his part, Fred had a similar mix of strong sexual desire and liking for Finky's personality. Here, in the parched precinct of '179,' a seed of genuine affection was sown. Now, Finky moved provocatively past Fred, as smiling, she glanced at him over her shoulder. He averted his eyes, pretending to be looking around the room.

"Boy, everything is sure pink in here, Finky."

"It makes me feel all—"

She finished the thought by swaying her body, punctuating it with a pleasurable grunt.

"But I'm crazy about purple even better."

"Purple?"

"Well, like... sort of like... lavender. Go ahead, take a look."

She motioned toward a partially open door, speaking breathily.

"I'll get a couple more beers opened and you'll owe me one."

"Ah-hah, Finky, now who's the cheapskate?"

She laughed appreciatively and Fred, feeling pleased with himself, got up to go to the bedroom door, turning his body slightly to hide his erection. He pushed gently at the door and it swung open, revealing a sudden splash of lavender. The walls. The furniture. The bedspread. The accessories, all purple hued.

"You like it, Freddie?"

Going by him, her body brushed heavily against him as she went to stand in the center of the small room. Looking around her, she turned in delight.

"Isn't it Boop-oop-a-doop, Freddie?"

She held her pouty Clara Bow imitation as she waited for his approval.

"It's Boop-oop-a-doop, all right, Finky."

The room was close and heavy with her scent. Extending a beer bottle toward him, he took it as she bounced down on the edge of the bed, gesturing that he should sit on a nearby chair.

As Fred settled down into the chair, Finky started to giggle and as it grew to a laugh, she pointed at him. He stammered uneasily.

"Whatsa matter, Finky?"

"Look at that."

Her bottle was pointing toward his lap.

"Look at that big funny thing sticking up."

Fred glanced down at the lower part of his body, his pants swelling up.

"Freddie, why does that thing keep wiggling around like that?"

Fred couldn't think of what to say. Was she just teasing him or what?

"The liddle boy is blushing."

She put her bottle on the floor and quickly knelt in front of him, between his knees, putting one hand on his penis, unbuttoning his fly with the other.

"Let's get it out so it won't get crushed in there."

Fred reached down to help her with the buttons, but she pushed his hand away.

"Just sit back and relax, honey."

The buttons undone, her fingers probed into his underwear, wrapping themselves around his erection, tugging it out where it jerked up to its full stiffness. Although she was extremely aroused, she hesitated, seeing that he was not circumcised; that he was a 'Goy'! Never having had sex with anybody but a Jew, she was excited by this novel experience. She pushed back Fred's foreskin, admiringly stroking his throbbing penis as she seductively murmured to Fred, "I'm sure glad to meet your good-looking friend, Honey."

Fred felt as if he were going to shoot off in a second. Sensing this, Finky suddenly took her hand away.

Fred quickly complained.

"Hey, c'mon."

Finky was already taking off her pink sweater. Fred gasped as he saw her full breasts spilling out over her brassiere. She reached behind her and quickly unhooked it, her breasts jumping out at him. Fred groaned in pleasure, leaning forward to touch her, but again she brushed his hand away.

"Don't shoot it yet, honey."

Finky's body writhed in pleasure, her hands sliding her dress to up high on her thighs. Fred sighed in pleasure as he watched Finky's fingers disappear underneath her panties. After a moment, she took her finger out, brushing its moist tip on the head of Fred's penis.

"Hold on, Honey."

She leaned forward, her tongue flicking at the head, before guiding its full length into her mouth.

Fred held her head down on him as he exploded into her mouth, his moans of pleasure echoing off the purple walls.

Spent, he attempted to withdraw, but Finky kept her mouth closed around him. Groaning, he finally pushed himself away.

Through half-slit eyes, he glanced around the purple room, feeling like some conqueror of a foreign land, the joy of victory mixed with the curiosity of what might now happen in this strange purple place. He closed his eyes again, watching her from beneath his lowered lids. She was completely naked now, as she pulled the lavender bed-spread from off the bed. Fred was surprised to see that even though her chest was full and round, her stomach was flat and firm, her thighs sturdy. She was even sexier without clothes, Fred thought, and the load she'd got from him should've emptied him for a long time, yet he was surprised to feel a stirring in his groin.

She came and stood in front of him. When he opened his eyes wide to get a better view, she smiled at him and pushed her breasts forward, moving her body slowly, suggestively, posing for him. She reached down and took his hands, helping him to stand up, before quickly removing his shirt. She stroked his chest, making muted sounds of approval, leading him to the bed and helping him to lower himself onto the pale lavender sheets.

She lay down next to him, taking him in her hand. He started to mutter that he thought it'd be a long time before it would stand up again, but he felt himself stiffen. Finky, with a triumphant moan, rolled him over on her, guiding his hardness into her ready wetness and warmth. She reached up and took his face between her hands, her eyes clouded with passion, pleased with the affection starting to lace her feelings, she moaned invitingly, "Now you're gonna fuck me, baby. Boy, are you gonna fuck!"

And Fred, also enveloped in the warmth embracing them both, did as Finky had requested.

31

WHEN NORMAN AND ALAN registered for the draft in 1918, they heatedly debated the probability of the Army choosing to assign two Jews to the same outfit. Alan offered a cynical "no!" When Norman voiced an optimistic "yes!" Alan caustically responded:

"You've got your head up your ass, Normie."

Now, in 1937, Alan's still strong opinion rode on the shoulders of the government's de facto anti-Semitism.

"When was the last Jew elected to Congress, huh? And what about the religious quota system in colleges?"

Alan also reminded Norman about a mutual friend, Gordon Halpern.

"Gordie was top of his graduating class, but finally had to settle for a half-ass medical school in cockamaymee Transylvania."

"I know that, Alan, and I'm also aware that there isn't a single well known Jewish-named actor in movies, so?"

"So don't argue with me, Normie. We both know it's a secret that everybody's in on; that our big Jewish movie star, John Garfield, was Jules Garfinkel on his birth certificate. And what about Paul Muni who couldn't use his Jewish name, Weisenfreund, even when he won the Oscar last year for that Louis Pasteur movie."

Alan switched to another area he was strongly sure of.

"And when Hank Greenberg won the home run championship last year, he was the only Yid in the majors!"

This drew them into another debate. Did Jews, as a race, genetically lack the natural athletic skills to complete on a professional level in sports?

Thirty years later, they felt they had an answer to that question when Jewish Sandy Koufax entered the pantheon of extraordinary baseball players, the Hall of Fame. Norman then pointed out that for a much longer time than Jews being excluded from playing in the Majors, Negro players like the great slugger, Josh Gibson, and pitching ace, Satchel Paige, were not allowed in; that Jackie Robinson finally became the first Negro in the Major Leagues. Now this was something else to dispute; did Negroes have a leg-up in sports because they had a natural talent for sports?

"Well, maybe..." Normie suggested, "... it's just that society forces them to nurture their athletic abilities in order to escape the racism that keeps them in lesser paying jobs."

"Is that a chapter from Karl Marx, Normie?"

"Well, look Alan, maybe special athletes like Koufax and Robinson prove that religion or race is not as important as the indiscriminate scrambling of genetic history."

"You going to give a sermon on that stuff at the D.C. rally with that Martin Luther King?

"I don't know, Alan."

"Good. Save some of your energy for Jewish pride. Yeah, save something from your liberal bullshit attitude about the "Schvartzes."

In any event, Norman was correct after all in his 1918 prediction of them getting into the same outfit: both of them going through basic training together.

It was during this time that Norman had a character defining experience. Although at thirteen he had been Bar Mitzvahed, Norman had since become almost secular in that he very rarely practiced his religion, attending Synagogue only at the strong behest of his parents, who themselves would only occasionally go to services on the very sacred once-a-year High Holy Day of Yom Kippur.

Their tight-lipped gentile Lieutenant had reluctantly permitted Norman and Alan to take off one Saturday morning in order to attend Jewish services.

The Rabbi led the congregation in the Kaddish prayer for the dead. When he was young, Norman had heard the prayer only in Hebrew, but now it was presented in English. When the Rabbi said, in reference to the departed, that they "should be remembered for their deeds of loving kindness," Norman was struck by the humanity of that simple statement.

Also, the prayer defined for him the Jewish virtue of not being concerned for material legacy, as much as for relating with decency towards others.

After basic training, Alan and Norman shipped out to France, serving in combat side by side right up to the armistice.

During their very first battle at Belleau Woods, the two scared eighteen-year olds were ordered, with the rest of 'C' Company, to advance from their trenches across a contested open area.

Their lieutenant had prepared them with the battle plan; an artillery unit would soften up the German resistance just prior to the attack. Alan, Norman and the other fresh recruits were partially reassured, their excitement pumping adrenaline to mask their fear.

When they heard the shrill piercing whistle signaling the attack, there was a moment of suspended animation; no words, breath held, and then a sudden intense rush to defend themselves; to kill the enemy.

The men, 'boys' really, with fixed bayonets on their Enfield rifles held stiffly in front of them, ran toward the German trenches, screaming to hide their terror and mute the staccato machine-gun fire; bullets tearing into young bodies, their flesh exploding in jagged pieces, soaked by gushing blood, as the boys' hands reflexively leapt to feel their wounds in questioning horror before they fell dead.

Alan and some of the other boys, to escape the withering fire, jumped into the shell holes dug by the bombardment as Norman fell to his stomach, hoping to avoid being hit.

Alan saw him over the lip of the shell hole, and risking his life, he reached toward Norman, dragging him in to share his protection. After several minutes more of intense machine-gun fire, the ground trembled as it clasped the fallen dead.

'C' Company's attack had failed, and waiting till dark, the pitiful few remaining crawled back to their trench, the screams of pain of the wounded and dying embedded forever in their memories.

32

AS MARSA STARED AT THE SECOND-HAND VICTROLA that Norman had just presented her with, she recalled the one she had used on her last day in Berlin just before starting on the trip to visit her aunt in New York.

She quickly noted that the Victrola now in front of her appeared similar to the one she had left behind, having the same blue painted case and metal handle used to wind up the record turntable. Only the faded, peeling paint was different from the memory of her beloved music player she had last seen over twenty years before. Idly lifting the cover of the Victrola, she glanced at its underside and was shocked to see the faded crayoned name there… Leo.

For a moment, Marsa could not accept the fact that this bruised antique was the same one she had used to play her treasured records on in that distant past life of graciousness and ease.

Norman observed Marsa's sudden change of expression, from the smiling light-hearted appreciation of his gift to a look of amazement which Norman perceived as one of disgust.

"Marsa, you look like I just handed you the dead Lindbergh baby."

"You should bite your tongue, Normie, to say such words. The poor Lindbergh's would vomit if they heard."

"You're right, Marsa," Norman, penitent, quickly responded. "I said an ugly thing… Sometimes I'm a shmuck."

Marsa's attention returned to the Victrola.

"This is my old music player, Normie… would you believe?"

"So, it is just like the one in Berlin you told me about?"

"Normie, this is the one he," pointing to Leo's name, "and I argued about who would play which record."

Their father, in his high position at the Philharmonic, had provided the family with an extensive collection of classical music, including a particular piece from Massenet's opera, Thaïs, the Meditation; its lovely plaintive melody becoming Marsa's favorite.

Norman explained how he had come to own the Victrola. He had helped Isaac Baumgarten study for his citizenship application, and so, in thanks, Isaac gave him the Victrola which he had bought for forty five cents from the desolate owner of a music store that was going out of business.

At first, Marsa happily embraced the extraordinary coincidence of her old Victrola finding its way back to her, but she quickly also saw it as an omen which she sadly explained to Norman.

"God is telling me that this is goodbye from Leo and my Papa and Mama. They are all toyt!" Dead!

It was not until after World War 2 that her prediction was confirmed. Her father, Abe, had died in the Dachau concentration camp; Esther and Leo had been on the shipload of Jews who, with all the other desperate passengers, had been refused entry into the United States and were returned to Germany. Her mother and Leo eventually were gassed in the Treblinka camp.

Only the spirits, she thought, of all those who died in the camps could know if Esther, Leo or Abe, at their final moment, touched the memory of their family having once been all together.

Marsa, finally accepting the unique journey of her Victrola, was astounded at an even greater coincidence: a moment after telling Norman about her reclaimed ownership of the music player, she opened the Victrola's small storage drawer which usually had held two or three records, oddly feeling only slight surprise that the single record now in the drawer was Meditation.

Incredulity! An old shellac record had traveled halfway across Europe and sailed the Atlantic to reach Brownsville!

Norman watched as Marsa wound up the turntable, carefully placing Meditation on it, and then lowered the arm with its needle placed on the record, but quickly removing it at the scratchy sound it made.

"A new needle I'll get!"

On her way to buy some needles at Murray's Music Store, she was somehow reminded of the Violin Man. At first, she was unclear as to what the purchase of needles had to do with him, but jogging her memory, she finally made the connection:

The Violin Man rarely repeated the same pieces that he played in the courtyards, but he had, on several occasions, played a few notes as a warm-up, then segueing into whatever piece he was to play.

The notes had seemed familiar to Marsa, but not until she listened to *Meditation* again on her new, old, Victrola, did she realize that those few notes were from a short section of it.

Now, realizing that made her feel even more respect for the Violin Man... he liked her favorite piece!

Replacement needles were very expensive; Marsa settling for a small five-cent packet of inexpensive wooden ones, each one guaranteed to be used for at least five times. She wore out three of them in just a few days. Norman, familiar with the piece, enjoyed listening to it again, along with Ira who had not heard much classical music on the one radio station which occasionally interspersed a classic composer with the big band sounds of Benny Goodman and Glenn Miller.

Marsa, pleased at Ira's genuine interest in the music, went searching in Madam J's thrift stores, finally finding two records for a nickel each; Puccini's sweet-sad 'O Mio Babbino Caro' aria, and the rousing overture from Wagner's

Tannhauser. Norman, long a fan of Wagner's music, decided however not to tell Marsa about the world becoming aware of the composer's bent toward the Master Race concept, Hitler adapting it to Nazism, growing the seed of hate in the already fertile soil of Germany's overt anti-Semitism.

Sometime later, Ira in a high-school European History class, learned of Wagner's racial bias and shared the information with Marsa. At first rejecting Ira's recounting of his class discussion as a 'crazy school joke,' she finally became convinced of the serious charge against Wagner and angrily rushed to break the Tannhauser record. She was stopped by Ira who tried to convince her that his love for the music's heartfelt sentiment was more important to him than Wagner's politics. Marsa became even more livid with anger at Ira's lack of allegiance to his Jewish roots.

"A Nazi in my own house!?"

"Mom, I say he's a Class A racist shmuck but also a Class A composer."

Marsa turned to Norman with a rhetorical demand, "Can you explain to your son that being a Class A mensch is more important then Class A anything else?"

Norman would later think of his volunteering to help Isaac as being the catalyst to this disagreement between Marsa and Ira. The discord between mother and son lingered only briefly, quickly being dissolved by their unconditional respectful love of each other.

Now, Norman finally decided he owed at least some measure of allegiance to Alan… to help him carry out his desperate, arson plan.

33

THE DALMATIAN RAN ITS TONGUE around its feeding bowl, licking up the last speck of food. Its hunger satisfied, it contentedly glanced up at Norman and Alan who had stopped outside of Firehouse 27.

Alan called out to a man who was energetically polishing the already gleaming, highly shined fire truck.

"Hey Sean," using his best Irish dialect, "how's it going m'boy?"

"Well, Mister Mulnick," Sean answered, playfully thickening his natural brogue as he proudly admired his work, neatly re-arranging a water hose on the truck, ensuring that it was stacked according to code. "It's goin' the way it should be goin'... m'boy."

"This, m'boy," Alan gestured to Norman, "is my good friend, Norman."

"Well, Norman," Sean said cordially, "you look like an honest man," continuing good-naturedly, "not like your buddy there."

Alan nervously tried to maintain an even tone as he answered, "How's that, Sean, m'boy?"

"Well," Sean addressed his answer to Norman. "How do you think I should feel if I asked you to buy a ticket to this year's Fireman's Ball and you tell me you can't, and I ask you why not, and you tell me you already spent your money on a ticket to the Policeman's 'cause they have bigger balls."

"Well," Alan smiled, "if you tell me next year that the *Fireman's* are bigger, maybe I'll dig up the dollar."

"Is that a fact?"

"Is the Pope Catholic?"

Norman, who had been patting the dog, glanced toward Sean.

"What's her name?"

"Trixie."

Alan had grown impatient. "C'mon, Normie, we've got to talk."

Trixie followed them for a few feet until Sean whistled quietly; the friendly, even-tempered dog, turning back in order to sit in front of the firehouse, a vigilant guardian of all her buddies at the station.

When Norman had come to Mulnick and Son earlier that afternoon to talk with Alan, he found him alone in the store, since Sam had gone to see the doctor because he had again been having chest pains.

Alan had seized the opportunity to show Norman how he planned to set fire to the store when his father was certain not to be there for the entire day. Using fur cleaning fluid for fuel, he would set the fuse for the fire while Norman, in the back alley, would alert him about anybody who might be passing by and become aware of what the arsonists were up to. If they were undetected, Alan would join Norman, and they would hurry away, joining other pedestrians with whom they would be able to, at a distance, observe the flames, evidence of the store burning.

"Okay, Alan," Norman said impatiently before they had walked halfway down the street from the fire house. "Why did you walk me past the firehouse?"

"Actually it was to say hello to Trixie."

"What's all this mystery about?"

The discussion with Alan at the store had been interrupted by Alan's father returning to the store.

"So, Pop," Alan asked. "What did the doctor say?"

"What does a doctor say, but the bill is two dollars."

"You're all right, Sam?" Norman, concerned, asked.

"According to Darwin, I'll be okay."

"What are you talking about, Pop?"

"It's the survival of the fittest, so I'll be able to open the doors here for another 30 years."

Now, as Alan and Norman walked back from the firehouse, Alan explained the mystery about Trixie.

"Sometimes Trixie wanders around the back alley of the store; there's a grassy area back there she likes to crap on."

"So?"

"Well, she barks when she smells even a match lighting, so if you see her while I'm inside and..."

"I didn't say I'm going to help you."

"You heard Pop. He's going to have another heart attack if he keeps working here."

"I have to really think this through, Alan."

"Normie, I've got to do this soon! I've got to get out of the trenches, and *you* have to help me this time when we go over the top."

34
New York, 1953

JULIUS AND ETHEL ROSENBERG were scheduled to be electrocuted, having been found guilty by the courts on espionage charges of stealing U.S. Government atomic-bomb secrets and delivering them to the Russian government.

Outside the unforgiving walls of Sing Sing prison, crowds of picketers engaged in shouting matches, expressing their passionate feelings, pro and con.

The abrasive sound of their conflict, a cacophony of accusations, recriminations, threats, statistics, was discordant accompaniment to the over-wrought 50s and the paranoia of the McCarthy Communist witch-hunt. Consequently, the public's sense of security was easily jangled by any threat to the *status quo* of political conformity. This turbulent climate of suspicion was grist for the mill of uncertainty and distrust, and when Norman applied to become a High-School Principal, his past association with the liberal activities of Local 5 of the Teachers' Union created, unknown to him, a target for the School Board's zeal to ensure that their ranks were pristine, clear of 'Red' influence. Norman, with optimistic anticipation based on his past record of meritorious teaching citations and his top-of-the-class grades on the exams he had taken earlier in the year, appeared before the Board's Finding Committee.

Chairman Comisky brusquely opened the proceedings, even as his three Board associates were still seriously arranging their notebooks and pencils in preparation for the meeting."Mr. Schecter, we are here, with your help, of course, to advance to the next step in your application."

Comisky's tone, and the aggressive body language of the other three Board members, signaled to Norman that the inviting sea he thought he was sailing into did not have the warmth of a friendly current, but rather a stormy one.

The first questions were sparring:

"How do you feel about the present cold war between our country and the Russians?... Mr. Schecter, do you feel at this time our teaching community should be free of Communist influence?"

Other innocuous questions followed:

"Should the U.S. continue under the Capitalist banner?... Should there be legislation outlawing the activities of political enemies within this country?"

And finally the question being asked of all teachers and civil servants: "ARE YOU NOW, OR HAVE YOU EVER BEEN, A MEMBER OF THE COMMUNIST PARTY?"

After Norman's quick answer, "No!" Comisky and the others nodded approvingly.

"Were there any Communists to your knowledge in Local 5?"

Since it was a well-known fact that Local 5 was riddled with Party members, it was a trick question in order to ascertain if the interviewee was being forthcoming. If the answer was a flat 'no,' the Board would have reason to doubt his veracity across the board. Aware of this, Norman was ready with his disclaimer.

"There *were* members who seemed to espouse Party-line concepts, but there were no cells, so to speak, that I was aware of."

"Then the question, Mr. Schecter, is if *you* personally knew any Communists in the Union?"

"There were one or two who identified themselves as Socialists."

"The question is, I repeat, did you, Mr. Schecter, personally know any Communists in the Union?"

Norman knew that Jerry Goldstein, who had been in his splinter group, had proudly identified himself as a Communist, but Norman had not been in touch with him since those early days in the 30's, therefore he wasn't aware of whether or not Goldstein had left the Party in disillusionment as many other Communists had done after the Russian German non-aggressive pact in 1939. Although Norman recalled that he had not particularly liked Goldstein for his condescending manner whenever he offered his views to the group, he was reluctant to offer to the Board information about him.

"Well, Mr Comisky, I never saw anybody who displayed their Communist Party card."

Mr. Comisky's patience was wearing thin.

"Mr. Schecter, I must remind you that you are applying for the very important position of High-School Principal and the Board expects total," the word was underlined as Comisky repeated it, "*Total* cooperation and candid, direct responses. Now, did you personally know…"

Norman debated in his mind as to whether or not he should give Goldstein's name to the Committee as having been a Communist. He felt that since Goldstein was Jewish, if he provided the Committee with his name, it might very well feed the already present public anti-Semitism generated by the Rosenbergs, convicted spies, who were also Jewish.

Norman reviewed his options as Comisky finished his question.

35

179 Amboy Street, 1937

THE VIOLIN MAN HADN'T PERFORMED in the '179-185' courtyard for several weeks, and Marsa had started to miss his mini-concerts.

One day, glancing out of her kitchen window, Marsa noticed that the courtyard had not been cleaned out recently, and she thought that perhaps because of its messiness, the Violin Man, offended by the schmutz, dirt, of his concert hall, had decided to stop performing here.

Marsa, distressed by that possibility, took a broom and large paper bag, resolutely going into the courtyard. Halfway through her self-imposed chore, the Violin Man entered as usual from the back lane. Marsa, flustered by his unexpected arrival, self-consciously left before she had completed the task.

By the time she returned to the apartment, the Violin Man had started his playing. As she tucked herself into her hiding place behind the kitchen window, she was struck by the coincidence of the Violin Man arriving just as she was removing the courtyard debris.

The piece that the Violin Man was playing stirred Marsa's memory, immediately recognizing the music from the opera, *Tristan Und Isolde*, which she was very familiar with, having sung in the chorus of a production of it in Berlin that her father had managed.

At the time, neither of them had known that its composer, Wagner, was to become the composer-centerpiece of Hitler's hatred of Jews.

Now listening to the music, she started to hum to herself, accompanying the soaring love melody of the opera's romantic aria, *Liebes Freude*, love's joy, unaware that her singing had become almost full voice.

The Violin Man, hearing Marsa, continued to play, at the same time glancing toward the Schecter's kitchen.

Marsa, noting the Violin Man's glance, and realizing that she had called attention to herself, stopped singing, quickly stepping back even more behind the kitchen curtain. Afraid that the Violin Man had somehow connected her presence earlier in the courtyard with her singing, she decided not to risk being discovered by throwing out her usual penny. Instead, she planned to make it up on his next visit, raising her offering to *two* cents.

On *his* part, the Violin Man, ending the piece with an extra flourish of rapidly plucked strings, wondered why he had selected this particular one from out of his extensive repertoire, insofar as he had never played it before in any courtyard.

As he walked to the next one, he suddenly recalled that he played it for Lula on their first date in Crete, and it had had the effect that he had hoped for... an aphrodisiac leading them to making love under the sparkling stars, on the cool grass beneath a trellis of ripe grapes surrounding them with the scent of romance.

Fragments of memory painfully stabbed at the raw awareness of what he had lost; of what he often attempted to resurrect unsuccessfully in his mind's eye.

36

Brownsville, 1937

MR. GAYNOR, one of the city relief investigators for the Brownsville area, visited his clients once each month in order to obtain the necessary information from people who were applying for financial assistance, and also to verify the status of those who were already on the rolls. In most instances, both the new and old cases were in dire need of the basics: rent, food, clothing. Many families, to struggle out of poverty, would become involved in different exotic activities for additional income.

One of the inventive entrepreneurs, Evelyn Wax's husband, Dave, sprang into action when Gaynor knocked on their door, announcing himself. Dave quickly hid the tobacco and leaf wrappings which he was using to make 'Hand Rolled in Havana Cigars,' as he called to his twin sons, Aaron and Shimmy, "Put the cigar boxes under the sink, fast."

By the time Evelyn, walking slowly down the hallway, opened the apartment door, Dave had time to sit down at the kitchen table, intently bent over a newspaper opened to the employment pages.

There was very little chance of being hired based on his past experience as a barber, people spending very little on how they looked, and many of them saving money by cutting each other's hair. A Negro religious leader, Father Divine, had stepped into the breach in the limited sphere of his ministry, charging only five and ten cents for haircuts, but business was severely limited because potential customers were required, under oath, not to swear, smoke, drink, or use cosmetics.

The sale of Dave's hand-rolled cigars when sold in neighborhood candy stores, provided him with as much money as most legitimate jobs he could possibly get.

By the time Gaynor reached the kitchen, Shimmy and Aaron were in the midst of a checkers game.

Whenever Gaynor was in the Wax's apartment, Evelyn managed to mask her usually acerbic manner, always the picture of genteel civility when she welcomed him.

"A glass of nice hot tea, Mr. Gaynor, brewed especially for our friends?"

Gaynor hesitated for a moment, but decided to take this early morning break before facing the usually difficult day he anticipated. At the meeting with his supervisor, Mr. Rhodes, early that morning he was warned to become more demanding of his clients about their having to report money earned 'under the table.'

As Gaynor sipped his tea, he thought about the fact that although he was very bitter about having been laid off from his job with SABBAR'S ARCHITECTURAL COMPANY for lack of assignments for the designing of new buildings, or even office renovations, he was fortunate in that his brother-in-law was a high ranking officer on the Civil Service Board, and was able to get him hired as an employment statistician, and subsequently had him moved up to his present interviewing position, enabling him to modestly support his family of four.

At the same time that the Wax's were entertaining Gaynor, little old Mrs. Cohen was welcoming Ira as a new employee in *her* unusual enterprise.

When Ira arrived at Cohen's apartment, she was at work with her sprightly, precocious teenaged daughter, Gloria, rolling condoms onto a metal stand shaped like a phallus. A small carton of unrolled condoms was in front of them, and they took out one at a time, placing it on the top of the phallus, tugging it down to the base of the stand, then rolling it up to the top and placing a narrow strip of cardboard around it that served as a container. As Ira watched the procedure, Mrs. Cohen admonished Gloria, "I told you to roll them tighter, my lovely Gloria."

Gloria turned toward Ira's questioning glance, "Remember that," flirtatiously, "dimples."

Mrs. Cohen gently addressed the confused boy. "So Mama's going to let the little boy work?... five cents an hour, good?"

Nervously, Ira stared blankly at the smiling woman as Gloria continued her teasing.

"Yeah, we're going to have some fun, right?"

The question provoked Ira finally to speak. "But not Tuesday or Thursday; I'm studying with the Rabbi for my Bar Mitzvah."

Mrs. Cohen nodded, accepting Ira's schedule, gesturing to him to stand where he could watch what she was doing.

"Today, for an hour first you will watch, please?"

Responding to Ira's apprehensive glance. "It's easy, like eating pumpkin seeds," taking one from her ever present small bag of them, as Gloria took over Ira's instruction.

"First ya take this —" picking up a condom, "you pull it down on this," patting the metal phallus.

"What's," Ira was puzzled, "that thing?"

Gloria smirked, "You don't know?" Mrs. Cohen was more understanding, "Oi, the little boy doesn't know, so he'll learn. Ask your papa what it's for."

Gloria was enjoying Ira's discomfort, "And if he won't tell you," teasing "I will."

Ira attempted to mask his uneasiness, "G'ahead, I know what it is."

Gloria recognized that Ira's response was an empty boast.

"Sure you do… dimples."

Mrs. Cohen joined Gloria in laughing at the flustered boy.

At the same time that Ira was serving his apprenticeship with Mrs. Cohen's improvised prophylactic industry selling condoms to neighborhood drug stores. Gaynor finished his tea with the Wax's, and gathered up his paperwork.

"I'll be back next month and I'm really hoping," focusing his gaze on Dave, "you will be able to find some kind of work."

"And so do I, Mr. Gaynor."

Gaynor nodded approvingly, accompanied by a professional fixed grin of encouragement.

Shimmy and Aaron followed Gaynor to the door, both speaking as one.

"I beat Aaron (Shimmy) in checkers alla time."

Mrs. Wax watched the twins close the door behind Gaynor, and was finally able to express her pent-up anger and frustration at the circumstances that had led the family to this painful edge of poverty.

"Gaynor should only evaporate with his fahkahta, Relief checks!" Turning to Dave, her voice lowered, but commanding, "Give the Schecters a knock… fast!"

A 'knock' was accomplished by Dave picking up the hammer that was always conveniently nearby, and using it to tap on the steam radiator in the living room. The particular 'knock' for the Schecters was a pre-arranged code of three taps, then a brief moment, followed by another tap.

The tapping sounds from Apartment 2's living room radiator alerted Marsa to Gaynor's presence in '179.' Springing into action, by the time Mrs. Wax had hurried down the stairs to the ground floor and stood in front of apartment 2's door, Marsa had managed to accomplish most of the necessary preparations for Gaynor's anticipated visit.

Marsa had taken the small tabletop Philco radio and put it into the small closet under the sink. This was the first thing that Marsa would always do, anticipating Gaynor's monthly visit.

Although Marsa resented having to hide the radio, it was necessary because on Gaynor's first visit he had noted that the family had no radio, the one they owned when living in East Flatbush having been broken in the move to

Brownsville. Since then, Norman had been able to buy a used one for two dollars, but he knew that if Gaynor learned of his spending money from the family allowance, on a 'luxury,' it could possibly affect their future allotment.

Marsa took out of the icebox the remains of the meat that Bennie the Butch had given Norman. Although Marsa knew that Gaynor and the city would not begrudge them some hamburger for dinner, she recalled that the three lamb chops that her father-in-law had given them were in the icebox the day Gaynor had come last visit, so now, not to appear too 'affluent,' Marsa put the package of meat on a plate, covered it with another plate and put it in the sink, running cold water over it. Gaynor would believe, Marsa thought, that she was preparing to wash the dishes.

Mrs. Wax, vigorously knocking on apartment 2's door, urgently called out.

"Mahk-Schnell, Marsa!"

As Marsa reached to open the door, her other hand suddenly went to her throat, nauseousness welling up.

Mrs. Wax, stepping into the apartment, aware of Marsa's pregnancy, immediately recognized Marsa's discomfort as being the usual early stages of her 'condition,' put her arm comfortingly around her friend's shoulder.

"Sit down on the couch here, sweetheart," clucking her sincere sympathy, "Oiy, a glass of tea will make the stomach better."

Marsa shrugged off the help. "In a minute, it's gone, Evelyn."

"That's right, honey, with the twins every morning nothing helped."

Glancing around the apartment, Mrs. Wax cautioned, "You need some help for Gaynor to get ready?"

"I already took care, Evelyn."

Over time, Evelyn, as many other tenants in '179,' had become familiar with the sound of Gaynor's leather heels on the floor tiles as he walked through the building and now, hearing him coming down the last flight of stairs, she murmured under her breath to Marsa, "He should only evaporate already with his papers."

Stepping out into the hallway, Mrs. Wax could see Gaynor approaching as she spoke gently to Marsa, "You sure I shouldn't come in a minute?"

Marsa, although still feeling sick, shook her head carefully, "Maybe he'll be quick this time."

Mrs. Wax's wry response was a classic neighborhood joke, "Like an Arab running from a Brownsville Jew!"

Marsa's appreciative chuckle was matched by Mrs. Wax's; the two women's deep feelings of warmth toward each other, a palpable bond of friendship.

Gaynor smiled to himself as he saw Mrs. Wax, sensing from experience that she had alerted Marsa about his presence in the building.

Marsa, sitting down with Gaynor at the kitchen table managed, in spite of her continued sick feeling, to answer the questions regarding the family's continued reliance on their monthly relief check.

Gaynor was concerned that Norman was not at home for the review of the Schecter claim, since it was necessary to corroborate the fact that he was not working. Marsa assured Gaynor that Norman was out looking for a job.

"Good, Mrs. Schecter; what are the chances of the School Board rehiring him?"

"It's a 'maybe'."

"Well, remember, if he substitutes for even one day, you have to report whatever income he makes."

"Believe me, Mr. Gaynor, being on relief is not a Mitzvah." Marsa, realizing that Gaynor was a 'goy,' translated her Yiddish into English, "good deed."

Gaynor nodded his understanding as he glanced impatiently at his watch.

"I have to go in a minute, so I won't be able to check," his pen poised threateningly over his official papers, "this space for Mr. Schecter's presence here today, and it's not good if it happens again, Mrs. Schecter."

"Don't worry your head, he'll be here."

"Very good, because my supervisor doesn't like it if the husband isn't home when we visit."

Gaynor was half out of the door as Norman entered.

"Sorry I'm late, Mr. Gaynor."

As Gaynor went by Norman, he spoke to him over his shoulder, "I reminded your wife about the regulations."

"I was out looking for a job."

Tumbling through Norman's memory were the abrasive events of the day; his conflicted feelings about Alan's arson plan; his awareness of his hypocrisy as measured against Ira's redemptive behavior, drying his wet newspapers.

Although he felt that Gaynor's manner was respectful, he nonetheless felt extremely depressed over the lack of dignity that he and his family were forced to suffer.

On Marsa's part, anger and bitterness stoked her despair-choking, desperate life.

By the time Gaynor had left, she had firmly decided what she would have to do… what she would definitely have to do… whatever the results might be because of what she certainly had to do.

37

NORMAN AND MARSA, dressed in some of their best clothes, spent several minutes convincing Ira that he would have to put on his one good pair of knickers because they were all going over to Bennie the Butch and his wife Yetta's apartment for their weekly dinner visit.

When they all arrived at the elder Schecter's apartment, they were surprised to see that Norman's sister, Elaine, and her husband had also arrived for Yetta's boiled-chicken dinner.

Norman had not seen his sister and her husband, Irving, since earlier in the year when he had participated in the memorial for Irving's sister, Annie, who had just died of stomach cancer.

During the week of ritualistic grieving, 'sitting shiva,' members of the family, along with close friends of Annie, met at Irving and Elaine's apartment, consoling one another, reminiscing about the 'departed,' and nibbling at the light buffet fare provided by the hosts.

Irving, being an orthodox Jew, sat on a wooden box for the proscribed seven days of 'shiva.'

Although Norman had never really liked Irving, having observed over the years his extremely controlling, abusive behavior with Elaine, demanding that her strong desire to have children be shunted aside for Irving's need to be the center of the family's universe.

One of the varied enterprises that he attempted was a bake shop which prominently featured the introduction of the first bread-slicing machine in Brownsville, U BUY WE SLICE. The novelty failed when the neighborhood grocers lowered their prices of the well-known pre-packaged WONDERBREAD, SILVERCUP, and other established name-brands. There was also the model airplane shop which quickly nose-dived for want of the public's willingness to occupy itself with trivial games, the business collapsing as suddenly as his haberdashery store quickly shuttered for lack of enough customers to pay even the second month's rent.

In spite of Norman's dislike of Irving's manner and personality, he granted him the fact that he was trying to make a dollar. After all, Norman thought, was he himself not in the same predicament, in pursuit of some way to earn money? However, he reasoned that because he spent much of his energy with Union activities, and not having much free time to find work, he found no contradiction with his placing his own behavior on a higher level than his brother-in-law.

When he saw Irving, he became angry at the memory of how his brother-in-law had acted toward Elaine in the midst of 'sitting shiva.'

"Elaine," Irving had curtly said, "I told you five times to make sure you bought some prune Danish for today."

"They ran out of them at Ebingers."

"Well, it was stupid for you not to go to another bakery."

Although Norman was upset at how Irving spoke to his sister, out of respect for his grieving, he said nothing. Since that time, Norman had thought of calling Irving and telling him about his strong negative feelings about his behavior toward Elaine; however he had decided not to waste a nickel on the phone call. Reconsidering it however, Norman thought that the larger reason for his not making the call was because Irving had somehow managed to afford getting a phone installed, and Norman had to admit to himself that he was envious, and didn't want to chance Irving making some slighting remark about his not having a phone.

What Norman was unable to really admit to himself was that although he was able to be outspoken about issues, like his union activities, he often felt uncomfortable about expressing his personal feelings.

38

THERE WAS AN ON-GOING, good-natured criticism of the culinary ability of Bennie's wife, Yetta.

As the family guests sat down expectantly for dinner, the comments usually were put into gear by Bennie.

"So, will somebody please tell me how my lovely wife, with lovely dimples, can take a first-class chicken, and cook it in a lovely pot, and make it taste like mein bubbas tahm!"

Responding to Ira's quizzical look, Bennie translated from the Yiddish: "It tastes like my grandmother."

Ira was puzzled by how a boiled chicken could taste like his grandmother, but as he had grown up, he learned that the richness of many Yiddish expressions carried multiple meanings, as did the colorful, extravagant 'curses' hurled at startled victims.

One such vivid example was when someone wanted to wish the worst for a person who they were at odds with: "Du zuhl vahksen vie a tzbila mit kup in dred, und fees auch himmel!"

Translation: "You should grow like an onion, head in hell, feet pointed to the sky!"

This menacing malediction was topped by the rejoinder of ultimate damnation: "Du zuhl vahksen vie a kartuflin, gahns in dred!" translated into "*You* should grow like a potato, *completely* in hell!"

Yetta placed another piece of chicken next to the half-finished one on Ira's plate.

"Ess, eat, mein keend. If you don't, your brain gets smaller!"

Yetta was the mother of all. All were her children, her children were all. All.

Ira, swallowing a piece of the bland-boiled chicken, glanced up at Norman dutifully chewing his piece, "Hey, Pop, tastes good huh?"

Norman, in mock amazement, exclaimed, "My own son," making certain that Yetta was out of earshot, "...a traitor."

Yetta, preparing the dessert of oatmeal cookies which were invariably over-baked almost to a burnt crisp, interpreted the exchange between Norman and his son to be one of genuine enjoyment of her meal.

"Ess, ess, mein boychiks," nodding toward Irving, including him in the invitation even though it gave her a 'sour taste in my mouth,' the way he 'never looked with kind eyes' at Elaine. Out of loyalty to her daughter, she 'bit her lip,' as she once told Norman, whenever she had to speak to her fahkahta son-in-law.

Ira suddenly sneezed, the sound morphing into Yetta's cataclysmic "Oiy!"

As all eyes turned to her, she segued the sound of dread into a foreboding prediction, "Mein grandson's got maybe pneumonia!"

Bennie quickly shook off Yetta's pronouncement of impending doom.

"It's not pneumonia; maybe he's giving a big sneeze because his body is growing so fast… one inch since last week!"

Although Yetta was conditioned to her husband's sometimes 'meshuga,' crazy ways, she was distressed by his ignoring her frightened warning. Bennie shrugged away Yetta's concern, glancing at the others for confirmation, his tone challenging them to disagree, "Bennie the Butch says Ira grew a whole inch!"

Yetta, in the matter-of-fact tone of royalty aware of its power, attempted to close the door on the discussion, "Not a smidgen inch my *lovely* husband."

Bennie, very certain about his estimate of Ira's growth, loudly reaffirmed his observation, "An absolute inch."

Very upset by her husband's insistent declaration, Yetta quickly corrected him again, "I got my own two eyes, and he's saying to me… an inch."

Bennie turned toward Ira, appealing for his tie-breaking vote, "Please tell the stubborn mule, your lovely grandmother… did you grow an inch?"

Having been drawn into similar polarized discussions in the past between his grandparents, Ira had acquired a statesmanship that would deal with such situations. He had learned a conciliatory approach during a stand-off between Bennie and Yetta as to the correct pronunciation of the Yiddish words for bread and butter.

Yetta, born and raised in the Galicia area of Poland and the Russian Ukraine, pronounced the word for bread… 'Broat.'

Bennie, coming from a more remote area of Russia, pronounced the Yiddish word for bread… 'Bright.'

As for the word butter, Yetta's version was 'pooter'; Bennie's was 'pitter.'

And so, bread and butter was either 'broat' and 'pooter' served up by Yetta, or 'bright' smeared with the 'pitter' of Bennie.

Both grandparents fought over which of them would control Ira's diction. Caught in the middle of this war of words, Ira recognized that his position in this struggle was a delicate and pivotal one, so he cleverly solved the problem: For the benefit of his grandfather, by saying 'bright' he pleased Bennie, dismaying Yetta; but by saying 'pooter' he was able to satisfy his grandmother. In this way, 'bread and butter' was split between the Galicians of Yetta's area of Europe and Bennie's section of Russia.

Ira managed in this way to make both his grandparents happy in the knowledge that each of them could claim part ownership and control of Ira's language and soul.

Now faced with the dispute over his height, Ira was ready to employ his 'bread and butter' experience as Bennie anxiously asked again, "So, an answer, please, about one inch higher, for you?"

"Well, grandpa —"

"So tell," Bennie interrupted, gesturing dismissively toward Yetta, "The Galiciana, that it's an inch, yes?"

Ira rushed through his answer, "maybe an inch."

Bennie, turning toward Yetta, barked his triumph, "See, my dollink?"

Glancing toward Ira, Yetta started to frown, but Ira quickly addressed her agitation, "And maybe it wasn't."

It was Yetta's turn to express *her* victory to Bennie.

"So, smart guy?"

"First," Bennie stood his ground, "he said an inch."

"Aha! But 'second'?"

Ira had learned his lesson well from the 'broat' and 'bright' experience, and all the future disagreements would employ that awareness of pleasing both of them. As a result, in his adult life, he would often find himself mediating conflicts in this manner, reconciling those in opposition with each other.

He would often pay the price of finding himself on the fence, both parties sometimes sniping at him. Whenever that happened, Ira would ease his pain with the pride of having 'done the right thing.'

~

During the 'bread and butter' discussion being held in the small dining room, Norman, Marsa, Elaine, and Irving had adjourned to the living room. The spare furnishings featured two handmade wooden chairs which Bennie had been given by one of his customers, Leon Sachs, who had owed him money for a few weeks of meat orders that he had been unable to pay for.

"Bennie," Leon had proudly said, "I made these chairs from a picture."

"A man makes pretty chairs like this from a picture?"

"My daughter, Irma, was studying in a history book."

"So?"

"I'm telling you, Bennie, I'm telling."

"So tell!"

"You never heard," Leon smugly asked, "from a Queen Anne chair?"

"From an *electric* chair, you should pardon the expression, I heard."

"Bennie the Butch, you know from lamb chops, but what else, may I ask?"

"So tell me 'what else' my friend."

"The picture was about a special chair from walnut."

Bennie, rubbing his hand along the rough pine arm of the chair, became an expert on the spot.

"This wood, my smart friend, Leon, is not walnut."

Now, as Irving and Elaine sat comfortably on the couch, Norman and Marsa squeezed into the crudely constructed replicas of Queen Anne chairs.

"So, Norman," Irving said in his usual pseudo-friendly manner, "here we are in the bosom of the family."

Norman questioned to himself Irving's sincerity. Based on Norman knowing that his father had once lent Irving seventy-five dollars for the bread-slicer enterprise, he anticipated that Irving's social visit would lead to a request for money for a new project.

Norman and Marsa had had several arguments about Bennie financially helping Elaine's family in the past, but giving Norman only a few pounds of hamburger meat once in awhile. Explaining his view on why his father appeared to slight him in favor of his sister, Norman, affectionately tolerant of Bennie's behavior, told Marsa that it was because underneath all his differences with his father, Bennie really respected him; that his father thought that though Norman's family was going through a great deal of financial and union problems, he would eventually solve them on his own.

Marsa would have none of Norman's rationale, claiming that Bennie wasn't smart enough to figure that out for himself. Norman, over the years, had come to realize that because of Marsa's extremely good education in Russia and Germany, she had often revealed a snobbishness toward the less educated, as Bennie was.

Later in the evening, when Irving took the opportunity to present his 'real killer idea' to Bennie, his plan was quickly shot down.

"Tell me," Bennie demanded, "how can a grown man think that people would spend twenty-five cents—"

"Maybe," Irving desperately interrupted, "I can charge less... maybe fifteen, twenty."

"Even a single dime... who would pay to play this midget golf?"

"*Miniature* golf, Bennie."

"Whatever... an investment... money I don't have... so I give you my best wishes for your midget golf, and that's all."

"Just listen to me, Bennie."

"Listen to me. A man who plays golf in the rain... putts."

Bennie laughed, repeating the joke, 'putts' becoming underlined with the Yiddish play on the word 'putz'... "penis."

~

Harvey Flanders, a motorman on the Brooklyn Surface Transit, always tried hard not to get assigned to car unit 2738 on the Ralph-Rockaway Avenue trolley line. The reason he avoided this run was because the connecting rod extending from the top of 2738 had a construction peculiarity which resulted in it often making faulty contact with the electric cable running above it, sometimes jumping off it, stopping the current, causing the trolley to stop. Flanders would be forced to get off the trolley and maneuver the rod back into place in order to start the electrical flow again. Flanders would hurry back into the car, grabbing the throttle, hoping that the rod would stay in place as the car accelerated. These occurrences would disrupt the running schedule, and the added hazard of bad weather would cause

Flanders to have to stand in the rain and snow while trying to correct the rod and cable connection.

Norman, Marsa, and Ira had boarded 2738 at Liberty Avenue, a few blocks walk from Bennie and Yetta's apartment. The car had had no cable derailment this evening, but as soon as the Schecters had seated themselves, the connector rod had slipped, Flanders exiting the car, calling over his shoulder toward the passengers, reassuring them.

"Flanders will fix."

Glancing around the car, Marsa saw Finky, who was sitting alone on a rear seat, and waved toward her but Norman did not try to get her attention, having had a disturbing conversation with her several days before.

He felt that this was an instance when he should not become involved in somebody else's troubles. Later on, after certain dramatic events that followed, he had regretfully to admit to himself that he had lacked sufficient compassion for Finky in a time of need. Earlier in the week, he had been leaving '179' when Finky, who had apparently waited for him, approached him.

"Mr. Schecter, can I please talk to you for a minute?"

"Sure, Mrs. Finklestein."

"It's about me n'Fred."

"Oh," Norman said non-commitedly.

"It's okay, Mr. Schecter, I think a lot of people know about him 'n me."

"It's none of my business."

"Well, maybe you're the only one around here who doesn't think I should be flushed down the sewer. Even my own father says—," Finky interrupted herself. "Anyway, I got this legal problem."

"Sorry, Mrs. Finklestein, I'm not a lawyer."

"Sure, but I know you're a smart man."

Although Norman felt sympathetic toward Finky, he thought it necessary to be careful, since he had met Charlie once, and immediately perceived him to be a dangerous person even before he was convicted of assault and sent to prison.

Oleshe's candy store was the center of the cultural, business, and ethical universe of Amboy Street. Here fortunes were made and lost; reputations shaped and shattered; relationships deepened and severed; goals established, compromised; friendships nurtured and ended; dreams and nightmares taking turns; all blending into, and spilling out of, a 200-square foot space. Oleshe's was a vibrant planet, spinning in an orbit sufficient unto itself.

Its connection to the rest of the world was the two payphones in the rear of the store, these lines of communication essential to conducting the affairs of Amboy Street.

Insofar as most of the Brownsville population was not able to afford a private phone, Oleshe's provided the only source of interaction with the outside world.

For the price of a three-cent stamp you could reach anyone in the country, but for a nickel, you could speak to anyone in New York and its environs.

And for a nickel, someone, somewhere, could reach a citizen of Amboy Street.

Mr. or Mrs. Oleshe would answer the phone, and invariably, it was someone calling one of the tenants in the tenements. On the street there were always a few boys 'hanging around,' discussing the merits of different professional athletes: was the New York Yankees' Joe DiMaggio a better outfielder than the Brooklyn Dodgers' Ducky Medwick?; was Johnny Van Demeer the best all-time pitcher because he had pitched two consecutive 'no-hitters'?; was the Knicks' basketball team the best in the east?

All discussions would stop when one of the Oleshes called out to the group: "Who wants to call Rosenspan, apartment 6, '185'?" or "Lensky, '179'?" Many of the people to be called to the phone had a known history, a two-cent tipper, or three, and in the case of Lensky, a sure five-cent tip, the catalogue of the different regular tenants and their tipping habits were well known by the boys, and there were often arguments as to which of them first agreed to call the tenant, especially for Lensky or any of the other big tippers. The tenants who were known to tip only a penny or two sometimes got a reluctant volunteer, and in several instances, the Oleshes had to threaten the group with withholding future 5 cent tipper calls if they weren't willing to call the 'cheapskate' tenants. Notwithstanding the pressure, sometimes there was nobody willing to do the job, and the Oleshes were forced to tell the caller that they weren't able to connect them with the one they hoped to speak to. In the rare instance when the caller pleaded an emergency need to speak to the tenant, if both the Oleshes were working in the store at the same time, one of them would hurry to the tenant to call them to the phone.

Norman had stopped by to purchase a newspaper just as Oleshe shouted out to the group loitering outside.

"Hey, any kid wants to go call Finklestein in '179'?"

Finky was known to usually tip 3 cents, maybe a nickel.

Bobbie Steiner quickly spoke up.

"I'll go, Mr. Oleshe."

Norman idly watched him hurry toward '179,' just as a man which Norman was later to learn was Finky's husband, Charlie Finklestein, grabbed Bobbie Steiner as he went by.

"Who you calling?"

"Somebody in '179.'"

"Yeah, who?"

"Somebody."

"You little shit, who?"

Bobbie hesitated, but seeing the harsh, threatening look on Charlie's face, he quickly supplied the information.

"Finklestein."

"Forget it."

"But I told Oleshe. I—"

"*I'll* answer the fucking phone."

Norman watched as Bobbie, frightened, went back, downcast, to join his friends.

Charlie, resolute, stalked past Norman, purposely using his shoulder to brush Norman back, glancing challengingly at him.

~

Earlier, talking to Norman in front of '179,' Finky had continued to try to enlist his help in dealing with Charlie.

"I just got this letter today." Smiling ruefully, Finky added, "Freddie delivered it." Her tone darkened, "Charlie wrote he's getting out next week, and I'm really afraid of him."

"How so, Mrs. Finklestein?"

Finky, pointing at her nose, started to tear up as she spoke, "He broke it twice."

Norman, glancing at her nose, which was misshapen, gently responded, "I'm really sorry about that."

"Thanks, Norman."

"Well, maybe you should tell the police about Charlie."

"If I did, he'd kill me. I'm really worried, Norman, when he gets here."

"Maybe the police can tell him not to come."

"He won't listen."

"Well, there's some kind of law, I think, that can order him not to bother you."

"That won't stop Charlie. I'm really frightened."

Notwithstanding her stress, she smiled warmly at Norman.

"Y'know, you're almost as nice as Freddie."

~

Flanders, having corrected the defective connection with the electrical cable, re-entered the trolley, announcing, "Flanders fixed."

As Flanders quickly turned the throttle up, Ira coughed, alerting his mother into action.

"A glass of hot tea for when we get home, my son, mein zindel."

Turning to Norman accusingly, "And if maybe we had a little honey to put in—"

Just the week before they had run out of the small bottle of honey that she had carefully rationed out through the hard winter coughs and sniffles. Now she reached up to pull the cord signaling the motorman to stop the trolley for passengers wanting to get off.

Surprised, Norman glanced out of the window.

"Was it mom's chicken or the burnt cookies that," he teasingly inquired, "confused you? This is not our stop, Marsa."

Marsa gently took Ira's hand.

"We're getting off here."

"But, Mom—"

"Come!"

Norman, concerned, asked, "Marsa, what's the matter?"

"My cousin Sarah is this stop. Some good cough syrup she's got."

"Let's go home, Marsa; I'll pick up some medicine at Gerson's Drugs."

"They're already closed."

The trolley had stopped. Taking Ira's reluctant hand, Marsa waited impatiently for the exit door to open as Norman protested, "Wait a minute, Marsa."

Marsa led Ira off the trolley, calling back to Norman, "I'll be home later."

39

THE VIOLIN MAN WAS VERY CONFUSED. At first it was only the problem of explaining to Norman that he wanted to be called George Dakis, and not Manos Pulyakis.

Now, Dakis was not too sure that he had completely understood the offer that Norman had made to him. The language problem made it difficult for them to communicate with each other, but Norman patiently explained that he would pay him a dollar-fifty if he would play his violin during the party that would follow Ira's upcoming Bar Mitzvah. Dakis was not clear about which tunes he should play besides the one that Norman asked for… Puccini's 'O

Mio Babbino Caro' which he knew very well. When he finally understood that the Bar Mitzvah was a happy celebration of Ira's 13th birthday, he decided that he would play some light Mozart tunes and the main theme from the Scottish Fantasy violin concerto because Dakis, knowing that Norman was Jewish, thought that he would like the fact that he would be playing music of the Jew composer, Bruch.

He now referred to himself as George Dakis, but rented a postal box under the name of Manos Pulyakis.

Occasionally, he would receive a letter from the symphony maestro Ignotis who would write him news about the different musician friends that Manos had known when he lived in Athens.

Answering a letter that he had written to his lover, Lula, in Heraklion, she reassured him of her undying love which would see them through his present problem with the law. Several letters would be exchanged, both of them looking forward to the time when they would again be able to be together. Manos had written asking her, if he managed to save enough money for her to travel to New York, would she come? At first she was excited by that possibility but after awhile, Manos started to sense a growing distance in her feelings, and when her letters became sparser with a greater time lapse between them, a chill started through his being, its intensity growing until there was a moment when he felt his mind freezing in his skull, the bones becoming brittle, ready to break under the slightest breeze, the slightest puff of air. Finally, brilliantly lit shards of thought bombarded his sensibilities, leaving him desperately flailing at the unkind air in order somehow to maintain his mind's balance… just barely.

He decided to write to his sister, Aglya, telling her that he had met a man here in New York, named George Dakis, and would she be interested in writing to him? Some time later, he received a letter from his sister Christina who had married the old wine merchant Kazanotzakis. She told Manos that Aglya had shown his letter to her, and they had considered it a cruel joke that he was playing, writing about this alive George Dakis. The two sisters had become drunk on several glasses of Retsina, and the next morning, a fisherman had found Aglya's body on the rocks where she had jumped from the place where their mother had fallen to her death years before.

Shortly after, Christina had given birth to her first born, a daughter she had named Aglya.

In her long letter, Christina said that because Manos was her older brother she had to respect him; that when he died, she would light a candle for him at the church, but until then she did not want to ever hear from him again.

He wrote Lula about his sister's death, and two months later, he received an answer.

"I have long known about the tragedy of Aglya's death. It was very, very sad. I offer condolences from my heart.

I hope you are well.

Fond regards,

Lula"

Enclosed with the envelope was a formal invitation to her marriage to Kazanotzakis's son which had been held a month earlier.

40

FROM THE CORNER where Flander's trolley stopped in order to drop off Norman and Finky, it was only a short walk to Amboy Street along Sutter Avenue with its small grocery, tailor, and barber shops. A modest sized fruit and vegetable stall shared a common wall with a radio repair store, sandwiched between the tenements pressing down on them fighting for the limited space.

When Finky asked Norman about Marsa and Ira getting off at the earlier stop, he explained, pleased that it averted Finky from again talking about Charlie. Instead, she spoke about the fact that she had just finished some overtime hours at GORDON'S APPAREL, sewing buttons on snow suits being readied for the winter season. The extra money would be used to buy a nice colorful dirndl dress she had seen on sale in an UNDER NEW MANAGEMENT store on busy Pitkin Avenue. She thought Freddie would really like her in it, and because their affection had quickly grown into a loving concern for each other, the overtime hours were very welcome, since she didn't want Freddie to think that she loved him only because she needed the help of his postman's steady salary to pay her bills.

Both Norman and Finky walked silently the rest of the way, the early evening shadow's cloaking the tired streets.

Although Norman was thinking about union problems and not counting on being rehired as a teacher in the near future, he was able at the same time to sense Finky's growing agitation as they neared Amboy Street.

She hurried ahead of him, turning the corner to glance apprehensively down the street, as if anticipating somebody or something bad would be waiting there. And it was... Charlie! Finky, immediately recognizing him anxiously standing in front of '179,' quickly put her hand behind her, signaling Norman to stop, feeling it would be unwise for him to accompany her as she walked toward Charlie. She was cautious because she was very aware that he was jealous of any man he saw interacting with her in any way, innocent as it might be.

Charlie, in his late 30s, was wearing an ill-fitting, inexpensive prison-issue suit of an indeterminate color.

Seeing Finky slowly, reluctantly walking toward him, he motioned her to hurry up. Agitated because she wasn't moving fast enough for him, he hurried toward her causing her to stop, frightened at his menacing look as he spoke, his voice strident with anger.

"Why the hell you coming home so late?"

"I was working."

Charlie sneered his response, "Bullshit makes the flowers grow."

"I'm telling you Charlie—"

"Aren't you glad to see me?"

"Well... yeah... I—"

As he roughly put his arms around her, Finky's stiffening body caused him to tense in anger.

Grabbing her arm, Charlie started toward '179' just as Norman walked down the street toward them. Acting casual, he gestured toward Finky.

"Good evening, Mrs. Finklestein."

As Norman approached them, Charlie glared his demand.

"Who the hell are you, Mister?"

Attempting to defuse the charged moment, Norman pretended an ease he certainly did not feel, answering nonchalantly.

"Schecter, apartment two."

"Hey," Charlie stopped him, "I'm Finklestein, apartment twelve."

"Hi," Norman smiled, "see ya," he said lightly as he went into '179.'

In apartment two, Norman put the light on as soon as he closed the door, his mind jumbled by what happened with

Marsa during the evening, and now the threateningly volatile incident with Charlie.

The sound of the raised voices of Charlie and Finky reached him as they walked down the hallway, Charlie's dark tone edged with anger.

"This is a real shit welcome home you're handing me."

Finky attempted to soothe him.

"No, Charlie, I'm really happy you're here."

Charlie, in a sardonic falsetto voice, mimicked her, "No Charlie, I'm really happy you're here."

As Finky started up the stairs, Charlie hungrily stared at her full body.

Norman put a kettle with water on the gas range, lit it and got a tea bag from a container on the kitchen table. As the water started to boil, Charlie's angry voice drifted in from the courtyard.

The *Daily News* that he hadn't finished reading that morning was still on the table, opened to the special feature story describing the tragic result of the strike between the Steel Workers Organizing Committee and Republic Steel in Chicago. The police had attacked the unarmed crowd of men and women, killing 10 people and wounding 80 in what became known as the Memorial Day Massacre. Although this sad event was in itself an obscene moment in the history of labor's struggle for parity, the fact was that after the sacrifice made by these protesters, the employees were finally forced to go back to work without Union recognition or other gains:

Blood soaked the ground; immolation with no benefits except, Norman hopefully thought, seeds had been planted for future change.

As Norman poured the boiling water into a glass with the tea bag in it, his mind leaped back in time to when his father had explained to him why tea should be drunk *only* in a glass.

"My father," Bennie had said reverentially, "God bless the good man, would be sick in his stomach if his eyes saw like my eyes saw in the newspaper, a picture of this Teddy Roosevelt president, drinking tea from a cup!"

He continued to shore up his argument, "my father, God bless the good man, told me that tea *tastes* like tea, *only* in a glass."

A very impressionable nine year old, Norman had accepted his father's pronouncement as an absolute truth, and over the years, he would often apply that term, as to a truism that his English teacher had solemnly imparted to the class, "People who read books are smarter than people who don't read"... an absolute truth! Later, he rejected that conclusion after he had read in a *Reader's Digest* article on LIVING BETTER, another 'absolute truth': "Sweeping generalizations tend to be flawed in the particulars." Applying *that* 'absolute truth' canceled out the 'reading books makes one smarter' generalization, making it no longer a viable one.

Tracking his convoluted reasoning, Norman was amused at his conflicted feelings about the wheels within wheels logic. Was this, he wondered, the rationale of a superior, inquisitive mind, or simply the wooly logic of a slightly demented one? He smiled to himself over his self-deprecating humor.

Charlie's loud voice ricocheted angrily off the courtyard walls, its sound floating through Norman's kitchen window, opened in order to hopefully draw in any breeze that managed to make its fetid way past the garbage cans. Charlie's words were firmly embedded in a harsh tone... sentences heard, clearly abusive.

"You bitch... who you giving it to?"

A neighbor's voice finally called out in protest. "Shut up there, will ya?"

Charlie stopped his tirade against Finky long enough to respond. "Kiss my rosie-red ass!"

"Fuck off!" the neighbor shot back.

Charlie was livid. "If I find out where you live, I'll tear you another asshole!"

The neighbor's wife, clattering some dinner dishes, shared the battle against Charlie. "We're trying to eat supper, so just shut up, okay?"

Charlie, his main concern of discovering if Finky had been unfaithful while he was in prison, turned back to her. "C'mon, who's been shtupping you?"

Norman glanced up toward where he knew Finky's apartment fronted on the courtyard as he sipped his tea and continued to read the newspaper.

Hearing Finky scream in pain, Norman glanced up toward the window again. As Finky desperately threw it open, Charlie grabbed her arm, dragging her back into the room.

"Charlie, please don't..."

"Get in the bed!"

Norman could hear someone knocking at Finky's apartment door. Charlie, releasing Finky's arm, hurried to the door, flinging it open, confronting Mrs. Wax, standing there, her face flushed in excitement, spitting out her demand.

"Enough already!"

"Stick your head in the shit bowl!"

Mrs. Wax, undaunted, raised her body up to its full five feet, pointing a rigid finger at Charlie.

"You... evaporate!"

She kept that stance for a moment, even after Charlie had slammed the door in her face.

Norman, concerned about Finky's plight, rushed to the front of the building, pushing open the heavy iron door, hurrying out toward Oleshe's candy store.

Norman, his adrenaline pumping on high, his mind racing in anxiety, flashed on his gut-wrenching first moments in combat in France, even as he searched quickly through his pocket change to get a nickel for his phone call to the police.

As Norman hurried up the stairway of '179,' Mrs. Wax was quickly coming out of her apartment, starting to speak as soon as she saw him.

"You heard the lunatic?"

"I called the police, Evelyn."

"A lot good they do."

As Norman started up the stairs to the next floor, he motioned to Mrs. Wax to follow him.

"Maybe we can help her, Evelyn."

"He's an animal... he should only evaporate!"

Norman hesitated for a moment as he stood facing Finky's apartment door, Mrs. Wax apprehensively standing behind him.

Norman's knock on the door was almost apologetic, his voice tentative.

"Finky?"

When there was no answer, Norman knocked again, calling urgently this time.

"Finky?"

Norman could hear the creaking hallway floor as Finky scurried quickly toward the door.

Identifying the light tread as being Finky's, Norman spoke comfortingly through the door.

"You all right, Finky?"

"It's okay, Normie."

"You sure?"

Charlie's heavy footsteps hurrying down the hallway alerted Norman that it was not okay. Norman, still very concerned, repeated his question.

"You sure, Finky?"

"I'm fine, Normie; I'm fine."

Charlie's rasping tone overrode Finky's assurance.

"That one of the guys shtupping you?"

"Stop it, Charlie!"

"Stop *this*," Charlie snarled, "you cunt!" slapping Finky across her face, her cry of pain only whetting his appetite for more violence. He raised his hand to strike again.

"Please Charlie," Finky pleaded, "that's enough."

"Is it enough Finky?" Charlie sardonically asked. "Is that enough?"

Norman tried again, calling out, "Don't hurt her, Charlie."

"Fuck off, buster!"

"He's like an ape, Normie," Mrs. Wax, frightened, offered.

Hearing scuffling on the other side of Finky's door, mixed with her cries of protest, Norman, in anger and frustration, turned away, hurrying down the stairway. Rushing into his apartment, he went directly to Ira's room grabbing his baseball bat, and moving as fast as he could, left the house taking two steps at a time going down the stairway to the courtyard, and then to the rear of the building. Leaping up to the lower rung of the fire-escape ladder, he climbed up, stopping at Finky's landing. Peering through the window of her apartment, he caught a glimpse of Charlie and Finky, who were now sitting at the kitchen table. Speaking in angry animation, Charlie suddenly reached across the table, slapping Finky. Yelping in pain, Finky rose, trying to get away from Charlie who grabbed her arm, roughly spinning her around, raising his hand to strike her again as Norman rapped his bat against the window. Startled, Charlie glanced in the direction of the sound as Norman struck the window again. Charlie, throwing Finky against the wall, snatched a long kitchen knife, leaping at Finky, holding it threateningly against her throat. Norman held his arms up, conciliatory, just as a police car, siren wailing, sped down Amboy Street, stopping at '179.' Charlie, shoving Finky away from him, threw the knife back into the drawer. Turning back to Finky, he warned, "Keep your fuckin' mouth shut!"

Norman, reassured of Finky's safety, started back down the fire-escape.

In front of '179,' Mrs. Wax and other neighbors milled around as two policemen entered the building. Norman, watching the small crowd grow larger with other people on the block curious for information about the police coming to Amboy Street, found himself thinking of another happier gathering one long-ago summertime when a group of people on Brooklyn's Coney Island Beach were watching a red-bearded man sculpting a body out of the sand. He industriously was shaping a male upper torso that magically seemed to take on life, flowing phoenix-like out of the dirty white grains.

Water was needed in order to moisten the dry, hot sand enough to mold it. In hurried trips to the edge of the beach, where the once high Atlantic waves finished their long journey across the ocean, gently lapping their way through sea shells, rotting seaweed, ice-cream wrappers and the occasional used condom, the red-bearded man fetched some of the brackish ocean, in a small children's pail.

At a critical moment, when the sun threatened to dry out his attempts to sculpt the body's stomach muscles, Norman had volunteered to fill the pail for him, rushing back with the precious water, feeling as if he was delivering life-saving serum to a dying child in some remote northern part of the Canadian wilderness.

The man nodded his gratitude, applied the finishing touches and stood up to appraise his work. Norman, awed by the results, thought it almost as good as any of the real sculpture he had seen at the Brooklyn Museum. Yet, even though it was clearly shaped by talented hands, the bearded man was only partially satisfied. Sitting down a few feet away, he appeared to welcome the rapidly rising high-tide that soon would wash away his creation and its flaws.

The first ripple of wave reached the sculpture. As soon as the sand started to dissolve, the man rose abruptly, striding away without a word.

At first, Norman had puzzled at the man's turning away from his intense handiwork. Later, reconsidering Red Beard's behavior, the realization formed that quality was paramount to existence for its own sake.

Norman sat in his kitchen while the police checked Finky's apartment to see that she was all right. He had done what he could, and there was nothing else to be done but wait and try to rest.

He thought again of Coney Island when he and Alan, celebrating their return from France, went swimming and showed off the different calisthenics they had learned from the *Charles Atlas: I Was a 97 Pound Weakling* body conditioning manual. They had chipped in, mailing two dollars for the training program, both of them having worked long hours on their Good Humor push wagons, earning 2-and-a-half cents for each ice cream sold.

Norman, although being somewhat athletic, never achieved the hard body he was promised, while Alan, naturally thick muscled, became more so. While exercising together, Alan often reminded Norman that he should stop using his jaw muscles so much, talking while they worked out, but instead, to concentrate on better doing the exercises.

It was at Coney that Norman first met Marsa. Both he and Alan, still wearing their Army summer khaki, bathing suit underneath, had brought Tag Along Hershey with them, since he had pestered them to let him come with them. It was Norman who had nicknamed him Tag Along because he always would plead to go with whoever was going to a party, picnic, or any other social function. His neediness was reluctantly tolerated because he always brought some Hershey bars to be shared by the others, none of whom ever took the trouble to learn Hershey's real name.

The three young Turks glanced around, studying the beach's ambiance, exploring the different possibilities of interaction with any of the young girls sunning themselves, who, on *their* part, were also studying the beach's ambiance, exploring the different possibilities of interacting with the energetic, prancing colts.

The boys spread their worn blanket, sprawling on it, nudging each other as they appreciatively eyed the three young girls draped across their colorful blanket decorated with Mickey and Minnie Mouse emblems. Tag Along, responding to Alan's gestured directive to test the waters of their neighbor's interest, addressed them with mock courtesy.

"Can you please tell me if the water is wet today, girls?"

He glanced toward Norman and Alan for their approval of his opening salvo for their "pick-up" campaign. Alan nodded encouragingly and although the girls didn't respond, Tag Along plunged ahead.

"Yez, look like ya gonna get sunburned like a lobster, y'know?"

Two of the girls, Rona and Marsa, the back of their heads propped up on sandy towels, glanced up indifferently shading their eyes from the noonday sun. The third member of the trio, Alma, who came along with her friends, but who was already engaged to Sheppy Diamond, lay on her stomach, removed from any need to flirt. Tag Along redirected his effort in her direction.

"Hey, looka Miss Stuck Up."

As Alma remained motionless and silent, Rona scraped at the red nail polish on one of her fingers as she casually 'uh huhd' her lack of interest, turning to Marsa to ask her if she was going to the dance at the Christie Street Settlement House that night. Marsa, in America less than five years, still speaking in a heavy German accent, replied that she thought she'd stay home to write a letter to her Papa and Mama in Germany. Tag Along, on his way to the water, saluted smartly and asked her to invite the Kaiser to the dance. Norman, who had been sneaking covert looks at Marsa's full bosom swelling over the top of her bathing suit, shoved Tag Along toward the water, shrugging an apology to Marsa before following his friends, threading their way through the mass of people on their crowded islands of blankets, towels, beach-chairs and newspapers.

Later, Norman asked Marsa if she was from Berlin and when she shrugged non-committedly, he rattled off Munich,

Hamburg, Frankfurt, finally deciding her home must have been in Dresden.

Marsa had a lovely, deep-throated laugh.

"But you haff never been—"

"I saw one of the Dresden Dolls you posed for."

Rona, lying on her back a couple of feet away, arching her face and body toward the sun, straining to absorb as much of the goldening rays as possible, cautioned Marsa.

"Boy, is he a lotta baloney."

Alan had been staring at Rona's full, fleshy behind, and excited by her, he opportunistically aligned himself with her, leaning close, stage-whispering.

"You're right, except it's more like kosher salami."

One of Rona's greased eyelids flicked open in his direction.

"Douglas Fairbanks you're not."

"But if you come under the boardwalk with me, I'll show you where I resemble him a lot."

"Oh, I can hardly wait, I'm having heart palpitations."

"Yeah, I can tell. Lemme use some of your oil lotion 'n I'll try to squeeze you in."

"Oh, you can have all you want, but only on one condition."

"Your wish is my command."

This time, Rona stared at him from under the other eyelid.

"Just don't bother squeezing me in."

Alan dramatically closed his left eye, the right one winking his sense of conquest as he sucked in his stomach, expanding his chest, and striking an athletic pose.

"Anything you desire, m'lady!"

Norman had started a sand sculpture of a man lying on his back. Marsa watched him as he crouched on his knees over his creation taking shape. After a few minutes, Norman glanced up at her, smiled, and went back to his work. He quietly spoke to her once, asking if she'd be nice enough to use her bathing cap to get him some water. Waving away Rona's disapproving glance, Marsa hurried to the water's edge. Then, returning with the brim-full bathing cap, she sat squat-legged, holding it so Norman could reach over and scoop a palm-full of water, sprinkling some as he worked it into the sand, making it mud for sculpting.

Only when he felt he was finished, and could do no more for his maiden effort, did he allow himself to speak, making the light-hearted comment that might befit even a serious artist.

"I doubt if Leonardo Da Vinci had to work with all these kids screaming around the place."

Marsa's warm, appreciative laughter reached out, encircling him. She stood up tip-toed in order to relax her cramped leg muscles. From where he sat, Norman could see the rounded shapeliness of her leg where it disappeared under the skirted folds of her bathing suit. The softness of her thigh was seen for just a breath-catching moment before it too was lost to his excited view as she lowered her heels to the ground.

She stretched her arms over her head, Norman enjoying her unselfconscious, guileless innocence.

Brushing sand off her arms as she turned toward the ocean, Marsa caught his attentive gaze.

"So, in the water I go."

"Go on, I'll catch up," Norman said, pleased with the introduction, "I've got a cramp in my leg."

Her animated laughter trailed behind her as she nimbly ran toward the water.

Dreamy eyed, Norman watched her elusively dodging around some card-playing men who flirted with her, playfully grabbing at her ankles as she went by, a romantic vision among earth-bound clods. It seemed to Norman that she had the gayest spirit of anyone he'd ever known.

The surf was crowded with people; one could barely make out patches of the brownish water between the clogs of bathers trying to cool off. Norman stood up, his erection gone down, and hurried to join Marsa, the foam eddying around her knees. He quite naturally, easily, extended his hand to her. Smiling warmly, she took his hand and they detoured around a group of yelping boys playing swim-tag.

A wave broke high on Marsa's body, the cold water causing her to draw her breath in sharply. She 'oohed' it out, her body shivering as she giggled. Still holding her hand, Norman immersed himself into the water completely, bobbing up and shaking his body in a playfully exaggerated imitation of Marsa. Laughing good-naturedly, she permitted herself to be led slowly out to the deeper part, squealing occasionally as the waves slapped at her.

A mountain of water suddenly engulfed them, throwing them off balance. Tumbling beneath it, they held on to each other, finally surfacing, bodies touching, their wetness conducting currents of feeling between them, sharper and stronger than any lightning flash.

They continued to play joyfully together, hardly speaking except for warnings of "Watch this one!" "Jump!" and occasional gleeful cries of "Great!" "Stupendous!" "I'm getting water-logged."

Finally spent, they started toward the beach, their shoulders grazing as they neared the shore. Marsa stumbled on a seashell, and Norman put his arm around her waist to steady her, her breast brushing against him. Marsa's body, trembling from the chill and excitement, stayed within the circle of his arm and he could feel the softness of her body through the clinging bathing suit. Their legs touched as they walked together. Glancing down, Norman could see her breasts rising over the top of her suit as she inhaled deep gulps of air. Feeling himself harden, he threw himself on the ground, melodramatically pretending fatigue.

"A horse, a horse! My kingdom for a horse!"

Laughing appreciatively, Marsa lowered herself down next to him, her head arching back over her shoulders, her wet neck glistening. As she glanced over at him, she smiled and took off her bathing cap, rays of brilliant sun playing a capricious game of flickering lights on her wet, shining hair.

Norman's physical excitement was joined, and then overwhelmed by an engulfing warm feeling. Only much later did he identify it as being one of love; a love which remained constant during their long life together.

At this unique instance for both of them, without thinking of consequences, without considering future obligations or responsibilities, they addressed that which had connected, bonded them forever.

Norman blurted out simply, "I'm going to marry you!"

Marsa, also taken with the moment, said simply, "Okay."

They had known each other for little over an hour, and many times over the years, they would refer to that moment, during the good *and* bad times, that singular instance remaining the foundation that stood strong against all the winds and inclement weather which stormed through their lives.

41
Amboy Street, 1937

PATROLMEN COMETTI AND HICKS were very familiar with Amboy Street problems. One of them that required their amused vigilance was the crap games taking place at least one night a week, weather permitting, under the street lamp in front of '179.' Sometimes, around 2 or 3 a.m., the gambling would stop due to several tenants' shouted complaints about the loud exchanges between the 10 or 12 intensely concentrated players calling out their bets. The neighbors' "Enough already!" was the staple plea.

However, the major reason for the game to end, more often than not, was because during the men's clustering under the dingy yellow light, the black-dotted white cubes rolling across the grimy pavement, a heated argument would ensue between Sammy Ash and Crazy Benjy. The angry dispute was usually about one of them putting twenty or thirty cents on a '6 and 8' bet, the other belligerently claiming that it was placed too late.

"The shooter already made his fuckin' point, shmuck!"

Cometti and Hicks would sometimes arrive, a bloody-nose fist fight in progress. The players quickly dispersed in order to avoid a possible citation for disturbing the peace, but often leaving on the ground their betting money, scooped up by the cops for their personal "Policeman's Benevolent Association.'

Three years earlier, Mrs. Wax, hearing Finky's screams of fear and pain, had rushed over to Oleshe's and called the police.

At that time, Cometti was alone on foot patrol, and after he had rapped hard on the Finkelstein apartment door, Charlie had let him in as he continued to curse violently at Finky.

"Just shut your trap, you fuckin' bitch!"

He turned to Cometti, his tone, 'man-to-man.'

"Hey, what can you do if the wife keeps yappin' all the time, right?"

Finky had followed Charlie to the door.

"Officer, he's been drinking again!"

Charlie backhanded her, even as he turned to Cometti, "See what I mean?"

Although Cometti, a church-going regular, agreed with the Good Book's perception of a woman's subservience to her husband, he definitely did not like women being mistreated, never having raised a hand in anger to his own wife.

"Well, sir, you can't..."

Charlie interrupted him to give a forceful push to Finky who had been whimpering in pain. He turned back to Cometti.

"Look, sir, I have to keep my wife on track, the way I see it, okay?"

Cometti spoke directly to Finky.

"You want to press charges about him assaulting you, Ma'am?"

Now as Cometti and Hicks stood outside of Finklestein's door, Cometti had a vague recollection of having been there before. However, after he had knocked, announced himself, and Charlie abruptly flung open the door, he immediately remembered him.

The low threshold of anger Cometti felt toward anybody who abused women or children usually produced a knee-jerk response of rage. He vividly recalled the last time he had heard Charlie's sneering reason for pushing his wife around, and the frustration he felt because the missus had refused to press charges against her husband.

Now Charlie was all smarmy smiles; insincere friendliness oozing out.

"What can I do for you, officer?"

Cometti tried not to allow his strong revulsion to mar his professional behavior.

"Well, sir, a neighbor phoned in to report a woman being beaten up in this apartment."

Charlie's eyes rounded in surprise.

"Not here, sir, absolutely not here!"

He called back over his shoulder, "Hey, honey, tell the officer how much you love me."

Finky, calling from the kitchen, unsuccessfully attempted an enthusiastic tone.

"Everything's okay, officer. Really."

Charlie smiled as he started to close the door.

"You heard the little lady, right?"

Cometti, reaching over to stop the door from closing, spoke sharply.

"Let me talk to the missus."

"C'mon officer, she ain't dressed," Charlie sneered, "ya know what I mean?"

Hicks, having seen Cometti flare up in similar situations, jumped in to quiet the waters.

"Look, sir, our orders are to talk to both parties in any domestic dispute."

"The wife's just not feeling good, officer. She's lying down… ya know what I mean?"

Actually, Cometti did know what Charlie meant, and it heightened his repugnance of his behavior.

"Well, sir, we'll just have to talk to her for a minute before we can leave."

"Hey, officer, I had a tough day; I just wanna get some shut eye."

Very slowly, deliberately, Cometti strongly underlined his position.

"Looks like my report will have to read that your wife was unable to talk to us."

"I'm really getting pissed off, officer." Charlie's voice rising in irritation, "I mean, this crap is—"

Finky, nervous about the argument accelerating, put her head around the edge of the kitchen wall, glancing down the hallway to where Charlie was talking to the cops. Trying to keep her face turned away from the hallway light, she called out.

"Everything's all right, officer."

As Finky started to turn back into the kitchen, the light caught her face, the heavy bruise on her cheek and dark discoloration around her eye repellently apparent.

Hicks had called into the station in order to check on Charlie's police record. Sentenced to three to five for assault and battery, he had been released earlier because of his, Hicks sardonically told Cometti, 'good behavior.'"

This information was enough for Cometti, the senior officer on the call, to haul Charlie down to the station where the supervisor on the watch would come down heavy on him; at the very least to make Charlie think twice about physically abusing his wife.

The fact that Charlie had been paroled meant that this domestic call would be enough cause to throw his ass back inside, or at least for a restraining order to be issued, even if Mrs. Finklestein didn't ask for one. This possibility eased Cometti's anger, restraining *him* from slapping Charlie around a little. Also, because Cometti knew that Hicks, on the Force for less than a year, was an eager beaver, always trying to kiss up to his superior officers. Even though Cometti believed that Hicks would probably look the other way if he used a little extra muscle on Charlie, he didn't want to take the chance that his partner might break the code of silence in order to score some Brownie points.

"Look, Mr. Finklestein, I'm going to have to take you down to the station, so let's just make it easy for all of us, and I don't have to cuff you."

Mrs. Wax was excitedly telling some of the neighbors standing on the sidewalk outside '179' about how Norman had called the cops, and then had stopped Charlie from using a knife on Finky. Cometti, firmly holding Charlie's arm, led him out of the house, and close behind them was Hicks and Finky. Charlie glared back over his shoulder, warning Finky to say the right thing. Although she felt some sense of security because of the police, she was frightened by Charlie's intimidating, threatening presence. Barely managing to speak, her words caught in her throat.

"He didn't really do anything."

Cometti glanced at Finky's purple-welted face, and shoved Charlie down the stoop step.

"Keep moving."

Charlie, all innocence, gestured toward Finky as he spoke to Cometti.

"Y'see, I told ya—"

Cometti brusquely moved Charlie along toward the police car at the curb.

"Move it!"

Charlie, using his free hand, made an awkward conciliatory gesture, his fingers poking at Cometti's chest. This was all the excuse Cometti needed. "Yes," his mind aware of what he would say to his supervising officer, "I put him in custody all right, but he acted physically like he was going to give me trouble, so I had to use force to restrain him."

All this barely flashing through his mind, he vented his feelings, his fist exploding in Charlie's face, blood spurting from his broken nose. Cometti hit him again, smashing his cheek and eye, Charlie collapsing onto the car. Cometti, grabbing Charlie by his shirt with one hand, and opening the car door with the other, threw him into the backseat.

"You scum bag!"

Finky and the others, stunned, watched the policemen pile into the car, quickly pulling away.

The crowd was silent for a moment longer before Mrs. Wax turned sympathetically to Finky.

"Oi! Your face!"

Curious about what was happening, Norman had returned to the street in front of '179' and spoke gently to Finky, still shaken.

"Come on in, I've got some hot tea on the stove."

Finky stared intently at the police car disappearing down the street.

Mrs. Wax and Norman, their emotional support apparent, watched Finky settle into a kitchen chair. Mrs. Wax, after staring at Finky's bruised face, the area around her left eye darkening into an ugly purplish black, turned to Norman, speaking quietly as if a louder voice would cause Finky even more pain.

"You maybe have a little Vaseline?"

Puzzled at the odd request, Norman finally managed a hesitant answer.

"What... Vaseline?"

"For her punim," explained Mrs. Wax, descriptively touching her own face, accompanied with an 'oo' of pain.

Quickly rummaging through the medicine chest in the bathroom, Norman could find only almost empty bottles of cough syrup and aspirin.

Returning to the kitchen empty-handed, Norman was greeted by Mrs. Wax's sarcastic response to Norman's unsuccessful search for the Vaseline.

"Normie, you're handy like poison ivy on a honeymoon."

Finky started to chuckle, but the sound became muffled by a groan of pain. Trembling, she started to stand up, Norman hurrying to reach out to support her.

"I'm shaking like a nothing, Normie."

"The police'll make Charlie stay away now, Finky."

"You don't know that crazy man."

"Then they'll put him back in prison."

Mrs. Wax had the final word.

"In a cage with the apes, he belongs!"

Marsa entered the apartment, and standing in the kitchen doorway she glanced at the others before speaking to Finky, her voice comforting.

"Sit, we'll take care."

Norman started to explain the situation, "That Charlie is a terrible—"

"From the neighbors," Marsa interrupted, "I already heard."

After staring at Finky's bruises, she headed to the bathroom.

"A little Vaseline to smear on."

Norman stopped her.

"I already looked, Marsa."

"In the soap dish on the bathtub?"

When Norman shook his head, Marsa went into the bathroom, Finky slowly starting toward the apartment door.

"I'll go lay down upstairs."

Mrs. Wax stood up, "I'll make you some more tea to wash down your nerves."

Marsa came in with a jar of Vaseline.

"Stay, Finky, there's friends here."

"Thanks, Marsa, I've got to fix the mess up there."

Mrs. Wax took the jar from Marsa.

"I'll bring back, tomorrow."

Gently taking Finky under her arm, she walked her to the door when Finky stopped, turning back to Norman and Marsa.

"Normie..."

She trailed off, then turning to Marsa in order to thank her also. "Marsa...," again emotionally unable to express her gratitude.

As soon as Mrs. Wax and Finky left the apartment, Norman, still puzzled by Marsa's behavior on the trolley earlier, quickly turned to her.

"Why'd you get off like that before?"

Not waiting for an answer, he pointed to the clock on the kitchen counter.

"It's late," he admonished her, "Ira isn't feeling well; he shouldn't be outside." quickly moving toward the door, annoyed, "Now I'll have to go get—"

Marsa's harsh tone stopped him in his tracks.

"He's sleeping already, thank you!"

"What are you talking about?"

"The sick boy is in bed by my cousin Sarah," openly combative, "So?"

"Why'd you leave him there?"

"'Why?' The extra room upstairs has sunshine coming in, not like," gesturing around the apartment, "And there's always good food in a *fridge* for Ira, God bless Sarah!"

"My boy belongs in his own room."

"*My* boy belongs where he can be healthy."

"You go get him right now, you hear me?"

"I'm deaf. The hearing maybe gets better if you take care of the family."

Angry, Norman raised his hand aggressively; Marsa's body stiffening defensively, her eyes defiant.

"So, Mr. Tarzan of the Apes? You see someone to hit?

Norman stared at Marsa for a long moment. Suddenly, as if his mind blinked, his bad temper started to dissolve, the sense of his many good years with Marsa warmly embracing him.

He gently reached toward Marsa who offered no resistance to his cautious embrace. Norman, emotional, held her.

"Marsa... please..."

Marsa leaned against him, his familiar smell and comforting body touching the memory of his hugging her as they came out of the water that day they first met at Coney Island.

Now Norman spoke gently, earnestly.

"I love you Marsa... I love you, my dark-eyed beauty."

Her eyes filling, Marsa tenderly returned his affection.

"Oh, Normie, I want what used to be with us."

"'Used to be' is not *now*, Marsa, and the change can be for the better."

Drawn in, Marsa questioned hopefully, "How *better*"?

"Well, for one thing, maybe it can bring us closer because the times are asking other things... more things of us."

Their fragile moment of intimacy fading, Marsa almost shouted her question, "Ask what? To do without so we can be close... to nothing?"

Abruptly pushing herself away from Norman, Marsa bitterly continued, "Who asks me *that*, I spit in their face!" Glaring directly at Norman, "Whoever!" Her words rushing out, "And then you tell this bubie-meiser to our new baby?"

"It's *not* a fairy tale, Marsa! It's just that sometimes we have to pay a price for self-respect."

"Oh? Then go shopping; see what you can buy with your self-respect, Mr. Union Philosopher!"

"Look, Marsa, don't crap on what I'm doing at the union, the work is very important, and somebody has to do it."

"Then it's time somebody else does it. My family is not going to starve because my husband wants to save the world, you hear me?"

"I'm listening to inside," tapping his heart, "here, and it says to me there're people counting on me, and I—"

"And your family *doesn't* count?"

"Of course," Norman adamant in his conviction, "and that's why I'm helping to organize the teachers, because in the long run—"

Marsa belligerently interrupted, "So you're telling me your final decision?"

"I'm telling!"

Marsa picked up a couple of towels from a kitchen cabinet, and tucking them under her arm, hurried toward the apartment door, speaking over her shoulder to where Norman stood nonplused.

"I'm staying with Ira until his body is not sick anymore."

That was all the 'goodbye' Marsa had time or inclination for, slamming the door behind her.

After a few moments of recovery from Marsa's short but potent attack, Norman idly left the kitchen, wandered through the small living-room, paused for an instant in the bedroom, then slowly went into Ira's, no larger than a walk-in closet-sized room. Earlier, he had tossed the bat he had used to threaten Charlie with onto the bed, now carefully placing it next to Ira's baseball glove which the boy always stored next to a couple of battered baseballs on the room's single chair.

A dog's loud bark from outside the window startled Norman. Glancing out into the courtyard, he worried about the dog's food and water now that Ira was away. Searching through the icebox, he found a small plate of mashed potatoes, and taking some corn flakes from a box in the kitchen cupboard, he mixed them together, and along with a glass of water, brought them out to the courtyard.

"Okay, Mutt, just don't bark anymore, all right?"

Pouring the water into a bowl that Ira had put there, he watched as the dog ravenously attacked the food. When the dog started to lap at the water, Norman, satisfied that the dog's needs had been taken care of, patted him on the head.

"Okay, Mutt?"

Accepting Norman's friendly touch, the dog licked at his hand.

"I'll send your regards to Ira, okay, Mutt?"

Receiving no answer but a slobbering tongue across his cheek, Norman continued his one-way conversation.

"Well, you'll have to spend the night out in—" Norman interrupted himself, untying the dog. "Okay Mutt, maybe I can use some company after all."

Glancing around the courtyard, Norman saw that the dog had not relieved itself.

"Good, Mutt; let's see if you can christen the Amboy Street gutter."

There were only a few tenants and pedestrians closing out the sticky summer night; the hush of people unspeaking, masked the churning unrest from the ugly violence of the encounter between Charlie and the police.

The back room of Mulnick and Son Fur Store was a small uncluttered area; a few empty cartons waiting hopefully to be used to pack any of the fur stock that the Mulnicks were able to sell.

"Remember, Alan, when I had to restock the new cartons at least once a month?"

Sam Mulnick would occasionally wax nostalgic about the good old '20s.

"Believe me, my son, when Coolidge, who spoke maybe 10 words altogether when he was President, and even that schmuck, President Hoover, for a few minutes, helped a business man make a dollar."

Yes, Alan remembered those years after he was discharged from the Army. With a keen eye on the restrictive demands of a limited budget, he was able to save some money, and was a year or so away from opening the new business he had been diligently planning, when the '29 stock market suddenly crashed around him and many other unsuspecting investors.

Homes, cars, college tuitions, vacations, and many other creature comforts were suddenly snatched away, and worse; eagerly expected bright futures, no longer floating colorfully in front of them, but fading away into what never would be; regrets of what could have been, and now, even pathetic dreams gone unattempted.

Unlike Norman, whom he often saw as striking a posture of great concern for everybody else's troubles, Alan was unshackled by considerations other than those which affected his own welfare; coming squarely down on the side of self-preservation, as he criticized Norman, "C'mon, Normie, you with your 'protests'... 'unions,' and all that crap, and your family ends up with less than zero. Yeah, my friend, climb out of your pity sandbox and wipe the sand out of your eyes so you can see the right thing to do for Marsa and Ira!"

Norman would argue back that Alan's views might be justifiably biased because of the tough times he was having, but, "Alan, you're just soured on everything since you lost everything in the market."

It was extremely difficult for Alan not to be grim about the situation he had found himself in. He had invested his savings in an ambitious plan to open an Army-Navy surplus store, buying some uniforms, mess gear, canteens and assorted equipment.

When Alan's surplus store idea fizzled out, Norman was secretly pleased, feeling that Alan might be forced into using his abilities to a higher purpose. Norman had always felt that Alan had a superior intelligence, and immediately after their Army discharge he had tried to persuade his friend to go to college, perhaps to major in City College's excellent Administrative program, which he himself eventually matriculated in. Alan, however, did not want to wait four years before he could make some 'real' money.

Measuring himself next to Norman's almost dedicated attitude toward helping others, he felt that after all there was nobody around who felt sorry for *him* when he was Captain of the school basketball team and the high scorer, threatening to break the all-time record only to have the playing schedule cut short because of Uncle Sam's decision to fight the Krauts. A lot of things just had to be left behind. Like the gold and crimson uniforms. Like other schmucky dreams. Like the proud hard muscles of youth which were sadly recalled by him from time to time, as they flabbed into the softness of his middle years.

Yet, the sharp edges of his mind had not become dulled, the twists and turns of survival honing them to animal alertness. Yes, his high-school grades suggested he go on to one of the professions, as his friend had, but his father's business promised richer returns. He quickly became one of the breed of men in the Fur District who stood outside their stores, hands behind their backs, sometimes strolling in small circles, discussing silk linings with other furriers and how to round a beaver collar.

When business had been good, he was pleased with his stenciled identity, but the Depression years had pulled the economic rug from under his ego. And the steep drop in income the last years had left him clawing to hold on to the little that was left; finally driving him to his arson plan.

"When would you do it, Alan?"

"*We* would do it maybe in a month... October... okay?"

Norman had come to Mulnick and Son as Alan was opening for the day, his father scheduled to come in later. Alan hurried Norman into the back room where he rapidly went over the same plans he had explained to him before, but wanting Norman to feel comfortable about what had to be done.

Alan's father, Sam, came through the front door, immediately calling out, "Alan?"

Alan hurried in from the back room, "Yeah, Pop?"

"Don't 'Pop' me. How many times I tell you already, an open store without a salesman in front is like a philosophy without an idea."

Pleased to see Norman with his son, he greeted him warmly.

"Norman, boychik."

"How you feeling, Mr. M.?"

"When Hoover was president, he made me sick everyday; with Roosevelt, at least he thinks Socialist, so I'm feeling a little less nauseous now."

"Sure," Alan said, concerned about his father's health, "and if you don't stop working so hard, we'll be buying a stone marker for you at BETH DAVID MEMORIAL."

"Your tongue should fall out, you talk to your father like that."

Sam turned to Norman, curious. "So what's the special honor, so early in the morning?"

When Norman hesitated, Alan quickly repeated the question. "What's the 'special honor,' Pop?"

Sam, for some reason he couldn't explain to himself, became suspicious.

"*I* asked."

Norman, to ease the situation, offered, "Oh, I just wanted to tell you both that Marsa is going to have a baby."

Alan, masking his surprise, was genuinely enthusiastic, "Yeah, isn't it great, Pop?"

"So when, my son, are *you* going to make me a grandfather again?"

"When I get enough money to pay the maternity bill."

Ignoring Alan, Sam turned to Norman, "So, next Shabbus, when you come over, we'll pour an extra glass of schnapps."

"But if you get me drunk, Mr. M., I'll kiss your beautiful wife when you're not looking."

"She should be so lucky, Norman."

Norman chuckled as he started toward the door, "I have to go. Zei gezunt. Stay healthy, Mr. M."

After Norman left, Sam wheeled on Alan.

"So, can you maybe answer me the question why he has more respect for me than my own son?"

42

OLESHE'S CANDY STORE carried only two morning newspapers, the *Daily News* and *Daily Mirror*, each costing two cents.

Glancing at the front page of the *News*, Norman angrily noted the picture of Henry Ford, the headline shouting, "FORD DENIES UNIONS." The story banner: "WE'LL NEVER RECOGNIZE THE UNITED AUTO WORKERS OR ANY OTHER UNION."

The *Mirror's* front page story featured a picture of Mayor La Guardia and a photo inset of the famous Burlesque Queen, Sally Rand, peeking out from between two large ostrich fans, which she was teasingly using on Fiorello, the Little Flower, in her renowned daring Fan Dance.

Norman, aware that Oleshe discouraged 'browsing' through the newspapers without buying, nonetheless sneaked a glance inside the *News*, then put a couple of pennies on the scarred wooden newspaper stand. He tucked the *Mirror* under his arm, hurrying around the corner to the H.E.S. where a meeting of his union group was scheduled to start in a few minutes.

Danny Watkins, Norman's second in command, had just started the proceedings, allowing Jerry Goldstein, the very vocal Communist, to recount a visit he had with an art group in Harlem. He had learned about Alan Locke, a professor at Howard University, the only American Negro to get a Rhodes' Scholarship at Oxford, through reading a book about Harlem's artistic activities, and the resultant influx of curious whites from upper-scale Manhattan. As Goldstein, reading from the book, described it, "Bustling, strong-minded matrons, in Sutton Place, on the Drive, even on staid Fifth Avenue, sent out informal notes and telephonic invitations: "THERE WILL BE PRESENT A FEW ARTISTIC NEGROES. IT'S REALLY THE THING. THEY RECITE WITH SUCH FEELING, AND WHEN THEY SING... SUCH DIVINE TONES. IMAGINE, A COLORED PERSON PLAYING DEBUSSY AND CHOPIN!!"

Dysart, the huge argumentive union man, whose main concern was related to further strengthening the workers' autonomy in order to get out from under the yolk of the Administration's oppressive stranglehold on teacher's initiative, shouted his objection. "So what the hell does that have to do with what we're trying to organize here?"

Goldstein, ready for Dysart's negativity, smugly replied, "Well, my dear counter-progressive, it might be to our advantage if we publicized our working relationship with the colored community and this Rhodes' Scholar.

Connie Washington, one of the Negro teachers in the group, stood up to speak, and in a soft but firm tone, spoke directly to Goldstein.

"I realize you mean well, Mr. Goldstein, but you don't seem to understand that the writer was actually being sardonic about the patronizing way that white folks act toward Negro artists."

"But, Connie," Goldstein patiently explained, "the book goes on to point out that the poems had such depth... primitive, you know, in a kind of exalted fashion."

"That's just more proof of what I'm talking about, Mr. Goldstein. Don't you see, that the writer is setting up the comparison with the Negro as in the story of the dancing dog. The applause given the dog is not because it does well, but merely that it dances at all."

Before the discussion could continue, Norman, concerned that although he agreed with Connie, the more important point of protesting against the School Board's constricting behavior was top of the agenda at this time.

He attempted to refocus the meeting's energy, soothing Connie's feelings. "We know that superlative Negro poets like Langston Hughes and Countee Cullen are wonderful examples of what good Negro poetry is all about. They represent—"

Norman stopped himself, realizing that he was just a step away from becoming condescending himself.

~

In the 60s, after Norman had become Superintendent of Schools in upscale Smithtown, Long Island, he became involved in an informal debate with Howard Zinn, one of the most militant left-wing activists in the country.

Although Norman had long admired Zinn for much of his pro-labor vigilance, when Zinn came to address a high-school student body, the meeting chaired by Norman as Regional Superintendent of Schools, a divide in the two men's hereto positive relationship became apparent. During the discussion, Zinn had come squarely down on the side of the teachers' need to have some control over the method of communicating the content of a class assignment, and not be hard-bound by the Administration's view, from a long distance, of how classes should be conducted.

As part of his argument, Zinn maintained that a teacher had the right, if not the obligation, to convey his or her philosophic perception of society, whether it be in math, history, English, or even phys-ed classes. It was of extreme importance, he felt, that the awareness of the vast 'class' wasteland, separating the 'haves' and 'have nots,' should always be part of the student's learning experience.

Although Norman's early liberal activities had involved him in the forefront of bettering teaching conditions, he had over the years become alerted to *other* significant priorities.

When he became a principal, and shortly after, Superintendent, he grew to feel that while teachers' concerns about hours, salary, and benefits were of course important, *his* overview was now of a *larger* canvas. Not only did he have to deal with the lack of sufficient public funding, but also with the Board of Education's stringent criteria, and having to balance the constant pressure from demanding-parents and complaining teachers. He had come to conclude that teachers were not nearly as concerned with the students' growth as they were with upgrading their salary, benefits, and being afforded more free periods. In his decision-making position, he found it necessary, sometimes reluctantly, to yield to many of the teachers' requests.

In rare instances, he had questioned his gradual shift away from his earlier campaigning for teachers' creative involvement in curriculum decisions, but now decided that teachers usually erred on the side of too much permissive student involvement. Norman would remind himself that sometimes one had to alter obsolete attitudes in order to adjust to the changing times.

Recently he had tried to contact Principal Mason of his old high school, Abraham Lincoln, but he had retired and didn't return the call that Norman left with his answering service. Perhaps, Norman thought, he was still angry about Norman's 'protest' behavior almost 30 years before. In fact, it had crossed Norman's mind several times to talk to Mason from the perspective of his 20-20 hindsight and his growing acceptance of the concept that in the final analysis, the best thing for the students and teachers was to remain under the administrator's control.

~

After Norman had agreed with Connie Washington about the error of patronizing the Negroes' accomplishments, Goldstein rushed to his own defense, maintaining that everyone, regardless of color, had to accept that for the greater good of the Teachers' Union, the over-sensitivity of different factions had to be subordinated to the welfare of the 'whole.'

Goldstein stubbornly continued to convince Connie, "I'm sure you can perceive the sense of sacrifice in your own Negro spiritual," and he launched into talk-singing, "You've got to cross that lonesome valley, nobody's going to cross it for you." With a small smile of triumph, he asked Connie, "You see what I mean?" then turned to the others. "You see what I mean?" Not waiting for corroboration, he continued to make his case.

"So you see, all our actions must be guided by our allegiance to our union, and eventually the state."

Dysart always laid in wait for Goldstein's 'red' propaganda to surface again, and now he appealed to Norman.

"If you don't tell Goldstein to stop this Commie crap, I might really lose my temper and do something to him, myself!"

Connie had been stunned into silence by Goldstein inappropriately invoking the words of a sacred hymn about facing death, in order to explain away his earlier patronizing attitude, now compounded, Connie thought, by his attempt to demonstrate what he thought was fellowship with his Negro 'comrade.'

"Mr. Goldstein," Connie tight-lipped, critical of the self-satisfied singer, coldly said, "All I can say is that when you pick a spiritual to make a point, you better know what you're singing about."

Norman, sensing that the meeting might now veer into unproductive argument, tried again to refocus the agenda.

"At the last meeting, we all agreed—"

"Only most of us, Schecter," Dysart shot in.

"'Most,' Dysart, is mandate enough for us to take action on."

"Like what, Schecter?"

"Like opening our membership to people who radically express their strong beliefs."

"Like who?"

Norman waved the newspaper to the group.

"Any of you read this about Sally Rand?"

Seymour Yanoff suddenly sprung up from the rear row of the small auditorium. He had been a member of the group since its first meeting and other than voting yea or nay on a proposed 'motion' or plan, had hardly said a word to anybody.

Now, Yanoff spoke out in one of his very infrequent times of communication.

"You mean the burlesque stripper?"

With mock severity, Norman corrected Yanoff.

"You mean exotic fan dancer."

"Yeah, I saw her last month."

"Yeah?" Dysart, smiling, challenged him, where'd you see the lady?"

"The Hudson Theatre in Newark," Yanoff shot back.

Goldstein, who had been the acknowledged expert on all things related to the arts, verified Yanoff's information.

"He's right; the expression of bourgeois decadence is still allowed there."

Dysart's derisive laughter joined the appreciative chuckles of several other members, and he became mockingly subservient.

"Oh, high Commissar of Culture Goldstein, I think you may have a real problem with sex, or maybe, not to be disrespectful, sir, it's just the lack of it."

As Goldstein sputtered his objection "Now, just a minute, Dysart—," Norman quickly jumped in, "Hold it down, fellas! I want to tell you about this headline. Rand offered to do her fan dance for Mayor La Guardia personally, so she could show him how 'pure' her art form is, so City Hall won't shut down all the burlesque houses."

Yanoff's "good for her!" was joined by some light-hearted approval from other members, one of them calling out, "the little guy is gonna have some fun!"

"Maybe," Norman cut off the laughter, "but don't you get it? She's going all the way... right down to the mat, so whatever happens, she'll always know she didn't back off from doing everything she could."

"Maybe," Dysart suggested, "Yanoff here might get all excited, but let's get back to business."

"This *is* business, Dysart, and maybe we can learn a lesson from the lady!" Norman had taken one of the pieces of cardboard paper from a small pile stored on a tripod that was used for lectures and demonstrations. Writing on the cardboard with a felt marker, he wrote in block letters:

TOTAL COMMITMENT

Holding it up high so that everybody in the group could see it, Norman, his eyes clearly expressing his dedication to the long journey ahead to achieve equity for the teaching profession, announced in a clear, resolute tone, "Total Commitment!"

Outlining an ambitious plan to align his group with the progressive policies of Local 5 of the Teachers' Union, Norman called for uniting all the union locals in a do-or-die walkout of all the New York teachers if their reasonable demands for salary hikes were not met.

Goldstein and Dysart both spoke out at the same time.

"It's about time—" Goldstein enthusiastically called out even as Dysart's booming voice overrode him, "This is no time for a revolution, Schecter."

Goldstein finished his support for Norman's proposal, his voice dramatically excited, "for all the struggling workers to unite!"

Norman and Connie joined ranks with Goldstein this once to convince the rest of the membership of the need for this next big step of action for the teachers' welfare.

43

ISAAC BAUMGARTEN WAS IN AWE of the Dewey Decimal System, which he discovered when he joined the Stone Avenue library.

Austria had not adapted this system of book classifying and cataloging that had become of enormous help to American library card holders, and Isaac was fascinated by the ease that the system provided for the reader.

He planned that when he returned to his beloved Austria at some future time after the Nazi nightmare was finally over, he would take it on himself as a labor of love to help institute this American ingenuity.

This system helped Isaac to catch up on learning something of the country which harbored him. His English was still limited, but with the help of some books that he was able to borrow from a German social club, he managed to piece together much about the country.

In his desire to find out more about the Dewey system he looked it up in the Encyclopaedia Britannica, but mistakenly read up on John Dewey instead of Melville Dewey who had actually originated the system. After reading about Melville, he became interested in the life of the philosopher, John Dewey, and was surprised and pleased to find out that Dewey had established the University-in-Exile which worked with scholars being persecuted in countries under totalitarian regimes.

Isaac, exploring this fact in the German club, could find no information about that program, deducing that the Nazi bias had eliminated that information in all the books that were on its shelves.

Returning to the Stone Avenue library, he was delighted to find Ira in the upstairs reading room.

Ira, influenced by his father's respect for Clarence Darrow, was avidly reading his published debate on Capital Punishment, brilliantly arguing against it. Isaac stood quietly near where Ira sat. Ira becoming aware of somebody staring at him, glanced up, immediately recognizing Isaac.

"Hello, Mister Baumgarten."

"Young Mister Schecter," Isaac warmly greeted the boy, "Sorry to interrupting you."

Isaac quickly realized his grammatical error, immediately correcting himself.

"I am very sorry to interrupt, Ira."

Ira, enjoying Isaac's attempt to improve himself, smiled in congratulation, "It is all right to interrupt me." He continued, gesturing to the book he was reading, "Do you have capital punishment in Austria?"

Isaac quickly answered, "Much more worser; we have Nazi murderers. Yes, they do terrible to the society."

"Were you able to be bar-mitzvahed in Austria, Mister Baumgarten?"

Nodding in affirmation, Isaac smiled at the pleasant memory of the ceremony in the warmth of Graz's Temple El- Emanuel, regarded not only as the premiere synagogue in the city, but one of the architectural beauties in all of Europe. It was not until several years later, after the end of the war, that he learned that the temple had been brutally razed by the German army engineers.

At this moment, in the safety of the Stone Avenue Library, he shared with Ira a special fact about this special birthday.

"—and my father gave to me a new set of tefillin blessed by the chief rabbi."

Ira, still several months away from *his* bar-mitzvah, wasn't sure if his parents would have enough money to buy *him* a set of tefillin, two very small black boxes of hide, one box placed on the forehead, the other on the arm, both secured by leather thongs in obedience to the commandments found in Deuteronomy and Exodus; the wearer protected from demons.

"Would you like to come to *my* bar-mitzvah, Mr. Baumgarten?"

"Thank you, Ira; that would give to *me* a good honor."

"I'll talk to my father about inviting you."

"Your father is a good man."

"Yes."

Agreeing with Isaac's assessment of his father made him think of a discussion he had had with Norman a few days earlier. Even as he continued to speak to Isaac, his mind raced around the talk he had with his father about their celebration of his achieving 'manhood.'

When Norman had spoken to him about this upcoming major event of his life he was at first very excited about planning it, but after talking to Marsa, he seemed less enthusiastic.

"Don't worry, Ira, it'll be a fine celebration. Maybe not as elaborate as we'd like, but after you make your bar-mitzvah speech, which I'll work on with Rabbi Mintz, all the relatives and friends will think they were at the grandest synagogue in New York."

A few years later, Ira learned that his father had wanted to spend a few dollars more for the use of a larger synagogue than what they finally ended up with: a very modest-sized one, converted from a gone-out of business law office.

Ira stumbled on this information after he graduated from high school and overheard Norman speaking to Marsa about it. His father, who had now started to earn more as a permanent tenured teacher, expressed his still angry regrets that his wife had successfully argued against them spending more than she claimed they could afford at the time.

"But Marsa, I knew that there would be a time when we'd be able to repay the loan."

Ira knew where they would have gone for the money: the Hebrew Free Loan Society. There had been times when the Schecters weren't able to pay the electric bill or the rent, so they had borrowed a few dollars from the Society. Marsa had on occasion sent him with fifty cents or a dollar to pay off some of their debt. Ira often thought about the fact that through some philanthropic contributions to the Society, no interest was charged to the lender. He would often think about the Society when confronted with a situation of one of his teenage friends wanting to borrow some money. He would usually lend the money if he had it, with the joking reminder that he was charging no interest.

"And do you know how I can do this without it costing you a penny?"

"Okay, Ira, how?"

"Very simple," Ira would say straight-faced. "I just don't spend anything on advertising."

44

FRED THE MAILMAN was 14 years old when he attended services with his parents in Manhattan's St. Patrick's Cathedral.

He had seen photos of the majestic cathedral, and pleaded with his father and mother to be taken there. Finally, each of them carrying their well-thumbed personal bibles, the Schlieper family took the IRT subway to East 42nd Street, and walked the several blocks up 5th Avenue to the church in the midst of the most fashionable expensive shops in the city.

Fred's father proudly carried with him the German Iron Cross that he had earned during his combat heroism in the Franco-Prussian War of 1871. He intended to have his medal blessed by the church's Bishop Delhanty, famous for having been invited to the White House by President Grover Cleveland.

Fred's parents, Erich and Clara, had migrated from Germany over 25 years earlier in order to escape the aggressive anti-Catholic climate in their country, particularly in Stuttgart, where Erich had been a draftsman in a top-flight architectural company.

Fred was extremely impressed by St. Patrick's High Mass conducted only in Latin.

After the service, the family spent some time touring the church's different chapels and prayer-candle displays, very much excited by what Fred would eventually describe to his friends when he'd returned in triumph from his inter-borough excursion.

"Fellas, Jesus himself would be proud to sit in one of the pews there."

Enriched by his adventure to St. Patrick's, Fred felt superior to the citizens of Ridgewood where the most exciting event afforded them was an occasional baseball game on a neighborhood sandlot by a semi-pro team, THE RIDGEWOOD PATRIOTS; the haphazard small bleachers erected by a local entrepreneur who charged 15 cents admission for a seat and a hot dog per customer.

After the Schlieper's left St. Patrick's, they walked up to Central Park and strolled through the zoo and stood for awhile admiring the people who had rented row boats which were gliding through the murky water. Fred smiled at the unusual ornamentation on the currentless lake; an unexpected wristwatch band and a shoelace tied to a popsicle stick dipping sluggishly in and out of the water.

In a few minutes, Mr. Schlieper importantly announced, "So, ten cents for the hour on this wooden ship," standing up heroically in the middle of the rocking row boat, "is much better, no? from that stinking steamship we came over on, yes, Carla?"

"Sit down, Erich, you will sink us into the water."

"Yeah, Poppa, let *me* row now."

"But do you have the muscles, little boy?"

"I'm not a little boy."

"Erich, leave him alone."

"Your good mother speaks loud for you."

And Erich abided, as he usually did, by his wife's gentle command. Later, making it a full outing, Carla and Erich lay on one of the large expanses of freshly mowed lawn, the family bibles carefully laid out beside them, as Fred joined a group of boys who invited him to join them in throwing rocks at the many windblown, colored kites arguing for space in uncertain patterns, zigging, zagging, dipping, soaring; busying the azure sky with their hopes for freedom from the earthbound grey. The high-spirited boys, eventually bored with their fruitless attempts at 'shooting down' the paper 'airplanes,' decided to chase some squirrels darting between the friendly elms.

Rejoining his parents, Fred was not surprised to find them affectionately playful with each other; hugging and laughingly darting kisses at each other. Their physical display, Fred knew, was the acting out of their steady love for each other.

Erich, stroking Carla's cheek, glanced up at his son, and winked as his wife cooed her pleasure.

Fred had rarely thought of that long ago moment since then, until he gently, lovingly touched Finky's bruised face where Charlie had brutally hit her.

"That son of a bitch!"

"Well, the cop came back, Freddie, and said that they told Charlie he better not come here again, or they'd put him back in jail!"

"Anyway, I'm moving in right now, honey."

"You sure?"

"I'm sure I love you!"

"Okay, but are you sure—"

Fred kissed her gently, stopping her mid-sentence, then spoke softly, genuinely, "I'm *sure* you're the best woman for my heart."

Fred almost blushed at his poetic words, but continued unabashedly, "You *are* my heart."

Finky stared at him.

Fred stared at her.

~

Charlie, who had quietly climbed up the fire-escape ladder, paused for a moment at Finky's landing and glancing in the bedroom, could see Finky and Fred, still dressed, asleep on the bed, in each other's arms. Suddenly, Charlie smashed the window with his foot, the glass pane flying into the room.

Startled, Finky and Fred sleepily turned toward the sound as Charlie continued to kick in the rest of the window, quickly stepping in past the remaining jagged spikes of glass, shouting, "You fuckin' whore!"

Fred, recovering from the shock of Charlie's crashing into the room, shouted back, "Get out of here!"

"You're screwing my wife 'n you're telling me to—?"

Fred had leapt out of bed to grapple with Charlie, who snarled threateningly as he pushed Fred away, slamming him against the wall.

"You little shit!"

Again Fred tried to wrestle Charlie, whose street-fighter tactics, kicking the smaller man in the groin, stopped him. Doubling up, Fred groaned in pain as Finky jumped at Charlie, attempting to stop his assault as he growled, "You scumbag bitch!" and smashed her across her face, then turning his attention back to pummeling Fred, who tried to crawl back toward Finky, bleeding from her nose and mouth. Charlie kicked at Fred who managed to hold Finky's hand protectively, starting to lead her toward the apartment door. As he passed his mail pouch which he had, as usual, hung up over a kitchen chair, he snatched at it, but the pouch hooked on the corner of the chair, the payroll bag falling out. Fred lunged to retrieve it, and Charlie sensing the bag's value, grabbed it. Fred also grabbed at it, and the two men, panting with the effort, fought tug of war over it.

Finky, blood gushing down her face, screamed, "Let him have the money, Fred!"

Fred glanced over at Finky, giving Charlie the opportunity to whip out from his pocket, a wicked-looking knife, and lunged at Fred who desperately twisted his body away… but not in time, the knife plunging deep into Fred's back. Finky screamed in horror, and Charlie pulled the knife from Fred's back, turned him over, and with one hand holding off the hysterically crying Finky, violently plunged the knife into Fred's chest. Freeing herself from Charlie's hold, Finky moved closer to Fred, holding her arms out to comfort him, his blood pouring out. Recoiling in horror, Finky stared in disbelief at her blood-darkened hands. Charlie grabbed the payroll bag and went to the window, stopping for a moment, turning back toward Finky who, reflexively, shrank from his poised hand still holding the bloody knife, Charlie pausing for a threatening moment before quickly stepping out onto the fire escape. Finky screamed in terror, as she saw Fred, his heart pierced, his eyes glazing in death, her strangled cries turning into deep, agonized moans.

45

NORMAN, AT 65, forced into mandatory retirement, concocted for his own amusement a fantasy scenario: President Johnson, aware of the planned festivities honoring Norman's 40 years in the New York Public School system, had devilishly, on that very same day, announced his withdrawal from the Presidential re-election campaign for 1968, in order to overshadow Norman's celebration.

The reality was that only a modest-sized group of administration colleagues attended the dinner held in the conference room at the sedately fashionable St. George Hotel in Brooklyn Heights.

Of course Norman realized that there was very little interest in a public-school figure fading into the sunset, so he graciously accepted the modest commemoration of his professional life.

Responding to the congratulatory speeches offered by the Board of Education Supervisor, and a highly placed Board member of the American Association of School Administrators, Norman expressed his genuine gratitude for their laudatory words, and particularly for the embossed gold-bound writing journal, his name spelled out in tiny ruby chips on its rich cordovan leather.

Later, at home, he was surprised at his self-consciousness about writing down any of his personal insights; recording for the most part, innocuous events of the past such as the date of his Army discharge after the World War; his first day of public-school teaching, and then his assuming the position of Principal following the School Board's interviewing him.

At first, Norman wrote about the reasons he had reluctantly decided to tell the Board of Inquiry about Jerry Goldstein being a card-carrying Communist; that he had felt that although Goldstein had been a valuable member of the Union group, he eventually lost his effectiveness, spinning his wheels by constantly introducing what Norman and most of the other members thought were counter-productive issues. It was for this reason that Norman had finally felt it was his duty to identify Goldstein's Communist affiliations.

After a moment of consideration, Norman crossed out the 'counterproductive issues' line, finally deciding to delete the entire section justifying his informing the Committee about Goldstein's 'Red' associations.

Recalling those early Union days, he thought about Elissa Jackman, and that after her accident he had stayed in touch with her during her painful convalescence. He sadly started a new page in the journal, writing down some of his memories of the several visits he had had with her. Hard on the heels of his jotting down his recollections, there was a wave of remembered conversations and events related to the 'Protests'; becoming excited by what he felt was the beginning of a short story.

He recalled Alan's belittling 'ahrt-shmart' comment when Norman had brought up the 'higher calling' of teaching, or once when he had shared with his friend the thought of one day writing a story or even a novel, again eliciting an 'ahrt-shmart.'

Now feeling challenged, Norman decided to plunge ahead with his writing, no matter Alan's slighting observations. Their friendship of over 50 years, despite occasional glitches in their intense relationship, served them both well; at times when either of them floundered through dark, desperate times, he was able to rely on the support of the other.

Norman had long before recounted to Alan the story of Fred's violent death; how his covered body was carried out on a stretcher; how Finky sobbed hysterically; how he had attempted to comfort her.

Norman now wrote down of what he recalled about that day… the high pitch of excitement… ambulance sirens… police cars screeching to the curb outside of '179'… milling jumble of curious neighbors… unsure whispers questioning the uncertain air… darting suspicious eyes demanding information… The identity of the dead body? … Who? … Man? … Woman? … Who?

Much later, Norman attempted to resurrect the melodramatic events for a short story, but failed to find a theme… a protagonist… but who?

He never wrote the story.

46

IN 1993, NORMAN, his age keeping step with the 20th century, watched President Clinton's inauguration on television, luring his memory back almost 70 years to the 1924 Presidential ceremony.

Although he had voted for Clinton, the "country boy" from Arkansas, and every other Democratic candidate way back into the late 20s, he still felt a twinge of guilt that the very first president he had voted for was the "return to normalcy" Republican, Coolidge.

The reason for this aberrational behavior from a Jew in predominantly Democratic Brooklyn was because he and Alan had been angry about the ex-president, Wilson, promising to keep the country out of the European war, but soon after he was elected in 1916... boom!... they were in it! So Alan convinced Norman that they should vote for Coolidge.

Many years later, Norman still blamed Alan for getting him to go Republican, although he had to admit to himself that, in the final analysis, he was *himself* responsible for his stupid action.

Over the years, Norman would try to keep his own mistakes in mind whenever he felt the impulse to condemn someone else's wrongdoing. In this way, he was able to develop a level of compassion by assessing a person's character and humanity on balance of *all* of their actions.

With this attitude in mind, Norman would periodically inventory his long life, which had been bombarded with an infinite number of experiences, sometimes imploding into a kaleidoscope of memories, fragmented, rearranged, forgotten, recaptured, lost, reinvented, discarded, reminisced.

47

1937 HAD VERY FEW EVENTS that were fondly recorded by Norman, but the excitement of that year: union activities; protest rallies; violent murder of Fred, laced these 365 days with a mix of dark and light.

Although this sultry summer day was very enervating, Norman and Mrs. Wax patiently tried to help Finky over her shock and grief after Fred's murder, at least to the point where she was able to get some rest.

Mrs. Wax led Finky, her sobs still racking her body, toward Norman's nearby ground floor.

"They gave Finky a pill, Normie, to make her less nervous. Can she maybe lay down by here?"

Norman nodded, gesturing toward the bedroom. Meeting with Mrs. Wax's approval, she helped Finky, heavily sedated, into the bed.

As Finky started to doze off, Mrs. Wax rejoined Norman in the living room.

"Normie, I'm going to make a bite for my Davie and the twins, so when Finky opens her eyes, give a yell up to me in my window."

After Mrs. Wax left, Norman glanced around the room, his eyes falling on the samovar, and lingering over its glistening surface, he perceived it as a symbol of not only Marsa's past, but of all elegance lost; just as Elissa's wheelchair, which he had seen on his last hospital visit, represented the present: a Throne of Protest.

Thirty years later, writing about Elissa in his journal, now metamorphosing into what he hoped could become a novel, he wrote, *"Elissa's body was a temple of pain but she managed a small degree of optimism. However, I sensed that she was paying a dreadful price. In order to survive the grueling physical workout her therapist put her through, she told me that sometimes, in order to cut down the pain, she pretended to herself that she was dead... that she could feel nothing. That must have done horrible things to her mind."*

Now, with Finky asleep in the Schecter bed, Norman switched on the light in the kitchen, a few roaches feeding on minute table crumbs, scurrying for cover.

Idly watching them for a moment before swatting them away with the back of his hand, he stepped on one of them as it hit the floor, crushing it into the grey marble linoleum. He filled the tea kettle under the kitchen faucet, the always-slow stream of water defying his impatient stare. From a small cardboard box on the counter, he took a wooden match, striking it on the hard abrasive strip on the side of the box, the match flaring up, lighting the oven burner. After placing the kettle on the flame, he suddenly reached down, opening the small cupboard under the sink. Tucked away behind a can of kitchen cleanser was a bottle of Four Roses, its label discolored because of the stored damp dish rags coming in constant contact with it. Since the bottle of Schnapps hadn't been opened for several months, Norman had to exert extra pressure in order to twist open the encrusted cap.

Norman couldn't remember how many months it had been since he last took even a partially filled shot-glass of the whiskey.

Because he had a very low tolerance for liquor, the family joke was that on the very rare occurrence of Norman taking out the bottle in honor of a birthday or holiday such as breaking the fast of Yom Kippur, there was *more* whiskey *now* in the bottle than was there months before.

Not able to find the shot glass in the kitchen closet, he poured the Four Roses into a water tumbler, almost half full.

Always disliking the taste of liquor, he quickly gulped down the whiskey. Having eaten very little during the day, the alcohol shot quickly to his senses and he became slightly dizzy within moments, sitting down quickly to retain his balance.

Finky, stirring in the bedroom, moaned loudly, the sound reaching Norman.

"Finky?"

This time Finky's sound was more of a scream. Norman turned off the oven burner, unsteadily going into the bedroom where Finky, still drugged, glanced up apprehensively. Recognizing Norman, she started to cry, speaking between sobs.

"He's dead?... He's dead?"

Norman nodded and Finky shook her head "No!" Norman, woozy, sat down on a chair near the bed.

"Finky..." he tried, comfortingly. She continued to shake her head more violently, her body trembling. Norman stood up woozily, stepping toward her, gently touching her on the shoulder. Off-balance, he stumbled, suddenly sitting down on the bed. Finky, still sobbing, reached toward Norman, putting her head on his chest. She was not being seductive, nor was Norman who held her tenderly in his embrace. He stroked her hair and her body started to relax, the drug taking effect. The whiskey had continued its dizzying effect on Norman, as he fell into the bed near Finky, who snuggled innocently next to him. Norman started to become aroused, hugging her close to him, tentatively caressing her, his hand moving up toward her breast. Finky, slipping into unconsciousness, frantically clawed at Norman.

"Freddie."

Norman, although still aroused, hesitated, holding Finky close. He closed his eyes, the whiskey taking its full effect. Later, both fell asleep.

48
Berlin, 1914

MARSA HAD A NIGHTMARE the night before she left Berlin, but she was able to recall only a few scattered, terrifying moments, which she put aside in order to prepare for this exerting day.

Her brother, Leo, and her parents, Frieda and Abe Slipoy, all left their home on Bleibtrue Strasse, sharing a taxi with her on the way to the train station to catch the special to Hamburg. Abe planned that the family would spend a night together in Hamburg before bidding Marsa *bon voyage* when she took the Liner Elbe for New York the next morning.

Abe excitedly chatted with his wife about his first important assignment as the newly appointed manager of the Berlin Philharmonic. An appointment had been arranged with Herr Vogel, his counterpart with the Hamburg Symphony, for them to discuss the Mendelssohn concert commemorating the 70th anniversary of the premiere of his famous violin concerto in E-minor.

Since Felix Mendelssohn had been born in Hamburg, it was generally felt that that city should have the privilege of having the very best presentation of the piece. Therefore, since the Berlin Philharmonic had engaged the world renowned Austrian violinist Fritz Kreisler for its performance of the Mendelssohn, the Orchestra's Board had decided to offer his services to the Hamburg Symphony if it agreed to specify the gift in their printed billboards and programs.

However, Slipoy had misgivings about honoring him because Mendelssohn, in the fashion of those days for Jews, in order to escape the ghetto, had become Lutheran, being baptized in a church. For Slipoy, who had a strong Jewish faith, this caused him to feel less about the man, though it did not affect his admiration of the magnificent lyricism of the piece, remaining a strong champion of the composer's music.

Leo, glancing out the taxi window, watched Nikolaikirche (St. Nicholas Church) as they drove by. He had recently learned in school that it was the oldest building in the city and he was excited to pass his knowledge on to the family, but his father was preparing some notes for the meeting with Herr Vogel, and Mrs. Slipoy was more interested in the fashionable shops along the broad avenue of Unter der Linden. Leo turned to Marsa, appealing for *her* attention, but Marsa's memory about the nightmare had been inexplicably jogged, now remembering it in detail: *She was working on a huge jigsaw puzzle of the sky, the pieces all exactly the same color of blue. She was almost able to complete the near impossible task of joining the unidentifiable pieces, but just as she was about to finish the puzzle, she was overwhelmed by a huge torrent of water. Gasping for breath, she started to swim expertly through the pieces which had become larger than her, threatening to slash her with their jagged edges. She managed to climb on top of one of the pieces, but Herr Schegel, her math teacher, whom she had a crush on, was poised on it, his long, long, very long arms stretched out toward her, his face set in leering invitation. Another large piece of the sky floated by, a faceless man on it, smiling in a friendly manner, but just as he reached his arms out to protect her, Herr Schegel threw him off his jigsaw puzzle raft. As the man desperately swam in the raging waters, Schegel turned malevolently toward her as she tore away from his grasp, but she started to drown.* She was saved from experiencing her death in the nightmare that she was starting to relive, by her mother turning her attention away from her window-shopping through the taxi window, speaking sharply to her.

"Why are you screaming, Marsa?"

The others had also turned toward Marsa's frightening sounds.

"What?" Marsa asked guardedly, "What?"

49
Brownsville, 1937

NORMAN FED THE DOG early in the day before the police and ambulance came for Fred's body.

Mutt had been tied up in the courtyard, and by evening when Norman had not taken it for a walk, he had finally done what he had to... right in the courtyard.

After awhile, Mutt barked a few times for more attention, producing a neighbor's agitated complaint, "Shut the fuckin' dog up!" followed by a loud, passionate indictment, "Charlie shoulda killed the mutt, too!"

The dog barked again. Finky and Norman asleep, did not respond at first, but when the barking continued, Norman stirred and shifted his body, his hand accidentally hitting the headboard. He grunted, his eyes opening, then closing... opening again quickly in order to focus on the person standing over him, rock still.

Norman's vision, still blurred because of his drinking, finally cleared enough for him to make out Marsa, her body taut in anger. Suddenly releasing her fury, she lunged at Norman, her words exploding in rage.

"Bastard! You... bastard! No good! ... Bastard!"

Norman, groggy, grabbed at Marsa's flailing arms, attempting to defend himself.

"What?!! Stop that, Marsa!"

Breathing with exertion, Marsa stopped just as Norman realized that he was lying next to Finky.

"Marsa, it's okay about Finky. Charlie —"

"The cop outside told me, and so right away, like two animals, you —"

Gesturing in disgust, Marsa left the thought unfinished.

"Marsa, we didn't —"

"And I rush over here like a crazy woman —"

"Marsa, listen, never once have I ever —"

"Like a crazy one from the hospital."

"Hospital?"

"Your son is lying there."

"What hospital? What?"

"To know 'what,' you don't deserve."

Desperate, Norman shouted, "What happened, Marsa?"

As Finky groaned, Norman pushed Marsa toward the living room.

"Tell me what happened to Ira."

"I can't stand anymore. I can't stand —"

"Marsa, what's the matter with him?"

"'What's the matter'? Polio, that's what!"

Her words hung between them like an ugly shroud, the very center of Norman freezing in terror, the diagnosis of polio in 1937 was often regarded as tantamount to a death sentence.

Marsa, barely able to speak through her sobs, managed, "The doctor says... it's very bad... bad, you hear? You hear what I said about Ira? ... You hear?"

Norman reached out comfortingly to Marsa, who pushed his arms away.

"Don't touch... monster!"

"All right, Marsa, all right. Everything will be —"

"Nothing will 'be'... nothing."

"I'll go tell Mrs. Wax to come down for Finky, and we'll go to the hospital, okay?"

Wordless, they walked rapidly toward the trolley stop. As they reached the corner, a taxicab, an unusual sight in money-pinched Brownsville, stopped for a red light. After staring in the direction of the empty streets of the trolley route, Norman hailed the cab.

Marsa was very conscious of the added expense. "We should wait for the trolley, Normie."

Taking Marsa by her arm, Norman walked them rapidly to the cab.

Marsa and Norman sat rigidly apart from each other as the cab drove through the dark streets, most of them deserted and as empty as the Schecters' lives felt to them, despair choking their terrified breathing.

The bright red-lettered emergency sign outside St. Mary's Hospital was a welcoming beacon for those in need of medical attention; a foreboding one to those concerned with the welfare of family and friends.

Marsa hurried out of the cab as Norman dug through his pockets, rounding up enough loose change to cover the seventy-five cents on the meter, handing it to the driver along with eight pennies he embarrassedly added for the tip. Staring apprehensively at the building, he tried to shrug off the barbed anxiety which had accelerated during the ten-minute ride. Marsa also paused for a moment in front of the entrance, her eyes darting around, desperately searching the friendless air for an omen that her son would be all right.

The well-polished glass entrance door reflected her face back to her. She was struck by its same look of fear that was the mirror image of what she had glimpsed in her mother's eyes twenty-five years earlier, when the Slipoys had said farewell to her at the gangplank of the Elbe.

Although she had always felt a profound love for Ira, it was now reinforced through the etched memory of her mother's face, the strength of the flesh-tempered steel of a mother's connection to her child. Taking Marsa by her reluctant arm, Norman led her through the hospital door which he had very slowly pushed open, as if deferring any bad news that could be waiting.

They cautiously, silently made their way through the old corridors, uneasy visitors to this alien land of black-dressed Sisters of Mercy. The Nuns nodded pleasantly at them as they went about their business, providing spiritual help to the patients of this crowded, under-endowed charity hospital.

Finally finding a nurse's station, Norman asked a harried nurse going over her records, for directions to Ira's room. She brusquely gestured to a passing Nun in habit, that she should help Norman and Marsa.

"The Schecters, Sister."

The Nun smiled comfortingly at them, introducing herself.

"I'm Sister Agatha, Mr. and Mrs. Schecter. I'll take you right to your son."

Marsa and Norman followed the Nun as she moved down the dim night-lit corridor, her gown's discretely rustling sound mixed with Norman and Marsa's shoes scuffing the waxed floors, sharing the hospital hush.

The night nurse's sympathetic glance followed them as Sister Agatha opened the swinging doors to Ward C, leading them into the dismal dungeon for ten children on their racks of pain, providing some small succor for the youngsters moaning in discomfort, homesickness and fear; a few of the lucky ones in a drugged, but fitful sleep.

Norman and Marsa nervously glanced around the semi-darkened ward, all of the beds similar with young bodies unidentifiable at a distance, one from the other.

Following Sister Agatha as she slowly moved down the center of the ward, five beds on each side, Norman and Marsa anxiously looked to their right and left for their son.

As Sister Agatha reached what appeared to be the end of the ward, she turned to face them.

Puzzled, Norman and Marsa stopped, silently inquiring of the nun as to where their son was. She answered by stepping aside, permitting them to get a clear view of the very end of the ward, shrouded in darkness.

What Norman and Marsa had thought was some hospital equipment that had been stored in the ward, turned out to be, as they adjusted their eyes to the light, what appeared to be an oversized, long metal box.

Marsa gasped, her breath drawn in uneven large gulps of air as Norman, stunned, his mind rejecting the idea of this metal-like coffin having anything to do with his son.

Sister Agatha gently motioned them closer, her glance leading their horrified eyes toward what seemed to be a disembodied head which, on closer examination, turned out to be the pale, waxed features of what was supposed to be their son. IT *WAS* THEIR SON!

His eyes closed in his death-like mask, his head sticking out from a tight neck-support attached to the large metal 'thing,' swallowing his entire body.

Norman, having read some medical journals at one time, was able to put a name to the 'THING'... the IRON LUNG!

He later learned some more information from Ira's Doctor Ronselli, who explained in some detail the workings of this artificial respirator for patients whose lungs were not able to function without its support.

Marsa was terrified at not knowing particulars about polio, other than that it was a deadly disease.

On the other hand, Norman had not long before read an article with its frighteningly graphic photos in the National Geographic, about different nerve sicknesses, like polio and leprosy.

He found it fascinating to learn about how the pathologies developed in both illnesses. In the case of leprosy, it was the destruction of peripheral nerves in the skin, leading to tissue degeneration.

The gradual change in a person infected by this Hansen's Disease, its medical term, produced a deformed, eroding, painful to look at, excruciating to be... a leper.

Many years later, when he had retired and had started to make entries in his journal, Norman recalled this information, applying it to the ongoing brouhaha of the Watergate scandal, and recorded his perceptions:

I think that in the eyes of the disapproving public and Congress, Nixon's overreaching need to control the government and the people, produced, if you will excuse the clumsy metaphor, an infection of another more potent, more viral sort... leprosy of the mind.

Many years later when Norman had his novel, "*There and Back*," accepted by Stein and Day publishers, he went to celebrate with Marsa at the Carnegie Deli. As they were sitting down, Marsa suddenly looked surprised, clutching at Norman's arm in pain as her eyeballs rolled upward. It was a major heart attack.

A week later, on the same day that Marsa's doctor told Norman that she might not survive the stroke, he was notified that Stein and Day had shut its presses... gone bankrupt. That day he made another journal entry.

So much for the history of my nearly published novel. I'm not going to mention it to Marsa; I'm really worried about her health.

Sister Agatha checked the iron-lung's gauges, finally turning to Marsa and Norman, explaining, "Doctor Ronselli will want to know these readings."

She abruptly started to walk toward the ward entrance.

"Sister Agatha—" Norman started to question her.

"I have to go, Mister Schecter."

Marsa added her anxiety to the moment.

"What about our sick boy?"

"There's nothing I can do right now, Mrs. Schecter."

Marsa and Norman could only watch the nun push through the ward's doors, and turning to each other, they then looked back to their son... and his iron 'coffin.'

Norman recalled how the National Geographic article explained polio: the virus affected the central nervous system. A warning was displayed in the magazine, underlining the need to 'wash your hands thoroughly after using the bathroom,' also 'there's NO KNOWN CURE!'

Norman and Marsa stood stiffly near Ira's head, the only part of their son that they could see. Neither of them cried, their hearts and feelings too frozen in fear for any overt expression to show itself.

Later, Doctor Ronselli would explain to them that in some cases, complications would include paralysis; most commonly of the legs. In many other cases, the nerves would be rendered unusable, the lungs collapsing, paralyzing the muscles needed for breathing and swallowing; very often leading to an excruciatingly painful death.

Now, the only sign that Ira was still alive was the slight tremor of his pursed, almost blue lips, as small breaths of air sighed their way out.

"Ira?" Marsa asked quietly, almost a whisper.

If Ira did indeed hear her, he was unable to answer.

Marsa hopefully called him by name again, this time in an even softer voice, as if in this way it would somehow coax him to consciousness.

A large electric fan on a pole stood in the center of the ward, its head rotating, the breeze an inadequate challenge to the overheated ward.

On one of its slowly revolving turns, a very faint breeze reached Marsa's face. Startled, her hand went to her ear, her fingers tugging at its lobe... like her mother would often do as a gesture of affectionate correction for Marsa's misbehavior.

Gasping, her imagination brought her mother to almost full presence at her side.

"Okay, Mom," she murmured.

"What?" Norman asked, glancing at her, annoyed by her *non-sequitur* comment.

"It's your fault, Normie."

"My fault? Ira being sick is *my* fault?"

"*Your* fault!"

Her answer allowed no margin for error, repeating it for even more effect.

"*Your* fault!!"

"Okay," Norman sighed, denying his responsibility by mockingly agreeing, "so it's *my* fault."

Sister Agatha, a moist cloth in her hand, hurried into the ward, stopping at one of the beds, quickly, efficiently tucking in the corner of an errant sheet, before continuing toward Norman and Marsa.

Nodding at them as she passed by, she gently wiped Ira's forehead, speaking to the Schecters.

"We're trying to keep his fever down."

"Thank you, Sister," Norman's appreciative tone was joined by Marsa's "Yes, yes, my dear, I thank you much... much."

"Don't worry, both of you; we will be doing everything we can," Sister Agatha's Southern drawl warming her assuring words. She was the cornerstone of the Catholic church's support for staff and patients of St. Mary's.

Aware of Ira's desperate life-threatening state, she knew that she would have to mobilize all of her prayers to help the highly agitated Schecters through this difficult moment of their son's terrible illness.

After absorbing the shock of seeing her son in the iron lung, Marsa again became the strong, vigilant mother protector. After all, she thought, I'm carrying another child, so I don't need this aggravation.

"Missus Agatha, what's going to be with my son?"

Norman, politely echoed his wife's concern, "We need more information, Sister."

"I told you, Mr. Schecter," Sister Agatha patiently answered, "we're doing everything we can."

Marsa was uneasy about Sister Agatha's vague reassurance. "'Doing,' is not the same as being healthy again, Missus."

Norman, attempting to ease the situation, quietly asked, "Where is the doctor in charge of Ira's case, Sister?"

"Doctor Ronselli has already examined your son... twice."

Marsa, feeling that Norman was acting much too politely regarding their son's welfare, became even more agitated, sharply demanding, "So, where's the nurse?"

"I'm sorry, but she has quite a few other patients she has to tend to."

Norman entered the fray, distressed.

"You mean there's not even one nurse for this ward?"

"Miss Templeton has four other wards she has to pay attention to, so I'll stay awhile until she's able to make her rounds here."

Marsa took over, "A nurse you're not!"

Norman again attempted to quiet the waters.

"Our son is very sick. Isn't he, Sister?"

Marsa couldn't believe that Norman was being so calm.

"You think this," gesturing toward the iron lung, "is because he's healthy?"

"Actually, Mrs. Schecter, that makes him feel better. When you see Doctor Ronselli, he'll explain exactly how it works."

"But I asked, Sister, if he's very sick."

"Well, to be honest, Mr. Schecter, polio *is* kind of dangerous."

Norman, noticing that Marsa appeared faint, staggering a bit, quickly reached over to a nearby chair, placing it behind Marsa.

"Sit, Marsa."

Reluctantly sitting, Marsa still continued her aggressive information-gathering.

"'Dangerous' is a big word, so tell me what it means with my son."

"The doctor will be here in an hour or so, and you can talk to him."

"An hour is a long time," Marsa complained.

"We'll wait," Norman added.

"Well, the visiting hours are over, but the doctor left instructions that you can see your son anytime."

"That's nice of him, but how come—?"

Sister Agatha shrugged, avoiding his eyes by dabbing her cloth at Ira's forehead again.

Marsa sat almost motionless and Norman stood in more or less the same spot until the doctor finally hurried in, starting to speak as he neared them.

"Mister and Mrs. Schecter?"

"Yes, Doctor?"

"Well, sir, we have a sick boy, but I think that we're going to get him well."

"How long does he have to," Marsa glanced at the iron lung, her voice trembling, "stay in that thing."

"We'll get him out as soon as possible, but right now his lung muscles are very weak, so he needs it to help him breathe."

"My heart doesn't feel good if he has to stay in there."

Marsa gestured toward Norman, his face frozen in frightened concern.

"My husband is also very worried, believe me, Doctor, so you must make Ira healthy again, you hear?"

"We're doing our very best, Missus Schecter."

"How long can we visit here?"

"You both can stay as long as you want to."

"What about our coming back tomorrow?"

"Anytime you want to, Mr. Schecter."

"Thank you, Doctor Ronselli."

"Can I bring him some food from the house?" Marsa asked, ever the good Jewish mother with her classic certainty that food solved everything.

"That's not necessary, Missus Schecter. We're putting him on a special diet. Do you usually feed him fruit, like oranges or grapefruits?"

"Sometimes when," glancing accusingly at Norman, "it's cheap, on sale."

"Don't worry, Missus Schecter, he'll get all the good food here he needs.

Marsa darted another angry look at Norman as Ronselli, speaking, turned to leave, "I'll be looking in on Ira in a little while."

Later, on the trolley, Norman and Marsa, except for both of them agreeing that Ira looked bad, hardly spoke to each other until Marsa pulled the signal cord to exit, Norman glancing up.

"Sarah," Marsa cryptically explained, as she exited to go to her cousin's apartment.

The rest of the ride was a gloomy one for Norman, and when he finally arrived at Amboy Street, he was upset that Mrs. Wax was approaching '179' too with a small bag of groceries. Not feeling like discussing Ira and the hospital, he slowed his pace, but so did Mrs. Wax, waiting for him to join her. After he briefly explained the situation to her, she let out an 'oy vey,' but quickly comforted him.

"Norman, listen to me; Ira will be making his Bar Mitzvah speech just like you regularly planned, believe me."

"I believe you."

"Good. A wise old Polish rabbi told me once that if you can't believe a neighbor's word, better you should move from your house."

When Norman entered the darkened apartment, he paused after switching on the light; something was odd. It took him a moment to figure it out. He went into the kitchen, picking up the clock that had wound down, winding it slowly, each creaking turn of the knob carrying with it a weight of significance: Ira is sick... creak... iron lung is good... creak... I love my son... creak... tomorrow he'll be better... creak.

He went into the bedroom. Finky had already left, but there was a note on the pillow, anchored with a small porcelain statue of Moses that Marsa had bought for 50 cents from Rabbi Mintz as a contribution to the Jewish National Fund.

As Norman read the note, he noticed that Finky had neatly made up the bed.

He read the note twice: *Dear Normie, I think I better go to my sister in the Bronx. (I just can't go upstairs again now.) You are a good guy. Love, Finky.*

Ronselli had asked Sister Agatha if she would wake him if he was able to grab a few winks on the operating room table (if it was not being used).

Understaffed, the Hospital Administrator had asked the Residents to take a double shift for the next month or so, and consequently, Ronselli had been on duty for over 25 hours.

Although he had not yet seen the results of the battery of blood tests that he had ordered for Ira, it was clear that the boy was ill, near terminal condition. If he was lucky, he might be able to get out of the lung and into a wheelchair... and perhaps linger on for a few years.

He tried as kindly as possible to explain to Marsa the reality of her son's condition.

"When your husband gets here, I'll explain it to him also."

"I'll tell him, believe me."

Marsa, after a fitful few hours of sleep at Sarah's apartment, had returned to the hospital early in the morning.

"When do I take my son home?"

"We'll see."

"Don't give me, 'we'll see.'"

"We have to wait."

"Take him out of that thing."

"He has to stay in there to keep him alive, Mrs. Schecter."

"He's like he's already dead laying there. I want you to take him out.

"I can't do that."

"Don't be a Mussolini with me."

"If you want to, you can talk to the Hospital Administrator, but I'm sure he'll agree with me that we're doing the best thing for your son's health. You just have to pray for him."

"To who? To your Jesus Christ?!"

~

As Norman left his apartment, the new mailman, who had replaced Fred, signaled the mail's arrival with a whistle hanging from a cord around his neck, a method commonly used by many neighborhood postmen. The whistle alerted the tenants, who hurried for the expected letters from relatives and friends; 'thank you' notes, wedding invitations, camping photos, one-page frantic onion skin requests from Berlin, Prague, Budapest, desperately pleading for immigration help, for money, for connections with U.S. officials who could assist in any way.

Today there were only some electric bills, a few advertisements from Thom McCann shoes, and the Relief checks for most of the building... and an official-looking letter for Norman Schecter from the Board of Education. Old Mrs. Cohen, happily clutching her relief check, smiled at Norman. Having heard about Ira's illness from Mrs. Wax, she offered words of comfort, "Tell the boychik he's still got his job and my Gloria will teach him good how to—," giggling as she winked at Norman, "you know."

When Norman entered Ira's ward, Marsa was applying rubbing alcohol to Ira's forehead. His eyes were closed, his breathing labored.

"He said 'Momma' to me before, and then he went back to sleep, mein bubila."

"Was the doctor here?"

"For a minute."

"And?"

"And nothing."

"Nothing?"

"He said everything is the same with Ira."

"That's good."

"Good with him laying there like a lox!"

Norman spoke softly to Ira, "Ira?"

Ira's lips weakly formed a word, "Pop."

Norman was pleased, proud that his son, in pain, would salute him. Norman turned toward Marsa again, started to speak, but hesitated as he fingered the Board of Education letter in his pocket.

Earlier he had hurried over to meet with his assistant, Danny Watkins, in order to consult with him about the letter's content: the Board offering to reinstate him as a permanent teacher.

"When do they want you to start, Norman?"

"As soon as I send in my letter of acceptance."

"Well, what do you think about it?"

"Look, I know they're just trying to buy me out, maybe get some information about our plans."

"But like you said, Norman, the time is right now for us to make a union-wide move, or we might lose everything we've fought for."

"I know that, Danny, but..."

"You're the one we're counting on to get us up on the barricades, Norman."

Watkins had picked up the TOTAL COMMITMENT sign that Norman had improvised at the last H.E.S. union meeting, and he now placed it on the table in front of Norman.

"This belong to you?"

~

Norman, facing Marsa, showed her the Board's letter.

"So, Normie?"

"So, I have to think."

"What's to think?"

Norman hesitated before silently putting the letter back into his pocket. There were the ward's usual morning activities; trays of food brought to the beds; Sister Agatha and a nurse's assistant straightening untidy bed sheets; the muffled moans of the aches and pains of the discomforted, lonely children.

"You know what, Normie?"

"What?"

"I can't even hold my son's hand."

Sister Agatha, her hands cupped around a bowl of hot cereal, approached them.

"Doctor Ronselli said that we should try to feed Ira some of this."

"I'll do this for you, missus," Marsa offered, taking the bowl out of Sister Agatha's hand. "With *me*, he'll eat better."

"Of course."

"Maybe you're a good person, but a mother is a mother."

She blew on the oats, cooling them before she carefully placed a spoonful of it into Ira's mouth, murmuring comfortingly. Ira's eyes, veiled with exhaustion, communicated little but a silent cry for help.

Forty years later, Norman shuddered in response to that same look he saw in his daughter, Edith's, eyes. Confused, questioning the mysterious deterioration of her once-strong body as it morphed into an emaciated, pain-wracked one.

By that time, Norman was happy that Marsa would not be able to see her daughter's life disappearing, wasting away, diseased by an illness he had barely come to learn about, reading an article in *Time Magazine*, describing the beginnings of this modern plague… AIDS.

Edith's daughter, Miriam, was only 11 years old when she started to visit her mother in the hospice.

~

Taking a break in the dingy hospital cafeteria, Norman and Marsa decided to 'grab a bite.' Toast and coffee was five cents, so they shared.

"Don't you want your own cup of coffee, Marsa?"

"I'll wait till I go have tea with my cousin, Sarah."

Glancing out of the cafeteria window, Norman smiled at a light drizzle that had started to darken the already overcast day.

"It's nice to be inside with your son on a day like this," he thought.

Marsa followed his glance, the weather also affecting *her*.

"It's miserable like my life," she thought.

When Norman and Marsa returned to the ward, Dr. Ronselli, Nurse Templeton at his side, were leaning over Ira. The doctor spoke hurriedly to the nurse who nodded and quickly walked past the Schecters as she left the ward.

Marsa and Norman sat watching Ira for any indication of change in his condition… the slightest head movement…

lip quiver… eye blink, would carry for them a significant implication for his recovery… or life-threatening danger.

Idly glancing around the ward, Norman, for the first time, noticed the variety of distressing problems of the different youngsters.

Three beds down from Ira was a boy whose two broken legs, casts up to their knees, sat on the side of the bed, gingerly massaging his upper thighs. Another bed cushioned a terrified teen-age girl whose bald head was swathed in a bulky bandage which she picked at as she moaned in agony because of her third-degree burns; a boy of five or six, recovering from an emergency appendectomy, his hands grimly clasped across his distended stomach, writhed in his bed, his anesthetic worn off.

The sound of the room comprised different discordant energies… wheeling medicine carts; nurses rushing to check the children's vital signs as they cried for surcease of their pains; the hushed, mumbled sympathy of family visits; children collecting their meager things to go home; attendants sadly packing the hopeful toys and games left behind by those children who did not survive their terminal illness.

The hospital… a temple of comfort and hopes… of despair, of life and death.

Marsa and Norman watched and waited… through most of that day and night, but nothing seemed to change in Ira's condition, even when Nurse Templeton gave him a hypodermic.

"What, Nurse… what?"

"It's to help him sleep, Mrs. Schecter."

"He sleeps all the time, Miss Templeton."

"His eyes are closed, but he is not sleeping, Mrs. Schecter. This makes him breathe easier."

Templeton left them watching their son in the silence of their terrified thoughts. The drizzle had become a heavy rain, and when Marsa decided to stay, Norman remembered that he had to get back home to feed and walk Mutt, Marsa admonishing him to get into dry clothes as soon as he got home.

"One sick person to a family is enough, Normie."

Although Norman felt he should save the five cent trolley fare, as he walked through the heavy rain, he realized that the real reason was that he was looking forward to letting the rain soak him, a kind of cleansing of his spirit, feeling that the inconvenience of being wet was little, weighed against his son's plight. As his shoes sounded a flop... flop... suctioning off of the pavement, bonding him closer to his son, he straightened up against the ever-increasing downpour, feeling that this present hardship would in some way help to cure his son.

~

When Norman had called Alan about Ira's sudden life-threatening illness, his friend was genuinely distressed by the news.

"I can catch a bus and be at the hospital in twenty minutes."

"Thanks, Alan, but right now me'n Marsa are going to spend all the time we can with Ira."

"What about money for the hospital?"

"Right now all I can think about is getting Ira healthy again."

"But it'll cost, my friend."

"'I have to hurry up and get back to him, Alan."

"Okay, but money—"

Norman had hung up.

50

SAM, IN THE FRONT ROOM OF MULNICK AND SON, was talking to a man nervously shifting his feet as he clutched a worn briefcase.

"You talk like a Cossack, Sokoloff!"

"Listen to the man talk. We came over on the boat together, Sam, so don't insult me."

Sam pantomimed a two-handed, sword-slashing gesture.

"Like a Cossack!"

"I'm doing my best, Sam, but the supervisor knows your payments are three months overdue, so he says that..."

Sam interrupted, "Thirty-two years, Sokoloff, *thirty-two years* I'm with your stinking Atlantic Fire Insurance, my old landsman, Harry."

"You know I'm not the one makes the rules, Sam."

Alan had entered the room.

"Bullshit with your rules!"

"Alan... respect, my son."

Fuming, Alan turned to Sokoloff.

"Every time your goddamn rates go up, we pay you the blood-money, right?"

"Up until May, your father did." Sokoloff ceded, but Sam was becoming short-fused.

"So after all these years," Sam protested, "a man is not good for the money a little longer?"

Sokoloff tugged a letter out of his briefcase. "Look," brandishing the piece of paper in Sam's face. "The supervisor," his voice almost pleading, "... yelled... my job... you have to pay!"

"Or what?" Alan challenged.

"I don't want it like this, Alan, believe me, but the insurance stops" — pushing the letter toward Sam — "...October first, unless..."

"That's nice," Sam's sarcasm made a painful point, "you give me till after Yom Kippur."

Sam's breathing was coming hard.

"Papa," Alan was very concerned, "... your heart."

Shaking Alan off, Sam still focused on Sokoloff, "My mother used to give you a piece strudel in the old country, remember?"

Sokoloff nodded in remembered appreciation, "God bless the good woman."

"On her grave, Sokoloff, I swear I don't have the money."

"I know, Sam, but the supervisor orders me."

Alan stepped between the two men, "Fuck you and the supervisor!"

"Alan," Sam admonished him, "... enough! Every man in society has a job to do."

"Yeah, Papa, there's always the guy who runs the electric chair, too."

Sam, fight leaving him, slumped in his chair, Alan watching him in concern.

51

"**I DON'T LIKE THIS, POP**." Ira said sharply.

Norman had arrived at the hospital just as Marsa finished feeding him some more oatmeal.

"But this stuff is good for you."

"I mean, I don't like being here, Pop."

"Don't worry, mein zindel," Marsa soothed him, "Home you'll be soon."

As she placed the empty bowl on a nearby table, Norman observed her unsteady movement."

"Marsa, get some rest; I'll stay with him."

"I don't need any rest."

"Marsa, please, you have to take care of yourself."

"Mom?"

"You want more oatmeal?"

Ira gasped, his breath stopping for a frightening moment before being pushed out again. Marsa glanced sharply at Norman.

"Go get the doctor!"

Norman hesitated, speaking apprehensively to his son," Ira?"

Impatient, Marsa hurried out of the ward as Norman stepped closer to the iron lung.

"Can you hear me, Ira?"

Ira's words were forced, but clear.

"I don't like this, Pop."

"Does Doctor Ronselli treat you well?"

Ira managed to nod, a weary struggle against engulfing terror.

Staring down at his son, Norman, more accepting of mortality than his son, put a name to his own frozen feeling... death.

Norman summoned up an encouraging tone, "I don't like this either, Ira, so we're going to do something about it, don't you worry."

Marsa returned in a few minutes, almost shoving Doctor Ronselli in front of her. After examining Ira, he gently patted him on his fevered forehead.

"Try to sleep."

Turning to Marsa and Norman, he half-smiled his attempted encouragement.

"I'll look in on him later." He gently patted the iron lung.

Only slightly relieved, Marsa and Norman sat near Ira for a couple of hours, watching his every facial movement, his labored breathing. Finally Norman convinced Marsa, obviously fatigued, to leave with him.

~

Marsa got off the trolley alone to visit her cousin Sarah where, over a glass of tea, she attempted, to hold back her tears as she spoke about Ira's condition, the word 'polio' being sobbed with awe and fear.

Norman went back to '179,' the apartment becoming more and more an alien space where his fitful sleep was laced with jumbled images of bird-like animals battling ferociously in a maze of mirrors, reflecting distorted, eerie images threatening to choke him.

~

Ira groggily awakened in the middle of the night, his eyes slowly adjusting, sleep still clogging his comprehension.

A candle wick suddenly flickered into a small flame, startling the ward's darkness, revealing in hazy silhouette Ronselli whispering to another man. The light from the candle held by Sister Agatha, standing at the head of Ira's bed, played around her somber face, her eyes staring compassionately at Ira. She rolled a six-foot-high portable screen to where it enclosed them and the iron lung, cutting off the area from the rest of the ward.

Ira suddenly became aware that the man who had been speaking with Ronselli was now seated on the floor As the man, wearing a white clerical collar, started to speak, Ira realized that he was actually kneeling next to the iron lung. As Ira's eyes focused, he saw the man's lips moving in speech, but was not able to make out the words.

Ira questioned the soft-spoken man, "What?"

The man raised his volume, carefully forming the words, "What's your faith, son?"

Ira was unable to fathom the meaning of the question. As he considered what the significance of the 'faith' reference was, eyeing the man's clerical collar, he recalled the movie he had seen recently in which a priest tried to get James Cagney, the killer, to go 'straight,' and he suddenly realized what the man meant, even as the priest at his bedside explained his question.

"What's your religion, son?"

Ira hesitated before answering nervously, aware that the man's religion was definitely not *his*.

He almost stuttered his reluctant answer, "I'm... I'm Jewish... mister."

The priest gently reassured him, "That's all right son," and started to pray.

Although Ira felt that the priest was well intentioned, he sensed that what was happening was *not* a good thing for him.

When Ira glanced apprehensively toward Sister Agatha, she quickly responded comfortingly to his uneasiness, "It's okay, Ira."

Ira, unconvinced, shook his head. "No!"

"Father Carey is just praying for you, Ira. You see, if you have to go to heaven, he's praying that—"

"No!"

"Ira, it's—"

"No!"

Ira, in protest, raised his head. "No!... I don't wanna! I don't wanna!..."

Sister Agatha stepped closer, as Ira strained his head forward as much as possible, the desperate force of his will seeming to move the iron lung itself. "I DON'T WANNA!"

A huge surge of resistance welled up in him even as the priest continued his earnestly voiced prayer to help the boy 'through this valley of pain and danger, keeping his soul alive.'

Ira repeated his rejection of the dark mist which was closing in on him.

"I don't wanna!" he heard himself say before his eyelids started to droop heavily, a strange feeling of peace coursing through his exhausted body as he struggled to take another breath.

52

AT THE TIME OF THE KENNEDY ASSASSINATION in November 1963, Norman hadn't spoken to his former union partner, Danny Watkins, since their argument several months earlier.

The heated disagreement had been over the fact that Watkins, who had become a union vice-president, asked Norman, now Superintendent of Schools if, since he had once been an active member of the Teachers' Union, he would join the delegation that would be going down to Washington, D.C. in August for the civil rights march, joining Reverend Martin Luther King, Jr.

Not having been in touch with each other since Norman had become a high school principal some 20 years before, at first they had cordially shared friendly reminiscences about the 'old days.'

Because Norman had resigned from the Union in order to join the Administrator's Guild, Watkins brought Norman up to date about some of their fellow union members:

Connie Washington, one of the few Negroes involved in the Union's activities, had gone on to become a successful lawyer dealing with medical malpractice cases, and several years later became the first black New York State Representative.

Dysart, vociferous conservative agitator during the mid-30's heated union debates, had become a real estate developer after World War II ended. The need for housing, coupled with the G.I. bill assisting veteran home buyers, led to a building boom. Early on, he innovated the concept of exercise facilities in some of the buildings, the idea soon becoming a standard for more luxurious complexes. In recent years, he had philanthropically supported the House of the Good Shepherd, a private religious home for delinquent teenagers and unwed mothers whose families had turned their backs on them.

As for Jerry Goldstein, the Red agitator, he had been working as a drill-press operator in a tool company since having been dismissed from the school system during the 50's McCarthy red-hunting hysteria. Watkins had been at the meeting with the committee, which was preparing the credential approval for teachers who were willing to declare, under oath, that they were not, nor ever had been, a member of the Communist party.

In Goldstein's case, they told Watkins that they had already obtained sworn testimony from a fellow union member that Goldstein was a card-carrying Communist.

"Do *you* know who did that, Schecter?"

"How the hell would I know."

"You sure, Normie?"

"What does that mean?"

"Anyway, you going to come with us to D.C.?"

"I asked you, what are you getting at?"

In that moment, Watkins knew who had turned in Goldstein.

"I'm not saying I wouldn't've done the same thing, Normie."

"You son of a bitch, you accusing me of feeding him to the lions?"

"C'mon, Normie, it was a long time ago when things were different."

"Well, some things always remain the same, Watkins."

"Like?"

"Like people who blame everything on somebody or something other than themselves."

"Like Jerry Goldstein?"

"You were always the cleverest one in the Union, Watkins."

"Don't minimize what I'm saying by smearing it on."

"You really think I'm doing that?"

"Guilt makes us do strange things."

"Well, you can give my space on the delegation to a more worthy person."

And *that* was *that* for Norman and Danny… until now that Watkins had come to Norman, hoping that the trauma of Kennedy's assassination would cause their past rancor to be subordinated to the common good, to respond responsibly to the country's needs at this fragile time. Prompted by the assassination, Watkins had organized a think-tank from among some civic leaders, scholars and intellectuals, to develop an agenda for dealing with the violence that had been surfacing even before the catastrophic tragedy; gang fights, racial turmoil, gun battles had long been woven into the fabric of society.

Explaining the program to Norman over a cup of coffee, their past differences seemed to slide away. Norman was impressed by Watkins's plan to organize citizen groups which hopefully would be tools for bridging differences in disparate areas of the city, hopefully, the country.

53

IT WAS NOT UNTIL MANY YEARS LATER, during the Vietnam War protests, that Norman confronted some of his past behavior which he felt reflected a mean-spiritedness… edged with dishonesty.

He struggled to reach a kinder self-evaluation, but cautioned himself that because he was aware of the instinct to justify wrong-doing, it would be wise for him to keep an exacting eye on his moral compass.

He sensed a twinge of regret, recalling instances when, as a high-school principal, he felt it his responsibility to file negative reports about teachers who were not in total compliance with the Board of Education regulations; then, as superintendent of schools, when it came to his attention that there were rule infractions and what he considered bald acts of insubordination, he quickly responded: some of the teachers had angrily argued against their having to teach from their assigned history books dealing with political dynamics. The point of contention was the text's indictment of the Communist systems of Russia, Cuba, and the growing threat of what promised to become the world's largest and most powerful Red regime… mainland China.

The growing groups of activists heatedly disapproved of the hard-line view of labeling these countries as imminent threats to the United States. The dissenting teachers judged this stance as dated and completely reactionary. In its place, they agitated for a conciliatory policy to be initiated in order to lessen the peril of a world nuclear catastrophe.

When several teachers attempted to introduce these opposing views into the curriculum, Norman contrived to have their credentials canceled.

The activists immediately hired a Teachers' Union lawyer to dispute Norman's 'arbitrary use of power' denying them the right to question the properness of the Board's decision.

Norman hastily circled the wagons, enlisting the support of two Councilmen and a New York State Supreme Court Judge. The lawsuit was quickly squelched by an impatient judge who, because of the 'frivolous charges,' held the union responsible for all court costs.

Norman, in an apparent gesture of reconciliation, arranged for those who had been involved and were now interested in returning to the school system as probational teachers, to re-earn their credentialed status by assisting in helping him form his innovative new program. It was to be built on classes designed for mentally handicapped children, working with professional people of varied child-care experience.

Norman saw this peace offering as evidence of his even-handedness, weighing this good intention 'on balance' with his prior severe disciplinary actions against these same teachers.

His conscience was genuinely at ease now… almost.

Eventually, this feeling of equanimity was jarred loose by what he found himself doing during the Vietnam protests.

Whenever he would think of those days, he would invariably link it to the day when Oleshe, the candy store owner, rushed to '179' in order to tell him that the doctor from St. Mary's hospital was on the phone.

Perhaps, Norman thought, it was nothing more than the fact that it was very hot and sunny that day, similar to this steamy summer afternoon when the war protestors marched in front of the Foley Square Courthouse in New York.

Some bystanders, several in their old military uniforms, linked arms as they marched alongside banners and signs: 'BRING THE TROOPS BACK... NIXON IS A TRAITOR... GENERAL WESTMORELAND LIES.'

Armed with the knowledge that many New York teachers had signed petitions against the conflict, Norman had decided to go to Foley Square and see for himself the extent of their objection to the war.

He was surprised at the force and energy of the demonstrators, and since he had brought the color Polaroid camera that Marsa had presented him with for his birthday, he took photos of some of the teachers who were participating. His mind went to Elissa Jackman and what she would have thought of the irony of him photographing war protestors.

Although he wasn't to consider writing as a vocation until a couple of years later when he retired, now watching the excited crowds milling around, ignited his desire to try his hand at fiction.

For the moment, he was interested only in getting back to his office in order to match the names of teachers that he knew to the photos he had taken.

At the time, he wasn't clear as to why he was doing this; but later, yielding to the pressure of the Board of Education and some government officials, he reluctantly shared his information with them about the protest marchers.

54

WHEN IRA HEARD FATHER CAREY, kneeling beside the iron lung, praying for him, he was uneasy with the fact that although the priest meant well and all that, at the same time he was saying things that made Ira feel that in some way, his life was in real danger.

His difficulty in breathing, and the heavy medication he had been given, overwhelmed him, his drugged thoughts tumbling over one another as they splintered into fragments, ricocheting off one another, sliding in and out of clarity trying to outrace confusion, an ephemeral contest.

Waves of sinuous mist threatened Ira's frightened air... screams of terror desperately clutched their echoes.

Panicked by being enticed into a bottomless dark pit which could snuff out his breath, Ira frantically scrambled to climb back out. In order to survive, he would have to battle against the priest and Sister Agatha's welcoming him into a heaven that he wanted no part of. The comfort it provided, luring the boy to surrender his life, was the incentive he desperately needed in order to fight off his imminent death. His back against the wall, Ira defiantly murmured, "I don't wanna... I don't wanna."

~

Norman rushed to take the trolley to St. Mary's where he met Marsa just as she also arrived at the main entrance to the hospital.

"What did that Ronselli call *you* about, Normie?"

"To hurry up here."

"Just 'hurry up' is an answer?"

"Maybe it's good news he wants to tell us himself."

"A goy speaks only bad things."

Norman gently guided Marsa into the small waiting room. A tired maintenance man was finishing mopping away the shoe scuff-marks of all the visitors who anxiously paced and worried their way to the reception desk to check on a patient's status. The pungent smell of strong ammonia cleanser hung heavy in the limited space, causing some of the visitors' eyes to tear. Norman, wiping at his eyes, impatiently jabbed at the elevator button as Marsa stood rigidly in front of its doors, as if commanding it to open quickly. The wizened old operator slid back the worn metal gate, scowling his impatient invitation.

"Awright... c'mon... c'mon... what floor?"

Marsa hesitated for a moment, apprehensive of what she might have to deal with when they reached Ira's floor. Norman hurried into the elevator, extending his hand toward Marsa as she joined him. Annoyed at the delay, the elevator operator drew shut the accordion-type gate, the grating sound punctuating Norman and Marsa's anxiety.

As soon as they got off the elevator, to the drone of the operator's "Watchya step," they somehow sensed that things were going to be very much different once they reached where their son was lying, "stretched out," Marsa had said more than once, "like a lox."

As they entered Ira's ward, their fear shrouding them made it seem as if their bodies had not really arrived with them. They were both shocked at seeing their friend Alan and his wife, Janet, talking seriously to Ronselli, the three of them huddled beside the iron lung.

"Oi," Marsa blurted out, frightened at the implication of what the discussion might be about. "They're waiting for the Mackamovitz."

"Don't worry, Marsa, your Jewish Angel of Death," Norman reassured her, "is not allowed in Christian hospitals."

"Funny you're not."

Ronselli waved them over to join him, and they quickly crossed toward him, their feelings of concern clearly etched in their faces and body language.

As Ronselli started to speak, they both stared hopefully at him.

"Your son is a pretty tough kid, y'know that?"

"Is he all right, Doctor?... Tell me, honest."

"Well, Mrs. Schecter, he's still sick. So he has to stay in the lung for awhile longer, but it looks like he's getting better."

Marsa and Norman quickly glanced over at Ira, his eyes closed, his face pink.

"He's breathing much easier," Ronselli hopefully offered, apparently pleased with Ira's condition.

Alan, excited, turned to Norman.

"The Schecters should celebrate; the doctor told me it's lucky he's alive."

Although Norman was extremely pleased with what appeared to be a good turn of events for Ira's health, he was nonetheless cautious.

"What does that mean, 'looks like he's getting better,' Doctor?"

"Do you believe in miracles, Mr. Schecter?"

"Miracles?"

"What's with the miracle?" Marsa interjected, trying to take over the discussion.

"It's very simple, Mrs. Schecter. Last night I told Sister Agatha to get the priest to come in and pray for Ira because I honestly thought that your son was not going to make it. Well, something happened during the night, because he suddenly has made a remarkable recovery. It's a miracle!"

"You sound, my good Doctor," Marsa rejoined the conversation, "like a rabbi, you should forgive the expression, who can take a piece of trayfe, and—"

Norman quickly translated for Ronselli, "Unkosher meat, for instance."

Marsa continued her example, "and with his blessings, turn it into a good kosher steak. *That's* a miracle."

Janet put her arm comfortingly around Marsa's shoulder.

"He's going to have a good Bar Mitzvah, Marsa, don't worry."

"You're a friend, Janet... a friend."

Ronselli motioned for Norman to accompany him to the iron lung, indicating a small window in its side.

"You can see when the air is pumped out of the casing, the reduction in pressure makes the chest rise, filling his lungs."

Marsa and Norman took turns looking in at their son, encased in this frightening metal cylinder, as Ronselli continued his clinical description, attempting a compassionate tone, "—and when the air is allowed back into the casement, the lungs empty, so Ira is actually well taken care of."

Marsa fondly patted the contraption that was saving her son's life, as Norman tapped Ronselli's shoulder.

"Good job, Doctor."

"So far."

Ronselli's reply worried Janet.

"'So far' doesn't sound too good to me."

"Well, Ira is a very sick boy."

"So what happens now, Doctor?"

Norman's glance at Ronselli asked the same question, the doctor hesitating a moment before answering.

"First of all, he's going to have to stay in the lung for awhile."

"But what about" Marsa angrily added, "the miracle?"

"It saved his life, Mrs. Schecter, but now we have to see what else we can do for him."

Norman reassuringly placed his hand on Marsa's.

"The doctor is doing everything he can, Marsa."

"When the boy gets out of the lung, he—," Ronselli started to explain.

"When? When?" Marsa anxiously asked.

"It could be in a few days if we're lucky... maybe longer," Ronselli explained.

"What's with this 'maybe'?"

"The truth is that if Ira continues to get better, eventually we'll be able to get him out to breathe on his own, but we can't be sure if and when that happens."

Norman, not wanting to upset Marsa anymore than necessary, spoke quietly to Ronselli.

"Exactly what does that 'if' mean, Doctor?"

"Well, maybe I shouldn't've got you so excited by what happened with Ira, last night."

Marsa's anxiety came back full force.

"You're getting me *crazy*. First it's a miracle and now it's a big 'if.'"

Ronselli started to feel sorry about having been so positive about Ira's condition and starting this questioning. After all, he had other patients he had to take care of, but he tried to curb his impatience at the Schecters' grilling him.

"I have to go now, but I'll talk to you tomorrow."

Norman nodded politely, but Alan blocked Ronselli's way as he started to leave.

"What happens to Ira *when* he gets out of this tin can?"

Ronselli spoke his words carefully, underlining their significance.

"I don't have an answer, but—" and then speaking ever slower, "But he... is... alive."

Alan reluctantly stepped aside for Ronselli, now agitated by the conversation.

"One other thing..."

Norman and Marsa spoke at the same time.

"What?"

"Once I get him out of here, it's up to you to feed him on a good healthy diet."

Norman was quick to respond, "Don't worry about that, Doctor."

Marsa was also quick to respond... to Norman.

"'Don't worry,' you say, so easy."

"Stop it, Marsa."

Ronselli hadn't slept for almost twenty hours, so his usual reasonableness had worn thin.

"Look, you two can work out your problems later, but right now Ira's the one who—"

Although Norman felt that Ronselli's point was well taken, he defensively turned toward him.

"I don't think you really understand what—"

"No!" Ronselli almost shouted, "*you* don't understand, Schecter. I've done everything I can, and if I finally get him out of the lung so he can go home, he'll be *your* responsibility. Do you know that every test we ran on Ira when he got here showed he was dangerously malnourished? Goddamnit, Schecter, you look like an educated man, you should know better. Use your brain, the boy will have to eat better, that's all. You're his father, you have to take care of him. You feed this boy, understand? You feed him, or save your pennies for his funeral… or if he's lucky, he can spend the rest of his life in a wheelchair."

Ronselli abruptly wheeled out of the ward, the humming sound of the iron lung a roar in the stillness.

55

NORMAN SAT NEXT TO ALAN on the trolley, the wooden seat they shared only partially cushioning the bumpy, clattering ride. Alan's wife, Janet, sitting behind them, tried unsuccessfully to eavesdrop on their conversation.

At the hospital, Janet had suggested that she accompany Marsa to Amboy Street, but when her friend had, in hushed tones, told her that she was living at her cousin Sarah's apartment, she had left with her husband and Norman.

Because Alan had told Janet about Norman having volunteered some possible help of a few dollars for Esther's braces, she assumed that that was what their whispered conversation was all about.

She was wrong.

Alan leaned very close to Norman.

"Like I told you, I've got it all worked out, okay?"

"I have to really think about it, Alan."

"You heard the doctor, didn't you?"

"I heard."

"So what's to think? Maybe *you* don't want some money for yourself, but what about your son?"

"Well—"

"'Well' is a hole in the ground."

"Anyway, Alan, there's something else."

"Of course there's something else, my friend."

"What, my friend?"

"Marsa."

"What about her, Alan?"

"Well, as it is, she's out of your apartment, right?"

"For now."

"What about the future?"

"What about it?"

"Well, there's something called divorce."

"Don't be a schmuck."

"No, *you* don't be a schmuck."

Janet, hearing Alan's raised voice, admonished them.

"Shh!... There's people."

Neither of the two men spoke for a minute until Norman, with a deep sigh, expelled his breath and spoke quietly to Alan.

"When?"

"Yom Kippur."

Janet, hearing Alan, leaned forward again.

"Are we going to the Utica Avenue Shul this year?"

Janet hoped that they would be able to afford the dollar tickets, a contribution to the synagogue for the services on this High Holiday.

Alan lowered his voice even more.

"Come to the store tomorrow morning."

"Tomorrow I'll be at the hospital."

"Yeah, but if he's feeling better and the doctor says it's okay to leave for 30-40 minutes, come on over, okay?"

"Thanks for coming to see Ira."

"Next to my daughter, Esther, he's the," sincerely, "best kid in Brownsville."

Alan, interpreting Norman's questioning glance as being critical, smilingly amended his comment, "maybe in Brooklyn."

When Norman good-naturedly shook his head, Alan added "in New York?... maybe the country?"

Norman's comment 'schmuck' was warmly offered, and Alan's returned 'schmuck' was more of the same.

They were friends, dedicated in their affection for each other.

56

August 24, 1937
Beth-El Hospital

Dear Ira,

I'm really sorry I didn't get to talk to you that time you came to visit me. Because they had just moved me to this hospital for special treatment on my back, I was very tired and fell asleep, but your father told me about your coming to meet me, so now I plan to visit ***you*** *in* ***your*** *hospital.*

(By the way, your father **and** *mother have been very kind to me. Your mother taught me different knitting stitches and your pop is a great chess teacher.)*

I'll be able to see you at St. Mary's hospital as soon as they get me well enough to put me in a wheelchair for the trip there. And your father told me that you are recovering from your attack and maybe you will be able to get out of that iron lung (I saw that thing when I was there) and maybe we can talk and have a wheelchair race, that would be great. Maybe we can get President Roosevelt (he has polio like you) to race with us. Ha! Ha!

Your father came to visit me and told me about your condition becoming a little better. From my own experience, I can give you a word of advice. Actually, it's something I read in a play once. A girl about my age asks a good question: Does any human being ever realize life as they live it, every, every single minute? Well that's something I copied on a piece of paper that I tacked up on the wall so I could read it once in a while. Sometimes, when I feel depressed, I look at those words and they remind me about all the good things that happen to me. So it makes me feel a little better. Oh sure, sometimes when I have a bad day it's hard to do that, but all I can say is that you should try to keep your mind on the good things that happen, and realize that you are lucky, 'every, every single minute.'

Well, I really look forward to finally meeting you.

Your friend to be,
Elissa.

57

IRA'S HOSPITAL STAY *was* called a miracle by Sister Agatha.

In a week he was out of the iron lung, and into his bed. In another week, he was sitting up, and a few days later was in a wheelchair, proudly wheeling around the ward, tagging along after the Sister as she served meals to the bed-ridden children.

Doctor Ronselli marveled at Ira's recovery, the hospital administration referring to his case as the $500 miracle, since it was estimated that Ira's hospitalization would ordinarily cost that much. Because of the family's financial difficulties, everything was provided free of charge, but the Schecters agreed that should their money problems improve, they would make some payments toward their bill. At the moment, it seemed to Marsa that it was unlikely that that would ever happen. Norman was more optimistic.

"You'll see, Marsa, it won't be too long."

"Just get me out of Brownsville, make *that* not too long."

Norman nodded encouragingly, his thoughts focusing on Alan's arson plan. Whatever problems Norman had wrestling with the legality and morality of that act, they were weighed and found wanting in the balance of Ira's health. Norman, having read Victor Hugo's novel, Les Miserables, in his youth had grappled intellectually with the ethical dilemma of Jean Valjean stealing food for his starving family, but *now* he struggled with his own *Les Miserables* history, perceiving the fire as being the much needed loaf of bread to save Ira's life.

In the meantime, the Schecters, in appreciation of St. Mary's life-saving treatment of Ira, expressed their thanks through Marsa's painstakingly embroidered pillow case in multi-colored threads, announcing that ST. MARY IS VERY GOOD, and Norman 'volunteering' to spend time in the children's wards, reading them books such as *The Three Musketeers*, *The Hardy Boys* and *Nancy Drew, Detective*.

Although his schedule was extremely busy with his work at the hospital; involvement with union activities; time spent at '179' with Ira now that he was home again; occasionally meeting with Alan in order to go over the specifics of the fire plans; his paramount concern became Ira's upcoming Bar-Mitzvah, the boy's entrance into manhood.

58

IN 1934, at about the same time that Norman was having his problems with Abraham Lincoln's Principal, Mason, regarding the school protests, Rabbi Mintz was opportunely taking advantage of a protest of another sort. Two local lawyers and an accountant had joined forces in arguing against Gergen Realty's raised rental demands for their office spaces in an aging building in the sluggish business area of Brownsville.

Gergens responded quickly and severely; ordering them out within 30 days.

Rabbi Mintz coincidentally, or in what he perceived as 'divine intervention,' in that his small storefront synagogue had been condemned by the Board of Health as uninhabitable, sending him desperately scouring the neighborhood for another location, just as the lawyers and accountants were vacating their offices.

Mintz moved quickly to rent the space, using the savings that he had managed over the years to accumulate from the fees from his Hebrew-school teaching of children, plus the proceeds from a small industry that his wife, Gladys, energetically organized. She had enlisted the help of several of his congregation who volunteered occasional use of their bathtubs which were then filled with grapes, sugar and yeast, fermenting into a concoction of wine, illegal, but as tasty as any manufactured brand, and far less expensive, although not considered kosher by Orthodox Jews.

59

"WHERE DID YOU GET THIS PICTURE, MIRIAM?"

Norman's granddaughter glanced at him as she opened the blinds of the North Tower window looking toward the river.

"What, Grandpa?"

"I haven't seen this one in over 20 years."

Miriam looked down at the photo on her desk.

"It was the only one mother had with her at the hospice."

They both studied the small black and white photo.

Crowded into the frame was Ira, about 18, wearing Marine Corps khaki, his arm lightly around the shoulders of a little dark-haired girl of five or six, Norman and Marsa in their mid-forties, smiling proudly.

"I'm sorry, Grandpa, I should have had a copy made for you."

"Don't worry, Miriam, I made a," tapping his forehead, "—duplicate I can look at anytime I want to."

Norman, stretching his legs, grunted his discomfort.

"You okay, Grandpa?"

"Uh huh."

"You know I always thought I looked a lot like Ira."

"You're right, my darling, especially when he was younger."

As he spoke, Norman had taken out his wallet. He opened one of its compartments, carefully removing a photo. Its corners were curled with age, razor-thin cracks streaking the faded black and white surface. Ira, wearing a yarmulke, a prayer shawl draped around his shoulders, stared solemnly into the camera, Norman and Marsa standing stiffly nearby.

As Miriam glanced at the photo, she nodded in agreement.

"Grandma was pregnant with Mother, right?"

"Very big."

"Yes."

"In that long time ago… long ago…"

Norman's voice trailed off, caught in that 'long ago.'

After a moment, Miriam gently prompted Norman.

"Grandpa?"

"Yes, my beautiful granddaughter?"

"I have some pictures of Mother in her teens, and she looked so much like this photo of Ira."

"They were like the same face."

Norman's eyes were filling, his voice faltering, but he continued with great effort.

"It has been said that I am an elderly person, which I admit is a possibility, but I am in possession of most of my senses, so I tell you that your Uncle Ira, and your mom, my sweet daughter, Edith…" His words muffled by his growing emotion, struggled out, as he continued.

"Ira will always be one of those stout hearted men."

He started to sing quietly, "Give me some men who are stout-hearted men, and I'll give you—"

Norman's sad mien was suddenly colored by a flicker of pleasure. Norman considered telling Miriam why this small feeling of joy had overtaken his melancholy, but he realized it would be impossible to explain why, at odd moments, his thoughts would go to the time when he sat with 5-year-old Ira under the limited protection of a tree that kept some of the rain off of them as he patiently taught his son the words to Stout-Hearted Men, singing…

"—And I'll soon give you 10 thousand more."

As his words melded into memory, he stopped, suddenly connected to the present moment.

"So, Miriam, you are a success here in your richly appointed office?"

"I'm very happy here, yes."

"Will you soon be married, and provide your grandfather a great grandchild, which I can enjoy when," he smiled, "I finally become old."

"It could happen… maybe, Grandpa."

"Why, is it better to make your way in the corporate world than—?"

"Grandpa," Miriam gently, lovingly, admonished Norman, "I've told you many times, my ambition doesn't preclude a family. After all, Grandpa, you managed to hold to your dreams without short-changing your family, right?"

Norman started to nod in agreement, but reached for Miriam's hand, "Were it but so." He looked long at her.

"When you look beautiful like that, you seem to be a Botticelli version of your black-eyed grandmother."

Tears suddenly filled his eyes, hesitating as they worked their way down past the deep wrinkles of his 100-year-old weatherbeaten face, which nonetheless still had the healthy color of a person who had eaten the right foods, taken the right vitamins, fought the right fights most of the time, as he would drift off to his right sleep... most of the time.

60

NORMAN STARED INCREDULOUSLY AT ALAN.

"You pick Yom Kippur night to do it? You crazy?"

"Like a fox, Normie; like a fox."

Alan quickly continued to seal the deal.

"My father... everybody... will be in Shul."

"That's just the point, Alan, *everybody* will be there, so—"

"That's *exactly* the point; when we sneak out, the streets'll be empty, so nobody'll be around the store to see us."

Yom Kippur, the highest holy day of the Jewish religion, produced an ambiance of sights and sounds unique to that day; as the sun set, the beginning of the observance of the holiday, the lights of the neighborhood businesses signaled the event. Oleshe's candy store, Shimmell's tailor shop, Stern's grocery store, Blau's Appetizing Delicacies, blinked out almost at the same time; a hesitant blackout... the street now lit by gathering dusk, painting a somber chiaroscuro portrait of the neighborhood, an eerie still life.

For 364 days of the year, the sounds of Brownsville were uniform in their assorted street noises; murmurs of pedestrians' conversation; children's playful shouts; vendors calling hopeful attention to their wares; rundown old Model T's and Studebakers growling their complaints as they clattered over potholed pavements; occasional police or fire sirens blending into the anxious rhythm of Brownsville during the Depression.

Yom Kippur was a reverential mosaic of atonement, a sincere repentance for one's sins against God.

Both Alan and Norman, although not deeply religious, being only infrequent visitors to the synagogue, nonetheless were aware that one of the tenets of Judaism was that on this day it was common practice for friends to ask and accept forgiveness from one another for past offenses. Neither Norman nor Alan would find it appropriate or necessary at this time to do so... until much later.

On this evening, as it was with all Yom Kippur nights, the sound of new shoes, bought for their first time use on this special day; the hard leather soles of the on-sale specials from Thom McCann shoes, clicked staccato announcement of all words and acts that did not carry out God's best intentions.

The clothes worn by the supplicants were, for the most part, either frugally bought or, for lack of money, the well-cared for old suits and dresses sparingly used on other lesser holidays, occasional weddings and funerals.

Amboy Street, like all of Brownsville, was almost deserted, the few people there dressed in their ceremonial best, behaved in the solemn, hushed manner prescribed by the significance of the day, nodded in approval as they passed Oleshe's crayoned sign in the door window: CLOSED FOR YOM KIPPUR.

Alan and Janet were among several people milling around the Synagogue's entrance as Marsa and Norman approached them. Janet smiled warmly at the Schecters.

"So when, my friend Marsa, is that little pisher coming home from the hospital?"

"The doctor says," Marsa was very pleased to pass on the information, "—another week to be sure."

Janet felt that it was time for a little levity.

"Like a horse he was eating yesterday when we went to visit. His big eyes were in everybody else's plate."

"He *likes*," Marsa complained, "that non-kosher food."

Alan spoke with mock severity.

"On this high holy day commanding us to fast, you speak of food?"

"That's right," Janet agreed with her husband, "I'm starving enough already with this fahkahta holiday."

Marsa and Janet took the stairway up to the segregated women's section, as Norman and Alan entering the main downstairs section met Sam, excited to report startling news.

"Your papa is giving the Rabbi such a spiel!"

"So, Pop is telling him how to run the shul?"

Sam pointed to where Bennie was earnestly speaking to the Rabbi who was attempting to start the service.

Norman shook his head affectionately.

"Bennie the Butch is Bennie the Butch."

"Well, your papa is telling the Rabbi that he should make a special prayer for Ira."

"Good for him." Norman smiled, "If Roosevelt listened to him, we could end the Depression by having a kosher chicken in every pot."

Alan glanced at his watch, then made eye contact with Norman, who glanced away, looking around the synagogue which he noted had had some much needed repairs and decorative alterations made in the past year.

He admired the repainting of the foyer leading into the main congregation foyer, solid blue walls with white trim. Another man was also glancing around the synagogue, and as he turned in Schecter's direction, they were both surprised at seeing each other here.

"Mister Baumgarten!"

Baumgarten nodded in friendly salutation.

"Mister Schecter, how are you my friend?"

For a moment, Norman forgot about his plans with Alan, genuinely pleased to meet Isaac again.

"I'm glad you found our little synagogue, Isaac."

"I am also much pleased, Norman."

As Alan stood off to the side, irritated with Norman for getting involved with this stranger, Norman continued his conversation with Isaac, who noted that the blue and white paint represented the colors of the Zionist movement, originating with a fellow Austrian, Theodore Herzl, who Isaac proudly mentioned, lived near his hometown of Graz.

Alan, exasperated, stared directly at Norman, firmly nodding to him that they should take their seat in the rapidly filling congregation pews. Norman averted his eyes, pretending not to have seen Alan's anxious signal.

Finally, realizing that he could no longer postpone the inevitable, Norman excused himself to Isaac, and took the empty seat next to Sam, Alan already seated on the other side of his father.

During the highly ritualistic service, the Cantor singing the beautiful Kol Nidre in excellent voice, a moving declaration of annulling all vows made during the year which concern oneself, although obligations toward others are excluded. God in his infinite compassion will forgive the sins of those who sincerely repent, expressing their enlightened state by improved behavior and the performance of good deeds.

Norman, moved by the Cantor's invocation of elevated humaneness, suddenly decided that he could not, would not, be part of the destruction of Mulnick and Son. He leaned forward, glancing past Sam, sending a silent message of his withdrawal from Alan's plans.

As Alan started to slide past Sam in order to reach the aisle, he was asked an annoyed question.

"What?"

"Pee-pee."

Now he whispered under his breath as he squeezed past Norman.

"Let's go."

Sam glanced at Norman shaking his head negatively.

For a reason he couldn't explain to himself, Sam felt uneasy about what appeared to be a surreptitious exchange between his son and Norman. He narrowed his eyes quizzically as Norman rose, preparing to move into the aisle.

"Norman… what?"

"I have to call the hospital, Sam."

Sam, relieved of his uneasiness, turned back to concentrate on the Rabbi conducting the services.

As Norman stood up in the aisle, he reviewed what he would say to Alan about his unwillingness to participate in the arson plan.

Glancing up toward the balcony where the women and children were, he noticed Marsa nervously gathering her dress around the spot where she had tried to mask a worn area on the once, long ago, fashionable material, that she had mended again for this Yom Kippur.

Norman, distressed by his wife's pathetic attempt to maintain some dignity, as quickly as he had decided just a moment before to withdraw his support for Alan's plan, now made a firm final commitment to go along with the arson… all the way.

Alan, waiting outside the Synagogue, had noticed a discarded empty tube of Colgate toothpaste on the sidewalk. As he idly nudged it with his foot, his thoughts went to his father who, several weeks before, had been suffering with a great deal of pain in a couple of his teeth, but when Alan accompanied him to a dentist, the quoted fee for one necessary filling, and the extraction for the other one, was four dollars; much too much money for Sam to spend.

A man who worked as a waiter along with Alan in the Catskill Hotel, had told him about the N.Y.U. Dental Clinic which did not charge anything.

Alan had gone there for a filling and was surprised that there were over 50 dental chairs in a very large cavernous inhospitable room.

A dental student was in charge of each station, supervised by a couple of professor-instructors who constantly moved around the room, observing the work, and providing guidance to the nervous neophytes attempting a professional manner in order to impress the clients of their expertise. The patients, realizing that they had surrendered the guardianship of their discomfort, if not excruciating pain, to a fresh-faced boy learning the ABC's of dentistry at their expense, would shudder in anticipation.

Sam, after he had been brusquely told to "open your mouth wide!" suddenly sat straight up and silently strode out of the room, not willing to accept what he perceived as charity.

Although Sam had often given help to people who were 'down and out,' his pride would not accept the fact that he was now in such financial difficulty himself.

He hurried over to Gerson's Drug Store, and bought a small bottle of oil of cloves which he applied to his teeth every hour or so in order to anesthetize the severe pain. Eventually, the tooth that had become infected loosened enough for him to wiggle it, finally able, using his fingers, to pull it out, bloody root and all.

Small victories like this gave Sam and others like him a sense of some control over their struggling existence.

In this way, the dark times were sometimes illuminated by painful accomplishments of this sort, elevating the spirits, feeding the will to survive.

Walking slowly, reluctantly, out of the synagogue, Norman stopped at the steps leading down to the sidewalk where Alan nodded approvingly, relieved that his friend had not backed out of helping him to set the fire.

Wordless, the two men hurriedly walked down the deserted street.

Glancing at his watch, Alan's thoughts raced over his plans; the excitement sharpening his wits, alerting his awareness, the apprehension underlining the danger.

Norman, noticing Alan checking his watch, nervously commented.

"They'll miss us at shul in a few minutes."

"Don't worry, Normie. I've got it all figured out down to the minute."

"What about Sam?"

"Once it's done, he'll be okay."

Alan started to step up the pace, Norman following suit. After a little over a block, Alan pointed to a lane off to their side. Norman nodded in recognition.

He furtively glanced over his shoulder at the sound of a car very slowly crawling along the empty street as if to apologize for violating the holiday's strict rule forbidding the use of transportation on this very special Sabbath.

Alan stopped, putting his hand up in order to shield his face from the view of the car driver, with his other hand signaling for Norman to do the same.

They both held their position until the car went out of sight around the corner and Alan quickly motioned to Norman to follow him into the lane.

Alan unlocked the rear door of Mulnik and Son, stepping inside, closing the door behind him. Norman, as arranged, remained in the lane.

Norman drew in his breath sharply; his gasp, a sound inviting fright to come, reminding him again of the battlefield terror of Belleau Woods, although in this instance, there was no enemy... but himself.

Inside the store, Alan went quickly to work preparing the fire; taking a string from his pocket that he had brought along to be used as a fuse, he dipped it into the can of cleaning fluid that he had set up for this purpose.

In the lane, Norman was suddenly surprised at a moving shadow on the wall. Catching his breath, he apprehensively traced it to where he stood. Coming slowly toward him was the fire-station dalmatian, Trixie. As the dog came closer to him, Norman recalled the time Alan had told him that the dog had been trained to bark in response to fire.

Norman quickly tapped at the rear door. In a moment, Alan cracked upon the door, anxiously whispering.

"What?"

"The dog."

"What?"

"The firehouse dog, I think."

"Trixie?"

"Maybe it's her, I don't know."

Alan glanced down the lane where Trixie was ambling toward them, her tail wagging.

"Shit."

"What do we do, Alan?"

"Get inside, close the door!" Norman quickly stepped into the store, slamming the door after him.

"Maybe we should call it off then?"

Alan considered that possibility for a brief moment, but the pressure of the store insurance lapsing in a few days forced him to rush past Norman's suggestion.

"We gotta do it *now*, Normie!"

Alan hurriedly finished the preparation for the fire. He had placed a small box of wooden matches on the floor near the end of the string. Taking out a cigarette, he opened the box.

"This set up'll give us at least two minutes."

Norman started to protest, but Alan had already lit the cigarette. As Alan puffed on it, there was a scratching sound at the door. The two men froze in place and as Alan puffed hard on the cigarette in order to get it to glow, the dog whimpered. Alan started to bring the cigarette down toward the string which, when the cigarette lit it, would combust the matches which in turn would ignite the cleaning fluid, which would explode in flames.

Alan had read about such a homemade fire in an Argosy magazine where different plans of arson were detailed, and now everything was depending on the efficacy of this particular method.

The dog had started to growl.

Alan's hand shook as he started to bring it down toward the string.

Norman anxiously spoke to him.

"We've got to get back, Alan."

Alan's hand, shaking even more, stopped in mid-air.

"Alan!"

The dog had started to bark.

Norman reached over to Alan's shaking hand, starting to direct it toward the string. Alan's hand, however, seemed locked in place. Norman pried open Alan's fingers, taking the cigarette out of them and placing it on the string, glancing up at Alan for his approval. Alan nodded.

The dog's barks had grown louder and more insistent as Alan and Norman opened the door, quickly stepping outside. The dog's barking continued as they rushed down the lane to where they had entered it.

Trixie appeared confused, hurrying after them, then rushing back to sit by the back door, her bark mounting in intensity.

As Norman and Alan approached the synagogue, the rabbi's assistant blew the Shofar made from a ram's horn, its sound an unusually harsh vibrato cutting through the still air.

Although the service was already in progress, it was the policy of the synagogue to 'blow Shofar' as an invitation to anybody in the neighborhood to join the congregation.

Norman and Alan hurried past the assistant, through the blue and white foyer leading to the pews, where Sam glanced angrily at Alan as he slid by him to take his seat.

"So, where was the bathroom my son, in Alaska?"

His glare softening, he turned to Norman.

"You made a phone call, or maybe you delivered personally a Western Union telegram?"

Before Norman could reply, Bennie had hurried over to him, excitedly whispering.

"So, when Bennie the Butch gives an order..."

Norman attempted to mask his lack of comprehension.

"Hm?"

Sam explained for Bennie.

"The special prayer the rabbi made for Ira."

Norman now had enough information to make a comment.

"Oh yeah, wonderful Pop."

As Sam glanced quizzically at Norman's uncertainty, Norman averted his eyes just as a siren screeched its announcement of a fire engine roaring past the synagogue.

Only Norman and Alan displayed any sort of interest since most of the people were accustomed to the police and firemen who were often called in to deal with crime and old structures lacking fireproofing, suddenly combusting.

Sam, catching a quick eye flick exchange between his son and Norman, made him uneasy for some reason he was unable to define, but when another fire engine, sirens wailing, stormed past the synagogue, he found himself suddenly standing up.

"What's the matter, Pop?"

"'What's the matter?' I don't know."

He started to step past Norman in order to reach the aisle.

"I need some air."

"You okay?"

Sam, not answering, walked silently up the aisle, Alan following him.

"Pop, take it easy; your heart."

Norman started to follow them. Bennie was puzzled.

"Normie, did you hear what I said about the rabbi and Ira?"

Alan and Norman caught up to Sam as he reached the sidewalk, his eyes riveting on a pink glow appearing in the area of Mulnick and Son's store.

Sam's sharp intake of breath seemed to suspend itself, hanging there for a moment, exhaling itself with a burst, causing his body to tremble.

"Pop?"

Sam turned to Alan as if asking, demanding, that what he thought had taken place was not so.

Alan pretended not to understand his father's silent message, returning his own one of blank innocence.

Sam turned to stare at the pink glow rapidly deepening to red. He turned back again toward Alan just as he was exchanging a meaningful glance with Norman. Sam stared at Norman, a request of this trusted friend of his son, for a denial of what he sensed had taken place. It was a silent plea to provide him some release from the vise of terror tightening around the center of his being.

Norman attempted a half-smile of reassurance, but it only confirmed for Sam what he had guessed, but now *knew*!

He started a half stumbling trot in the direction of his store, another fire-engine siren accompanying his inner shrieks.

He began to run, his breathing becoming more labored, his hand going toward his chest as Alan ran alongside him.

"Papa — please... stop!"

Sam continued to run, his pace slowed only by his stumbling step.

"Papa!"

Gasping for breath, Sam managed just a few words.

"I'm... not... your... papa!"

They passed the laneway where a fire truck had already connected their hoses to a nearby hydrant, water shooting into the back of the store. Norman stopped for a moment, staring at the fire before rejoining Sam and Alan.

Sam, physically spent by the time he reached the corner, could see the flames shooting from his store which was ablaze; the adjoining shoe store also engulfed by the fire.

A policeman stopped the three men by guiding them across the street, away from the now nearly demolished store, the sign above blackened as the flames licked at it, the letters 'MUL' catching fire, quickly wrapping itself around the rest of the sign, the 'SON' suddenly incinerating, dropping down, disappearing into the rest of the charcoaled ruins.

Across the street, Sam wearily sat down on the curb, realizing that the rest of the store; the furs, the shipping boxes, the worn 'FOR SALE' signs... everything... a lifetime's work... all gone.

Through his inner roar of despair, he barely heard his son mumble, "I did it for you, Papa."

"For *me*?"

Sam continued to stare straight ahead into nothingness, a tear attempting to struggle its way out was turned back by the anguished man's memory fixed on the image of the "GRAND OPENING" sign hanging across the window of 'MULNICK'S FURRIERS' almost 35 years before.

Alan, too, stared at the fire consuming not only his father's history of work and dreams unrealized, but also his own failures, now disappearing into the ashes.

He fervently hoped that Phoenix-like, his ambitious plans would rise again, but for days Sam would not even acknowledge Alan's presence or talk to him.

Many weeks passed before Sam even grudgingly allowed Alan to come over to his house.

Many more weeks would pass before he allowed Alan to try again to explain his motive for setting the fire.

It was less than a year before the love Sam always had had for his son was rekindled.

61

SEVERAL DAYS AFTER THE FIRE, Norman considered its results.

Having read many of Clarence Darrow's court cases, Norman had been in accord with most of his compassionate and non-judgmental views, but there was one instance in which his own opinion differed widely from the famous lawyer's.

Attempting to support his contrary view, Norman tried to find the speech Darrow had once made about the consequences of severe economic stress, but his research was unsuccessful. However, he reconstructed it as best he could from memory:

Darrow's premise was that people, when pressured by extreme need for money to maintain themselves and their families, would often forego considerate humanistic behavior in order to acquire financial relief which, like sex, Norman recalled Darrow writing, would provide only an immediate, passing feeling of well-being or ecstasy.

Although Norman might agree with the sexual analogy, he felt that Darrow had omitted an extenuating ingredient. What, Norman asked himself, at the same time supplying the answer, if the acquiring of money was for preventing a very good friend from being dragged over an economic cliff, plummeting to his financial ruin?

62

SISTER AGATHA, as an acolyte in the Catholic church had, along with several others in her order, once been escorted into a Jewish synagogue by their Mother Superior as part of their training in learning about Hebrew rites.

It surprised Sister Agatha that Jewish ritual was in many ways as ornate as the Catholic church's; the rabbi's chanting his prayers as the replica of the Torah scrolls was paraded around the congregation was, it seemed to her, as elaborate as High Mass; the richly embroidered cloth tallis draped over the Rabbi's shoulders, the clothing equivalent of a priest's vestments.

Anticipating Ira's bar mitzvah, to which the Schecters had invited her, would provide additional exotic information about Jews, she had pleaded with the staff administration to allow her to borrow the hospital's Eastman Kodak box camera in order to take some photos of the ceremony.

Doctor Ronselli had also been invited, but was forced to leave a week earlier for his long-sought appointment to the famous Mayo Clinic in Minnesota. However, he asked Sister Agatha to deliver his congratulatory note to Ira.

When she sent Ronselli copies of some of the photos she had taken during the festivities, she explained the one of Ira wearing his yarmulke, his arms outstretched, smiling broadly as he delivered his well-rehearsed bar mitzvah speech to the appreciative audience of aunts, uncles, cousins, Mr. and Mrs. Wax, Bennie the Butch, and Yetta and of course the proud, glowing parents.

Impressed by Ira's elocution and energy, especially since he had been out of the hospital for less than a month, Sister Agatha asked him about some of the things he had talked of in his confirmation speech.

She wrote Ronselli of the high points of Ira's 'becoming a man' address, phonetically spelling out the opening lines of Yiddish, including their translation.

"*Tyare eltern* (worthy old folks), *vetera freint* (dependable friends), and *ahla fahzhamelta* (all congregated).

Sister Agatha was able to sketch in several of Ira's remarks itemizing some of the religious edicts passed on from biblical law: to be a dedicated Jew, honoring not only his parents, but all of those he would come in contact with; to walk the path of righteous morality as he meets many challenges. Sister Agatha commented in her note to Ronselli that the values espoused by the boy could very well be identified as similar to the Christian ethic of 'doing unto others.'

In her letter to Ronselli, she also listed the foods that, although spare, were proudly served: at least one piece of gefilte fish for each of the celebrants, along with either a plate of boiled chicken or a hot pastrami sandwich.

Mr. and Mrs. Schecter, she wrote, were highly excited by the bounty of having their son miraculously out of the hospital, not even needing the help of a wheelchair.

Rabbi Mintz spoke at some length about Ira's good citizenship "both as an American and a good Jew," collecting money for the "Fight Against Hitler." He continued solemnly, "This boy, now a man, has through his stalwart behavior, painted for us a picture of a truly, truly, exceptional person."

The Rabbi, understanding that people looked to him to articulate great issues at all ceremonies, felt that because of Ira's recovery, he could point to it as a miracle, created by the boy's avowing his Jewishness "in the face of a Christian priest!"

It struck Ira that Rabbi Mintz had not spoken correctly about what happened at St. Mary's hospital. Ira could not quite explain to himself what was wrong with the Rabbi's comment about the priest's involvement with him, except that he felt that he himself was *not* against the priest, as the rabbi seemed to suggest.

After the Rabbi had finished to respectful applause, Norman nodded to the Violin Man, who had been standing in the rear, attempting not to be noticed, but now he boldly stepped forward with his violin, once again sure of himself.

As in the courtyard, he tucked the violin under his chin, raised his bow for a moment, then brought it down surely, stroking the opening plaintive notes of Bruch's Scottish Fantasy.

Immediately on hearing the first few bars of music, Marsa's eyes filled, her memory transported to her home on Bleibtrue Strasse in Berlin.

Under Norman's instruction, only the first few bars of the piece were played, segueing into a *'frailach'* melody as Bennie and Yetta led several of the guests into a 'hora' dance, Mrs. Wax executing difficult, but sensual steps, the others laughing good naturedly at her exhibitionist version.

Isaac Baumgarten, who had immediately recognized the Violin Man as his one-time travel companion, waved in a friendly fashion at him as he happily joined the dancers; Marsa and Norman, each holding one of Ira's hands, joyfully joining the guests on the limited dance area, hemmed in by several plain wooden tables, gaily decorated in Woolworth-purchased, party-designed paper tablecloths.

The violin music having stopped, the guests sat down at the makeshift tables, while Marsa and Norman, assisted by Mrs. Wax and Finky, served the plates of gefilte fish, cooked by Marsa and chilled in the neighbors' ice boxes.

Norman directed Isaac to sit at the family table with himself and his sister Elaine (her husband Irving unable to attend because of a business meeting with a prospective 'backer' for a new venture he was promoting).

The Violin Man, averting his eyes from making contact with Isaac, took the envelope with a dollar-fifty that Norman had given him for his playing, and feeling out of place, abruptly left.

Norman gestured for Finky to join his table where Isaac hesitantly spoke with her, Finky attempting to be friendly but still subject to recurring flashes of Fred's violent murder and surges of grief that would still suddenly grip her.

Ira, the center of attention, was too nervous to eat very much as the family and friends congratulated the bar mitzvah boy.

Norman and Marsa basked in the attention as if *they* were the ones who had achieved the honor, as indeed they *had*, through their constant support and love for their son.

Years later, Marsa would tell her daughter, Edith, *she* had also attended her brother's bar mitzvah in the comfort of her mother's stomach.

Later, after the guests had left, the Schecters inspected the different gifts which had been given Ira.

There were seven of the ever presentable present, the highly regarded fountain pen; three wallets; several envelopes with two crisp dollar bills enclosed... one envelope with a five and ten dollar bill from Bennie and Yetta.

Ira, for his part, had feelings of well-being at his achieving 'manhood,' at the same time thinking that Jewishness carried with it responsibility, which would be necessary for him to learn about as he grew older.

63

STUDYING THE FIGURES she was writing on the sheet of loose-leaf paper she had taken from Ira's school notebook, Marsa expressed her satisfaction.

"In less than a year, Normie, all our debts — pht! Then maybe we can look for a nice apartment in, maybe, Flatbush."

Glancing down where his hand rested on an official-looking envelope, Norman picked it up gingerly, smoothing it out before placing it carefully next to the letter from the Board of Education.

"Why not *now*?"

Marsa glanced affectionately at her husband as she good-naturedly criticized him.

"Oh, Normie, practical you're not."

She underlined a number she had already written over twice, darkening it in order for it to stand out boldly.

"Your salary," glancing down at the letter, "for teaching this year is enough for now and for a little of what we owe, and you should know I want to leave Brownsville, Normie, but we have to save a few dollars to put in the pocket first."

"Well, Marsa, Sam'll be putting a few dollars in *his* pocket... from the insurance when it's finally settled."

"That's nice... for *him*."

"He's planning to buy another store."

"An old man in a new store?"

"He has to do it to stay alive, Marsa."

"But his pockets will be full."

"And his heart, empty."

"Don't philosophize me, Normie, practical is practical."

"Maybe 'practical' doesn't always have to do with what's in the bank, Marsa. Sometimes 'practical' can be the dreams you put in—"

Norman left the sentence unfinished as he tapped his chest. He idly started to glance at the newspaper he had brought in with him from Oleshe's candy store because the front-page story was about Charles Lindberg. Visiting Germany, he had been very impressed with their air force and Norman was about to turn the page when a four-column story about Clarence Darrow caught his eye. He moaned in shock as he read: LAWYER, HUMANIST, DEFENDER OF UNPOPULAR CAUSES DIES AT 80.

Marsa glanced at Norman and then down to the newspaper article. Shaking her head sadly, she placed her hand on Norman's shoulder.

"You all right, Normie?"

Norman managed a nod. Marsa sat down on the chair next to him. Aware of his reverence for Darrow, she gently touched his hand.

"He was a good man, Normie."

Agitated, Norman hurried to the apartment door, inadvertently brushing against the FULL COMMITMENT sign he had hung on the wall. Noticing that the sign was now askew, he hesitated for a moment, considering straightening it out.

"What's the matter, Normie? You still with the fighting City Hall idea?"

"It's up to somebody else now, Marsa." Speaking over his shoulders wearily as he closed the door behind him.

"I'm going up to the roof."

Marsa glanced down at her notes, still pleased with her calculations, underlining the figures once again.

~

Alan was very pleased that he had been able to tell Janet to take Esther to the dentist to have her measured for the braces that would stop her from looking like a squirrel. He stopped by his friend's apartment to share the good news with him, but when Marsa explained about where he was, Alan started out, glancing down at her stomach.

"You're really getting big, Marsa."

"Well, maybe," patting herself, Marsa was pleased at an idea that crossed her mind, "it's twins."

"When you due?"

"Maybe two months… April… May."

"Well, when the oven pops… Janet'll be over."

Norman, sitting on the tar roof, stared off into space, attempting to justify to himself his accepting the Board of Education's ultimatum that in order to be reinstated as a teacher, he would have to stop his Union agitating.

His concern with needing money to take care of Ira's health did not give him cause enough to rid himself of the feeling that he was shirking his union responsibilities. And now, being reminded of Darrow's life of uncompromising principle, he tried to weigh this perception of his own lack of integrity against those acts of his that he could consider carried some small degree of honor, but he was unable to reconcile his self-criticism to his satisfaction.

Alan spoke to Norman from the doorway opening to the roof.

"I hear you can see the Statue of Liberty's left tit from up here."

Norman glanced up, apparently distressed.

Alan continued, "Well, if you let those morbid eyes glance at *my* left," patting his left breast pocket area, "you'll see something that'll make you feel a little better."

Disinterested, Norman managed a "Hm?"

"Yup, the insurance company," Alan continued, "made noises like a Model T, but they finally paid off."

"Hm?"

"Yesiree," Alan's excitement was growing, "there are five one hundred dollar bills here," tapping his breast pocket, "that belong to you."

When Norman shook his head 'no,' Alan smiled.

"Hey, you're not raising the ante, are you?"

"No, buddy."

"Then, what?"

"I'm just not taking *any* of the money."

"Oh yeah, I know you said before you didn't want any, but—"

"I was lying."

"What the hell does that mean, Normie?"

"Well, it means that I was handing you a line of bullshit. It's just that I didn't mean it when I said I was helping you with the fire because I was a great big friend of yours."

Alan was becoming more confused.

"I asked you, what the hell—?"

"And if I fooled you with that crap, Alan, it was because I even believed it myself, but that night when everything went 'poof,' I realized I *was* doing it for the money. You see, if I really *was* your friend, I would've seen you *didn't* want to do it."

"F'chrissake, it was just for a second, Normie. I just—"

"No! I should've stopped you, but instead I did it! I have to face it! *I did it for the money!*"

"So what?"

"So that's why I can't take it, Alan!"

"Wait a minute! Pop got some money; I got some gelt, and *this*," Alan was taking out an envelope from his jacket, "belongs to you and your family."

Norman waved away the envelope; Alan starting to lose his temper.

"Normie, don't be like a little Bo-Peep all your life! Here," extending the envelope toward Norman. "Here, I'm handing you your sheep, take! Look, when I planned the fire, it was for my pop, but a part of it was I needed the money. So what?"

"That's just the point, Alan. *You* were honest about it all the way. Me, I was posing as Mister Morality when underneath it, I was willing to buy any reason you gave me so

I could sell out without disturbing my 'ethics.' Well, the only way I can buy back my honesty is to," Norman pushed Alan's hand away holding the envelope.

"Well, then I'm going down to Marsa with it!"

"No! If you told her she'd want me to take it, and I don't think I'd be strong enough. So please, my friend, in this, okay?"

"You are one crazy son of a bitch! Well, I'm going to make a present of one of these," taking out a $100 bill from the envelope, "for the hospital so she doesn't have to give birth in a charity ward. Is *that* okay with you?"

Norman hesitated for a moment. "Okay, but don't tell her about the rest of the envelope."

Alan nodded as he went to the roof door.

"You crazy son of a bitch!"

"What do *you* plan on doing with your money, Alan?"

"Well, remember the army surplus idea that I worked on years ago?"

"Yes, it was a good idea."

"Well, I'm going for it now, Yeah, no more settling for crumbs for this boy."

"Good luck, buddy."

"Back atchya, Normie."

"I owe you, Alan."

"For what?"

"For helping me realize that maybe, just maybe... Brutus *is* an honorable man."

Alan stared respectfully at Norman for a moment before leaving. Norman, standing near a drainpipe, noticed some water that had accumulated at the mouth of the pipe, some debris blocking its flow. Norman pushed the debris away with his foot.

The water started to flow easily down the drain. He watched it for a long moment.

64

"GRANDPA?"

Norman glanced up from reading the editorial page of the *New York Times* which was open on his granddaughter's desk.

"Well, Miriam my sweetheart, I thought that the only newspaper allowed in these hallowed business halls was the *Wall Street Journal*. I thought—"

His throat tightening in discomfort, Norman was unable to continue his light-hearted teasing of his granddaughter. The throat spray he always carried with him to cope with the problem was now immediately used by him in order to ease the severe irritation.

"You want me to get you some water, Grandpa?"

Not waiting for an answer, Miriam quickly poured a glass from the decanter on her desk, anxiously watching Norman as he gulped it down. Concerned, she asked him how he was feeling.

"I'm okay, Miriam. I'm definitely okay." But years before he had been made aware of a dangerous health factor. He had just turned 80 and some blood tests had alerted his doctor that Norman's prostate was in the early stages of cancer.

Doctor Saladoff had prescribed some medications which had serious side-effects, so he had suggested the alternative therapy of watchful waiting, not taking any medication at all, since at Norman's age he would probably die from other health causes before the cancer would kill him. However, Norman fancifully declared that he intended to live until at least 107, and decided to suffer the side effects of the medication in order to limit the growth of the malignancy of the prostate.

Other than the throat soreness and some stiffness in his legs that challenged his mobility, he was okay. By the time he was 90, he finally reluctantly accepted the fact that his flexibility of movement had started to diminish; his shoulders' arthritis limiting the full use of his upper body. Heading into his one-hundred-and-first birthday, Norman counted himself fortunate in that his vital organs, on balance, were okay.

Evaluating his physical capabilities measured against men much younger than himself made Norman feel somewhat superior. He had been a good caretaker of his body, exercising regularly, not smoking at all, drinking only an occasional glass of wine, diligently observing a diet of healthy food, and not feeling any sacrifice because of this behavior, thoroughly enjoying his lifestyle and its results.

Asking himself why he had arbitrarily chosen one hundred and seven for the cut-off of his life span, he answered the question: based on the math of adding a few years to Miriam's age and hoping that by that time he would become a great grandfather, this title being the one that would provide him with the comforting sense of life's continuity. Since he had, many years before, ruled out 'heaven' or any other religious concept which held out an eternal life of any kind, being reminded of the Kaddish prayer of a person being remembered for their 'deeds of loving kindness' which could be considered their life's legacy, Norman was at peace with his choice of 107.

65

OVER THE RECENT PAST, Norman had had several good natured discussions with Miriam about what he perceived was her gradual slide toward a Republican bias. Now he pointed to an article in the financial section which took President Bush to task about his tax cut for the upper two percent of income earners.

"So, my dear nascent Republican, what do you think of this latest benevolent move to ease the burden of our financially stressed millionaires?"

"Well, Grandpa, since I fall short a million or two, it doesn't really apply to me."

Miriam enjoyed the light-hearted political banter she would often have with Norman, maintaining for his benefit a pose of possibly being weaned away from the Schecter family's long-standing membership in the Democratic party.

"Well, Miriam, maybe Bush is laying the groundwork for when his tax cut will be more appealing to you as you enter your more affluent period."

"You know, Grandpa, the older you get, the more you really amaze me."

"How so, my sweet girl?"

"Oh, the way you make your points so comically."

"Well, as I've grown elderly, I've figured out that it's the best way to face the serious world."

"Well, so when you get real old, you'll be ready for a comedy-club gig."

"So young, Miriam, and already a quick mouth."

"Well, I've been taught by a master."

Norman stared lovingly at his granddaughter who, after a moment, returned a warm, knowing look.

"Grandpa?"

"My dear?"

"You're not going to sing 'Sunrise, Sunset' are you?"

Norman quickly understood her reference to the song from *Fiddler on the Roof* when Tevya, the father, lovingly sings about the passage of time in a child's growth.

Perhaps Miriam didn't remember when their truly caring for one another started. Norman did. It was during Miriam's second birthday party. She was feeding Norman a piece of her birthday cake, her eye-hand coordination not matching her enthusiasm for putting the whipped cream cake into her grandfather's mouth. Norman playfully licked the overflow from his lips. Miriam giggled, and staring at him in a simple straightforward, knowing manner, unadorned with any sophistication, spoke directly into his heart.

"You love me, Grandpa!"

It happened as easily as that, and forever after, although she did not recall it exactly as it happened, she did remember the feeling of connection between them.

As for Norman, that moment became an indelible part of his memories, no less than what had happened 60 years before.

66
December 8, 1941

THE FRONT-PAGE HEADLINE of the *New York Times* shouted, "JAPAN MAKES WAR ON U.S. AND BRITAIN."

Norman had hurried in with the newspaper, he and Ira hungrily reading about the details of Roosevelt's "DAY OF INFAMY" speech he had made the day before, on Sunday December 7.

Shaking his head in anger, Ira read aloud the caption underneath the large, grainy wire photo of a battleship sunk in Pearl Harbor.

"Over a thousand sailors were killed on the Arizona alone!"

"And those poor kids weren't even in a war, Ira."

"Well, President Roosevelt says we are now, so I'm going to join up."

"We'll maybe talk about it when you're 18," Marsa stated firmly, attempting to cut off any further discussion.

Ira was prepared and held up a well-worn piece of paper for Norman and Marsa to see that it was his birth certificate. Over the years it had been folded, unfolded, for school purposes, his hospital stay, vaccination shots and other instances when proof of birth had been necessary. The frequent use of the certificate had resulted in the creases almost wearing through the aging, thin paper.

"See this, Pop?" Ira excitedly pointed to the spot where the constant wear and tear had almost obliterated some of the letters and numbers.

"According to this, I was born in 1925 or 1924, so my next birthday I'm gonna be 16 or 17."

Marsa felt a flutter of panic. She stared at Ira, her questioning "So?" supplying its own answer: fear.

"So, Mom, I'm going down to the Army recruiting office."

Before Marsa could protest, Norman quickly interceded.

"If you're not 18, you need your parent's consent!"

"Is that true, Pop?"

"Oh, yes," and calming Marsa's fear, "so don't worry."

"I don't sign anything, believe me."

Ira pleaded his case, "But Pop, *you* were only 18 when you went to France."

"Sixteen is not 18, and anyway, I was drafted!"

"Well, in a year, I'll be 18."

"*Seventeen*, mein zindel," Marsa corrected him.

Ira, triumphantly waving the certificate, declared that, "In one year, I'll be 18..."

"In *two* years," Marsa insisted, "and *then* we will sit down and discuss this mishaghas."

"Yeah, Mom, it's a crazy mess, but it's a war."

And so Ira, who had been precociously academic in school, 'skipping' several classes and graduating from the highest rated High School in the state, if not country, Townsend Harris Hall, at 16, decided to go to work until he was able to go into the army.

Although at this time Norman had been working as a regular fully credentialed teacher, earning enough to support the family, Ira nonetheless felt by working he would be able to contribute some of his earnings to improve the Schecter's living conditions, especially since his sister Edith, age three, would eventually need corrective surgery because of her club foot.

Since the draft had already started to deplete the work force, it was not difficult for Ira to find a job in a small defense plant manufacturing radio-testing equipment.

Working 56 hours a week at 45 cents an hour, Ira was proudly able to earn about 25 dollars weekly, contributing 10 dollars a week to the Schecter household.

A bonus for Ira was that he could proudly wear a button that stated he worked at PRECISION APPARATUS COMPANY—

DEFENSE PLANT, which he wore until he finally went into the service.

When he turned 17, because both Marsa and Norman had made it clear that they would not sign their permission, Ira had gone down to the Draft Board, presenting his birth certificate, quickly answering one of the Board's not really probing questions about the indistinct birth date.

It would not be the first time that a Draft Board would look the other way; not only about dates, but name changes or even jail time.

Ira had kept close attention to intercepting the Schecter's mail, and the letter from the United States Selective Service when it came with the famous "Greetings" from the President announcing the draftee's induction into the Armed Services.

Grabbing the letter without being seen by his parents, he hurried down to Grand Central Station where, in a cordoned-off area, several hundred anxious draftees had come for induction.

A gravel voiced Army Sergeant boomed an invitation, "Who's going into the Army today?"

Most of the men raised their hands and a number of others raised *theirs* in answer to "who wants to go into the pansy Navy?"

Ira had been reading the newspaper accounts of the last few weeks of the Battle of Guadalcanal in the South Pacific, and the bloody final victory of the Marines. He had also recently seen the movie about the U.S. defeat at Wake Island where the movie heroes were about to be slaughtered, and the commandant of the doomed Marines, bravely portrayed by the chesty actor, Brian Donlevy, declared valiantly 'SEND US MORE JAPS' and with the turned-up volume of the Japanese bombardment and blaring martial music, the movie heroically ended.

The gravel voiced Sergeant, in a jocular manner, asked the small remaining group.

"Anybody wanna commit suicide with the Marines?"

Ira was one of the very few who raised their hands.

After the physical, Ira was given two weeks to get his civilian life in order and report for duty at the train going to Parris Island, South Carolina for his basic training.

A few days before his reporting date, Ira showed his induction notice to his shocked parents, and although both Marsa and Norman angrily argued against his behavior, when he explained to them that if his actions about his age fraud was brought to the authorities attention, he might be prosecuted and jailed, they very grudgingly listened.

Although Marsa completely accepted Ira's version of his legal position, Norman had serious doubts about the fraud charges, but deciding that Ira's strong stance about his patriotic duty, and the vague rumors that Norman and the general public had become aware of about the horrors of Hitler's Nazi regime and its systematic terrorizing cruelty of not only the Jewish population, but Catholics, gypsies and homosexuals, all were reasons for Norman to convince Marsa to allow Ira to carry out his commitment to the Marine Corps and the country.

67

Saipan, Mariana Islands, 1944

"MOVE YOUR ASS, SCHECTER!"

Corporal Porter had desperately barked his order as Ira double-timed to the nearby pile of howitzer ordnance.

Ira grabbed a 105-millimeter shell, pivoted with it, slapping the shell into the breech of the canon.

Porter quickly, expertly pulled the lanyard, the cut fuses exploding just 50 yards from the howitzer, mowing down the Japanese soldiers screaming banzai as they ran toward Able Battery of the third battalion, 10th Marine Regiment.

The suicide avalanche of the Japanese troops had broken through the 10th, overrunning much of the infantry support.

Japanese rifle fire and bayonets had killed many of the Marines of Able Company and now, if the attack was not stopped, the entire battalion was in danger of being wiped out.

A PFC in Ira's battalion, Agerholm, jumped into an abandoned ambulance and, under heavy fire, evacuated about 40 wounded Marines. His actions helped stop the tide, but he was finally killed, and posthumously awarded the Medal of Honor.

Ira vowed to himself that when he shipped home, he would contact Agerholm's parents and tell them firsthand about their son's bravery, but realized that it would be at least a year, maybe more, before that could happen. This made him feel immeasurably sad because later, after he would have made it through the campaign, which he knew in the way that only an 18-year-old with his cloak of immortality could be sure, that by that time, the parents' grief would have been dealt with, and therefore he would only be reopening the painful wounds of loss and grief.

Because of the Second Division's strict censorship restrictions, Ira was unable to write home about the specifics of where his outfit was stationed or anything about the Saipan campaign, but when about a month later, his outfit received the *Time Magazine's* detailed recounting of the entire battle, Ira wrote Norman and Marsa and alerted them to the article, so they were able to track where Ira was, and the battle over now, was safe... for the time being.

When Ira thought about Agerholm, or any of the other Marines who were buried in the Saipan cemetery, he took some small pleasure in the fact that his parents would not have to suffer the ultimate grief... *he* was coming back. However, he could not shake the dark feelings he had about all the guys who would not be returning to the States.

Empathy for their families would often depress Ira, although he sometimes would manage to push aside all these considerations, achieving some equanimity. On one occasion, he was prodded into a vague memory of an instance that could possibly explain his conflicted vision of seeing both uneasiness and comfort at the same time.

Could it be similar to how his father had, many years before, explained about his seeing two things at the same time because of being born on the cusp of 1900?

Or could what he felt be because of Bessie and Jack on Amboy Street?

Bessie was tall, a very attractive blonde. Jack also was tall, attractive, and very black.

In the mid-30s, in this all-white neighborhood of Brownsville, before civil rights had started to make its small glacial movements toward tolerance, an interracial couple was not only startling, but more than that, an anomaly of the most incredible sort.

In all the time the Schecters lived in the area, never once had they ever seen a single white-black couple. The union of Bessie and Jack was rarer than a unicorn. The neighbors' surreptitious glances followed them as they walked through the building and up to their small top floor apartment.

Neither Bessie nor Jack seemed to take any notice of the veiled curious looks in their direction.

It seemed to Ira that Bessie would brace her trim, athletic body in an aggressive manner, like a baseball player would take as he got into the batter's box... like Babe Ruth seemed to invite the pitcher to 'throw one past him'; so did Bessie challenge the neighbors' 'curve ball' glance.

Norman was the first tenant to make a neighborly gesture to Bessie and Jack, after he had tentatively said 'hello' to them.

"How you two feel about coming down to our place for a cup of coffee?"

When Bessie seemed to hesitate in accepting the invitation, Jack alertly took over, his tone appreciative.

"Sounds good, Mister—?"

"Schecter."

Jack, gesturing toward Bessie, included her in the introduction.

"Powers."

Norman rolled the name through his lips; friendly, welcoming.

"Powers."

Ira recalled how nervous his mother was preparing for the Powers' visit. Although Ira was aware of his father's relaxed behavior with their visitors, the boy also became aware of his mother's strained manner as she offered them her favorite, a slice of muenster cheese with a strong cup of coffee served in the special-for-guests dinnerware, rarely used; that Bennie and Yetta had given Norman and his bride for their wedding gift 15 years before.

Ira thought that the conversation about Marsa and Bessie exchanging complaints about the need for more exterminator's visits to control the bugs and mice was something he'd heard many times before. More interesting was Jack's recounting how he worked for a couple of years in a radio-repair store and was now going into business for himself, asking Norman his opinion about a business card he was going to have printed up calling himself 'POWERS' TOP RADIO REPAIRS, INEXPENSIVE.'

Ira came to admire his mother's behavior at all the frequent exchanged 'coffee' meetings between the two families. He saw that his father had an easier rapport with the Powers, but because he felt that his mother was not as 'liberally' at ease with the couple, he actually had more respect for her because, in spite of her unease, she was able to struggle through it and be cordial.

Was that the reason, Ira thought, for his being, almost 10 years later, confronted with an event which had at least two opposing feelings, each threatening to cancel out the other? Were the conflicted feelings he had about the death of some of his buddies based on empathy and/or guilt? Although he made efforts to sort it out, he was unable to come closer to a clear view of his mixed feelings.

He considered his ambivalence a promissory note for future clarification, to be cashed in at some appropriate time.

68

1945

BY THE TIME NORMAN AND MARSA received the letter from Ira about his outfit 'hitting' Okinawa on April 1, he had returned to Saipan, which after the island had been 'secured,' was now being used as a rest area for the Second Division.

Ira's letter in hand, Norman hurried over to where Alan was celebrating the opening of the third branch of his prospering Army-Navy stores.

As Norman came into the store preparing to congratulate Alan, and also share the good news about Ira, his friend waved the newspaper at him that he had been reading.

"You see this, Normie?"

"You see *this*?" Norman asked cheerfully, holding up the letter.

"Wonderful Normie… beautiful!"

Norman in turn inquisitively read the newspaper headline which jumped out at him.

"KILLER OF POSTMAN SCHLEIFER FREED"

The story went on to explain that the convicted murderer, Charles Finklestein, on death row for over 6 years was released due to a technicality: an inadequate legal defense.

A photo of Charlie being met at the prison gates by his parents was captioned: "PARENTS SPEND SAVINGS FOR APPEALS." The story went on to recount how Charles had been abused by his alcoholic father, and a mother who had been able to support the family by part-time prostitution.

The newspaper prompted Alan to ask Norman about how Finky was doing.

"Well, she dropped me a line from Los Angeles last year and told me about the good money she was making at Boeing Aircraft."

"Good for her."

"She wrote me about this soldier she married just before he shipped out to the Pacific."

"Well, I hope the sexy lady gets lucky this time around."

"She sure deserves it."

~

Some weeks later, on the same day, June 6th, that the headlines trumpeted the announcement that the Allies' European invasion had been launched in Normandy, a feature story on an inside page was about Charles Finklestein, recently freed convicted murderer, who had been killed by a hit-and-run driver.

Eric Schleiper, Fred's father, who coincidentally lived in the neighborhood of the accident, did not pretend any grief when interviewed, being quoted as saying that what the driver did, "Speaks loud for me."

A neighbor had caught a quick glimpse of the hit-and-run vehicle leaving the scene of the accident, describing the car as being dark colored, with no hubcaps.

The next day Schleiper repainted his Ford a light blue, finishing it off with some used hubcaps. The police, aware of Finklestein's murder conviction, without any further investigation of the hit and run, closed the case.

~

As Alan gave Norman the grand tour of his new store, Norman, very impressed, clapped his friend's shoulder.

"Great, Alan, but I wonder how the hell the army has enough supplies left over for the troops, after you empty out the quartermaster's warehouses."

Alan laughed at what he knew was a compliment, enjoying the moment. "There's always something lying around to pick up if you know who's hungry for a little," his thumb and forefinger describing the 'money' gesture.

Norman pointed to a stack of folding cots that were 'ON SALE SPECIAL.'

"What are you charging?"

"What? Marsa finally kicked you out of bed?"

"Funny. How much?"

"For old friends… zero."

"Thanks, it sounds like a good price."

"And why don't you take home one of *these*?"

Alan reached over to a mound of cloth silver stars sewed onto 10 X 10 inch cloth backgrounds; each one, when displayed in a window, represented a member of the family who was in one of the branches of the Armed Services.

"No thanks, Alan. Marsa doesn't like the idea of hanging up one of those."

"Why?"

"I think it's because in some way it would be an admission that Ira is actually in the war."

"Fine, then you'll never need one of *those*," pointing to a group of gold stars on cloth, which were sadly used to represent an Armed Service death.

"That's right, Alan, we won't need one of those."

"Absolutely, my friend!"

An unusual scraping sound floated through the night silence of the Schecter's bedroom.

Marsa stirred awake, mumbling in apprehension.

"What... what?"

Norman quietly reassured her.

"Go back to sleep, Marsa."

The street's lamplight, filtering through the Venetian blinds, provided a dim glow around Norman, bent over the canvas cot he had brought with him from Alan's store.

Adjusting her eyes, Marsa could make out Norman sliding the wooden rod through the cloth slats, forming one end of the cot. She watched Norman as he connected the other end.

She clicked on the bedroom light, enabling her to see clearly what Norman was doing.

Puzzled and irritated, Marsa sat up in bed; speaking sharply.

"Whatever crazy thing you're doing... why in the middle of the night?"

"It was on my mind."

"So you drive *me* crazy?"

"Go to sleep. I'll explain in the morning."

"Explain now, Normie. So I *can* go to sleep."

Realizing that he could no longer sidestep the issue, Norman searched for words which could describe his reasoning.

"Remember the picture of me and Alan in France?"

"Maybe."

"Well, it was the one of us both in the tent."

"So?"

"Each of us was lying on a cot."

"So?"

"It was a canvas cot like this one."

"Oi, Normie, in the middle of the night, this is too much."

"Well, look at this," Norman pointed to a photo that they had recently received from Ira in Saipan.

"So he's lying on a cot, Normie, so?"

"So, I decided that I'm going to sleep on a cot, too."

"Meshugga."

"I'm *not* crazy. Maybe if I sometimes sleep on this cot like *he* has to, it'll be sort of protecting him."

"You protecting him? *Du bist ein nahr.*"

"I am *not* a fool, Marsa. It's just that I know what a kid goes through in war, so maybe I'm kind of sharing it with him."

"And you're going to sleep there every night?"

"Maybe just once in awhile."

Marsa didn't speak for a long moment before turning away, shutting the light and stretching out in the bed to try to go back to sleep.

Norman waited for a moment before he lay on the cot.

Within a week, he put the cot in the bedroom that Ira had used, and would sleep on it occasionally.

One time, Marsa could hear what she thought were quiet sobs, and deciding against going into the room, she lay there, staring at the ceiling.

She never cried; her tears dammed up by the same terror that had lived in her for over 20 years, choking the memories of her parents and Leo.

69
August, 1945

Dear Elissa,

By the time you receive this, I will be on my way to Japan. I've written, (as usual) to my father and mother about my favorite organization, the Marines, arranging this trip for me and my buddies. But please call them in case my letter to them is held up.

I figure that the newspapers are full of the news of the atomic bomb ending the war.

What are your feelings about it?

I remember the last time I saw you at the hospital when you were celebrating the great new steps you were literally taking. My pop writes me that your being able to get around more is improving. Congratulations.

I realize that I've seen you only a few times over the years but I figure you're one of the funniest people I know.

That joke you told me about what you get when you cross a School Board with Edgar Bergen's Charlie McCarthy was a lollapalooza. None of the guys in my squad got it, but that's okay because they couldn't get the connection about dummies talking to each other.

About the bomb, soon as they announced the news. (I had 'volunteered' to build the PA System because they knew about my radio defense plant experience.) I realized that eventually dropping the bomb meant that we all would be going home soon. There was something, I can't really explain it, that was wrong in incinerating all of those Japs, maybe 150,000 civilians, but it was to end the war, and maybe that made a difference. Anyway, maybe it'll be clearer when my outfit gets to Nagasaki. Yes, they already told us we were going to be the first troops to land there. Wow!

I'm looking forward to it because of my points (campaigns and service time). It means that I'm going to ship back to the States from there real soon.

When you get a chance, drop me a line okay? It's very good to hear from friends.

I remember you used to be in the peace protest movement (my father told me), so I wonder what you think about what I said about the A-bomb.

You can use my old Second Division address and they'll forward it to me.

After fighting Saipan and Okinawa, this Japan duty will be a big difference.

Now my parents won't have to worry about me anymore.

The way I figure it, when I finally get back, I maybe might not even be 21.

Regards,
Pfc. Ira Schecter

70
1956

THE SCHECTER'S YOUNGER CHILD, EDITH, had an unusual problem to deal with from birth.

She was born with a club foot, its heel bent upward and the front part of the foot turned inward and bent toward the heel, a malformation which can usually be corrected by splints and a plaster cast prior to the child starting to walk.

However, in Edith's case, by the time she was four, her doctor told the Schecters that it would be necessary to operate surgically on the tendon, hoping to correct the condition.

Lacking the finances, it appeared that they would not be able to afford the procedure, but Ira's salary at the defense plant enabled them to go ahead with the operation.

After several years of special exercises, both Marsa and Norman spending long hours supervising her, Edith finally was able to walk almost normally.

The Schecters felt blessed by her recovery, relating it to Ira's illness of several years before.

"Marsa, that's *two* miracles in the same family!"

Marsa sharply admonished her husband.

"Don't give us a kineahora, Normie!"

A 'kineahora' (jinx) could set off terrible consequences for a person who had the temerity to comment on their good fortune, and thereby set into motion the most dreadful negative turn around in their fortunes.

However, the Schecters escaped any bad results of *this* 'kineahora,' although Marsa vigilantly watched over Norman's behavior so that nothing he would say or do could possibly lead them into the deep waters of bad luck.

When Edith was 17, and one of the shining lights in her high school drama club, the management of the Broadway play, *Bus Stop*, because of the dwindling audience in the latter days of the show's run, gave tickets to the school's English department.

Edith quickly recommended her father to be the necessary chaperone for their theater outing.

The show's press agent told the group they were welcome to visit the star, Kim Stanley, backstage after the show.

Although the group was apprehensive about it, Norman encouraged them to take advantage of this exciting adventure.

They were graciously invited by Kim Stanley herself into her small, hot dressing room, offering them all cool cokes.

"You were just great, Miss Stanley," Edith admiringly observed.

"As usual," a man, seated in a corner chair, quietly agreed.

Stanley, genuinely modest, waved away the compliment. "I'm sorry you all saw this performance; I was not all there," turning to the man. "Bill, I didn't do right for you."

It was Bill's turn to wave away *her* comment. "It was one of your best, Kim."

She introduced the man, Bill Inge, the author of the play.

"Kim," he said to the others, "cannot accept that she's never less than brilliant."

Stanley smiled her answer. "You haven't seen the show for a few weeks, Bill, so you're just enjoying your words."

"And they certainly are excellent ones," Norman offered, adding, "Also, your *Come Back Little Sheba'* was really a poignant, moving play."

Inge, like Stanley, was extremely modest in his manner. "Thank you, sir."

Edith joined the conversation.

"*Sheba* was one of my favorites. We read it last year in our drama club."

"That's very nice...?"

"Edith... I played the college girl, Marie."

One of the other youngsters in her group produced a camera, and politely asked if they would be allowed to take a picture with Stanley.

"Well, I still have on some of my costume."

"That's great," Edith said, turning to Norman. "Can you take the picture, Dad?"

"Yes, Dad," Stanley warmly said, posing with Edith.

Al Salmi, the play's co-star, stuck his head into the dressing room.

"Kim, you wanna go to Downey's for a beer?"

"Albert," Kim lightly reproved him, "say hello to my guests."

"I'm sorry, folks," Albert genuinely apologized. "I've just got a case of the uglies."

Stanley, taking off her make up, glanced in the mirror, smiling at him.

"All is forgiven, and I *can* use a drink, or two." She turned to her guests. "I've been rude, sorry. Would you all like to join us?"

The students seemed to light up in pleasure at the invitation, but Norman reluctantly, graciously, demurred.

"Thank you, Miss Stanley, but they're not permitted to go to a bar."

"Neither am I," Salmi protested, quickly explaining, "My girlfriend wants me home early for a change."

"Well," Stanley offered, "Maybe it's just because she misses her 'loving boyfriend.'"

The students were excited by being privy to theater backstage life, but Norman felt it was time for him to escort his charges out.

"I think we have to go now, Miss Stanley, but I do want to repeat our pleasure at you and," including Salmi, "everybody for letting us see very fine actors in," turning to Inge, "a very entertaining play."

Later, Edith argued earnestly with her father about what she felt was his old fashioned attitude at what he had called, "just backstage gossip."

"You think me some kind of prude?"

"Not exactly, Dad."

"Well, as you grow up, I hope you get to realize that parents do some strange things in order to protect their children."

"I'll keep that in mind, Dad."

"Good."

They hugged each other affectionately.

71

1963

SHORTLY AFTER EDITH'S INVOLVEMENT with James Baldwin and the Civil Rights march on Washington, she met her husband, Barry, a theatre stage-manager. Edith, who had been able to get several small roles on television, jumped at the opportunity of joining Barry when he went on tour with a revival of *South Pacific*, which happily ended up with her playing the small role of one of the nurses.

She called her parents from Minneapolis and said how truly sorry she was that she had not been able to arrange for them to come out in time for her impulsively planned marriage to Barry. However, by the following year, when the *South Pacific* run was over, she happily returned with Barry to announce the news… she was pregnant!

Norman and Marsa were ecstatic. A grandchild!

Unfortunately, Barry was not able to be there for the birth. The army had conscripted him for active duty. He was able to get a furlough to spend a week with Edith and their child, Miriam, whose spell he quickly fell under, adoring them both completely before he had to ship out to Vietnam where he was killed on his first day of duty.

72
1973

IT WAS NOT UNTIL ALMOST 18 YEARS after Edith and Norman had first met William Inge backstage after the *Bus Stop* performance, that there was an unusual end to the story.

Edith had lovingly planned a day for her and her daughter to celebrate Miriam's 9th birthday, but she suddenly became ill and called Norman for him to take her to the doctor's office.

Although Norman had been concerned for his daughter's constant health problems over recent months, he was very pleased to have the opportunity to spend some time with Miriam.

Norman had bought her a birthday gift, a children's crossword puzzle book. Waiting at the doctor's office for Edith to finish her examination, grandfather and granddaughter had a fun time working on the puzzle together.

Giggling in victory, Miriam announced "I can work *this* answer out all by myself, Grandpa."

"Yes?"

"Do *you* know it?"

When Norman shook his head in dramatic ignorance, Miriam triumphantly supplied a clue in disbelief.

"You don't know a four letter word for 'story'?"

"I just don't know, but I bet my smart granddaughter does."

"I told you I did."

"Well?"

"The word is," Miriam proudly displayed her knowledge, "tale."

"But that doesn't make sense."

Worried, Miriam asked, "What do you mean, Grandpa?"

Norman pretended obtuseness.

"Well, I just don't see how an animal with a T-A-I-L has anything to do with a story."

Patiently, Miriam explained, "No Grandpa, it's T-A-L-E."

"That's a strange way of spelling a cat's T-A-I-L."

Miriam saw the twinkle in her grandfather's eyes.

"Oh, Grandpa."

After Edith's examination, she joined Miriam and Norman, masking her concern.

"Well, let's have my daughter's birthday party."

"Okay, Mother."

Norman, observing Edith's hesitation, jumped in with a suggestion.

"It's a lovely day, so how about us going to Riis Park and enjoy the beach?"

Norman phoned Marsa and invited her to join them.

"It's too hot for an old lady, but enjoy, enjoy, and I'll be here with a large glass of Lipton's iced tea for your hot tongues."

The IRT train and two bus rides deposited Norman, Edith and Miriam in the Riis Park Beach, several steps up in the clean sand, ocean, and general beach ambiance compared with tatty Coney Island.

Attempting to develop this relatively new beach area into something special, the management had initiated a novel way, at that time, of buying the hot dogs, cokes and assorted food knick-knacks. Instead of the standard method of paying with sandy change dug up from the wet bathing trunks and suits or paper money, soggy with the surf, the bathers would purchase tickets from a booth manned by a guardian of rolls of cardboard tickets with denominations of 5, 10, 25 and 50 cents each. People would line up patiently, buying the amount of tickets that they would anticipate needing for the different food items at the refreshment stands. This meant of course that they would have to gauge their needs for that afternoon. Redeeming any extra tickets not needed for food was not permitted, therefore one would be forced to sell their unused tickets to other bathers, or save them for use on another day.

This sunny afternoon, Norman had rented a large sun umbrella for them, another special feature of Riis Park.

They had a refreshing swim in the clean surf, which had not yet been polluted by years of many thousands, millions, of bathers depositing the remains of unfinished hot dog buns, wax-candy wrappers, assorted debris and of course the constant deposits of natural waste.

Glancing up from where he was lying, he noticed a man who was walking past their area and immediately recognized him as William Inge, the playwright of *Bus Stop*, who in turn glanced at Norman, a flicker of recognition passing through his eyes.

Norman smiled at him, "Hello, Mr. Inge."

Inge paused, rifling through his memories in order to place the man who apparently knew him. Was he, Inge thought, an actor who had auditioned for one of his plays or a backer he had casually met at a fundraiser?

"Mr. Inge, I'm sorry if I've intruded, but we," gesturing toward Edith, "were lucky enough to meet you backstage a very long time ago at *Bus Stop*."

Inge's memory was jogged, but not until Edith supplied an additional piece of information about Albert Salmi meeting them also, was he able to recall in vague detail their meeting.

"And today," Norman proudly announced, "We're celebrating my granddaughter Miriam's birthday."

"Well, how about her using these?" Inge asked, offering Miriam some 'refreshment' tickets, "as *my* birthday present."

"Oh, no, Mr. Inge," Edith politely rejected the offer.

"No, please, take them."

"But it's for *your* food."

"Oh, no, I've had enough today. Don't worry, I won't need these anymore."

Edith finally, graciously accepted the tickets, Miriam voicing *her* thanks also.

After Inge left, Norman and Edith agreed not only because of his gift, he seemed a gentle, considerate person.

Later, when she would recount to her friends the story about this Broadway playwright who remembered her, it was always tinged with a dark note of sadness... the theater section of the *New York Times* carried a glowing tribute to him in the obituary of the award-winning writer who had committed suicide. It had happened just two days after their Riis Park meeting... giving her the food tickets that he 'didn't need anymore.'

73

1946

Dear Pop and Mom,

Well, here I am in Nagasaki!!! It's been five days since I landed here with the first MP Company which is made up from our different used-to-be combat units. Well, it's much safer and better duty here, believe me.

I'll tell you more later, but how are both of you and my kid sister, Edith? Is she walking even better now? Tell her to send a letter to her big brother. Hey, she's over seven years old and it's about time she didn't just say 'hello' in your letters to me.

Mom, you remember that girl, Bonnie, who came to my farewell party that you gave me (thanks)? Anyway, she's been writing me a lot, but when we shipped out of Saipan, I lost her address.

I remember she lives on Herzl Street, maybe 31 or 37. So, will one of you look her up, her name is Levin, and give her my new address, or send me her address. Okay? I suddenly realized maybe she met another guy stateside so she doesn't write anymore to poor, lonely Marines.

Mom, I know about you getting worried a lot before about me, but now everything is okay, so just keep taking your pills, and it's no reason to worry about me anymore.

Pop, I'm sure glad that you and the other teachers are getting more money. You're worth it.

I should be coming stateside in a few months, so we've got a lot to talk about. It's been two years!! I've sure missed you and Mom, and everybody.

I read one of the books that the chaplain got for us aboard the ship on the way here. I was really impressed. It was a book, YOU CAN'T GO HOME AGAIN.

Oh, the writer was a southerner, Thomas Wolfe, and he has a very sensitive way of expressing feelings. Do you know the book? But if I know you, Pop, you always read everything that's good.

Anyway, I think you can go home again, and I'm going to prove it in a little while.

Well, we'll sit around and talk about it, okay? And give my funny kid sister a hug for me.

You know, I love you all, but I don't really miss you right now because I know I'll be seeing you all soon.

How's that for a peculiar philosophical point?

I'll write more about Nagasaki next letter.

Your wandering boy,
Ira
885601 — my serial number which I don't think I'll ever forget, or you, after all these letters addressed to —
Ira Schecter-H + S Company
10th Marines
2nd Division
Fleet Marine Force (FMF) in the Pacific

~

At just the same time that Norman and Marsa received Ira's letter, the junkman, Isaac Baumgarten, sent a letter of acceptance to the president of Graz University in Austria, confirming his appointment to the History Department. Once again he would be on staff; once again part of the academic milieu which had given him such feelings of fulfillment in those years before the Nazis had come.

During the 10 years since he had left Austria, he had never given up on the dream of his once more teaching there; but hovering over this fancy was the fact that when it finally came to pass it would be without Emma and their daughter, Rebecca, killed by German sentries in the Brenner Pass when they too all tried to escape into Switzerland.

He and Norman shared their good news with each other during a dinner that Marsa cooked in celebration of the happy news of Ira's imminent return from Japan.

Joining in the festivities were Ira's grandparents, Bennie, who had recently, reluctantly, retired; Yetta, who, hobbled by the advanced stage of Parkinson's; both still bickering about whatever would come up that they could possibly dispute. The latest bone of contention was their strong disagreement over how fluent in Japanese Ira had become. Bennie pointed to one of Ira's letters which ended with sayonara; that Bennie offered as proof that his 'brilliant boychik' had a great knowledge of Japanese.

"So, Bennie," Yetta argued, "he tells you one word in Jap talk and you say he knows the whole language?"

"Who says the 'whole language'? He knows a lot, believe me."

"*A lot* is not *everything*." Marsa stated conclusively, ending her participation in the discussion.

Norman's sister, Elaine, came along with her jubilant husband, Irving, who had become a partner in a thriving company which was serving mothers with infants who, as Irving loudly stated, "shit enough in their diapers," to make A-1 Diaper service the biggest in the borough.

The dinner was a joyous one which Yetta exclaimed was almost as well cooked as one of her meals. Norman glanced at Marsa, pleading that she not disagree with his mother's assessment.

Many years later, Norman was to recall nostalgically this family get-together as the last one that they were all together with this feeling of great joy and happiness.

74
1946

Dear Mom, Pop and Edith (when are you going to write your big brother?),

How do you like this? I ran into Maurey Lassen here in Nagasaki. Remember him, Pop? He was on my baseball team, the Canarsie Cardinals. He was the first baseman (very good hitter) when I played 'third.'

The problem I had was in throwing to first in the last couple of months just before I enlisted. I think that it was this shoulder bursitis I got suddenly.

I remember you were there for the last game I played, and when they hit to me at third, some of my 'funny' teammates would sort of kneel like they were praying for me to reach first base with my throw. Remember that? It was *funny.*

Well, Maurey wasn't really a big buddy of mine and I didn't even know that he joined the Corps (after me), but it was great to see him here suddenly.

I remember him as being kind of quiet, but the last few years he sure became a kind of big mouth.

I wonder if I changed much. You will have to tell me when I get home, but personally I guess I'm about the same, I think.

Anyway, he was in the Marine band (bugler) in the States, but in the islands he actually had it worse than me because all the band members became 'runners' during combat, which meant that sometimes when radio contact was out, the 'runner' would be used to get messages to different officers or squad leaders. It was a very dangerous job. He told me some pretty tough things that happened to him at Iwo Jima. (I was lucky I missed that one.)

Well, here in Nagasaki, some of the Japs built a baseball field in an old schoolyard where the bomb destroyed everything but a set of kids' monkey bars which melted and twisted into a weird shape. It was something!

Well, one time, Maurey and me went to watch them practice. It doesn't take too much for Maurey to show how much he knows — especially about baseball. We didn't know too much Japanese, but we sort of asked to play with them. They were pretty good, but Maurey wanted to show off as usual. (He's a very good ball player.) So he grabbed a bat. At first the Japs were very polite, but after awhile, they wanted to get a few licks themselves, so they asked for the bat, but Maurey didn't want to give it up, so one of them reached for it, and *Maurey shoved him away. The Japs (some of them still wore part of their old Army uniform) were always polite and not threatening at all. In fact, eventually none of us even carried any firearms when we went into town. It was that safe, but when Maurey acted the way he did, almost challenging these 5-6 Japs, I felt he might be pushing us into a problem with them.*

I even mumbled, "The war is over, Maurey," and I got him to leave before a fight started.

What do you think? Maurey thought I was too easy with the Japs.

"Hey, we won the war, didn't we? And we don't have to be nice to the gooks anyway," he said.

To tell you the truth, Mom and Pop, there were other times I can talk about now because our letters are not censored anymore. I mean, I know that the Japs acted very bad with our troops a lot (like prisoners), but it wasn't as if our guys didn't sometimes act wrong.

One time, after Saipan was 'secured,' we had to go in and clear out some caves. This was maybe even a month later, when one time a squad of us flushed out a single Jap. I couldn't tell if he was a soldier or just one of the civilians, because his clothes were all torn up. I remember his arms were filthy, and all covered with mud and dirt as he held them up over his head, surrendering.

Corporal Hanson was in charge of our flame thrower and without even waiting for an order from our Lieutenant, McDonald, he turned the blast of fire right on the Jap, and screaming in pain, the poor guy went up in flames.

I'm sorry that I went into all this, folks, but it's been on my mind for almost two years.

I was only a new replacement in the company so I didn't say anything and maybe Hanson would have laughed at me if I said why did he have to do what he did? Maybe. But I figure not to say anything was wrong, and maybe now (being an old vet) I hope I would say something. Who knows?

Anyway Maurey got a couple of baseball gloves and a ball and asked me today to go into town and throw a few around.

Our Chaplain here in Nagasaki has some magazines. I dropped around to pick up one of the dictionaries that was being issued to anybody who was interested in improving their English. (Even if their father was an English teacher!) Or even helping them to write something like this long letter.

Anyway, in a Time *magazine article it talked about the devastated City of Nagasaki, as if the A-bomb destroyed the whole city. Well, let me tell you that even though the blast did horribly kill thousands of people (and I've seen some of them with burned faces, which is, believe me, a sad thing to see), but just to keep facts straight, only a small section of the city went boom! It's like as if an A-bomb was dropped on Brooklyn, wiping out Brownsville, but Flatbush, Williamsburg, Bensonhurst, Canarsie, and every other section was still standing.*

I was talking to the Chaplain (a Christian) and he was not too happy to tell me that the area in Nagasaki, which was one of the few Christian ones in whole of Japan, was the largest part of the city that was wiped out. Well, if I were a good Christian, I would wonder what this meant. As you know, Pop, and I know you, Mom, don't like my attitude about all religions. Well, I think that there's nothing to wonder about, that it's not a sign of anything but something like a tragic coincidence.

You know, I don't know whether you've noticed, but since I started out at 17 like most of the other kids, to do what we had to do, to beat Germany and Japan, I've sort of grown up. (Heck, I'm going to be an old man of 21 soon! It's about time.) Hey, I sound like an expert, but I hope I get to learn more about things like A-bombs. But right now, even though I know that dropping it saved a lot of American lives, all I can figure out is if they dropped it like, say on one of the small Japanese islands with maybe just a few civilians, the example of a big mushroom cloud would have frightened the Japs enough so that they would have got the message.

This must be the longest letter I've ever written. Maybe I should wait until I get back to the U.S. soon, but maybe I'm just growing up now that the war is over, and I feel like talking. Yes, maybe without even thinking about it for the last three years I wasn't really thinking like I would have if I went to college. Yes, maybe my thinking of cleaning my rifle and digging foxholes and playing poker with my buddies and trying to find a dry place during the rainy, rainy, rainy season was not everything.

Oh, something else. When we first landed in Nagasaki I noticed something very strange... there were no girls around. I figured out fast that because all of us for almost two years did not meet any girls (except in the movies or fantasies). Well, then I saw some Japanese posters that were still up on the walls, which showed drawings of Marines tearing clothes off Japanese women and spearing bleeding babies on their rifle bayonets.

In about a couple of weeks or so, when women started to feel safe that we wouldn't just rape any girl we met, we started to see women come out from behind their closed doors. Well, things changed when we tried our few words that we learned; like ohio *(that's pronounced just like Ohio), and* Ko-neech-ee-wah *for another version like good morning or something like that.*

When I get home, I'll tell you about some of the girls I met, like Terukio (I've got a picture of her. Kind of pretty), but she got mad at me once when she invited me into her little house (her parents were there too, and they served me some real strong tea), but when she showed me her room and a kind of small shrine with some candles around a photo of a Japanese man in uniform, then she sort of trusted me, I guess, and she took a couple of sheets of paper from in front of the photo and almost like it was a religious object, she held it up like it was more important than the Declaration of Independence, and she sort of cried and emotionally translated what turned out to be his farewell letter to her because he was a Kamikaze pilot who was going on his mission that day. Wow! Then she explained to me that he was going to do his duty at Okinawa. Well, I told her that I was at Okinawa, too, and she became very upset, calling me a Riksentie *(Marine) son a bitch. I tried, in my limited Japanese, to explain that I was only doing* my *duty, but she still was very angry, so I tried to tell her that the war was, sumimashita, over, but all she could say was, anata, son a bitch (you are a son of a bitch). All I could say was that my buddies* (tomadachi) *and I were just trying to stay alive. Well, that didn't make any difference as far as her anger was concerned, so I finally had to say sayonara, and that was the end of our friendship.*

Well, that's all for now, so I'm going to have to find a big envelope to mail all this latest info from me. I'll be home before too long now.

All my good thoughts to all of you — I love the whole Schecter family.

Ira

Hold everything. Great news! I was about to mail all of the above, when Sergeant Cushming came in with some wonderful news. One of the men scheduled to go back to the States tomorrow suddenly got sick and can't travel right now, so because I was supposed to go in the next batch, if I could get my sea bag packed by the morning, I could take his place, so of course I said yes and I'll be back in Brooklyn in a few weeks! Wow! You know what? I'm not going to mail this after all — yes, I'll deliver it in person.

75

MARSA WAS PREPARING EDITH'S FAVORITE LUNCH, an egg omelette of smoked salmon and onions, its pungent aroma wafting through the kitchen and drifting into the rest of the apartment, when a polite knock at the door caused her to stop her favorite moment, testing the results of her loving concoction.

Holding the fork carefully in her hand, a small piece of her prized cooking on its prongs, Marsa went to the door, opening it for a man whom she thought for a moment was Ira.

In his dress blues, Lieutenant O'Connor stood facing the door, his shoulders squared, his face attempting a blank stare.

It was going to be only the third time he had drawn this duty and the chaplain couldn't come with him… an emergency… so it was going to be difficult to handle himself.

Marsa glanced behind him, expecting that he wasn't alone.

"So, Ira is with you?"

"Mrs. Schecter?"

With a flicker of apprehension, Marsa managed a nervous, "So?"

"I am Lieutenant O'Connor. May I come in, please?"

Cold dread enveloped her, heartbeats seeming to freeze in place.

Mothers live the violence of childbirth, and its joy; the warmth and nurture of the flesh of its flesh; embraced by timeless maternal bonds.

Even death cannot separate these joined spirits, they remain connected; the grief of either one's loss of the other forever threading their eternal memory.

Marsa heard words... Nagasaki... Investigation of beating to death of Ira by Japanese... condolences... letter found on him.

Resisting comprehension of the terror of acceptance, Marsa mindlessly, gently invited Lieutenant O'Connor to sit at the table.

"You like a taste of lox and eggs?"

When Norman came home, Edith was doing her homework as Marsa sat wordlessly, staring at Ira's opened letter on her lap.

Marsa was only 45-years old when Ira was killed. His death co-mingled with her recurring nightmares of her family's deaths in the concentration camps.

She once darkly remarked to Norman, "My world is one big cemetery."

It was only Norman's attempts to buoy Marsa's spirits that were able to alter, to some degree, her grim view of her existence. Norman's support and her loving concern for their daughter, Edith, provided balm for her damaged spirits, but Marsa was unable to really embrace even small moments of joy, pushing them into the hiding place of her parched soul.

In the same manner she had refused to place a silver star in her window for Ira's Marine Corps service, Marsa was now in complete denial of what happened to him in Nagasaki.

Along with Ira's final letter, his dog tag was included, and she stared at it for several minutes:

IRA SCHECTER
885601
Blood Type A
H

She was pleased to see that the Marine Corps identified Ira's Jewishness: H for Hebrew.

She carefully placed the dog tag into the envelope. It was the last time she ever looked at it or the letter.

Norman would sometimes attempt to talk to her about Ira, but other than her once telling Edith that her big brother would never come home to them, she would never again speak of Ira.

Marsa's pain, all internalized, clouded the Schecter family, just as Norman's devastated feelings, often tearfully expressed, surrounded them.

This remained constant even when Norman would attempt to break through the malaise.

"Marsa, let's give Edith a big birthday party this year."

"So '10' is so important?"

"Well, she has a few friends in her girl-scout troop that she always has a good time with."

Marsa was indignant.

"A big party *this* year?"

Norman managed to prevail, taking Edith and her friends to see the movie, *The Best Years of Our Lives,* which he, not having read the reviews, was unprepared for: the story followed the lives of several servicemen re-entering civilian life.

Although the events underlined the many vicissitudes that veterans were confronted with, it saddened Norman to be reminded of Ira's being denied facing those problems.

Confronting his grief head on, Norman wondered how Marsa was able to bury the expression of what he knew was an overwhelming anguish.

Often, when he sensed that the agony of her grief was threatening to break the bounds of her worn spirit, he would comfort her by holding her hand. At those times, Norman would stare at Marsa who returned his gaze, their intense exchange connecting them in silent commemoration of the shared pain of losing their son.

76
1977

MIRIAM WAS UNABLE to shake off completely her feeling of being responsible for her mother, Edith's, acute illness.

A Caesarian had been performed on Edith during Miriam's birth, and because of a uterine tear during the procedure, a blood transfusion was necessary.

Not until many years later, after several bouts of unexplained illnesses, Edith's doctor finally discovered that they were due to the weakening of her immune system. The condition was finally traced to be the tainted transfusion of blood that she had received. Although medication was able to slow the complete breakdown of her body's organs, the prognosis was negative.

When Edith became too ill to continue working, Norman and Marsa helped tend to her physical needs, cooking, and bathing, and even enlisting Miriam's willing assistance.

When the doctor became concerned that Edith's health problems might be contagious, he advised Marsa that Miriam should be taken out of the environment.

As she left Edith's apartment that very day, accompanied by Miriam's sobbing, she reassuringly turned at the door.

"Edith, my lovely daughter, I'll bring her back to you as soon as you become healthy again."

Finally, the doctor, baffled by Edith's downward spiraling health, decided that she should go into Riverside Comfort, a rest home that had excellent medical facilities and a small wing for patients whose condition resisted all medical remedies, their immune system so compromised, that the patient's life was in danger.

Riverside was one of the first hospices in New York to deal with the growing scourge of AIDS.

On the first day of Edith's admittance, Marsa gloomily glanced around the ward, and although she recognized its significance, she assumed a positive attitude.

"There's some bad sick in your system, Edith, but don't worry, the doctors are very good here, believe me, and—"

Edith realized that Marsa was unable to express overtly her deepest feelings, but nonetheless she would sometimes erupt.

"Mom, you know I'm very sick, so stop this crap!"

"Crap? You use this language to your mother?"

"Will you take care of Miriam?"

"Do I breathe? And when you get out of this place—"

"I'm dying, Mom! I'm dying!"

Marsa's face, because of her very high blood pressure, now became even more flushed than usual. Feeling faint, she carefully sat down.

Concerned, Edith quickly questioned her.

"You all right, Mom?"

"If my daughter didn't open such a big mouth, I can be okay."

After resting a bit under Edith's apprehensive eye, Marsa started to get up to leave.

"Mom, don't take the bus."

"What? You want me to walk home?"

"I want you to treat yourself for a change… Take a taxi."

Marsa, always economy-minded, waved away the suggestion, but Edith persisted.

"Please, Mom, it would make me feel better."

"For mein daughter, who will be healthy soon, I'll go in a taxi."

Edith watched her mother wearily leave, then hurriedly got the nurse to tell the doctor she needed more morphine for the pain that was becoming worse by the minute.

~

When Marsa got off the bus, she rested for a few minutes before making the long three-block walk to the apartment.

Norman was studying a newspaper editorial, the article was questioning the 'coincidence' of Menachem Begin taking over as Israel's Prime Minister because the more moderate Yitzak Rabin had resigned even as the Palestine National Council insisted on establishing an independent national state on "National Soil".

Norman had had several heated discussions with Alan about the urgent Middle East problem, or as Alan mockingly referred to it as the MEDDLING SHIT PROBLEM, because the U.S. should, he strongly felt, just leave it up to Israel to beat down the Palestinians, including the crazy man, Yasir Arafat, and not, as Norman usually argued, find some validity in the Palestinian demand for parity in what, after all, was once originally their land.

"Normie, you're turning into the poster boy for self-hating Jews."

The thought struck home and he wondered about it now.

Marsa came into the living room, and visibly fatigued, sat down heavily.

Norman, glancing up from the newspaper, worried about Marsa's apparent illness.

"I'll make you a cup of your favorite Lipton's, Marsa my dear."

"But in a glass."

Returning with the glass of tea, Norman noticed the overhead light reflecting off Marsa's now stark white hair in the same way, he reminisced, as it did so many years before when they had first met at Coney Island.

As he watched her, Marsa's lips moved; her breathing weak, the words almost inaudible.

Norman leaned down closer to her in order to be able to hear, but to no avail. However, the soundless words were loud enough for Marsa's heart to hear, "Ira, mein son."

As Norman leaned even closer to Marsa, her eyes suddenly rolled back in their sockets and just as suddenly stared straight ahead. Her body sagged, all of her muscles surrendering even as a huge moan forced its way through her protesting throat.

As Norman quickly reached toward her to provide support for her collapsing body, he could see that his wife of 50 years had come to the end of her troubled life.

He gently closed her eyes and sat next to her on the couch, lovingly embracing her, his taut face contorted in anguish for a long moment, suddenly starting to weep uncontrollably.

Ira's death over 30 years before had been seared into his memory, now Marsa's sudden passing, and the sure knowledge of Edith's imminent death, froze his tears in place.

77
World Trade Center

NORMAN, IDLY FLIPPING THROUGH the *New York Times,* noticed that a section of the Social Activities page had been scissored out. He held up the page, glancing questioningly at Miriam.

Miriam pointed to a newspaper photo pinned to a small cork bulletin board on the office wall.

Norman adapted the same teasing, quizzical tone that he had occasionally used with Ira when he was a child.

"You know, that woman in the picture looks like... no, don't give me any clue, but I think... yes... it looks just like my granddaughter, Miriam, who, now that I think about it, is you!"

Echoes of Ira's "Oh, Pop," laced his memory often, in a similar way, enjoying his father's humor.

Many moments triggering the long ago were happening to him more and more in recent years:

Sunlight filtering between his fingers as he held his hand up, glancing toward Ira across the street singing his original song, PLEASE HELP THE JEWISH NATIONAL FUND.

The smell of Bennie the Butch's sawdust-covered floor and the fresh cut meat in the showcase.

The fragrance of his mother's burnt oatmeal cookies.

The sharp, abrasive tone of Alan's arguments.

The clatter of the hospital gurney as he watched the nurse wheel his daughter's pain-wracked body.

The odor of death pungently floating over NO MAN'S LAND, in France's Belleau Woods.

The twinkling light in the knowing eyes of two-year-old Miriam, as she told Norman, "You love me, Grandpa."

Now, Norman put on his eyeglasses in order to adjust his near-sightedness, as he studied the newspaper photo.

"Was this AIDS party you went to last night the same as the one that Elizabeth Taylor is involved in?"

"No, Grandpa. My friend," Miriam pointed at the woman standing next to her, "Christine Khalafian is the chairperson of this fund-raising event."

"Good for her."

"Oh yes, she's very nice."

"Was she the one who went with us last year when you took me to the Windows of the World restaurant upstairs?"

"You remember?"

"Believe me, my granddaughter, I am many years away from Alzheimer's."

"I can only hope, Grandpa, that I'll be as sharp as you when I reach… even 60."

"Do not worry, you have the Schecter DNA."

"Yes, if I'm lucky…"

"And that's the reason I often ask about you propagating the family."

"Oh, Grandpa," Miriam said with a grin, "You're incredible."

"Well, you have to remember that you're the last of the Schecter's."

Miriam nodded in agreement, hesitated, taking a full breath before she spoke.

"Well, Grandpa, you may get your wish after all."

"So, you're going," Norman excitedly asked, "with somebody after all?"

Again Miriam hesitated, unsure of going further, but finally bravely continued.

"Grandpa, my friend Christine and I are working on an adoption."

Norman was pleased, but at the same time, puzzled.

"But who's the lucky guy?"

Miriam was not sure how to answer, her eyes unconsciously flicking toward the photo. When she noticed

Norman's glancing at it, and then back at her, Miriam perceived comprehension, and she continued carefully.

"Yes, me and Christine have been trying very hard to get the adoption agency to give us their final approval."

Norman stared straight ahead, digesting this unexpected news. Putting all the pieces together took him only a moment or two, before turning back to Miriam.

"Not only do I not have Alzheimer's, but I am *au courant* about different modern behavioral developments. So if I am correct in my assessment, you are... gay."

Relieved at what she had been very apprehensive about... a negative response, she was timid about pushing the revelation any further.

Norman spoke mock severely, "My granddaughter will please step forward closer to me—"

Miriam, smiling, took a half step toward him, and Norman took one towards her, his arms stretched out to her.

Grandfather and granddaughter embraced, their love for each other transcending any cultural divide, any struggle with moral concepts, any differing views of sexual preference, of autumns bleeding into winters with no end; Springs hiding behind Summer warmth; everything fusing into a brilliant flash... parent and child, joined, indivisible.

78
1977

WHEN MARSA DIED, Norman, despite his extreme grief, marshaled his energy and focus in order to guide Edith toward what the doctor told him to expect shortly... that her life was rapidly coming to an end, that he was prescribing large quantities of morphine to ease her excruciating pain.

As soon as Norman arrived for his daily visit, Edith greeted him with an urgent demand to get Miriam to the hospital as soon as possible. Because Edith had told him not to bring her to see her mother's suffering, Norman understood her request now to mean that she was feeling her life slipping away.

While he rushed off to phone Miriam to get a cab and hurry to the hospital, the nurse helped Edith to sit up in bed and applied still another layer of rouge on her cheeks, in a vain attempt to mask her gaunt, sallow complexion.

Edith had started to keep a journal shortly after she had arrived at RIVERSIDE COMFORT, but because of her general fatigue, she hadn't been able to record much of what had been happening to her, but anticipating Miriam's arrival, she managed to write her a note.

By the time Miriam reached Edith's room, Norman was sitting on her bed, his arm around her, whispering consolation.

"Here's your beautiful daughter, Miriam, *my* beautiful daughter, Edith."

Miriam, very frightened, stood stiffly by the bed and Edith extended her hand toward her, inviting her to join them.

Miriam carefully sat down next to her mother, experiencing her comforting warmth.

Other than Miriam softly murmuring her support, "Mother, don't worry, we'll take care of you," the three sat quietly for a moment. Suddenly, with a great moan, Edith's body arched in a paroxysm of pain, her head thrusting upward, unsuccessfully attempting to draw away from the body's intense sensation, her arms stretched upward, her hands stiff in supplication, as she asked, "When?"

Norman and Miriam were unsure of what Edith meant by the question, but when her face contorted even more, crying out again, "When?!!," they realized that she was pleading for the termination of her terrifying nightmare of life… for death to answer her question.

Norman quickly rose and rushed to the nurse's station.

"Please, she needs more morphine. The nurse nodded compassionately, but made no move.

Norman urgently repeated, "PLEASE!"

"The doctor," the nurse started to explain patiently, but Norman waved away her objections, his voice rising in demanding, "She needs something right now!"

"I'm not allowed to give her anything until the doctor authorizes—"

Norman desperately reached toward the tray of medication beside the nurse.

"Don't do that, Mr. Schecter!"

As he started to pull the tray toward him, he spoke threateningly, "I'm not going to wait for the doctor, she's in too much pain."

"It's dangerous if I give her more."

"Dangerous?"

"Yes, it might mean that she—"

Norman paused for a brief moment.

"I understand, but that has to happen eventually. I'm not going to let her—"

"All right, Mr. Schecter."

Norman gently took Miriam's hand, holding her close to him as the nurse inserted the hypodermic needle.

Almost immediately Edith's body stopped convulsing; her eyes starting to close.

As Norman and Miriam watched, Edith's eyes fluttered open, finally opening wide enough to focus on her daughter standing at the head of the bed.

Many years later, Norman would remember that moment when his daughter managed a half smile at *her* daughter before she closed her eyes... forever.

79

NORMAN DECIDED TO REVISIT BROWNSVILLE.

Many times since the Schecters had moved to the more upscale neighborhood of Brooklyn Heights 30 years before, he had thought about going back there but Marsa had been adamantly against the idea of returning to that *fahkahta* place, now that they were able to 'live like a person.'

Although Norman realized that it was unlikely that many of the people he had known would still be living there, a nostalgic feeling drew him to take the EL and get off at the SARATOGA AVENUE stop which he had used countless times before.

As soon as Norman started to walk toward Amboy Street, he quickly realized how much the area had changed. Whereas in the past, just about everybody in the neighborhood was white, Norman could readily see that now just about everyone was black.

Many other things had changed: several of the small food and confectionery stores had been shuttered; only the once majestic pool room, ACE BILLIARDS, its lettering fading, the sign now slightly askew, still inviting young men in to challenge their skill.

The intent players studiously competed in a game of 'eight ball' in order to create for the winner some degree of self-respect, in short supply in this extremely run down, impoverished area.

It crossed Norman's mind that he and those others who were, in the 30s, caught in the iron jaws of the Depression, had been much better off than these people, who had inherited decaying blighted streets and their inexorable deterioration.

But here at ACE'S, the experts at straight pool or 3-cushion billiards hungrily chalked their cue sticks, hoping for victory... a nirvana in the midst of the defeats of daily existence.

Norman passed BETSY HEAD PARK'S 10-foot high chain link fence separating it from the street. It was still intact, although the metal had long needed a re-coating, the many winter snows and grime having worn away at it.

The used-to-be well-tended grass had burnt out years before, scattered clumps of dirt patterning the ill-kept baseball field.

The city's budget for low-income, politically expedient areas was limited; funds for re-seeding the turf, used elsewhere, perhaps for hiring another much needed security guard for the volatile temperament of the angry youths' despair, or perhaps simply finding the graft pocket of a local politician.

The other half of BETSY HEAD PARK was the city-block-long swimming pool which remained much like it had been since its construction by the government's WORKS PROGRESS ADMINISTRATION during the Depression, affording many men some much needed paychecks.

People from the neighboring areas, such as East New York, Carnarsie and East Flatbush, flocked to the pool during the stifling summers, at the same time often feeling like peasants being appeased, enviously wondering about the rich people enjoying the comfort of their private pools and their attendants catering to the wealthy.

As soon as Norman took his first step into Amboy Street, he immediately sensed that his pilgrimage to this other time was going to have unexpected significance.

Having recently been impressed with several movies in which the director had utilized the slow-motion technique in order to punctuate the action, now Norman's every step seemed to him to be played in that mode.

His eyes slowly 'panned' to a dilapidated building, coming to rest on the mottled number '179' on the glass front door. Keeping it in 'close-up' for a moment, he tried to recapture the memory of what the building had once looked like, when, with his vice principal's appointment in his pocket; the family's meager belongings; Marsa's samovar from Germany; his books along with Ira's carefully preserved letter from Nagasaki; with a sense of loss that he would only much later understand, the family left Brownsville for an easier life.

Now, Norman stared at the boarded door and windows of the Schecter ground-floor apartment. The charcoal-singed front of the building was a souvenir of a recent fire, probably caused by an area kerosene heater used to supplement the insufficient heat provided through corroded steam pipes.

Recalling Ira's long-ago refutation of not being able to go home again, Norman was now unsure of *his* ability to do so.

Finding himself staring down at the stairwell leading to the courtyard, Norman suddenly realized the underlying reason for his return to Amboy Street... to solve once and for all the riddle of why Marsa had hidden behind the curtain whenever she threw her penny into the courtyard for the violin man.

On one hand, Norman considered it essential that both the 'giver' and 'receiver' of a gift be known to each other. However, he then argued against himself: An anonymous donation *also* had value, even though gratitude for it is not able to be expressed to the 'giver.'

When all was said and done, Marsa's unique behavior, Norman felt, was probably the better way. After all, she would always reply simply to the perplexed inquiry as to why she hid behind the curtain, "Well, he gets the penny, doesn't he?"

This logic was all that Marsa needed to enjoy her contribution which placed her, Norman decided, as close to a pure act of altruism as one could get.

For a moment he was struck by his insight, until his memory flipped through the pages of his occasional Bible reading, and was reminded of the moving story of the Samaritans and their 'giving' without 'receiving.'

Norman smiled deprecatingly at himself, "So much for my philosophically reinventing the wheel."

Slowly taking the few steps into the courtyard, his thoughts went to the Violin Man, whom he had not seen for many years.

~

Edith's husband, Barry, had died in Vietnam just a few months before and Norman thought to cheer her up, so his sister Elaine babysat the year-old Miriam and he, Marsa, and Edith went to eat dinner at the city-famous JACK DEMPSEY

RESTAURANT, topping it off with the even more famous cheesecake.

They strolled uptown to Carnegie Hall to take the box seats that Norman had purchased, knowing that Edith always enjoyed the specialness of sitting in what she playfully referred to as the Royal Box.

They enjoyed Isaac Stern's superb playing of the Brahm's *Violin Concerto*, and to round out the evening, Norman had reserved a table at the nearby elegant RUSSIAN TEA ROOM.

As they settled in, they were rewarded by observing a meeting between the Russian violinist, David Oistrakh, who Norman considered to be the greatest modern violinist, and Stern, who entered the restaurant to appreciative murmurs of approval from the customers.

Oistrakh, who had attended the performance, stood up, crossing directly toward Stern, and his hand extended, spoke quietly, one artist to another, "Shalom."

Stern, as amiably, answered "Shalom." They shook hands and Oistrakh, desiring not to take the spotlight away from his fellow artist, returned to his table, as Stern joined his family at their table.

It was only a passing moment, but Norman felt that he had just witnessed a shining example of artistic camaraderie and admiration.

He recalled a line that one of his favorite poets, Edna St. Vincent Millay, had written, "When something really fine comes along, all jealousies are pooled in a common admiration."

Norman fancifully thought: if only life's conflicts were dealt with in the same respectful and considerate manner.

With this moment still lingering in his mind, they exited the restaurant and Norman noticed a shabbily dressed elderly man sitting on a canvas stool, expertly playing his highly polished violin.

It was not unusual for street musicians to play in front of Carnegie Hall, but this violinist, it seemed to Norman, was of very superior musicianship.

As Norman passed the discreet donation box set in front of the man, he put a dollar in it and the violinist nodded his gratitude, continuing to play.

Marsa suddenly stopped, glancing at the violinist who was still concentrating on playing her favorite, the *Meditation* from *Thais*. She peered at the grizzled old man, a full beard masking his identity.

Norman's memory played around in the past as he noticed Marsa's intent gaze, and suddenly a name from the past jumped to his lips, "Pulyakis," he blurted out.

The man stopped playing, hurriedly picking up his donations and hastily walked down the street.

Norman and Marsa exchanged glances, tacitly agreeing on the fact that they had just seen the Violin Man whom they had last seen when he played at Ira's Bar-mitzvah.

Now, as Norman entered 179's courtyard, he was almost oppressively aware of the years that had galloped by and the memory of Marsa watching from behind the kitchen curtain, standing out in bolder relief than many other events which he had thought were more in the forefront of his growing storehouse of memories.

Glancing around at the heavily littered, garbaged courtyard, Norman felt a mix of pleasure and sadness, and the clear realization that he would never again… never again go home, perhaps not even in memory.

80
World Trade Center 9/11

"I'LL BE BACK IN A FEW MINUTES, GRANDPA."

"I think my hot pastrami sandwich is getting cold."

"I just have to pick up this market report for a client."

"How do you turn on the TV?"

Miriam pressed the power button of the desk TV.

"Katie Couric is on Channel 4, Grandpa."

"Well, I'm sure a *Law and Order* rerun is on."

Miriam smiled, recalling the many discussions they had had regarding the vagaries of the law and ethical dilemmas that were dramatized on the show.

"You've seen so many of them, Grandpa, I'll bet you could write a good script for the show."

"Maybe, but at my advanced years it would be about an elderly neanderthal claiming age discrimination because he was forced to live in a cave for senior citizens."

"You're really funny, Grandpa. Anyway, if I get held up, I'll give you a call."

After Miriam left, Norman surfed the channels until he found his favorite program.

For years, he had been an avid viewer of *Law and Order*, enjoying its mix of mystery and trial by jury resolution.

Although a number of the leading roles had been recast several times, Norman had developed a loyalty to all of them, feeling that they seemed to possess a personal decency which appealed to his sense of fair play. However, considering the several times he himself had been confronted with choices that placed him between what he thought might be the 'right' thing to do and the expedient one which permitted him to go in the opposite direction, he was forced to accept that he would not likely be 'upright' enough to be cast in *Law and Order.*

Glancing around Miriam's modest-sized office, Norman watched the hazy morning window light glinting off a glass-framed photo hanging on the wall.

Not having seen the photo since a year earlier when he had arrived for his annual pastrami, Norman stared intensely at the picture which he had snapped many years before.

He nursed the memory of that sunshine afternoon when he, Marsa, Edith and Miriam strolled through the glorious colors of the idyllic landscaped BROOKLYN BOTANICAL GARDENS.

He bought a large bouquet of multi-colored tulips for Marsa who, after warmly thanking him, gave a tulip each to her daughter and granddaughter.

Norman recalled Edith holding the vivid orange one; Miriam, the brilliant red one, but the photo showed it actually in reverse; Edith holding the red one; Miriam the orange one.

Chuckling at the game his recollections were playing with him, he vowed that this time he would make sure to record which one held the red tulip, which one the orange.

He looked forward to next year when he would test his memory again. Although he felt that his mind was still intact, Norman was forced to admit that it had started to fray around the edges as the years passed.

Below the photo was the framed note that Edith had written on the last day of her life and left for Miriam.

My Dear Beautiful Grown-Up Daughter Miriam,
Twelve years old, and so smart, but you were very bright from the moment you were born. As

soon as you came out you put your thumb into your mouth, and the nurse said she had never seen a newborn baby who was able to figure out how to do that so young. If you keep on studying, you will continue to grow. I'm so proud of you. I guarantee you I will always be watching you do great things.

I have to rest now—I'm tired.

And in a barely legible scrawl, Edith managed to finish—

I love you. Grandpa will always help you.

Norman, glancing up from reading the note, caught a movement outside the window, several stories up, and he idly watched an airplane until it passed out of the range of his sight. In a moment, there was a dull thump as if something had been dropped on a floor above.

Out of the corner of his eye, he noticed the newspaper photo of Miriam and her friend, Christine, flutter as if in a breeze.

Because Norman had the cataracts removed from both of his eyes many years before, he ascribed the clipping's unusual movement to the fact that his eyesight was failing, reluctantly accepting it as further evidence that his body's machinery was breaking down. He had recently come to realize also that his sense of balance was poor, noting it whenever he would uneasily bend over to pick up an article he had dropped from his trembling hand.

'The tyranny of the body,' Norman protested to himself as he scanned the political editorial.

The door of the office was suddenly flung open and a nervous-looking man holding a paper cup in his hand, trying not to let any of the coffee spill over as he excitedly called out to Norman, "We've got to get out, there's a fire upstairs!"

Norman quickly stood up preparing to leave, but as he stepped toward the door, the phone rang. When Norman hesitated, the man spoke urgently, "You better get going, sir!"

The phone rang again, and as Norman picked it up, the man decided to let the old guy do whatever he wanted to, and sipping his coffee, he joined several other office staff, speaking intensely to each other as they hurried by.

"Yes?" Norman inquired quickly into the phone.

"Grandpa, I want you to take the elevator right now and leave the building."

"So there is a fire?"

"Yes, go right now!"

"Are you okay?"

"Yes, go right now."

"You coming too?"

"Yes, I'll meet you downstairs."

The phone clicked off, but immediately rang again, Norman answering immediately.

"Miriam?"

"No, is she there?"

"She just called me."

"Is this her grandfather?"

"Absolutely."

"Good, she told me you were coming over to see her."

"You're her friend?" glancing at the newspaper clipping, "Christine Khalafian?"

"Yes, Mr Schecter."

"She told me about you."

"Oh."

"Don't worry, my dear, she told me all about both of you."

"I'm glad, Mr Schecter."

"I'm going to meet her downstairs right now."

"Good, tell her to call me right away. You have the TV on?"

Norman glanced at the TV screen, the *Law and Order* show had been interrupted and a man's voice was speaking excitedly as film of a plane crashing into the World Trade Center was played.

The concerned newscaster crisply explained, but Norman's nervousness jumbled the words 'Plane has crashed into Tower 1 … Accident?' … 'Another plane crashed into Tower 2.' … 'Two accidents?' …'Fire shooting out of upper floors.' …'No more information.' …'Fire engine equipment arriving… Firemen met by Twin Tower security personnel… Police… People rushing out of building. Chaos.'

The phone ringing again startled Norman. He grabbed the phone.

"Yes?"

"Grandpa, I told you to go."

"Christine called. Said you should call her."

"I will, but you have to go right now. You understand?"

"Where are you?"

"I said I'll meet you downstairs. Please, Grandpa, leave right now!"

"Okay… I'm going… I'm going, okay?"

"Good!"

"You know why I'm doing this?"

"Yes."

"So tell me!"

Miriam paused for only a moment before repeating her long ago, two year old's insight.

"You love me, Grandpa."

"I'm going out the door right now."

Norman hung up, hurrying out of the office.

The man with the coffee cup, along with several other people from the office, stared at the elevator door as it opened, revealing the passengers crammed together.

Mr. Coffee Man saw that it was hopeless for any of them to crowd in. He quickly hurried to the stairway exit, calling over his shoulder to the others.

"Come on, it's only four flights."

A young woman started to follow Mr. Coffee, but noticing Norman walking slowly to join the group, spoke to him solicitously.

"You need some help, sir?"

"Thanks Miss, but I figured out how to walk by myself 99 years ago."

The woman smiled. "I thought so," extending her hand toward Norman, "Then I'm sure it'll be easy for us to figure out going down the stairway together."

Norman, smiling, took her hand.

"You're very persuasive."

Although his muscles protested, Norman started to move more quickly. He grasped at this opportunity to feel as if he, an ancient gallant knight, was being helpful to her, leaving danger behind them.

By the time they reached the second landing, the murmurs of the office personnel were joined by people from that floor, their scattered conversations adding to the mounting concern.

As the people headed to the first floor, strong voices came up toward them…

Firemen, suited up with all their weighty gear and paraphernalia, were rushing upstairs, with perfunctory apologies to the people they were pushing past.

"Sorry folks!"

"Just keep moving down!"

"Everything's okay."

"Everybody all right?"

One of the firemen stopped in front of Norman long enough to speak quickly to him.

"Need any help, old timer?"

Norman retorted quickly.

"Go do your duty."

As the firemen, moving as rapidly as they were able to, brushed past the people descending in the now-crowded stairway; everybody started to feed off the tension of the fire alarm; the firemen's business-like but grimly focused behavior enveloping all in an unnamed fear.

The terrifying events that would follow shredded the bounds of what could be imagined…

The unimaginable.

~

"Hurry up, sir! You too, lady… over here!"

Norman, feeling proud of himself for not having to hold on to the young lady's arm as they left the building, smiled cheerfully at the policeman who was waving them over toward the nearby parked ambulance.

"Thanks, officer, it looks like—" gesturing toward the people following them out of the building and joining the milling crowd, "it's a busy day."

"Come on, sir, hurry up!"

"I'm waiting for my daughter, and she—" gesturing toward the young lady, "is a very nice person, but she is not in the family."

The policeman, shaking his head in exasperation, started to bark another command, but the young lady quickly defused the situation, again taking Norman's hand.

"Why don't we just walk over to the ambulance so your daughter will be able to see you when she gets out, too."

"But why is everybody so excited about a little fire?"

A woman in the crowd suddenly screamed as she pointed up toward one of the floors of the tower where flames were billowing out.

She violently shook her head as if the effort could rescue the man who was standing outside a smashed window, desperately cringing away from the flames licking at him.

Terrified, he shouted an agonized protest of pain, the sound gurgling in his throat as he jumped out of the window, his clothes smoldering, smoke trailing him comet-like as he hurtled down to the street.

Norman's sense of denial blocked the full meaning of what he had just seen, even as a man and woman, holding each other's hands, perched rigidly on the ledge outside of another window, flames shooting out toward them. They seemed to pose for a moment, suddenly silently plummeting toward the sidewalk and the concrete grave waiting for their smashed bodies.

The full significance of what was happening enveloped Norman and the others, who finally accepted the overwhelming horror.

They stared in hypnotic fixation at the building, its upper floors engulfed in flames; some people frantically backing away; others anxiously inquiring of the police and firemen as to what emergency measures were being taken. The security police provided them with curt assurances that everything would be all right, as firehoses were hurriedly connected, and personal equipment was expertly organized by the firefighters and strapped to their bodies. The firemen started to rush toward the building and as they pushed through the crowd, questions were hurled at them, receiving only brusquely professional replies and growled orders to get as far away from the building as fast as possible.

The police herded the crowd toward the street as an ambulance attendant motioned to Norman.

"Let's get you into this ambulance, sir."

"Don't worry, young man, I'm top of the line."

"You're breathing kind of hard, sir."

"I just walked down four flights, that's all."

"I'll get the doctor to check you out anyway." Norman almost shouted his objection, "Look, there are people," gesturing toward the agitated crowd, "who really need some help."

"Right, sir, so as soon as you get into the ambulance, I'll get them all to move to safety, okay?"

Norman, dizzy with the exertion and tension of the last several minutes, decided on a *noblesse oblige* gesture and stepped toward the ambulance. The crowd's eyes were riveted on the tower, which for a moment seemed to sag before imploding into an eerie rumbling, the whole structure slowly collapsing on itself in a huge wave of mortar and glass, finally disappearing into its own instant pile of rubble on the sidewalk.

Up to this moment, Norman had felt that he was observing an event which he was not really part of, like watching an exciting movie, but now he was shocked into awareness by the building's blackened dust swirling toward them, and through the cacophony of rescue noises, he heard the whisper of mortality. He gasped in sudden terror that Miriam might be smothered by the ominous cloud enveloping them.

He took a long, deep breath, as if he could swallow this danger that threatened to destroy his granddaughter.

81

"MR. SCHECTER?"

The nurse checked the IV to be sure that it was flowing steadily into Norman's vein as he lay sleeping.

"Mr. Schecter?" she repeated gently.

"Hm?" Norman mumbled.

"We feeling better, Mr. Schecter?"

Norman's eyes flickered open, "Wha?"

"We managed to get all that dust out of your lungs."

"Miriam?"

"I'm nurse Alianak, Mr. Schecter."

"Miriam?"

"A woman's hanging around a couple of hours to see you."

"Miriam?"

"You rest and I'll go to the waiting room and get her."

Relieved, Norman closed his eyes, but just as he started to doze off, he was startled to hear his name called again. Immediately alert, Norman excitedly attempted to sit up, but his breathing labored, he fell back immediately.

It was not Miriam standing at the head of the bed.

"Mr. Schecter, I'm Christine."

Norman narrowed his eyes apprehensively, but said nothing.

"I spoke to you this morning, Mr. Schecter."

After a moment of silence, Christine tried again.

"I'm Miriam's friend, Christine."

Finally realizing that this woman was a link to his granddaughter, Norman sensed that her worried manner was not about his welfare.

"You spoke with Miriam?"

"Yes, after I talked to you. She was in the restaurant."

"The restaurant?"

"Where the three of us had lunch, remember?"

"The Windows on the World, right?"

"You have a good memory."

Norman hesitated, hoping that Christine would provide information that would ease his obvious growing concern.

After a moment, Christine offered news she thought would lessen his anxiety.

"The fire chief told the news media that he thought most of the people got out safely."

"What about Miriam? Is she in this hospital, too?"

"No, but I'm checking all the other ones. Don't worry, Mr. Schecter, I'm on top of it."

"That's not good enough. I want to see her right now!"

"But, Mr. Schecter—"

"No!" Norman sharply interrupted, "I'm absolutely not interested in your speculations about different hospitals."

Christine, quickly aware that Norman was too distraught to be rational, remembered knowledge about him that Miriam had once shared with her.

"My grandfather," Miriam had lovingly explained, "just can't accept the fact that bad things *can* happen to good people."

Now Christine spoke to Norman, "Mr. Schecter, I'm sure that Miriam will turn up all right, so I'll be checking for some good news from the rescue teams, but we just have to be prepared."

"For what?"

"For anything."

"'Anything' means what?"

"Whatever is on the shelf."

Norman became incensed.

"We're talking about my granddaughter, and you sound like a grocery clerk."

"I just meant, Mr. Schecter, that there's no way of being sure what's happened."

Norman, extremely distressed, almost hissed, "I don't need your gratuitous analysis."

"I just mean—"

"Now I remember Miriam showing me the picture of you at that AIDS party."

"Good."

"Do you have that thing?"

"What, Mr. Schecter?"

"AIDS."

"No."

"Miriam?"

"Absolutely not."

"Well, then all we have to do is find out which hospital they took her to."

"I'll do that as soon as I leave here."

"Yes, Christine, yes. You know what this means to me."

Christine nodded solemnly and stopped at the door, turning back toward Norman.

"And *me*."

"Then I count on you, Christine."

Norman and Christine's eyes met in a mutual bond of love and fear for granddaughter… for mate.

After Christine left, Norman grimly shook his head, rejecting any negative about his granddaughter's well-being, as he again recalled "you love me, Grandpa."

82

THE MANAGEMENT OF SHALOM ASSISTED LIVING had established a strict policy, that so long as a resident did not have medical conditions that required constant doctor's visits, he would be welcome to stay at the facility.

In Norman's case, his general good health did not pose any problem, but since the Trade Center disaster, because of his often rude behavior to the staff and other residents, it was reluctantly decided that the rules would be stretched a bit, on one condition: "Mr. Schecter, you must be more polite."

Norman, to avoid any further conflict, confined himself to his room, occasionally venturing out to the dining room. Not able to tolerate sharing his thoughts or feelings with others, he would wait until everybody left, before eating by himself.

Finally, he came to accept that the once-promising journey of shared joy with his grandchild that he had eagerly anticipated, Miriam providing loving comfort as he headed toward the end of his life, was not to be.

All of his dreams were aborted by the greatest obscenity: Miriam's young heart, along with several thousand others, had been stopped tragically on September 11, 2001.

Overwhelming grief settled into Norman's spirit, dragging him into a dark cave of depression. Any attempt to escape from the constant state of mourning was cut off by oppressive hopelessness. Only rarely was he able to touch a moment unburdened by despair.

He lived isolated in this way for almost a year. Only Christine, who came to visit him weekly, could manage to lift his spirits. However, there were instances after she had left him that he would feel flashes of anger toward her, that

Miriam had recently died, and here Christine was dashing around on various social 'do-good' projects.

It was an easy leap back in time for him to recall Elissa Jackman and *her* activism.

After years of painful operations and grueling rehabilitative exercises, she had finally been discharged from the hospital.

She phoned Norman, who congratulated her, and he and Marsa took her to crowded, buzzing KATZ'S DELICATESSEN in Manhattan's lower East Side which had, according to Marsa's culinary expertise, a bigger and better hot pastrami sandwich than the more famous Carnegie Deli.

Elissa had become highly agitated at reading the newspaper reports; the high profile German-American Bund meeting at New York's Madison Square Garden, extolling Hitler and Germany's fevered nationalistic drive for *'liebensraum'* in pursuit of becoming Europe's super-power.

The Bund meetings were led by the vitriolic and bombastic Fritz Kuhn, the American 'Führer,' leading the noisy support for Hitler's takeover of Czechoslovakia's Sudetenland, a highly attractive industrial area.

England's Prime Minister, Neville Chamberlain's, famous 'PEACE IN OUR TIME' declaration in Munich eased Germany's acquisition.

Elissa hand-painted several signs parodying Chamberlain's capitulation.

**A PIECE OF CZECHOSLOVAKIA
IS NO PEACE**

A few weeks later, she enrolled in Princeton and even as she was achieving honors grades, she became energetically involved in negotiations with the teachers' union for upgrading salary and benefits.

She invited the Schecters to her informal City Hall marriage to Simon Davis, philosophy professor at NYU, who shortly after became a Jewish Army Chaplain.

Immediately assigned to the Normandy invasion, he accompanied the first troops into the Buchenwald death camp.

When he returned to New York he recounted the dolorous experience to Elissa; the emaciated prisoners, the horrible stench of its unhygienic conditions. He told her with revulsion about one of the camp's rooms that was filled with piles of the shoes of children who had been sent to the gas chamber for their painful extermination. The pitiful image of the mounds of shoes, which Simon had photographed, evoked a cry of great sorrow and pain from Elissa. Later, she told Norman about the argument she had with Simon about his showing the photos to her.

"I think he knew how upset I'd be, Norman, and he showed them to me anyhow."

Another 'blow up' she had with Simon was because he defended the U.N.'s decision to go along with England's plan to divide Palestine between Arabs and Jews. She phoned Norman after she finally decided to divorce Simon.

"Norman, do you think I can live in the same house with a man who is willing to prepare us for concentration camps?"

When Norman suggested to her, "Perhaps you're still blaming him, the messenger, for the genocide," she hung up abruptly, angry with herself because she hadn't directly expressed her wrath. Regretting that she hadn't told Norman, "I never really did trust you and now you've proven again to be a Goddamn apologist for the anti-Semites."

Elissa would not have known about the many heated discussions between Norman and his friend, Alan, over this same Israel-Palestine issue. Nor would she be aware of the many disagreements between the two of them on any subject which they could tacitly agree on that was worthy of them to arm-wrestle their brains over.

Over 50 years after Elissa had hung up on Norman, his memory connected with the innocuous dispute he had had with Alan in the 30s over the grand chess master's 'Alekhine gambit,' the argument moving into the serious concern of Alan's drawing Norman into his arson plan to burn down his father's fur store. Years later, all that morphed into Norman's visiting Alan in the hospital after he had a stroke, which debilitated the entire right side of his face and body, leaving his ability to speak damaged, but allowing him to communicate with halting clarity.

Drawing himself up into an awkward sitting position, he proceeded to harangue Norman about the growing threat and deadly damage of the different militant Palestinian groups like Hamas and Hezbolla.

"They have to be wiped out," his words spat out in short bunches as he fought to align his all but frozen jaw and twisted mouth to shape the words, "before we can even talk to that lunatic Arafat!"

"I don't know about *that*, Alan. After all, he has unified the Palestinian people and given them a sense of national pride."

"You really piss me off, Normie."

Alan was finding it hard to speak, not only because of the struggle to move his reluctant lips, but because of his frustration at having so much to say to his 'stupid liberal ass' friend, but lacking the muscle control to get the ideas out of his mouth as quickly as he would have preferred, since he was politically engaged and passionate about the 'MEDDLING SHIT PROBLEM.'

"So they manufacture this fahkahta name, the Palestinian Authority, to give them the right to kill Jews." Gulping in an elusive breath, he painfully exhaled his rejoinder, "And you try to invent an excuse for them to do it."

"Don't be an idiot, Alan! It's just that we should keep in mind that *they* also want to live in *their* Holy Land."

"Now, I'm getting really angry," Alan managed to shout out, "You great big fuckin' mediator between us and them." Pausing for a moment in order to catch his breath, Alan shot out his clinching argument. "You can't go through life pleasing both sides. The Jews need a place they can feel safe in, so none of them has to be afraid of the gas chamber and ovens being turned on again."

"Paranoia is an excuse for everything, right?"

"I don't even want to discuss this with you anymore, Normie. You have this self-image you carry around... Mister Fair Play; well I've got a name for you and your fuckin' balancing act... loser!"

Norman was not surprised that he suddenly thought about Ira. In the over 30 years since his son had been killed in Nagasaki, Norman had thought of him often, hardly a day passing without some poignant memory of his son. Sometimes it was an image of a pair of bronzed infant's shoes on the coffee table; an old children's carriage in the cellar of '179'; Ira singing *Stout Hearted Men*; a faded official Marine Corps photograph of Ira and a few Jewish buddies in his outfit in Saipan celebrating a Passover ceremony under a battered canvas awning; in the back- ground a small improvised cemetery, its makeshift crosses and six-pointed Jewish stars poignantly marking 'the last full measure of devotion' of the very young men who had come over 9,000 miles to the battle… and their death.

Now, when Alan had disdainfully accused him of being a 'fuckin' mediator' trying to please both sides, he realized that although he had felt that he had in some way created some positive guidelines for Ira's behavior during the 17 years before he had gone overseas, he was now pleasantly aware of how much he, the father, had learned from the son: Recalling Ira's mediating between his grandfather, Bennie the Butch, and his grandmother, Yetta, in the big pronunciation battle over bread, 'brot,' and butter, 'pitter,' diplomatically reconciling their opposing views, he gladly accepted the fact that Ira had influenced *him*.

Norman was pleased that Ira's legacy lived on in him.

Here he was, almost 80 years old, and still open to learning.

He rolled the idea around.

"Hooray for you, you old, old man."

Norman turned away from Alan, the argument about Israel and Palestine tabled for another time.

"I've got to get over to visit Edith in the hospice."

Alan's tone softened, "Give the good girl my very best."

When Norman hesitated, Alan glanced warmly at his friend. "So go over there, shmuck."

Three days later, Alan's wife, Janet, phoned Norman. Alan had died in his sleep and the funeral was being held the next day.

"Will you say a few words at the service, Norman?"

"Me?"

"Who else but his best friend?"

"Okay. And how are you doing, Janet?"

"Unfortunately I'll live."

As Norman finished delivering the eulogy at Alan's memorial, his thoughts somehow found their way back to another speech he had given at the service held for his father, Bennie the Butch, some 25 years earlier.

The people at Alan's funeral were puzzled at Norman's smiling as he concluded his speech, "I'm sure Janet and the rest of the family will grieve the loss of Alan's special company, but although I am not blood, I'll truly miss my best friend and everything we shared over the years."

Although Norman's words were genuine, his smile grew to an inadvertent chuckle as he recalled telling his father's favorite joke to a different congregation of mourners.

"So Bennie the Butch always got a great big kick out of asking all of his customers, 'How could five men stand under an umbrella and not get wet?'"

Norman acted out his father's superior manner as he would answer his own question, "It wasn't raining!"

As Norman, in the limousine provided by the mortuary, drove to the cemetery, he took inventory of the many times over the years he had made the sad journey to bury a friend, a relative.

He had begun to realize that he had outlived most of his contemporaries, starting to feel the disturbing pangs of aloneness.

83
Los Angeles 2003

THE PUBLIC ADDRESS SYSTEM in the airport terminal had been malfunctioning for about 10 minutes, causing anxiety among many of the waiting ticket holders.

Anticipating problems, a number of security guards were put on alert. Some of the waiting passengers were upset due to the lack of PA announcements which would ordinarily clarify whether their flights were boarding, delayed, or having equipment difficulties.

Because there had been recent terrorist bomb scares, the PA situation added to the tension created by the impact of 9-11 and Homeland Security's various color alerts. The large electronic board listed arrival and departure times but the uncertainty of travelers who were concerned about the status of flight connections or the expected arrival of a friend, family member, or loved one, hung heavy in the terminal.

Christine Khalafian was very worried.

Although the flight from New York was listed on the arrival board, no announcement had been able to be made confirming it.

She had managed to convince the security supervisors that because she was coming to pick up a man who was 103 years old, they should allow her to stand by at his arrival gate.

As she waited along with an attendant to push the wheelchair she had requested, Christine sighed in relief as the PA, its defects finally repaired, declared that the New York flight was arriving on time.

Relieved that she now knew when Norman would arrive, Christine reviewed the events leading up to this moment: About six months earlier, her position at the non-profit AIDS fund raising organization was transferred to Los Angeles. Her supervisor had decided that Christine's ability to attract and deal with celebrities would be put to even better use in the glamour-land of high profile movie stars attaching their names and reputations to 'good causes'; also billionaire studio heads; airplane production CEOs; communication executives looking to donate to a worthy cause which could then be linked to their products.

Christine was cynically aware of the transparent opportunism of some of the contributors, but since she was genuinely dedicated to raising money to deal with this growing health scourge, she would focus all her efforts on the benefits of her activities.

It was the middle of winter when she packed for the trip to LA.

She had been having at least once a week lunches or dinners with Norman, and they were times that meant a good deal to both of them.

Norman, in addition to having lost all of his family members, his few friends at Shalom Assisted Living were also 'dropping out of the race,' as he characterized the thinning ranks to Christine.

"The trees are falling all around us."

"But *you've* been in good health, haven't you?" Christine asked, concerned.

"The aches and pains are really..." Norman left his comment unfinished, using his sagging energy to massage his knees which had been causing him more and more discomfort.

"You in pain, Norman?"

"The winter has really been tough on these old bones."

"You need some warm climate, Norman."

"Israel is warmer than New York."

"What, Norman?"

Norman explained that his friend, Alan, had visited Israel once to explore the possibility of opening a branch of his Army-Navy surplus store, and eventually convinced Norman to accompany him on a 10-day vacation.

"Normie," Alan had said, "haven't you been even a little bit curious about visiting the land of your ancestors?"

"Which would mean *me* going to Russia, land of my father and mother."

"Oh, the country of Czars and communists is your *real* homeland?"

"The *U.S.* is, my entrepreneurial friend."

"You trying to tell me that you don't have any allegiance to Israel?"

"Look, Alan, from what I've read and heard, Israel has my admiration for what they've been able to do against all odds. I mean, they've developed their country that manages somehow to exist in the face of constant threats and pressure."

"Then what else do you need?"

"Nothing, it's a great country from what I understand."

"And the only democracy in the middle of monarchies, dictators, and crazy sheiks!"

"Well, yes, almost."

"What the hell does that mean *almost*."

"Well, for one thing, I understand Israeli Arabs don't have full voting rights."

"What the hell you doing, Norman? Counting which pimple on your ass is bigger than the other ones?"

"I'll go with you, okay?"

"Hey, don't do me a favor."

"I really would like to visit some of the historical sites."

"Well, maybe if you got a load of the wailing wall, you'd get a little old-time religion."

"Probably, Alan, and I'd like to get a look at some of the settlements in the West Bank."

"But I think we'd better stay out of the Gaza Strip; the Arabs there are lunatics."

So the two of them went to Israel and stayed in a house of a man Alan had befriended on his last trip.

They had a lovely time there in the sea coast town of Haifa, and after visiting a number of other tourist 'musts' Norman convinced Alan to accompany him in a guarded escorted journey into Gaza. The trip, while a tense one, went without any negative problem.

"Well, Normie, you had fun over there?"

"You're right, those refugee camps are not pretty."

"Maybe if they stopped making trouble with the settlements, and just took the time to fix up their areas."

"But they don't have the money."

"And I don't have the time to discuss this crap."

On the flight back to New York, they both avoided any more discussions after Norman had brought up what he called the 'Palestine problem' and Alan had shot back that the only problem was that the Arabs weren't smart enough to realize that they should be happy with what Israel set up for them, and just stop their trouble-making Intifada.

~

"Maybe it's too long a trip for you to go back to Israel," Christine delicately offered, "but Los Angeles is only a few hours. So what if when I get there, I check out some senior housing for you?"

"What are you talking about?"

"Well, I thought if you came out there, we would be able to have our lunches like normal."

"No, I don't want that, Christine."

"Oh, I'm sorry. I thought you enjoyed—"

Norman quickly interrupted, "I meant I don't think California is for me."

"I know you love New York, Norman, but Los Angeles is more than just movie stars and sunny weather. It has theater, opera, good museums, etcetera.

"But you need a car out there and I can't drive, remember?"

"Well, I can drive you around sometimes, or maybe find a good senior place for you that has a shuttle service."

"But I'm used to New York, 103-years worth."

"I realize that moving out there could have problems, but—"

"Well, let me know if there's a nice place for me out there, and then we'll talk, okay?"

"Good enough; we'll talk."

~

Norman glanced again at the photos that Christine had sent him along with a letter explaining that she had done a great deal of research in LA and had come up with a novel idea.

At first she had checked several assisted living complexes which had reasonable accommodations and monthly rates. She then cruised around another neighborhood in the nearby San Fernando Valley where she had gone to inspect an apartment-hotel that she had seen listed in the *LA Times*. The manager of the unit told her that because of Norman's age, they weren't enthusiastic about accepting him, and suggested that when he arrived in *LA*, and had been examined by their doctor, they might consider allowing him to become a tenant.

Disheartened, she left, driving past a row of what appeared to be bungalows. A sign read: Concord MHP.

Driving into the driveway, she followed a wooden cut-out of an arrow, discreet lettering announcing 'MANAGER.' The manager, Gladys, showed Christine around the MOBILE HOME PARK which was made up of about 75 'manufactured houses,' each on a small plot of land complete with attractively landscaped flower beds, shrubbery, and even a small yard for a dog to exercise in.

The mobile homes ranged from two bedrooms up to three and even four bedrooms in a few of the more elaborate ones.

"So, Norman, instead of paying $1,800 a month for your one little room and meals, if you bought a two bedroom mobile home, you would own your own house, no rent to pay. Maintenance is about $500 per month. A 'plus' is the fact that Concord is a senior park, so there aren't noisy kids running around. And something else you'd like Norman; they have a very nice clubhouse and swimming pool, and I know you always like to do a little swimming. People meet socially in the clubhouse and I think you once told me you always like to play poker: the 'alter khakers' at Shalom Assisted Living don't play, but there's a once a week penny poker game in the clubhouse. How does this sound? Also, a lot of the tenants have cars, so whenever I'm not available, one of them could take you for shopping, etc. It's a very nice situation, Norman. I really think you should take advantage of buying the mobile home. Keep in mind, Norman, that your aching knees could become a thing of the past. Imagine living in the warm climate without the pain you have to go through every winter in New York. I know it would make me feel good to know that you won't have to put up with all that, and besides, who would I talk to about politics and the fact that our president is against all the sensible things that we agree on."

84

AFTER THE POLISH PHYSICIST, COPERNICUS, had established the fact that the earth revolves around the sun, Galileo, the Italian mathematician and astronomer, attempted to spread the concept of a sun-centered universe. He was eventually forced by the Inquisition to recant his position, spending the last eight years of his life under house arrest.

Norman, in the face of the dire punishment meted out to outspoken Galileo, had nonetheless developed *his* personal theory: that the entire country circled around Brooklyn, its three million inhabitants, the center of the American universe.

Norman's heretical opposition to Manhattan's claim to be the hub of all of the U.S.'s meaningful action seemed, on its face, to be nothing more than a whistle arguing against a strong majority wind, but many who dwelt in the proud borough of Brooklyn shared a common delusion of superiority over all that was not blessed with Brooklynese.

Recently, a representative of the 9-11 Commission had interviewed Norman about his personal experience on that tragic day, and he described his view of the events.

"As far as I'm concerned," Norman, with a mix of sadness and anger, declared, "No matter what they've taken from me, the United States still stands like a colossus astride the world!"

When he read his published comment in the newspaper, Norman thought that he sounded like a pedantic patriot.

A bit ashamed of what struck him as flag-waving nationalistic fervor, he managed to excuse his purple rhetoric as the ramblings of an old man.

He had often thought of himself as not being provincial until now, but after all, a bereaved person could be allowed some moment of being less than himself.

Marsa had never been that way, Norman unexpectedly recollected… never less than herself.

His memory watched as she hid behind the kitchen curtain and threw out a penny to the Violin Man. A moment of what she truly was. Unadorned by words. A simple act of giving. Pure.

The nostalgic sadness was overtaken by the more immediate grief over his granddaughter Miriam's death, still a deep, bottomless wound.

85

CHRISTINE HAD SUGGESTED TO NORMAN that since he wasn't certain that he would able to 'make it' away from Shalom Assisted Living and the support and caring of its staff, that until he made a final decision, he should invest only in inexpensive house furnishings at the Salvation Army store (30 percent off for seniors on Tuesdays).

Selecting some furniture and pots and pans, Norman thought nostalgically about the decorating ideas that Marsa would have made for his new home.

In a tribute to her memory, Norman carefully packed the samovar which had followed her from the Ukraine and Berlin, then Brownsville, Flatbush and in its final journey to Brooklyn Heights. He lovingly set it in a place of honor in his small living room.

He also packed several of his books and the manuscript of the novel which he almost had published years earlier.

His favorite picture of his father, Bennie the Butch, his arm affectionately around his wife, Yetta, was also carefully packed along with the photo of Ira taken during his Bar Mitzvah speech; Edith in her wedding picture with Barry, who shortly after was killed in Vietnam, and another one holding her newborn Miriam, his granddaughter.

Norman had managed to repair a very old photo that Marsa had treasured, taping together crumbling pieces of the picture of her in a peasant blouse, playing piano along with her brother, Leo.

Carefully placing the photos in different areas of the mobile home; Norman was able to see one or another of them at all times.

By the end of his first week in L.A., Norman was feeling positive about his move to sunny California, where its warmth quickly helped rid him of much of his ongoing joint pain.

"Yes," he brightly said to Christine, "You were right. This weather adds some extra years to my Superman body."

To some degree, Norman *meant* his playful self-characterization of his physical condition; proud of his regularly exercising at Shalom Assisted Living's small but well equipped workout room. Although the years had taken their toll, he was pleased that his body had maintained some flexibility and that he was still able to walk a slow mile without becoming winded or his legs cramping up.

The move to Los Angeles, where he intended to celebrate his 104th birthday, also had helped lift his spirits from out of the deep depression he had been trapped in since Miriam's death on 9-11.

Moving to Los Angeles also reminded him of Finky, who had relocated here after leaving Brooklyn, and remarried. Settling down, she had mentioned to Norman during one of his phone calls, "like a Jewish princess with this goy, Leland, and popping out babies."

She had sent him a photo of her, Leland and their brood of six children.

Although he had learned of her death some 30 years before, when Leland had dutifully written him about it, Norman now called the phone number he had on occasion used to speak with Finky during the HIGH HOLIDAYS, YOM KIPPUR.

Her first born, named Norman, just starting his Social Security retirement, was pleased to hear from Norman since his mother, Finky, had spoken warmly about him over the years.

They exchanged family photos, and Norman was flattered not only by the fact that Finky had named her son Norman, but studying his photo taken only recently, that to his ancient eyes, was uncannily reminiscent of himself when *he* was that age.

Shocked at the apparent resemblance, his memory galloped back to the time when Finky, very distressed after the violent murder of her mailman lover, Fred, came down to the Schecter apartment for solace and he, after a few drinks, had dizzily stretched out in the bed next to her. He recalled embracing her in comfort, and then... ? Was Norman's fancy of having a replacement son for his tragically killed Ira, over 60 years ago, being shaped to embrace a new memory, fathering his namesake, Norman.

He had come to realize that the abundance of memories that he had warehoused over his long life would sometimes play different tricks on him.

Was Norman speaking to younger Norman after all these years just another one?

~

Christine, sensitive to Norman's problems in being transplanted from the comfort of his Brooklyn home, visited him as often as her schedule permitted, bringing some groceries and helping him make decisions as to the different arrangement possibilities of the furniture; both of them enjoying the lighthearted time spent together.

Christine invited several people from the mobile home park's other residents to welcome their new neighbor, Norman.

He was pleased not only for the conviviality, but that one of the couples, Roy and Francine Dawes, were prime movers in the Teachers' Union's struggle against the Governor's attempt to cut heavily into the teachers' budget.

The 'warrior' in Norman had been lulled by his retirement years; his lack of resolve caused by 'watching' rather than 'doing.'

"I've been sleeping on my memories for a long time, Christine, so I appreciate your helping me to wake up. Thanks."

The several meetings he had with the Dawes, and other members of the union activists, led his thoughts back to the early volatile days of Local 5 of the Teachers' Union in New York.

He shared, with the Dawes' group, several stories of those times and the different methods they had used to win eventually some of those teachers' battles with management, i.e., Principals, Superintendent of Schools, Board of Education officials, and of course, legislative bodies.

"Mr Schecter—"

"Norman."

"Norman, you've had very varied experiences which I think we can benefit from. Yes, I really think that."

Roy Dawes liked to underline the importance of what he said, by commenting on its value and in instances such as this, would repeat his assessment.

"Yes, I really think that."

Francine Dawes, who unlike her husband, tended to express herself in almost cryptic language, agreed with her husband.

"Correct."

Serious as they were about their dedication to their union work, the Dawes had a personal love… the theater.

As theater arts high school teachers, they had earlier worked on stage presentations at the two different high schools where they were on staff.

Roy had worked on an ambitious concert performance of *West Side Story* at El Camino Real High, and Francine, at Taft High, had directed a production of the William Inge play, *Bus Stop*, the same play Norman had seen on Broadway, with the author present. They briefly told Norman about their love of theater, then shared some of their ideas arguing against the Governor's plans to cut back on teachers' and firemen's benefits.

Norman was pleased at the Dawes involving him in their discussions, and was invited over to their nearby mobile home, where he noticed a production photo of *Bus Stop*, and vaguely remembered his meeting with Inge many years earlier.

Roy told him that his interest in the play dated back to when his father told him about his uncle who had been in the original Broadway production of the play, and committed suicide.

A photo of a performance of the play hung on a wall and Roy pointed out a cast member.

"My great uncle, Al Salmi, was the one who killed himself."

Norman was shocked at the coincidence of having met William Inge just before *he* committed suicide, and now finding out that Al Salmi, whom he couldn't really remember, had also killed himself.

On occasion, Norman had thought about the logic of a person killing himself.

Although he could understand how someone with a terminal medical condition and ongoing excruciating pain could be so driven, he could not fathom what would impel a healthy person to take his own life.

He had recently read a newspaper story which somehow suggested to him a suicide of another sort.

The columnist had written a moving account of how a young American woman, Rachel Corrie, had bravely stood in front of an Israeli bulldozer that was about to demolish a Palestinian's home.

The bulldozing was retribution for the fact that the house owner's son had been involved in an Intifada attack on Israeli soldiers.

The bulldozer moved slowly but relentlessly forward as the Israeli driver shouted a warning to her, but she determinedly stood in protest, her fluorescent orange jacket clearly visible.

The bulldozer moved forward... In a moment, Rachel Corrie's body was crushed in a painful death.

Was there a commonality, Norman thought, in the suicide deaths of William Inge, Al Salmi and Rachel Corrie?

Was there a subtle link between them, some expression of a societal inability to cope with life's pressures?

Norman, moved by the woman's hopeless sacrifice for her beliefs, perceived that there was little similarity with the other suicides... But who was he to judge what lay in the heart of anyone else? Someone who may not have been driven by noble impulses, but by painful anguish; Stygian darkness of the spirit.

Or was it, as Alan might have tartly said, nothing more than three people who just had their heads screwed on wrong.

Later, Norman came up with an idea that had him questioning whether or not *his* head was on straight.

Impulsively, he wrote to the Israeli whom he had visited with Alan many years before, and promptly received an answer from Lev Meskin.

"Mr. Schecter, I am much truthfully sorry to have to give you the information that my dear father, Amnon, died over 20 years ago.

I hope I will be able to help you with your plan to visit here again in our country.

Haifa is usually a city where there is good relations between Jews and Arabs, but even this quiet city has started to have dangerous problems. There is tension, more about the plans to remove the Gaza settlements. I do not know how much information you have about this very major problem we possess in our country.

I thought at first that the Prime Minister, Sharon, was maybe correct in starting the settlements, but because of the present situation maybe it is right that they do not stay now. There are many citizens who do not agree. Do you know about our Likud Party? They are very religious and strong in their belief that God has declared this land is for us alone.

I think that your idea to come here and visit, as you wrote me, is a nice idea.

I realize that you are an elderly person, but I assure you that we have excellent doctors and medical facilities if you should need them. Your question about going into the Gaza area as you did many years ago is not a very good idea at this time.

Yes, I have heard about that woman, Corrie, you mention. Yes, I have heard stories of that woman and that unhappy experience. Some people say that she could have been saved but she on purpose stepped in front of the bulldozer to be a martyr to stop them tearing down the Palestine house.

It was just like those suicide bombers who blew themselves up — for what?

When you were here with your friend many years ago, I was very young but I remember you, Mr. Schecter, and you are welcome to visit us again to see our country."

Norman asked himself what the reason was even to have thought about taking his tired, aching old body to Israel, especially now that he was becoming more involved with Mr. and Mrs. Dawes and their activist work with the teachers' demonstrations.

He put off exploring his thoughts about Israel once he became involved in a project that the Dawes had asked Christine to manage.

Learning that Christine was Armenian, they asked her to help them with the teachers' protest demonstration in the city of Glendale, whose Armenian population was 40 percent of the city's, one of the largest outside Armenia itself.

Christine asked Norman if he was interested in accompanying them on the hour-long trip to Glendale.

"I realize that L.A. is not as exciting as New York normally is, so I thought this could be a way of showing you an exotic part of our California's culture."

The Dawes suggested that at the same time Christine used her familiarity with Armenian history and folklore to help them set up communication lines with the public, the Dawes would help her to engage the untapped population for contributions to her AIDS project.

One of the wealthy community leaders, Albert Sarkisian, often had given large donations to the St. Peter's Armenian church.

When Christine introduced Norman to Sarkisian, Norman noticed a red, white and blue colored crest: 'I SUPPORT OUR TROOPS,' proudly worn on the other man's jacket lapel.

"There's quite a war going on," Norman said, eyeing the patriotic emblem.

"I don't like it, Mr. Schecter."

"Those poor kids," Norman agreed, and Sarkisian nodded, "Well, I'm for *them* but —" not finishing the sentence, underlined his distress.

Norman gently asked, "Are there many boys from Glendale there?"

"Enough."

"War is nasty, Mr. Sarkisian."

"I know, Mr. Schecter, I know."

Norman glanced at him questioningly, and Sarkisian joylessly answered.

"Two tours in Vietnam."

"I know it must have been very bad."

"You know?"

"I'm an old man but once I was young enough for the Army in 1918."

"'The war to end all wars,'" Sarkisian growled. Norman's bitterness matched his.

"It sure wasn't, was it?"

After a moment, Sarkisian politely asked, "Mr. Schecter, are you Jewish?"

"Absolutely."

"Well, Armenians have the greatest sympathy for all those who died in the Holocaust, because we had the same thing done to us in 1915... and for many years longer... many."

"Yes, I've read about the Armenian genocide, Mr. Sarkisian."

"But the good heart of Armenians is still alive."

"Yes, I understand that you've been an extremely gracious benefactor for the Armenian community."

Sarkisian's tone was sharp, "Mr. Schecter, whatever I did is private business."

"Well, I've been told that many have benefitted from your help."

"I ask you, Mr. Schecter, has even a single person said they have seen me actually give anybody money?"

"Well, no, but —"

"It's *my* business, Mr. Schecter... my business."

"Of course, Mr. Sarkisian."

Norman felt as if he was in a long ago taut discussion with Marsa about her hiding behind the kitchen curtain as she made her anonymous contribution to the Violin Man.

Now Norman's hand seemed to move aimlessly out in front of him; whoever noticing it would possibly think it was only the involuntary gesture of an old man, not guessing that it was only Norman's reaching out to touch Marsa's cheek.

In recent years, Norman more and more had found himself physically acting out another sort of fantasy, sometimes with a leg movement which meant, but only to him, a step alongside Marsa as they strolled through the leafy comfort of the Prospect Park lane, leading to the boat house where a rowboat would be rented for twenty-five cents worth of romantically gliding through the friendly rippling lake.

The Dawes, with Christine's help, organized a strong unit of teachers, businessmen and several women homemakers who seemed very committed to demonstrate actively and spread the word around the tightly knitted community in opposition to the Governor's plans. A fireman, Aram Karak, was particularly angry at the situation.

Sarkisian took Karak off to the side and spoke intently to him; Norman watching as Sarkisian wrote down his name, then earnestly shook his hand.

On the ride home, Christine appreciatively thanked Norman for his help, but noticed that he had started to seem uncomfortable, holding his head and having difficulty swallowing.

By the time they reached Los Angeles, Christine had decided to pull into Tarzana Hospital's emergency room, in spite of Norman's objection.

After Christine stopped the car, she gently reached over to feel Norman's forehead; a raging fever had taken over. Holding his reluctant hand, she guided him past a disinterested security guard.

The emergency room doctor checked Norman's very sore throat and after quickly running several tests, glanced worriedly over to Christine.

"He has a very bad case of pneumonia."

Norman was rushed onto a gurney and wheeled up to his bed in the quarantined wing. Slipping into unconsciousness, he was barely able to hear Christine say that she would be able to come to see him the next day, immediately after her appointment to help manage still another AIDS fund-raiser.

Norman spent a racking, distressing night, restlessly tossing, moaning—through disjointed images.

Several weeks earlier, he had delicately asked Christine if she had considered finding another partner to live with since 9/11 had killed Miriam.

Shocked at Norman's bald question, she nonetheless answered angrily.

"Did *you* run out to find somebody after your beloved Marsa, passed away?"

Now, snatches of memory glided through Norman's fretful thoughts, hazy recollections of his trip back to see Brownsville one last time after Marsa died, nostalgically dropping into the Benjamin Franklin Bank where he had, 30 years before, deposited 50-60 cents a week into the Christmas Club and chatted with Maureen Dickens about *A Tale of Two Cities*.

This day, the rest of the bank employees were giving her an informal retirement party.

Norman drank a ginger-ale toast with her before walking her to the bus stop. They exchanged telephone numbers and although Norman did call her up, planning to ask her if she would like to go to a movie with him, he hung up when he heard her voice.

Now, his feverish stream of memory was jangled by the zig-zag of Miriam phoning him on that fateful day at the Trade Center.

"Grandpa, take the elevator! Leave right now!"

And firemen rushing up the steps.

"Everybody all right?"

And Norman hesitating, firemen insisting.

"Need any help, old timer?"

Now, nightmare images tumbled over one another, cutting into shadows of blinding light, indistinct edges crushed into distorted shapes, stitched together with eerie sounds, splintering words bouncing off the surrounding void, the meaning… terrifying silence.

Defying all odds, Norman, nearing 104, defiantly struggled for his health over the next several weeks and in a little more than two months, the hospital assigned him to their rehab ward, and other than needing a cane to support his frail body, he was, as he proudly declared, in better shape than he was when he turned 100 after 9-11.

86

IT WAS NORMAN'S 105TH BIRTHDAY.

Many years before, Norman had estimated that his life span would reach 107, but his recent bout with pneumonia forced him to accept the fact that his time might be foreshortened by circumstances beyond his control. Therefore, on his birthday, he had decided to take inventory of his life up to that moment, and so leaving behind some document of his existence for anybody who might be interested. But for whom? Christine, whom he had become close to? Who else? Everyone he had known had died, so it would have to be for an unseen, unknown audience.

Perhaps it was only for himself? Perhaps, in the final analysis, he would be the most important, only one, to see his testament, so he bought a fresh new school composition book to write down his estimate of his attempts to balance out his life.

Acts of Value	Husband, father, grandfather… acquitted moral responsibilities reasonably well. Teacher, union activist, principal, superintendent, soldier, 1918, WW1.
Acts of Dubious Morality	Assisting Alan to start fur store fire… Shifting loyalties between teachers and school administration.
Personal Doubts	Causing intense pressure on Marsa in the 30's because of his lack of earning power due to union activities.
Proud Achievements	Good relationships with daughter Edith and son, Ira, and Miriam, of course.
Negatives	Frightened by Edith's illness and not being supportive enough. Not being able to dissuade Ira from joining the Marines.

Regrets	Not to have taken Miriam out to eat just one hour earlier on 9-11, and so avoiding the suicide plane
Regrets of Fancy	Not being young and strong enough to go to Israel to see if he could stop the bulldozing of Palestinian buildings and their tenants.
Honest Regret	That he would not be able to possess the courage to do that even if he were young enough.
Accomplishments	That he had succeeded in some small way to honor what was good in those he had met. That he now would use his energy to help the teachers and firemen.

As he finished his inventory, Norman realized that even now he had managed to achieve whatever insight he had, standing on the shoulders of others who had fought the good fight. He had read and shared their experiences: Plato, Voltaire, Jefferson, Clarence Darrow, Martin Luther King, the firefighters who heroically rushed up the stairs of the burning Trade Center and the Armenian playwright, William Saroyan, whom Christine had spoken about and had suggested to him to read his play, *The Time of Your Life*, a rich, eccentric character-based celebration of life.

Norman recalled reading it 60 years before, when he was instructing an English lit seminar.

Now, Christine drew his attention to Saroyan's preface to the play, its words resonating with the struggle to discover goodness everywhere, bringing it out of its hiding place, letting it be free and unashamed... Like Finky and Freddie the mailman finding real affection, lifting their spirits in the midst of the tragic odds stacked against them.

"Encourage virtue in whatever heart it may have been driven into secrecy and sorrow by the falseness and terror of the world." ... like the street bully, Walter who, propelled by the desperate economics of the Depression, menaced Ira for his few cents earned at Big Nose Nathanson's junk yard.

"Have no shame in being kindly and gentle, but if the time comes to kill, kill and have no regrets." ... like dear Ira did in the few years of his briefly explored life. "In the time of your life, live so that in that wondrous time you shall not add to the misery and sorrow of the world, but shall smile to the infinite delight and mystery of it."

Like Marsa did, as she hid behind the kitchen curtain and listened to the music, her secret appreciation and help, a penny wrapped in a piece of newspaper.

Like Norman who had tried to, feebly, he felt, help in any way *he* could.

Like the Jewish Kaddish for the dead imploring, 'to be remembered for your deeds of loving kindness—'

THE END

About the Author

Eli Rill

During World War II, Rill served three years in the South Pacific, Second Marine Division (Saipan, Okinawa and Nagasaki). After the war he began his writing and acting career on both stage and screen.

Eli adapted and directed Lee Strasberg's Actors' Studio Production of both Edna St. Vincent Millay's *Conversation at Midnight,* and James Baldwin's *Giovanni's Room* and also three successful children's musicals in New York, Toronto, and Los Angeles.

He and Philip Yordan co-wrote the screenplay for *The Harder They Fall,* Humphrey Bogart's last film. Rill also worked on the film as Bogart's acting coach.

Rill co-founded with Elia Kazan and Arthur Penn, the Actors' Studio Playwrights Unit in New York. He was Artistic Director of Drama Development for the National Film Board of Canada in Montreal, and for eight years, Chairman of the Drama Department, Ontario College of Art. In addition to Bogart, he has coached and directed Barbra Streisand, Paul Newman, Marilyn Monroe, Shelly Winters, John Candy, Rip Torn and Kevin McCarthy.

His acting credits include work with Peter O'Toole, Rod Steiger, Roddy McDowall, Barry Sullivan and Patricia Neal, among other prominent actors.

Eli Rill now writes novels in his studio in Canoga Park, California.

"**Eli Rill** has always surprised me. As an actor, I have always been impressed with his rich inventive work. As a director, he is always insightful, sensitive and invigorating. Now, once again, he has shown a completely different side of his spectrum of talent – as a novelist.

"I was captivated by *A Penny for the Violin Man* and couldn't put it down. The very same qualities that make his work in the theatre jump off the stage, now make his characters spring off the page.

"I highly recommend the *Violin Man.* It is a great read and a wonderful engrossing trip to another time and place, and a mirror of the problems that face us today."

~ Martin Landau, Actor

Additional copies of *A Penny For The Violin Man*
are available through your favorite
book dealer or from the publisher:

Circle of Life Publishing
8901 Eton Ave., #109
Canoga Park, CA 91304

Phone/Fax: 818-341-7713
Website: www.apennyfortheviolinman.com
E-mail: info@apennyfortheviolinman.com

A Penny For The Violin Man
(ISBN: 978-0-615-33807-1)
is $24.95 for softbound edition, plus
$5.50 shipping for first copy
($2.00 each additional copy)
and sales tax for CA orders.